"A marvellous, confounding debut that moves from eerie Vietnamese forests to rundown zoos and crowded nightclubs . . . Kupersmith has been compared to David Mitchell for her novel's time-hopping characters and sweeping ambition. . . . The novel's descriptive powers and sense of place are vivid and intoxicating. . . . Enjoy the funhouse ride."
—*The Guardian*

"Each chapter disorients and disturbs but also entices. . . . The novel develops its characters with relatable and sympathetic plights and thickens its supernatural mystery with carefully placed hints and literary breadcrumbs. . . . [The] talented author . . . knows how to frighten her readers and intertwine a wide-ranging story. Kupersmith's ability to balance character development with a thickening plot, conflict and suspense is extraordinary."
—*Bookreporter*

"*Build Your House Around My Body* is a beautifully written page-turner that takes possession to an unexpected place."
—*Book Riot*

"A rich and dazzling spectacle [that] peels back the layers of a haunted Vietnam."
—*Kirkus Reviews*

"[An] exceptional debut . . . Magic can be both benevolent and monstrous in Kupersmith's work, and here she indelibly illustrates the ways in which Vietnam's legacies of colonialism, war, and violence against women continue to haunt. . . . Surprising and satisfying."
—*Publishers Weekly* (starred review)

"Strange and wondrous . . . [Kupersmith] magically manages to create a story both epic and intensely intimate. Patient and observant readers will be richly rewarded."
—*Booklist* (starred review)

"Unsettling and powerful."
—*BookPage*

"Take one psycho-history of Vietnam; add hungry ghosts and an expat on the brink of a breakdown; then mix in two brothers, love and jealousy, spilt colonial blood, doomy ennui, satire, and a slithering, unguessable plot: *Build Your House Around My Body* is the dark, smart, vivid result. Fiction as daring and accomplished as Violet Kupersmith's first novel reignites my love of the form and its kaleidoscopic possibilities." —DAVID MITCHELL

"There are so many things I love about Violet Kupersmith's brilliant debut novel. The language is beautiful, and the plot is complex and rich, but best of all, it's a real page-turner. I completely fell into this book." —RUTH OZEKI

"A brilliant, sweeping epic that swaps spirits and sheds time like snake-skin, *Build Your House Around My Body* is a marvel. Thrilling, witty, disturbing, righteous—I won't be able to shut up about how damned awesome this book is. Neither will you."
—PAUL TREMBLAY, author of *A Head Full of Ghosts* and *Survivor Song*

"A heady, gothic spellbinder of a book."
—KELLY LINK, author of *Get in Trouble*

"This impressively constructed weave of stories, haunted by the ghosts of history and family, is gorgeous, completely original, and quite disturbing—usually all at the same time. Beware! This book might swallow you up."
—KAREN JOY FOWLER, author of
We Are All Completely Beside Ourselves

"I loved this epic book—beautiful, brilliant, powerful, and shivery-back-of-the-neck terrifying." —MADELINE MILLER

"This lush, sultry phantasmagoria of a novel is as playful, hypnotic, and bone-chilling as a cobra rising to strike."
—ELISABETH THOMAS, author of *Catherine House*

"Violet Kupersmith has elevated the ghost story into an art form. Her intricately plotted, flamboyantly original novel is by turns steamy, grisly, comic, horrific, and touching. This haunting tale will stay with you long after the last page is turned."
—VALERIE MARTIN, author of
Property and *I Give It to You*

BUILD

YOUR

HOUSE

AROUND

MY

BODY

BUILD

YOUR

HOUSE

AROUND

MY

BODY

A

NOVEL

Violet
Kupersmith

RANDOM HOUSE

NEW YORK

2022 Random House Trade Paperback Edition

Copyright © 2021 by Violet Kupersmith

Maps and illustrations © 2021 by David Lindroth

Published in the United States by
Random House, an imprint and division of
Penguin Random House LLC, New York.

RANDOM HOUSE and the HOUSE colophon
are registered trademarks of
Penguin Random House LLC.

Originally published in hardcover in the United
States by Random House, an imprint and division
of Penguin Random House LLC, in 2021.

ISBN 9780812983487
Ebook ISBN 9780679645153

Printed in the United States of America
on acid-free paper

randomhousebooks.com

Book design by Barbara M. Bachman

For

my grandparents,

and for M

LIST OF
CHARACTERS

—

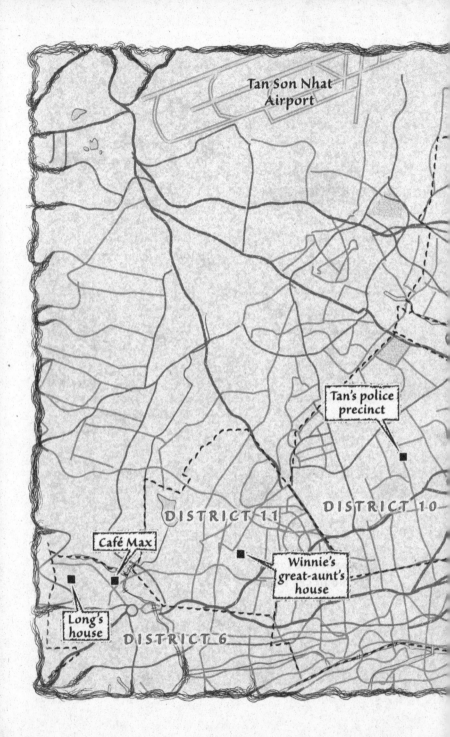

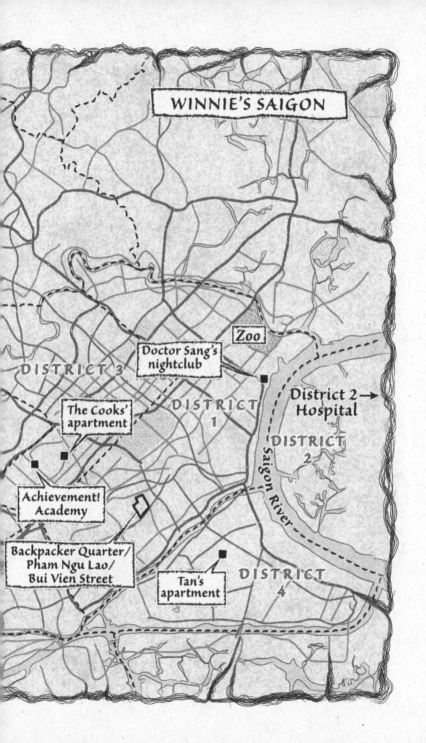

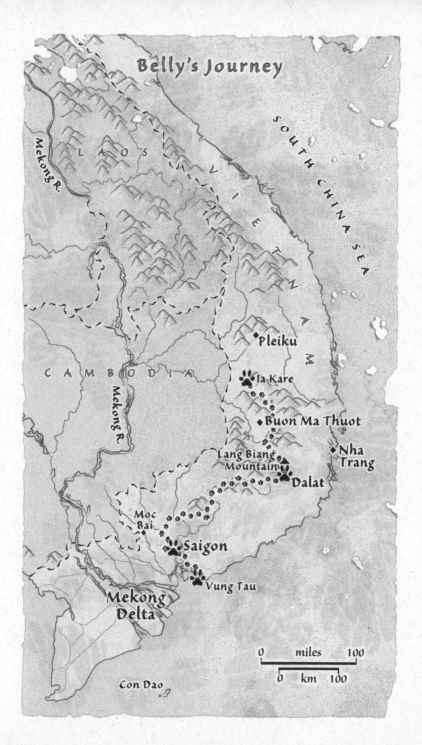

BUILD

YOUR

HOUSE

AROUND

MY

BODY

SOMETHING WAS MOVING IN THE SHRUBS IN FRONT OF
Tan Son Nhat Airport. It was one in the morning, and Winnie had
stepped off a plane twenty minutes ago. Her connecting flight had been
held up by a summer thunderstorm in Hong Kong and now her plans
were all awry from the start.

Leaving the air-conditioning of the baggage claim, she had felt her
edges soften immediately in the humidity. The yellow-uniformed taxi
drivers, like half-spilled yolks in their cracked-open car doors, stretched
out their necks in unison as they followed the movements of the new
passengers exiting the airport. Winnie had seen one of them stare at
her, and when she accidentally returned his eye contact he opened his
mouth to call out before abruptly closing it again, and Winnie knew he
was debating whether to use Vietnamese or English on her. She'd
turned and started walking away from the taxi queue before she could
hear his final verdict.

And now she was standing in the dark, on the shorn grass of the
small, half-neglected greenery by the motorbike parking lot, watching
the leaves on this low bush quivering strangely. Just one bush—the rest
of the shrubbery was still, and there was no discernible wind that could
be responsible for the shaking. She contemplated finding something to

prod it with, wondering what would come out if she did, wondering what she should do now.

Winnie leaned on the handle of her suitcase. She was supposed to be staying at the house of a great-aunt she'd never met before but doubted that the old woman was up at this hour or would appreciate Winnie arriving at her home in the middle of the night. All Winnie had been told about the great-aunt was that she was a former nun, was still deeply devout and, if she missed her five A.M. mass, deeply irritable.

Her curiosity had gotten the better of her: Winnie took a step toward the rustling shrub and bent over to pull back a branch and peer inside. But before her hand could make contact with it, she heard a sudden, low hiss from somewhere within the leafy shadows, a sound like an angry radiator. Winnie jerked away. It could have just been a jet-lagged auditory hallucination, but if it was not, it would be better if she and whatever was inside the bush remained strangers to each other. Winnie quickly turned and began dragging her suitcase toward the smeary yellow streetlights of Tan Binh.

The farther she got from the airport the cheaper the hotels would be, so she planned to walk for at least ten blocks. Whenever she passed a hotel that still had lights on, she would look into its lobby and see how big its couches were in order to determine whether or not it was too expensive. The pay-by-the-hour sex motel was fully illuminated and conspicuously couchless, but it had a yawning motorbike guard sitting on a stool and a woman with her hair set in pink rollers behind a desk and a large, glass-paned refrigerator full of beer. Winnie didn't see the sign advertising an hourly rate or the condoms for sale next to bags of beef jerky on top of the fridge until she was already halfway through the door and the woman in curlers raised an eyebrow at her. But when she hastily calculated that it would cost her less than five dollars to have a room until six in the morning, she decided to stay. She would have plenty of cash left over for the taxi to her great-aunt's house, and she would arrive right as the old woman was returning from church.

The receptionist took Winnie's passport, gave her a room key, and sold her an overpriced can of 333 from the beer fridge and a bag of jerky. The motorbike guard took the handle of her suitcase, about to offer to carry it up the stairs for her, but when he realized how little it actually weighed, he returned it unchivalrously to Winnie.

The polycarbonate clamshell thumped hollowly against the stairs as Winnie dragged it behind her one-handed. Buying a suitcase so large now seemed like an overconfident gamble she had made back in America. She had assumed that one day she would fill all of this space. That her life here would provide things worth keeping. That she herself would become someone worthy of being kept. But now she feared that she had jinxed herself. Her arrogance had earned her the ire of a fickle god, and her life would continue to be as empty as her luggage, wherever she went. Winnie was twenty-two. She had brought with her a passport, two sets of clean clothes, and her own flesh. All the rest she would acquire.

The key opened a windowless room that smelled like dried sweat. Its walls and floor tiles were the color of the inside of a lip, and there was a large mirror mounted on the ceiling above the bed. The wheeled suitcase drifted on its own over to a far corner. The truth was, she had paused by the airport bush in the first place because she was considering folding herself up inside her hollow bag and hiding in the hedges until morning. Winnie lay back on the mattress and opened the beef jerky. She spent her first meal in Vietnam staring up at her own reflection.

THE NIGHT BEFORE SHE WENT MISSING, LONG DREAMED that Winnie turned into a rubber tree. The dream would have felt portentous even if Winnie hadn't vanished the following day, as Long hardly ever remembered his dreams, and the few times he did, they were prosaic to the point of embarrassment: banal nightmares about misplacing something at the office or trying to play soccer but being unable to move his feet.

In this dream, Long woke up in his own bed. He rolled over to his right side and saw an empty expanse of mattress beside him where Winnie should have been. He got up and descended the narrow staircase to the kitchen. There he found her growing out of the slight depression in the floor tiles where, six months ago, the landlord had dug a hole and never filled it in properly. Her trifoliate leaves brushed the ceiling. While the tree did not have a human face, the trunk boasted two curved, breast-like protrusions and tapered in an approximation of a waist. Its lower half was partially bifurcated to suggest legs, complete with a vaginal bark cleft. When he leaned in closer to examine the Winnie Tree, Long saw that, most disturbing of all, it even had a tiny knot where her belly button should have been.

He immediately recognized that she was a rubber tree. He would have been able to identify the breed anywhere after a childhood spent in close proximity to plantations full of their spindly silhouettes. There was a knife in his hand now—a tapping knife, short and curled at the end like an ice skate or an unusual punctuation mark—and Long knew this meant he must make a cut. What would run out of her, latex or blood? He would find out. And what should he collect it in? Long reached for a mostly empty beer can lying on its side on the counter—even in his dream, the kitchen was a mess—and shook the last of the fusty lager droplets out into the sink. But where should he cut her? This was the hardest question. Long didn't know whether or not the Winnie Tree could feel pain, and even though she lacked a mouth, he couldn't shake the feeling that she might still be able to scream. He let the crimped tip of the blade rest experimentally on the soft, mottled skin between her bark-breasts. Pressed it in tentatively. Panicked and then quickly retracted it. He decided that it would be safest to stay away from her heart, and so he moved the knife down to the soft swell of her lower abdomen instead, just south of that repulsive belly button. The stomach was a safe place to make a shallow incision, wasn't it? Like a cesarean, only without the baby? Long angled the knife carefully. He had never witnessed the tapping of a tree before but was familiar with the curved lesions it left behind. The scar provided the blueprint for the new wound. He steadied his hand, inhaled, and sliced.

Long opened his eyes. It was the morning of March the 17th, and he was no longer dreaming. He was in bed, in his small room overlooking a nondescript District 6 alley, and when he automatically rolled over onto his right side he saw Winnie lying six inches away from him, asleep and—from what bits of her were poking out from the blanket—still human. Long now had to guiltily acknowledge that there was a part of him that wished the dream hadn't ended before he could see what happened when he cut. To apologize for being disappointed, he tenderly drew up the blanket to Winnie's chin and tucked it snugly around her sides. While doing so, he noticed that Winnie's hair was damp.

Long always took pains not to disturb Winnie when he got ready in the mornings. He had become an expert at opening and closing the closet doors noiselessly. When he brushed his teeth, he leaned in close to the sink and dribbled the toothpaste into the drain instead of spitting. He tiptoed down the stairs. But this morning, catastrophe struck when he reached the kitchen: unwilling to cross the dip in the tiles where the dream tree had grown, Long decided to circumnavigate it instead, and, while creeping along the edges of the room, he accidentally elbowed one of the half dozen crinkled-up beer cans on the counter, sending them all raining down onto the floor. There was a sproingy quality to the sound of the aluminum striking tile, and Long hated it. It made his teeth clench. It felt like paper cuts to the eardrum. When it was finally over, he listened for Winnie stirring upstairs but heard nothing. Noise traveled oddly in the house. The Saigon traffic a few feet from his doorstep was inaudible from every room except the upstairs toilet, where the motorbike honks and the reedy siren song crackling from the ice cream man's speakers were always perfectly clear despite the fact that the bathroom window did not face the street. Long didn't like having conversations in either the foyer or the spare bedroom, because the walls there had a muffling effect, and everything had to be repeated twice. But in other rooms, there was too much echo. When he was lying in bed upstairs he was able to hear the slow, intermittent drip of the leaky kitchen faucet on the ground floor, and yet not the sound of monsoon-season rain hitting the roof. Long didn't know what the acoustics of the attic crawl space were, because he was mildly claustrophobic and never went up there.

He left the fallen beer cans on the floor, his excuse being that it would only make more noise if he collected them and put them back on the counter, no matter how carefully he did it. Truthfully, he was also hoping that Winnie would pick them up later, and that doing so might inspire her to continue cleaning the rest of the filthy kitchen too. But he knew this was unlikely. Now that she no longer had her teaching job, Winnie didn't do much apart from sleep and eat, and she didn't adhere to a regular schedule when performing these activities either—she was often awake for long stretches between midnight and dawn and made up for it by napping during the day. At least, this was what Long inferred from what Winnie had told him; Long slept like the dead, so he had never witnessed her insomnia firsthand. He didn't know when she slipped in and out of bed, or how she spent the currency of her restless nocturnal hours.

Long reached his front door and gave the steel gate a polite but firm tug, hoping that it would accordion itself open without screeching today. Sometimes it behaved. But this morning it was noncompliant and gave a drawn-out, rusty groan that made heads turn on the street. Long still didn't mind this sound as much as he did the crashing aluminum cans. He rolled his motorbike down the small ramp built into the front steps, stared at the sky to try and determine the probability of rain, donned his driving jacket, and went to work. On his drive home that evening, he purchased two takeaway dinners from a cart.

When he returned to the house at half past six, Winnie was gone. At first, he didn't realize that the house was empty—he just assumed that all the lights were off because Winnie was upstairs napping. After wheeling his motorbike back inside the house, he felt his way to the kitchen (for months now, the landlord had been making excuses for why he hadn't fixed the broken ceiling light in the entryway), plopped the dinner boxes onto the counter, and tripped over the fallen beer cans, which were still on the floor. With a sigh, Long began picking them up. He didn't bother to do it quietly, because he wanted Winnie to wake up and come downstairs so he wouldn't have to eat alone. When the rattling did not summon her, he went up to the bedroom, knocked softly on the door, then pushed it open when she did not respond.

With surprised delight, he saw that Winnie had made the bed. It was the first time since moving in that she had bothered to do it. A lonely strand of black hair was clinging to the pillowcase, and he plucked it off and dropped it into the wastebasket. Then he realized that if the bed did not contain Winnie, he did not know where Winnie was. To what would later be his first great shame, his immediate emotional response was not alarm but more delight; days would pass—weeks, even—where Winnie wouldn't leave the house, and he was hopeful that this indicated an end to her agoraphobia.

Long returned to the kitchen, where he ate his dinner and began watching a pirated Korean horror movie that he found enjoyable despite the poor video quality and mistimed Vietnamese subtitles. He wondered if Winnie was out shopping. Could she have gone to meet someone? He didn't think that she had any friends in Saigon. He very much doubted that she would go visit her great-aunt on a whim. The Korean movie was now beginning to get too grisly for him—there was some sort of goblin living in the family's attic, and Long could already tell that at least one of the children was going to get eaten. It was now nearly eight and Winnie still hadn't returned. Long shut his laptop and sent Winnie a text. He worded it carefully—he didn't want her to think that he was worried and therefore discourage her from going out again in the future.

Ten seconds later, Long discovered a new auditory enigma of his house: from the kitchen, he could hear Winnie's phone vibrating upstairs in the pocket of a dress that had been discarded on a chair.

He raced up the stairs, back to the bedroom. *She just forgot her phone at home when she went out,* he told himself, even as he frantically threw open the doors to the closet, to the bathroom, to the spare bedroom full of junk that he'd been planning to sublet for a year and a half now but still hadn't gotten around to clearing out. Winnie was not in any of them. Long had to mentally prepare for a minute before he could bring himself to climb the steps to the attic. She was not in there—and to his relief, no goblins were either—but the air smelled rank. He returned to the bedroom and got down on all fours. Her suitcase was still under the bed, her passport zippered snugly in one of its interior pockets. Long took it out and ran a thumb over the gold embossing on the front. American eagles always looked spatchcocked to him. He opened to the photo page, where the glossy face of a long-haired Winnie he could barely recognize gazed back at him through the laminate.

Long went back downstairs and checked for her in the cupboard-like space beneath the staircase with the broken toilet and then the cabinet under the kitchen sink, just in case. Then, because he did not know what else to do, he sat in the kitchen and waited. Periodically, he rose to get himself a beer from the fridge. By midnight he had drunk five of them yet didn't feel tipsy. Winnie still hadn't returned. Long lined the empty cans up on his countertop, then went upstairs and got ready for bed. He told himself that if Winnie wasn't back by morning, he would call the police. His second great shame was that he then proceeded to sleep for a full and untroubled six and a half hours. He did not lie awake sick with worry, he did not get up during the night to see if she had come home, and if he dreamed again, he did not remember it.

In the morning, Long opened his eyes and rolled over on his right side, as he did every day. He saw that the space next to him was still empty. He already knew that he was not going to call the police, and this was his third great shame. Not yet, at least. He would wait a little longer before getting them involved. He was not going to run the risk of encountering his older brother, however negligible the odds, until he had no other choice. But while he brushed his teeth (quietly, still; it would have felt rude to take advantage of Winnie's absence by being purposefully noisy) he started preparing his answers to the questions they would ask him. *How long have you known the American girl?* Not quite a year. Nine months, maybe. *What is your relationship with her?* (Long paused to inaudibly release a foamy plop of toothpaste.) We are romantically involved. *How long have you lived together?* About three months. *Has this residence been properly registered with the police to rent to foreigners?*

Long scowled and rinsed vigorously. The answer was no. His landlord would be fined, Long would be evicted, and who knew if they would ever find Winnie.

He left for work. On the way home that evening, he stopped to buy two dinners from the same cart as before. It felt too pessimistic to just buy one. A rat ran along the edge of the tarp awning that sagged above the rice cart, and Long was so startled that he nearly fell off his motorbike and the woman bagging up his takeaway boxes looked at him strangely. At home, he drank the last two beers in the fridge to settle his nerves. Winnie still had not returned. Long turned out all the lights and wandered around the house with his ear pressed against the walls, rapping them softly with his knuckles. He was now genuinely convinced that she might be trapped inside them. The building was old; perhaps its walls were hollow, and this was why things never sounded right. No one knocked back.

The next day was a Saturday. Winnie still had not returned. Long decided that it was time to begin searching for her beyond the perimeter of his own home. He drove in widening concentric circles around the neighborhood on his motorbike, scanning sidewalks and coffee-shop windows for her face. In the afternoon, he set out for District 11, where Winnie's great-aunt lived. The old woman did not remember who Long was, but the cousin who answered the door did and gave him an unpleasant stare. No, she had not seen Winnie since she'd moved out. The cousin closed the door so abruptly that she almost caught Long's fingers in the frame.

Long decided he did not trust them. The great-aunt was at least eighty-five years old, and the cousins looked like they collectively weighed seventy kilos, but perhaps the three of them together could have overpowered Winnie. After pretending to drive away, he circled back to the block and then found a seat at a café with a view of the house's front gate. A stakeout. Maybe he should have become the policeman instead of his brother. Long spent the entire afternoon there before admitting to himself that he did not really believe that they were responsible for Winnie's disappearance.

He couldn't bring himself to go back to District 6 yet, so he parked next to a canal and practiced his dialogue with the police again. *When was the last time you saw Winnie?* In the house, in bed, on Thursday morning. *What did you do that day?* I went to my office. I had *hủ tiếu* for lunch at a place around the corner and then an iced coffee next door. I left work at five-thirty, arrived back at the house just after six, and by then she was gone. *Is there anybody who can vouch for your whereabouts on the seventeenth?* My boss and several coworkers. And the owners of the *hủ tiếu* shop and the café. They know me because I spend my lunch hour the same way every day. *Why didn't you report that she was missing sooner?* I don't know! I was giving her time to come back to me! It would be embarrassing if I went to the police and then found out that she'd just gone to live with a secret boyfriend. *Did you assume that Winnie left you because Binh left you too?* Why are you bringing up Binh? How do you know about Binh? She has nothing to do with this.

He was hyperventilating over the canal railing. The water below was unspeakably polluted, but the sidewalks were lined with beautiful old cast-iron streetlamps, and their glass globes gave off a soft, tea-colored glow that disguised the floating garbage.

Long drove back to his small, dark, empty house. Winnie still had not returned. Should he go door-to-door, asking his neighbors if they'd seen her? He shook his head. Every single one of them would reply that they did not know her and then promptly and anonymously report him to the police after he'd left. People did not get involved in others' business in the alley. Except for one person, it suddenly occurred to Long. He poked his head back outside and looked down the street to see if the *xe ôm* man was lurking at his usual corner like the neighborhood vulture. Tonight, the spot on the sidewalk where he parked his motorbike was empty. Long went back inside, slightly relieved.

Another wild idea, because wild ideas were all that he had now. Long got his tool kit from the spare room. He would pry up the wonky kitchen tiles with a chisel and dig for her. He could picture exactly how it had happened: the landlord had finally showed up to fix the broken light on Thursday morning, discovered that there was an unregistered foreigner living in his house, murdered her because he did not want to deal with the local police, buried her in the spot where he'd already been mucking about in the house's foundation, and then tiled back over it. The dream of the Winnie Tree had been a premonition; all along, she'd been underneath it. Long should have figured it out the first night. He was a psychic as well as a detective. Someone ought to give him a TV show.

But when he opened the toolbox, he discovered something that did not belong there. Something he had not put inside, something he had never seen before. It was a clumsily coiled piece of aluminum wire. A cruel-looking thing, nearly a meter when unfurled. There was dried blood streaking the length of it. No, it was not red paint. Long knew blood like he knew rubber trees. He stared at the wire, and then silently rolled it back up and returned it to the toolbox. He pushed the toolbox back into the corner where it lived. He exited the room and shut the door. Two minutes ago, he hadn't actually believed that he would find Winnie if he dug up the kitchen. Until now, he hadn't seriously considered that real harm had come to her. He could imagine Winnie dead, but he could not handle being confronted by the evidence of things he thought were imaginary being true.

Long went to sleep. He woke up in the morning and rolled onto his right side. Winnie still had not returned.

TWELVE HOURS NORTH OF SAIGON BY BUS AND FIFTEEN BY motorbike, low red hills covered the land like a maculopapular rash. Their slopes were horizontally striped with rows of coffee plants and staked peppercorn vines, and in the flat stretches between the hills farmers also tended patchy plantations of durian, lychee, cashew, and avocado trees. But the widest, evenest expanse of land—just west of Ia Kare, the small and unremarkable town to which it belonged—was occupied by the cemetery. The local people's council would occasionally petition for the graves to be exhumed and their contents relocated so that the valuable acreage could be converted into more farmland, but they were never successful. Here, the living looked after the departed. Though they themselves lived in drab boxes of brick and thatch, they enshrined their dead in tombs painted peach and celadon and gold, with eaves that curled heavenward like lotus petals. From a distance, the cemetery resembled a dazzling miniature city with a skyline formed from the layered angles of crosses and stupa spires. On important anniversaries, painstaking care was taken to clean the graves and offerings were burned by the interred inhabitants' progeny, so the air was usually spiced with smoke and sandalwood from somebody's devotions. There were some, of course, whose families had not been able to afford stones, so they lay beneath simple mounds of earth ringed with bricks, their incense sticks jabbed directly into the ground instead of arranged carefully in ceramic vases. One wealthy local clan with several well-polished tombs to their name had cultivated an elaborate cactus garden around the perimeter of their plot, designed to shield from view the five small dirt heaps of the adjacent tract where five children were buried, all of them dead from malnutrition back in the early eighties. A thumb-shaped chunk of pale limestone, worn egg-smooth, marked the final resting place of an elephant named Su-Su, who had passed away in 1953.

Towering dark and noble over the graves at the center of the cemetery was the envy of all the neighboring towns: the new war monument. The statue was over fifteen feet high, carved out of sumptuous black granite. It depicted a dead or dying soldier draped across the lap of a seated woman, his fingers still clenched around his rifle, the shirt of his uniform falling open to reveal the artist's careful rendering of his abdominal muscles. Because it was unclear whether the woman was supposed to be the soldier's mother or his wife—her head was bowed, the face obscured by a conical hat the size of a fishing boat—she had been given the grandiose appointment of "An Emblem of Vietnamese Womanhood." Storks used to try and nest on top of her hat until the local branch of the Fatherland Front's Commission for the Defense and Preservation of Meaningful Landmarks hired someone to chase them all away.

The man whose funeral was being held this afternoon would not have his name engraved under the granite woman's toes on the base of the monument with the other war martyrs, even though he, too, was once a soldier, and now he, too, was dead. He would not be immortalized with his friends in the black granite because, instead of dying facedown in an unfamiliar rice paddy, he returned home after the war mostly intact, then fathered a dozen children in fifteen years and drank himself to early liver failure. Now his widow, their twelve offspring, and an assembly of other family members in the mourning party, their heads swathed in ceremonial white bands, wailed as they carried him to the waiting tomb.

Watching the funeral party from a distance were three dirty children in school uniforms, aged seven, eight, and nine. Two boys and one girl, squatting atop a turquoise-colored tomb, barefoot and balancing on their heels with their toes hanging over the edge of the large headstone. The boys were clearly brothers, for their lips and ears and noses were identically shaped. But the eyes of the bigger boy were narrow and heavy lidded like a contented house cat's, while the smaller boy had the bulging eyes of a goldfish. They wore navy trousers rolled to the knee and button-up shirts that were not quite filthy enough to disguise the fact that they had once been white. The girl was wedged between the two brothers, one scrawny arm draped casually over the shoulders of the larger one. Someone had made a valiant earlier attempt to contain her hair in two thick plaits, but dark locks had broken free and were sticking out at odd angles, as if she had recently been electrocuted. Her white blouse was the dirtiest of all, and she had taken it upon herself to deflate its poofy cap sleeves by snipping slits all around their cuffs. Their massacred edges flapped sadly when she moved her arms. All three of the children had taken the red neck scarves of their school uniforms and knotted them around their heads with the tails dangling down their backs in a parody of the mourners' headcloths.

As the funeral party wound its way through the cemetery like a line of ants, the children watched them carefully: the elders preoccupied with their displays of grief up near the coffin, and the younger, lower-ranked women of the family trailing toward the back. Far from the elders and safe from their reproaches, these women were noticeably less enthusiastic in their lamentations, stopping periodically to fan themselves or have a covert chat. But behind them there was one other: a man, alone. Both of these details were unusual. The children's eyes narrowed in unison, puzzled. He should have been with the other men toward the front of the line, impatient for the burial to be over so that the postceremony drinking and gambling could start. Or, if he were a relatively new in-law—say, the husband of one of the dead man's nieces—he should have been staying close to her, attentive and careful not to offend anybody. But this man did not seem to mind that he was lagging farther and farther behind.

He was not an immediate family member of the deceased, for instead of a white cloth, the man was sporting a cowboy hat of dust-colored suede with a tattered brim. Everything about him was slightly ill-fitting and askew: the hat was too big, so he wore it far at the back of his head, tilted at an angle that was more precarious than jaunty; the sleeves of his dark suit were too short, making his hands appear disproportionately large, which in turn made the too-small leather briefcase he carried seem even smaller. His hair was long, worn in a low ponytail that would have been stylish at this point in the early nineties were it not quite so greasy. It was barely gray—only lightly streaked in a couple patches—but the man's lined face suggested that he was much older. The children could not fathom his true age. He was not a handsome man; if considered separately, and belonging to a different individual, the features of his face might have been charming—the eyes were framed by long, dramatic, almost feminine lashes and thick lids, the mouth wide, with strangely plump lips that curved up at the edges, the nose of a noble height—but collectively gave an unpleasant, almost mannequin-like impression.

The funeral party was drifting farther away, but the man still did not appear concerned. As he passed the great granite statue, he stopped for a moment in the shade provided by the dead soldier's bottom to fish a cigarette out of his jacket pocket and light it. Then he strolled on again, taking languid puffs of the cigarette and pausing now and then to read a name on a tombstone. At one point he frowned, stooped, picked something up from the ground, and then slipped it into his pocket. He did this several more times, and the children craned their necks to try and see what it was that the man was collecting, but he was too far away to tell. The girl knew they should watch him a little bit longer, just to be certain that he was the right choice, but her curiosity made her hasty. She gave an executive smack to the boys' backs and they hopped down from their perch in unison and landed noiselessly. Because the scrubby ground of the graveyard had been baked to burning by the midafternoon sun and their feet were bare, they needed to move fast. They ran in a tight triangle with the girl in the lead, only breaking formation to dart around the graves that lay in their path. When they were within twenty yards of the man in the suede hat, they slowed down, first to a lope, then a slink, dividing and circling like a trio of jackals.

By now, the man had run out of room in his pockets. He set his small briefcase down on top of a squarish, moderately sized stone (but not before patting it gently to thank its occupant, the late Mr. Le Van An, for allowing him to borrow it momentarily) and began fiddling with the combination lock. Then he heard the sound of someone clearing their throat behind him and his hand froze.

Each of the children was staring at him from atop an individual gravestone. The girl, of course, had chosen the tallest and most imposing one—a slab of gray stone guarded by two painted lions whose heads she now employed as handholds. She cleared her throat again, more authoritatively, and the man in the hat finally turned. He looked from the girl to the two boys flanking her on their smaller graves and then back to the girl again. The younger of the brothers was regretting the stone he had chosen; its top was curved and finely polished, and he was struggling not to slide off. He hoped that this would not take too long.

The man in the hat removed his cigarette from his mouth. "Hello there," he offered, after a beat.

"Hello there," the girl parroted with a grin. Her voice was disconcertingly husky and low for someone so young. "Hello, hello, hello." Then she dropped the smile. "What's in your pocket?"

"I've been tidying," the man replied, though it wasn't really an answer to her question. He didn't seem sure whether he should be addressing just the girl, as she was the apparent ringleader, or her two silent comrades as well. He set his still-lit cigarette down next to his briefcase on the stone (mentally apologizing to Mr. Le Van An), then reached into his jacket and showed them a handful of what appeared at first to be red and saffron-colored confetti. After a moment the children recognized that they were scraps (corners, mostly) of joss paper—fake money for burnt offerings—though what the man was doing with all of them was unclear. An unexpected breeze suddenly lifted a few of the paper scraps from his fingers and sent them floating down to the hot ground, causing the man to curse under his breath as he scrambled to collect them again. When he had recovered each piece, he unlocked his briefcase, emptied all the paper particles into an unseen compartment inside, checked in his pockets for any that might have escaped or were hiding, and then clicked the briefcase shut once more. He finally retrieved his neglected cigarette and took a careful drag, then looked up, seemingly surprised to see the children still there.

"Why?" rasped the girl in that alarming voice of hers, suspicious.

The man lifted his hat to tuck a few stray hairs in place behind his ears. "To finish the offerings, of course. People are so careless these days—they don't bother to burn the papers completely. How do they imagine that makes their ancestors feel?

"I know it doesn't seem all that important," continued the man, half to himself, "but something burned should be burned completely. Unfinished business leaves dangerous openings. And in my experience, it will always come back to haunt you." Then he looked at the children and frowned. "You should be in school!" he said, as if just realizing it.

The little girl was confident that they had chosen an ideal victim: superstitious, absentminded, and not a very important member of the funeral party—now grown small in the distance—for they had not sent anyone back to come and look for him. "We're here to protect the cemetery," she said to him, grin back on.

The man in the hat was fascinated. Could the children be guardian spirits, perhaps?

"That one getting buried over there," the girl continued, gesturing with her thumb toward the far-off mourners. "He must have been pretty important. We know because we saw the size of the flowers they were carrying. Those are the expensive kind. He was probably part of the Ma family. Maybe a cousin." She chewed pensively on the inside of her cheek for a moment. "Okay," she finally said, "five thousand đồng."

"Pardon?" The man frowned again.

"Five thousand đồng. That's what you're going to give us in order to keep his grave safe."

"I'm afraid I don't understand."

The girl leaned forward ever so slightly. "Here's the deal: if you don't pay us the money to protect it, something *bad* could happen. My friend"—she pointed to the larger of the two boys—"might come back here after sunset with a bucket of buffalo shit and empty it"— here she made a grand, expansive gesture with her hands—"aaaaaall over the spot where that important man is buried. Or," she continued, gleefully, "it might not even be buffalo shit. My friend here loves to eat, but he has a very bad stomach." The older brother contributed a doleful shrug. "For dinner tonight," the girl went on, "I think he's going to eat cabbages and eggs—a *lot* of eggs—in fish sauce and, hmm, a little bit of durian, and maybe a couple river eels too. And then, when his belly is good and bubbly, he'll come and squat on top of the tombstone himself!" The little girl emitted a gravelly chuckle, and it was a truly dreadful sound. "Just think how angry that would make that fancy man's ghost! And it would be all your fault for not protecting him when you had the chance, wouldn't it? So, when his spirit comes back looking to get even, he'll come for *you*!" The older brother laughed along with her this time, his eyes turning into crescent moons. The younger brother was soundless, but he gave a very gummy smile as he struggled to stay mounted on his tombstone.

The man sighed. "Yes, yes, enough, I understand." He couldn't help but be slightly disappointed that he had not stumbled across a new kind of guardian spirit, after all, but junior racketeers. Good ones—he was so impressed by their bravado that he was tempted to just hand over the money. He imagined that they would probably go on to find great success in local politics. A twinkle appeared in his eyes. He checked the position of the sun over his shoulder and estimated that there was a safe two-hour window before it set. Blue-black clouds, the exact same shade as the granite statue, were beginning to gather in the southwest, foretelling the impending arrival of the afternoon monsoon.

"You drive a hard bargain," he said, "but could I counter with an offer of my own?"

This was the first time that someone had ever tried negotiating with the children. Nine times out of ten, their victim would decide that it was better to be safe than sorry where the spirit world was concerned and pull their wallet out for the little graveyard hooligans, though there were a couple times in the past that they picked the wrong mourner—someone a little too cantankerous and not superstitious enough—and were chased out of the cemetery and pelted with rocks. They were always prepared for this other possibility, though they were sure that they were too fast to ever get caught. But the man in the hat, unexpectedly, was neither cooperating nor attacking them, and this made the two boys visibly nervous. Their leader, however, remained unflappable.

"What's the offer?" said the girl.

It was the man's turn to smile now. He dropped his finished cigarette into an incense pot and then put his briefcase down on the tombstone once more and twisted the dials. Embossed golden initials in the leather flashed in the sunlight, and the girl squinted but couldn't read them. "You are clever children," he said brightly. "I can see that. Calculating. Entrepreneurial. But foolish—talking about desecrating tombs, provoking spirits . . . most people would be too afraid to do that here. You think you're not afraid of this place . . ." He swept out a hand to indicate the cemetery around them. The briefcase clicked open. "But how brave *are* you? My offer—my wager, really—is that I can show you something that will frighten you so badly you'll run away screaming, and you'll never be the same again. If not, I'll give you *each* five thousand đồng. What do you say?"

The little girl scoffed at him. "There's nothing that can frighten us in the daylight," she said without hesitation.

"Are you sure?"

The looks on the faces of the two brothers certainly indicated that *they* were not sure. While the older boy had a penknife in his pocket, they had never had to use a weapon before. The girl's swagger did not reassure the boys. Something new and sinister was at hand, something that they did not know, and did not want to know.

But the girl's response was to rise and stand up on top of her headstone with her arms crossed defiantly. She did not wobble once. She nodded.

The man shrugged. He removed his hat with a deliberate flourish and laid it down next to his briefcase. The younger brother shivered.

"I had something of an accident when I was younger," the man began. "When I was about your age, in fact. Or a bit older. I had an encounter with what I will call a *bad thing*, for lack of a better word." He reached into the briefcase, dug around, and recovered a few scraps of the joss paper from earlier. "But I was lucky; it left me mostly myself, but with . . . well, I just call it my little party trick. Care to see?"

He held the paper bits in one palm, pulled out his lighter with the other, and then swiftly brought the flame down to his cupped hand. One of the brothers audibly gasped. The little scraps ignited and turned to ash almost immediately, releasing little gray smoke plumes. Quickly, the man bent his head down and inhaled the smoke before it could dissipate completely. He closed his eyes and held his breath for four, five, six long seconds. Then he swallowed, coughed several times, and he yawned.

The children waited. Then they realized that the yawn was not stopping; the man's mouth opened all the way, and then his lower jaw unhinged and kept opening. The skin on his face grew taut and his lips shrank to a thin line, exposing the entirety of his nicotine-yellowed teeth and mottled pink-and-white gums as the mandible dropped farther, farther, down past the neck to the collarbone. The children watched. Terror tightened the boys' chests and dried sharp and sour in the backs of their own open mouths, but the girl did not move, and her face betrayed no sign of fear. She was clenching her teeth a bit hard though, perhaps in response to seeing the jaw in front of her being stretched like rubber. The hole in the man's face finally stopped growing when it was the size of a large papaya and the base of his chin was resting at mid sternum. His stretched-out cheek flesh rippled slightly each time he inhaled. The man opened his eyes again, blinking as they readjusted to the sun, and this grotesque juxtaposition—long, delicate eyelashes fluttering, with a monster mouth gaping beneath them—was at last too much for the two boys to take.

They leapt backward off their gravestones, the larger, older boy slightly faster, his younger brother slipping down and running two steps behind. They tripped over themselves as they fled. The girl remained standing on her stone, unaffected by her friends' cowardice. Only when he was a safe distance away did the smaller boy turn and risk a last, pleading look back. "Binh!" he called out to her, a feeble bleat that she could not hear. But when he caught another glimpse of that ruddy, yawning maw, he abandoned what little sense of loyalty remained and kept following his older brother.

The girl only smirked. She was the kind of child who had come to the realization very early on that in her world, fear was rarely useful, and so, being in possession of precociously strong willpower, had nearly completely exorcised the emotion from herself by age five. This man, this creature in front of her, was disturbing, yes, but also ridiculous and a little sad. Tendrils of dark, slightly stinky smoke were now trickling out from the mouth and wafting toward her. She waved one smoke frond away from her face with her little hand, and it dissolved harmlessly in the humid air.

The man heaved a gigantic sigh, lifted his chin with one hand, and started putting his face back together. It was a delicate process involving a lot of wiggling and waiting for the skin to shrink back into place.

"What are you really doing here, Thing?" demanded the girl.

"I'm looking for my . . . hmm." The man paused, massaged his jaw, and reconsidered his phrasing. "I'm trying to find somebody."

"Are you gonna eat them?" she asked coolly.

"Perhaps. Does *that* frighten you?"

She didn't bother responding; the smirk just grew wider.

The man looked a little crestfallen. "I'm not sure who wins the bet. Your friends are going to have nightmares about me for years, but you're impossible to scare. Shall we call it a draw?" He dug around in his jacket for his wallet, removed a note and held it out to the girl.

"No," said the girl. "No, Thing. We do not have a draw." She did not know what he was, but she hated him. She knew that she would never play in the graveyard with the boys again because of his mouth. They would always remember what they saw this afternoon, but they would never speak of it, because they had run away and she had not—and this, more than the monster itself, was the fact that the boys could not face. It was because shame had now entered their friendship, and it had put its first crack in their trio. The crack was permanent, and it would be the first of many. Years later, the girl would look back on this day as the end of her childhood—already, in this moment, she sensed a kind of curtain being drawn across it—and though it was a scabby and meager and delinquent childhood, its loss filled her with rage. Anger leached into all the parts of her where fear should have been but was missing. The anger was so hot, she imagined that it would burn her up into a heap of ash, and then the wind would blow her away with the cemetery dust and the old cinders of incense and dried flower petals and paper scraps that may have been missed by the strange man. "You can keep your money," she hissed at him, "but remember that *I* won our bet today."

With that, she threw herself backward off the tomb, away from the man, and landed on her feet running. The man watched her go. He almost smiled, but he respected the integrity of her fury too much to do so. He packed up his briefcase, dropped his hat back onto his head, and looked up to check the position of the sun but found that it had been swallowed by the clouds. The rain would begin any minute now. As the girl passed the great black statue, she kicked it impulsively even though she knew it would hurt, and it did, much worse than she had expected. But when she couldn't stop herself from screaming afterward, a scream so loud that it echoed off the tombstones and made heads turn far away in the funeral party, it was not just because her foot hurt.

EVEN BEFORE MOVING TO SAIGON, WINNIE HAD ANTICIPATED that she would be a mediocre English teacher at best, as she lacked any prior experience or real interest in the job. But after only a couple weeks of working at Achievement! International Language Academy, it was clear that she would fail to surpass even her own low expectations. Winnie was incompetent. She went blank when confronted with the unnerving stares of twenty bored teenagers. Her own English came out sounding wrong, her students couldn't understand her, and if she tried switching into halting Vietnamese for them—gleaned from seven years of childhood Sundays spent at language classes in the purple-carpeted basement of suburban Maryland's Our Lady of La Vang church alongside two dozen other young American Nguyens and Phams and Trans whose parents feared they were losing their mother tongue—it only confused them more.

In the beginning she had tried her best. Or, at least, had tried her best at trying. She prepared activities, printed out worksheets that she copied from online teaching blogs, and one Saturday she spent an hour in the bookstore on Le Loi Street picking out a perfect grading note-book. But her first lessons went so poorly that by week two she gave up on planning them altogether and re-designated the entirety of the hour-long class as "Unstructured English Conversation Time." Her students were the kind of wealthy urban high schoolers who had grown up secure in knowing that they would eventually go to college but either weren't quite smart or quite wealthy enough to attend one overseas. There was little incentive for them to excel at the extra English courses they were being forced by their parents to take at a third-rate academy. Most of them spent Unstructured English Conversation Time playing on their phones, but a few enterprising ones used the period to work on their homework from other classes, and one group of older boys who sat at the back of the room would occupy themselves by meticulously filling the pages of their vocabulary workbooks with lewd doodles, which they then left behind for Winnie to crumple up and hide at the bottom of the trash can after class.

Winnie spent her own class time reading unevenly translated Japanese crime novels that she bought from the secondhand paperback stalls near the backpacker quarter. Whenever she finished a book, she gave it to one of her more advanced students in hopes that they would enjoy it one day after their reading comprehension had improved under the tutelage of a more capable educator. It was a gesture she made to try and offset her guilt about the fact that they weren't learning anything from her. Teaching English was what most of the other unmoored expats seemed to do in Vietnam, qualified or not, and Winnie didn't see why they were able to manage it when she could not.

Luckily, the owner of her academy—a morose Singapore-educated man in his forties named Mr. Quy—hadn't caught on to Winnie's sham yet because he struggled to keep his non-Vietnamese employees straight; there were seven other foreign teachers at Achievement!, two of them were both named Alex, and Mr. Quy was frequently day drunk, because his job primarily consisted of wooing prospective investors over beers at eleven A.M. If he was ever in the teachers' lounge it was to take a nap on the foldaway cot he stored in their broom closet. He regularly confused Winnie with Dao, another Vietnamese American teacher in her early twenties, and Winnie never corrected him. After the second time it happened, she had even started pulling her long hair back into a low, disheveled bun—the way that Dao always wore hers—so that they would be indistinguishable from behind. She stopped putting sunscreen on her arms and let them darken to a Dao-ish shade, and she toted her untouched grading notebook around in a straw bag she had purchased because it was similar to one she had seen Dao carrying.

She tended to stay away from other teachers. It was easy to avoid interacting with Nikhil, American Alex, and a middle-aged blond woman whose name she had forgotten; their classes were on Tuesdays and Thursdays and Winnie's were on Wednesdays and Fridays. But Dutch Alex, Dao, and Jeff and Anna Cook were harder to hide from.

She wasn't exactly sure how old Dutch Alex was. He was bald, with a deeply tanned but curiously unwrinkled face, and his wardrobe was made up entirely of zip-off cargo pants and shirts with dragons on them. His wife was Saigonese, and every Friday he brought their roly-poly mixed-race baby to the academy and let the students and other teachers coo over it. Winnie took particular care to stay away from Dutch Alex when he had his small, gurgling accessory in tow after one afternoon when she had accidentally gotten caught in his crosshairs while he was parading down the hallway, brandishing his infant at everyone he encountered and expecting them to squeal with excitement and squeeze the child's saliva-slick fingers.

"Winnie!" he had boomed. Dutch Alex's voice could fell pine trees. Winnie hadn't been able to dart into a side room in time. "Here—hold him!" He thrust the hairless nine-month-old at her, and Winnie was polite enough to stop herself from recoiling. The baby had taken one look at her and then emitted a loud, saurian screech of displeasure. "Awww, he's laughing!" Dutch Alex had said. "He likes you because he knows you're a halfie too!"

Luckily, the baby had begun wailing. This allowed Winnie to slip away unnoticed with her face burning slightly.

Her halfness was the reason she hated getting confused for Dao, even as she gamely played up their slight physical resemblance in order to continue slacking off at work. By pure coincidence, Winnie and Dao were both in their early twenties, originally from the D.C. suburbs, and Vietnamese American. But while both of Dao's parents were Việt, Winnie's mother was white. Their similarities continued to unravel from there: Dao was from a charming tree-lined town in northern Virginia, and Winnie was from the part of Maryland that was entirely strip malls. Dao currently lived in a large apartment full of charming, shabby-chic rattan furniture and had a balcony overlooking the Saigon River. Winnie's unfurnished spare room in her great-aunt's house was deep in the distant warren of District 11. She shared a bathroom with two second cousins from the countryside who had moved to the city to attend university and barely spoke to her when they were home. And her balcony overlooked a garbage-filled alley behind a hospital. Dao was an excellent teacher, bubbly and beloved by her students. Her Vietnamese was superior, her feet were smaller, her complexion was brighter, and her boobs were perkier. Winnie resented Dao for being a better, full-blooded version of herself, but she hated herself more for the involuntary swell of joy she felt whenever she was mistaken for her colleague.

It was a relief for Winnie to be able to loathe the Cooks in the purest and least complicated of ways. Originally from Oregon, Jeff and Anna Cook had been living in Saigon for six years, and the first time they met Winnie they introduced themselves, unprompted, as "the *good* kind of expat." Over the following weeks they had made sure to list all the evidence they had gathered to support this claim: 1) Unlike most of their colleagues (including Winnie), the Cooks had gone to the trouble of acquiring English teaching certifications. 2) They had taken a year and a half of Vietnamese lessons and reached semiproficiency, though their language skills were primarily inflicted upon Bà Khanh, their housekeeper. 3) They never went to Bui Vien to sweat on plastic stools next to other foreigners and get drunk on candy-colored vodka cocktails served in plastic buckets. 4) Neither did they spend their holidays at the coastal resort towns whose shorelines were crowded with clubs and whose white sands were strewn with the beer-barf of kitesurfing English gap-year students. 5) Instead, they donned elaborately velcroed trekking sandals and went tramping through nature preserves in forgotten rural stretches of the North. 6) They documented all of their kayaking and karst-climbing and rappelling and put the photographs up on their travel blog. 7) Somehow in six years they'd only ever gotten their fancy blogging camera stolen once. 8) They had rescued a one-eyed alley dog and named him Goji, and he was now more vaccinated and better fed than most of their students. 9) They smelled like the aloe-scented hand sanitizer with which they anointed themselves constantly, and this was probably the reason why 10) the Cooks had never, ever gotten food poisoning, a fact they particularly enjoyed reminding others of.

The Cooks were also the hardest for Winnie to evade. Both of them taught on the same days that she did, and they always seemed to be waiting to pounce on her with questions about her weekend plans or unsolicited advice about which Saigon pizza restaurant had the best imported cheese or very long stories about spelunking in Quang Ngai. They would pop up behind her unexpectedly in the teachers' lounge, or the bathroom, or the balcony that she liked to disappear to between classes. Their persistent social overtures puzzled Winnie, because she could tell that the Cooks liked her as little as she liked them. Mrs. Cook's classroom was located directly opposite hers, and sometimes, when Winnie was reading her detective novels, her feet up on her desk and her students left to their own devices, she would glance out the door and see the other woman watching her from across the corridor, lips pursed disapprovingly. But for unknown reasons, Mrs. Cook hadn't snitched on her yet to Mr. Quy. Winnie had the troubling hunch that she was just waiting for the right moment to blackmail her with the information.

BY HER FIFTH WEEK, Winnie no longer felt guilty when she cashed her paychecks. She had adopted a uniform of black and indigo and dung-colored linen sack dresses, purchased for five dollars apiece from an airless, sepulchral semibasement boutique in the shadowlands around Binh Tay Market. Winnie thought they helped her blend in with the dark academy walls. If she was successful at avoiding the Cooks, entire days could pass where she didn't speak to another human being. Her students no longer needed the pretense of her faux instructions, and would file into the room and begin doodling or texting or napping on their own, then leave quietly when the period was over. At home, Winnie's two cousins treated her like an American ghost who happened to live with them; they either seemed slightly frightened when she appeared in the hall or just ignored her completely. She was proactive about hiding from her great-aunt, who would interrogate her about how often she attended mass every time their paths crossed. Most days, the house smelled like the steamed sardines that Winnie's great-aunt ate wrapped in rice paper for every meal. On extra-hot days, it smelled like the biomedical waste dumpster of the hospital next door.

Because she dreaded being at home so much, Winnie had started spending most of her free time in coffee shops. She chose a new one each day, leery of becoming a regular somewhere and losing any of the anonymity she was working so hard to achieve. After leaving the academy for the day she would take a motorbike taxi out to an unfamiliar district, amble along until she found a place that she liked, then loiter for as many hours as she could, only returning to the house after her great-aunt went to bed at nine. Sometimes she chose little coffee shops that were cached down narrow alleys—four tables packed into the front sitting room of a family's house, pantsless toddlers capering about underfoot, roasted watermelon seeds—complimentary but never touched—slowly going stale in red plastic bowls next to the unused ashtrays of card-playing men in undershirts who tapped their cigarettes out onto the floor tiles instead. On other days, Winnie chose one of the large chain coffee shops: glossy, air-conditioned boxes with maroon-and-beige interiors and particle board furniture and Wi-Fi-seeking backpackers. She discovered sprawling garden cafés hidden behind inconspicuous gates on mundane-looking avenues, where well-heeled professionals and housewives met to drink pastel-hued smoothies and pose for photos next to the manicured fig trees and plumeria shrubs and miniature waterfalls. She sat on the sidewalk on plastic stools, beneath makeshift tarp roofs strung up between scrawny elms, drinking coffee poured over gray ice that she had to pick gravel out of. She studied faces. She read her detective novels. She switched to soy milk or beer when she had drunk too much coffee. She walked streets until they ran out, and then she chose a new direction. She ducked under awnings during sudden downpours. When she got hungry there was always someone on a street corner selling grilled porkchops on rice or bánh mì or soup iridescent with chicken fat. Winnie believed that this was the best way to absorb the entirety of the city, inch by humid inch, and she applied herself to the task with all the energy that she was not devoting to her actual teaching job.

WINNIE'S FORTY-NINTH DAY IN Vietnam found her once again among the shelves of a used book stall on Pham Ngu Lao, searching for crime novels between the blue spines of the Lonely Planets.

She purchased two (per their back covers: "Haunted by the memory of his murdered wife who he could not save, Detective Kusakawa searches for a serial killer on the loose in Osaka," and "A salaryman is seen getting onto a train at Tokyo Station bound for Aomori at nine in the morning but his corpse is discovered in Yokohama one hour later . . ." Winnie could tell that it was going to be twins, but she didn't really read the books for the mystery) and, as she was putting away her change, felt a fat droplet of rain sting the skin on her forearm. She and the bookseller tilted their heads back in unison. Above them: an ambush of dark clouds. Winnie and the bookseller glanced at each other for a nanosecond of panicked solidarity before the sky opened up, the bookseller ran to pull protective tarps over his shelves, and Winnie dashed toward the internet café a few doors down—no time to find a coffee shop—for shelter.

Inside, the patter of teenage fingers on keyboards drowned out the patter of the rain outside. Winnie found a free computer and decided to check her email.

The state of her inbox was one of such extreme neglect that her fourteen-year-old neighbor, flicking his eyes away from his game and over to her monitor for what he had only intended to be a half second of perfunctory snooping, pursed his lips and let out an unvoiced whistle of horror and awe. There were over six thousand unread messages.

Winnie did not notice him. She was unbothered by the clutter of her own emails and hadn't deleted a single one in at least three years. Was it apathy, was it nostalgia, or was it because if Winnie ever cleared out her arsenal of old promotions and newsletters and phishing scams, the scant handful of real correspondences that remained would be a painful testament to the smallness and loneliness of her life? Because she already knew the answer, there was no need for Winnie to ask herself this question.

Today, however, two new emails had arrived that could be added to that scant handful. The first was from her mother. Winnie only skimmed it, because all emails from her mother were identical: an exuberant greeting followed by a brief chastisement for not responding more often and in greater detail, and then several paragraphs of gushing updates about Winnie's three (much) older siblings and their families. When she got around to it later, Winnie would reply with the same bland reassurances she had deployed five weeks ago in response to the last one. In the imaginary Saigon of Winnie's six-sentence responses, her classes were great. Everything, in fact, was great. Her room at her *bà cố*'s house was great. Her new friends (who, in email world, existed) were great, and her coworkers were great too. Her two cousins? Great!

The second one was from her brother Thien, and while Winnie had been expecting this particular message, she still felt her stomach tighten when she saw his name nestled among the spam.

HEY! HOPE YOU'RE DOING WELL OVER IN THE FATHERLAND! WANTED TO LET YOU KNOW THAT I REACHED OUT TO MY OLD FRIEND FROM MEDICAL SCHOOL, SANG, THE ONE I MENTIONED BEFORE. HE'S BEEN LIVING IN DISTRICT I FOR THE PAST SEVEN YEARS AND HE SAID HE'D BE MORE THAN HAPPY TO SHOW YOU THE ROPES

AND HELP YOU OUT WITH ANYTHING YOU NEED. SO PLEASE GIVE
HIM A CALL AS SOON AS YOU CAN. BIG LOVE, T

Winnie scowled at the phone number at the bottom. Along with
staying at her great-aunt's place, the promise to meet Sang from Medical School was the familial appeasement tax she had agreed to pay before leaving America. Her parents had been so relieved to hear that
there was a successful Vietnamese American doctor in Saigon who
could keep an eye on their substandard daughter, they hadn't even
minded that Winnie only had a one-way ticket and no concrete plans
for returning.

As she grudgingly took out her phone and began composing the
message (*Hi. This is Thien's sister . . .*), Winnie consoled herself with
the thought that this Sang was undoubtedly very busy with his doctoring, and had only agreed to meet her out of politeness. With luck, he
wouldn't even respond. And even if he did get back to her, his schedule
was probably so full that she would not have to endure any of his rope-
showing for at least several weeks. Winnie hit send.

She was wrong. Two minutes later, her phone chirped. *Are u free
now? Text me ur location and I'll come meet u*

While Winnie was put off by his unwillingness to write out "you,"
the brisk impatience of his message verged intriguingly on the creepy.
She briefly considered telling him she was working, but she was now,
despite herself, a little curious. And more importantly, once she had
paid her family the Sang fee, their grip on her, already loosening,
would become even flimsier.

She logged out of her email and gave 3,000đ to the front desk for
her seventeen minutes of internet use. During this time, the rain had
stopped, and Winnie stepped outside into a Saigon in the act of drying
itself off. The bookseller was dumping the pooled water from his tarps.
A woman was wringing out the end of her ponytail into the gutter. A
man taking his postdownpour constitutional did not observe the low,
raindrop-laden branches of a tree growing out of the sidewalk until it
was too late; he accidentally walked into one and cursed loudly as it

released its miniature shower upon him. There was a transient crystal-line quality to the light. The heat had not yet relaunched its offensive. Winnie found the street number of the internet café and texted it to Sang. *I'm free*, she wrote, even though it did not feel particularly true.

While Winnie was debating whether she should buy a coffee from a woman with a pushcart, she heard the squeak of taxi wheels coming to a halt on the wet asphalt.

Sang rolled down the window, quickly scanned the sidewalk for his half-American, and nodded when he saw Winnie. "Ngoan!" he called, "Hop in."

Ngoan. She flinched when she heard it, and then chastised herself for being taken aback. Of course he would know her by her Vietnam-ese name; it was what Thien and the rest of her family called her. Mouth set in a grim line, she rose from her stool and began walking over to the taxi.

Ngoan. The name on all her paperwork. The name she couldn't quite kick. A jarring cohesion of letters that could not be easily molded into something more Western sounding. In its various distortions on the lips of her American peers and teachers and neighbors growing up, it was a croak, or a yawn interrupted by something phlegmy in the throat. And it was made even worse in conjunction with her surname, Nguyen. Ngoan Nguyen. A double helping of letter combinations that were jarring to the American eye and nonsoluble to the American tongue. She could recall in perfect detail every awkward roll call, every raised-eyebrows-and-pursed-lips look of panic on the attendance-taker's face at the beginning of the semester when they arrived at the *n*'s. "Winnie" had been the gradual result of years of explaining how to say her last name. "Nguyen" became "Win," which by high school became "Winnie," which stuck.

Even if Winnie had wanted to ask Sang to call her by her preferred name, she didn't have the chance to:

"Glad you could make it," he said as she climbed into the back seat of the cab. From the front, he reached around and offered her an abrupt and awkwardly angled left-handed shake. His right hand was holding a

flip phone up to his ear. "You can call me Dr. Sang. Everyone does."
He pointed to the phone. "I'll be done with this in two minutes."

He proceeded to have a sixteen-minute conversation conducted entirely in what Winnie inferred was slightly halting Thai, which she
wished she didn't find impressive but did. She spent this time trying to
figure out their location by looking at street signs. Her mental map of
Saigon was too patchy to guess where they were going.

After Dr. Sang had finished his phone call and hung up, the window
for introductions and name corrections had closed. "Ngoan," he said
(she almost flinched again but was able to stop herself in time), studying her via the taxi's rearview mirror, "You're all grown up. I almost
didn't recognize you."

"Oh," said Winnie, embarrassed, "Have we met before?"

"Only once, very briefly," he said with a smile. Winnie thought that
his teeth were too long and the hair on the sides of his head was too
short. She didn't like that she could see his scalp through it. Pink-white
skin, like a scallop. "You probably don't remember. Thien introduced
me to your family at our graduation. That would have been, what, ten
years ago? You were just a kid."

Winnie nodded slowly, an imprecisely edged memory beginning to
reassemble itself in her mind against her will. The graduation: She,
surly and thirteen. Her thighs sticking to a wooden auditorium seat.
Thien in golden academic regalia that matched his status as golden
child. Their father struggling to figure out the buttons on the camcorder
he'd bought the week before, a used Sony the size of a loaf of bread.
Thien posing for the video with Winnie's other older brother and sister, who were twenty-four and twenty-one, respectively, while Winnie
watched, resenting the three of them for their closeness in age and in
every other way that mattered. Resenting the three of them for taking
up all the space in their family for nearly all of her young life and then
vanishing in quick succession, leaving behind a vacuum that she could
not fill. Thien posing with his friends from the Vietnamese Student As-
sociation, all the fellow golden children with refugee parents and bright
medical futures—*ah yes*, she thought, twisting the mental lens of her

memory into focus—there was Dr. Sang with his long teeth, standing next to her brother. Greeting her family in formal Vietnamese, even her white mother, because golden boys were always polite boys.

"Do you work around here?" she asked, hoping he would provide a clue about where they were headed. "Are you at one of the big hospitals?"

"Oh, no," said Dr. Sang. "You could say that I run a private practice. More money and better hours, so I can pursue some of my other business ventures on the side."

"Is that why you moved to Vietnam?" In the mirror, Winnie saw Dr. Sang's eyes flick sideways. Her question had accidentally brushed up against something it should not have.

But then he just laughed. "Why would I settle for simply doing well in America when I can have the run of the entire playground here?" he said. From his jacket pocket he produced a small pink bottle, rattled out two pills, and swallowed them dry, seemingly without any difficulty. Winnie felt her own throat seize up reflexively just from watching. Then the doctor squinted out of the taxi window. "Oh, good, we're here."

The taxi had turned down a side street and was pulling up in front of a moderately sized pagoda with walls painted the mealy red-pink of an overripe guava. Winnie looked at Dr. Sang for some sort of explanation ("Your Vietnamese education requires a temple blessing" or "I am now going to perform surgery on a monk"), but he just gave her an encouraging smile and gestured for her to exit the vehicle.

"Go ahead," he said.

Winnie hesitated, her hand on the door handle. "Is this a special pagoda?" she asked, hoping it was an effective way of disguising the question "Why are we here?"

Dr. Sang flashed her a look of exasperation. "It's a pagoda. It's a very nice pagoda. What more do you want?" There was a sharp edge to his voice that took Winnie by surprise. "All Americans who visit Vietnam like to see the pagodas," he added, enunciating carefully, as if reciting something he had memorized from a book.

"I'm very excited to see it," Winnie said quickly, and got out of the taxi. Dr. Sang remained seated. It appeared that he did not intend to leave the car. "Are you . . ." Winnie began, apprehensively.

Dr. Sang pointed to his phone. "I have to make another quick call. You go have a look around. Take as long as you like. Enjoy yourself!" The sharpness in his voice still had not dissolved completely, causing the last line to sound vaguely like a threat.

Relieved to get away from her host, Winnie bolted for the pagoda gate. She now understood that Dr. Sang had never been eager to meet her, just eager to get their meeting over with. This half-guided tour was his own version of paying a tax.

The pitiful thing was that she had nowhere better to be than this largely empty pagoda, in the middle of the afternoon, with the kind of man who asked people to call him "Doctor" outside of the office. In forty-nine days, this was the first time that she had gone somewhere besides her great-aunt's house or the academy and not been alone. Winnie was determined not to enjoy herself, purely because it was what Dr. Sang had told her to do and she disliked him, but as she passed through the stone archway and into a shaded courtyard, she felt a hush fall over her heart. It did not feel like stepping back in time but like stepping sideways into a protected pocket that existed outside of it. Banyans flanked the courtyard, cauled with tangles of aerial roots that resembled dripping candle wax. In a walled, circular pool at its center, the silhouettes of three geriatric turtles moved slowly through cloudy green water. Long wires had been strung up between the archway and the entrance to the actual temple; every few feet, lanterns bobbed like buoys, their exposed wooden ribs peeking out in spots where the silk had rotted away. Winnie followed them inside.

The only light within the temple came from offertory candles and a single glowing recess that housed a statue of the Buddha with blank, bronze eyes, framed by concentric circles of psychedelic flashing yellow and purple tube lights. The air was stagnant and agarwood scented from the bedspring-shaped coils of burning incense that dangled from the ceiling. In the darkness, distorted by the strobe of disco Buddha, the shadowy figures of the few other visitors to the pagoda—all of them women and most of them on their knees—took on a touch of menace. Despite the heat, Winnie felt a strange chill burrowing its way across her shoulder blades, and the longer she stood there, her skin turning violet, gold, violet, gold with each flash of the lights, the more the feeling spread. She exited the temple quickly and found a banyan to regain her composure beneath.

Winnie felt better in the sunlight. She let her hand rest on the tree's ropy trunk. The bark was smooth beneath her fingers. These were the breed of strangling ficus that spent two hundred years braiding their bodies around a host tree, killing it while gradually assuming its form. Parasite, doppelgänger, sarcophagus. Winnie admired it. What she wished, she reflected dreamily, her whole back now leaning against the tree, was for the same thing to happen to her. For the new self she'd hoped she would become in Saigon—a better self, a banyan self, resilient and impenetrable—to encase Old Winnie completely in its cage-like lattice of roots and then let her wither away inside. She wanted there to be no trace left of that thirteen-year-old girl that Dr. Sang had remembered.

But now her daydream had been interrupted by the reminder that the doctor was still sitting in a taxi on the other side of the gate. Winnie wondered how many minutes she should wait before returning to him. How long was long enough to have believably pretended to enjoy oneself at a pagoda? She pushed herself up from the trunk and headed toward the turtle pond, thinking that she would pass the time by staring at them, but just then, in the corner of her eye, something glinted.

It was sunshine on metal spokes. A woman in a wheelchair was sitting just to the side of the same tree that Winnie had been leaning against. Winnie didn't know why she hadn't noticed her earlier. Her face had been powdered to ageless, poreless immaculacy, and she had the kind of hair that was a black so pure, all the light that touched it was swallowed up instead of reflected. The woman smiled at Winnie, and Winnie smiled back automatically before she realized that the woman was selling lottery tickets. Winnie felt it would be rude not to buy one

from her after making eye contact. She sheepishly searched for a
10,000-đồng note in her wallet and walked over. With a graceful nod,
the lottery woman held out her booklet of glossy red slips for Winnie
to choose from and then folded her hands atop the blanket on her lap
while she waited.

Winnie could not remember which numbers were supposed to be
lucky. She thumbed through the tickets, looking for a 22, her age, or a
30, her birthday, in any of the six-digit combinations. When she
couldn't find either, she decided to base her decision on the accompanying illustrations, for each ticket had a different picture—lotuses, a
heap of melons, boats in a harbor, a massive carp. The one she found
herself pausing at, 2 5 0 1 2 9, had a seated dog on it, depicted with a
cheerful curve to the tail that suggested wagging, and an orangey-
brown patch over one eye. It reminded her of the kind of dog she used
to draw over and over again when she was a child, filling entire pads of
construction paper. Growing up, Young Winnie had longed for a
puppy with an intensity that had occasionally frightened her parents,
who were "not pet people." Winnie gave the dog on the lottery ticket
an imaginary little scratch on the head with a fingertip and then handed
the rest of the booklet back to the woman along with her 10,000đ. She
looked at the woman a little nervously, part of her irrationally hoping
that she would receive some kind of small signal to show that she had
chosen a good number.

To her surprise, the woman's facial expression did, in fact, change.
As she continued gazing unblinkingly back at Winnie, the corners of
her lips began curling upward, like guitar strings being slowly pulled
taut on tuning pegs. It shifted her smile from pleasantly serene to something that Winnie could not describe but which made her stomach suddenly feel icy. It was triumphant, but there was a detached, almost
clinical element of pity in it as well. It was not even really a smile anymore.

Clutching her ticket, Winnie backed away from the woman, who,
she noted with fresh alarm, still hadn't blinked. Away from the temple, away from the trees, away from that face. She backed through the

gate, the prospect of Dr. Sang now preferable to remaining in that courtyard a minute longer.

The doctor was no longer talking on the phone—he was texting rapidly, but he was standing outside the taxi now, leaning against its hood at an uncomfortable-looking 140-degree angle that Winnie was sure he thought looked alluringly louche. This was not being done for her sake though, but for the five attractive young women working at the electronics store next to the pagoda who had an unobstructed view of him through their large glass window.

"Done already?" he said, pushing himself up from his deep lean with visible difficulty. "Did you take any photos for your family? If you didn't remember to take photos, you should go back and get some," he warned, humorlessly.

"I took a lot," lied Winnie. She folded her lottery ticket in thirds, so that she wouldn't crease the dog, and placed it in her wallet. Dr. Sang watched this with the most interest he had shown all afternoon.

"We'll have to remember to check that tonight to see if you've won anything," he said. Then he slid back inside the taxi. "Ready for the second stop?"

WINNIE HAD NOT ANTICIPATED that the pagoda was part of a larger itinerary. The second stop was the old presidential palace ("All Americans who visit Vietnam like to see the presidential palace," he declared on the way over, taking out his pill bottle from his jacket and eating two more capsules like they were candy). They didn't actually stop for a tour of the building, which Winnie was thankful for—the doctor just ordered the taxi to drive slowly around the block three times so Winnie could look at it. He did the same thing at the cathedral, but at stop number four, the post office, he told the driver to pull up onto a curb and then instructed Winnie to go into the building and take photos. ("*All* Americans like to take photos of the post office.") While he waited in the car, she strolled around the main hall for ten minutes, admiring the colonial curvature of its paneled ceiling.

When she returned, Dr. Sang announced that they would end with dinner at a hot pot restaurant. It was just past five, but Winnie was already hungry. The promise of both a meal and of the end of the Dr. Sang Saigon Experience cheered her up right away. "Do all Americans visiting Vietnam like to eat hot pot?" she ventured playfully.

Dr. Sang just blinked at her, confused. "What do you mean?" he said. "Americans don't come here to eat hot pot." He turned back around in his seat. "What a weird question," he muttered to himself under his breath.

THE RESTAURANT HE HAD chosen was on the top floor of a newly constructed shopping complex. They had to ride eight gleaming escalators in order to get to it, and so Winnie was disappointed when they arrived and there were no windows. It was her first time being this high up in the city—she lived her life in Vietnam horizontally and at sidewalk level—and she had been curious about the view. The restaurant was decorated in a color palette of lacquered blacks and brothel reds, with framed swords on the dark walls, and Winnie and the doctor were the only customers there. Winnie was not surprised at all when Dr. Sang immediately took the sole menu on their table and then ordered for them without consulting her, but she was taken aback when he told the waiter to remove his bowl and chopsticks.

"I have to save my appetite," he explained to Winnie. "After this I'm taking a group of investors out to dinner. Bird's nest soup. Have you ever tried it?" He asked this with a waxy little smile, knowing perfectly well that she hadn't. "A hundred U.S. dollars for one bowl of bird spit. It doesn't even taste like anything; it's all texture. Very slippery. Like raw egg whites." Winnie no longer felt guilty about the afternoon's astronomical taxi bill, which the doctor had paid. Across the table, he was taking his pills out again. Now that she was closer, Winnie saw that it was a bottle of Pepto-Bismol.

Dr. Sang noticed her staring. "Oh, this?" he said, giving the bottle a jaunty shake. "Three years ago I decided to quit cigarettes and alcohol and all my other substances cold turkey—better for the brain and the body, et cetera—and to make it easier, I got in the habit of popping a couple of these every time I got the itch, just to take the edge off. And now they've grown on me." He unscrewed the cap and tipped out a chalky capsule. "I even like the taste. But I prefer the pills to the chewable tablets. Swallowing is just more satisfying." He took the pill between his thumb and index finger, placed it in his mouth with the kind of delicacy usually reserved for tabs of LSD, and then smiled.

Winnie was struggling to keep her face neutral. It was one of the more insane things she had ever heard. In her head she calculated that the doctor had taken five Peptos during their three hours together, so he was going through at least half a bottle a day. She pictured his luxurious apartment somewhere in District 1; imagined his penthouse views, his imported flooring, a rooftop pool, perhaps, and then, in a capacious bathroom, a closet stocked entirely with little pink bottles. With horror, she tried to contemplate what his bowel movements were like. At that moment, two waiters arrived with a tabletop burner and a large vat of broth. They ignited a white puck of paraffin beneath the hot pot and then vanished again.

"So," said Dr. Sang, "your brother's email said you're an English teacher here."

It appeared that this part of the proceedings would involve more small talk than Winnie liked. "Yes." The less said about her teaching career, the better.

"And your mom teaches too, if I remember correctly?"

Winnie fidgeted with her chopsticks. "Middle school language arts now," she said. "But she used to teach ESL. That's how she met my dad—she volunteered at the refugee camp where his family ended up. He was one of her students."

The waiters had returned, this time with three platters. One was heaped entirely with noodles. One was shingled with thin slices of raw beef, pork balls, fish cakes, gray apostrophes of uncooked shrimp, puffs of fried tofu. The last was overflowing with vegetables: watercress and shaved banana flower, a whole head's worth of cabbage, a mountain of okra. It was enough food for six people.

Dr. Sang was nodding to himself. "I remember Thien telling me about your parents. I thought it was such a cute story." There was that sharpness in his voice again, just beneath the skin of his words. "My parents weren't American enough to have a cute story. They both just worked at the same nail salon when they came over."

But isn't it just the same story? thought Winnie to herself. A four-word story: *"It was the war."*

Dr. Sang was still going. "We grew up too poor for cuteness. Whenever your brother talked about your family, it sounded like a fairy tale to me. Especially you guys and your rhyming names. Like the dwarves in *Snow White*."

"Well, not all of us rhymed," demurred Winnie. The names of the seven dwarves didn't rhyme either, but she knew he would not like to be corrected. "I came along and ruined the pattern." Thien, Hien, Lien, and then, eight years later, Ngoan, like an intrusive trombone in what was supposed to be a string quartet. "I don't think they were planning on having to name a fourth child."

The hot pot was now bubbling. "Load it up while it boils," ordered Dr. Sang. "Veggies first. Then shrimp and meatballs." Winnie tentatively began to choose her morsels and lower them in. Impatient with her slow chopsticking, the doctor grabbed the ladle himself and dumped all of the cabbage into the soup.

Winnie's appetite was faltering in the presence of an insurmountable quantity of food. Because it was impossible to consume this much by herself, her stomach was giving up already. She felt angry now. It was a trap. The doctor had known she would never be able to finish it. He had planned to prove that Winnie was the girl he'd thought she was: spoiled, half white, wasteful. But she was going to prove him wrong instead.

"It never felt like a fairy tale to me," she said, as she poked all the floating greenery down below the surface of the liquid to finish cooking.

"Hmm?"

"Or if it did, it felt like one that I had accidentally wandered into by mistake. Thien, Hien, Lien. Doctor, lawyer, engineer," she recited. "Well, technically, doctor, engineer, lawyer, but still. No one needed a Ngoan." She laughed and began rolling the meatballs into the soup from the platter, ignoring the painful coiling in her stomach. "Between the three of them, they accomplished everything that my parents ever wanted, and they're all married with their own kids already. There weren't any American expectations left over for me." She didn't know why she was telling him this. The doctor had taken his phone out again and wasn't really listening.

Or maybe he was. "Is that why you moved to Vietnam?" he asked, without looking up from his screen. Everything was in the hot pot now. Too many things—the soup had risen and was boiling over now, rivulets of orange-hued liquid hitting the burning paraffin and hissing. When Winnie did not reply, he clicked the phone shut and gave her a slightly reproachful glance. "I answered when you asked me the same question earlier," he reminded her.

"I came here to teach English," Winnie said lamely.

The doctor snorted. "That's a justification, not a reason. No one comes here to teach English, least of all the actual English teachers. They're in Asia to find themselves."

"I didn't come here to find myself," protested Winnie quickly. "I don't want to find anything."

Dr. Sang gave her a look that was nearly as unsettling as the lottery woman's, back at the temple. It pierced through her, but there was something in it adjacent to kindness, and she was unprepared for that. He took the ladle and dealt her a bowlful of broth, making sure that it contained at least one of every ingredient. "Then just be careful nothing finds you instead," he finally said, handing it to her. "Eat."

Winnie picked up a shrimp with shaky chopsticks. She brought it to her lips and, even though her throat was trying to tie itself shut, she chewed it into sludge and swallowed. She would waste nothing, she told herself. She shoveled down all the beef next, bringing the bowl up with her free hand to wash the meat down with spicy broth. Winnie ate the okra, ate the gooey strings of what had once been sliced tomato, ate the tofu, transformed during its sojourn in the soup into pouches of boiling liquid that burned her tongue when she bit down, ate the banana flower that felt like coarse, curly hairs in her mouth. Dr. Sang watched her and said nothing.

Once she had drained her bowl, Winnie took hold of the ladle herself and refilled it. She wiped her eyes with the back of her hand, not sure if what she was wiping were the beginnings of tears but wanting to head them off early if they were. This time she had unwittingly served herself an entire bowl of dripping cabbage. Still, she was determined to consume all of it, and she did, bite by torturous wet bite. Winnie wanted to throw up, but she reached for the ladle once more.

"Ngoan. Stop," Dr. Sang said quietly. It still took her a moment to remember that the name he had called her by was her own.

Her hand fell back. "Thank you," she whispered. She couldn't even look at what was left in the pot. None of it could be saved.

THEY RODE THE EIGHT escalators back down in silence.

At the bottom, Dr. Sang asked the doorman to hail two taxis for them. "You take the first one," he said to Winnie. "I have to go directly to my dinner. Will you be able to get home from here? Do you live close by?"

Winnie nodded, even though she still wasn't certain which district they were currently in.

"Here," said Dr. Sang, pulling out two 200,000đ notes and handing them to her. "That's enough to get you halfway to Ba Ria." He laughed. "Oh, wait!" he said suddenly, "I forgot—your lottery ticket. I'll show you how to check the results. Take it out."

Winnie unzipped her wallet, putting away the 400,000đ from the doctor and pulling out the ticket.

"So, first you look and see which province it's for. It should say it somewhere along the top. It's usually Dong Nai or Tien Giang."

Winnie frowned. "It doesn't have a province." She flipped the ticket over, examined the back, then returned to the front again. There was the dog, there was the number, but there was no sign of a province.

"Let me see." The doctor took the ticket, glanced down at it, then handed it back. He couldn't quite keep the smile off of his face. "Oh, Ngoan. You got scammed. This is a fake. I didn't even know people went to the trouble of printing their own lottery tickets to trick foreigners. And I thought I knew all the grifts here!" He handed it back to Winnie and laughed when she put it carefully in her purse. "Why are you keeping that? Throw it away."

"It's a souvenir," said Winnie. But the truth was that even though she couldn't explain it, she knew that the ticket was hers now. She couldn't just get rid of it.

By now, their taxis had arrived. Dr. Sang waved goodbye to Winnie as she climbed into her car.

"Feel free to contact me if you want help with anything," he said. "I'm sure that you won't need to though." It was polite, but his meaning was clear. The two of them were finished with each other now.

In the taxi, Winnie felt so sick that she wrapped her arms tightly around herself and squeezed like she was holding the seams of her skin together to keep the soup from exploding out of her. The concerned driver asked her if she was cold, and she could not answer because she was sure that if she opened her mouth, hot pot would bubble up. He turned off the air-conditioning, thinking that she hadn't understood his Vietnamese, and so Winnie spent the rest of the ride back to her great-aunt's house as sweaty as she was nauseous.

THE NEXT MORNING, WINNIE went to a phone store and spent the leftover taxi money from Dr. Sang on a new SIM card. She dropped her old one in the gutter on her walk to the academy. Now he would not be able to contact her again even if he wanted to. Winnie told herself that the uneasy fluttering she still felt in her stomach was just the sensation of her old roots finally starting to come loose.

T WAS A SLOW WEEKDAY AT CAFÉ MAX, AND AN EVEN SLOWER one at the Fortune Teller's office, which was located in the coffee shop's back storage closet; the owner—Max himself—let him rent it in exchange for weekly horoscopes. Though the Fortune Teller's horoscopes were always alarmingly accurate, whenever he bet on soccer games he lost. On this particular afternoon he was at the front of the coffee shop, gambling away his assistants' paychecks on Liverpool vs. Arsenal with the other middle-aged men who whiled away their daytime there, sipping iced tea until it was an acceptable hour to begin drinking liquor, all of them elbowing each other for a better view of the tiny television.

Back in the storage closet, Second Assistant squished his leftover coffee grounds around with a spoon and glared at First Assistant over the desk that they were forced to share. He had never forgiven her for the fact that, while he had to put up with a plastic stool, she got a real chair with a cushioned seat because she claimed to have a bad back. Probably from all the flailing she did during her trances, which Second Assistant was certain she faked. He was also convinced that the Fortune Teller didn't believe in First Assistant's "ghost possessions" either but allowed them to continue because all of the wailing and spasming and rolling around on the floor impressed their clients (and guaranteed a bit of boob jiggling).

First Assistant's alleged clairvoyance was the reason that she had been promoted above Second Assistant, leaving him with all the shitty tasks: he was the one who had to chase after sacrificial chickens when they escaped, drag heavy teak furniture into arrangements the Fortune Teller deemed more pleasing to the spirits, and revive old women with eucalyptus oil when they fainted during exorcisms. He was the one sent outside to burn joss paper during a monsoon, crouching damp and miserable beneath a rusty umbrella while, inside, First Assistant draped herself over a sofa next to the Fortune Teller and pretended to chat with the dead.

Second Assistant was starting to regret not studying English in university like his parents had wanted him to. He could have been a tour guide by now, getting paid to take drunk Australians around on a boat in Ha Long Bay. He wouldn't live in a crumbling apartment complex, or have to wear cumbersome protective amulets while he slept because his job made him susceptible to psychic interference from spirits. He might even have a real chair. Second Assistant gave his coffee grounds another jab. He made a mental note to look up night classes at the nearby language academies when he got home.

And then the office phone rang.

"Saigon Spirit Eradication, Second Assistant speaking, please describe your supernatural predicament," he rattled off in his most brisk, businesslike tone. On the other side of the desk, First Assistant rolled her eyes and continued thumbing through a magazine. Second Assistant made sure that the pen he chose from the communal pen jar was one of her fancy ballpoints.

From the other end of the line there was nothing but light, crackly silence. *Another prank caller,* thought Second Assistant, sticking the pen in his mouth and chewing absently for two seconds, before:

Cracklecrackle. "Hello? Hello?" A man's voice.

Second Assistant spat out the pen. "Yes, hello? How may I help you?"

"Hello. My house has sounds," the man said abruptly. "My wife and I don't know where they're coming from."

Second Assistant could now identify his accent—the slippery Central Highlands cadence characterized by a general sloshiness of speech, punctuated intermittently with hard, phlegmy consonants. *Noises—disembodied,* he jotted down on a notepad. He waited for further elaboration, and when none came, offered: "Voices? Thumping? Footsteps? Weeping?"

"Dripping."

Second Assistant stopped writing. "Dripping?"

"Dripping. You know, *plip, plip, plip,* those kinds of water sounds?"

"Yes, I obviously know what dripping sounds like!" said Second Assistant crossly. "I just think that perhaps you should be talking to a plumber instead of wasting the time of the premier ghost-catching agency in southern Vietnam!"

The man was not offended. "I would agree," he chuckled, "if it weren't for the fact that my house doesn't have indoor plumbing. That makes the dripping a little more unusual, no?"

"Well couldn't it just be . . . erm, trapped rainwater?" Second Assistant persisted halfheartedly.

"Believe me, I wish it was—I'm a pepper farmer. It's the middle of the rainy season but we've barely seen any of the stuff. Driest August since the 2005 drought."

"Well, how come you have a cell phone but no running water in your house?" Second Assistant demanded petulantly. The man snorted.

"It's 2010! *Everyone* has a phone. What kind of hillbillies do you take us for? Maybe it sounds strange to you Saigonese, but I grew up without indoor plumbing, and it suits me just fine. There's a well in the garden where we get all our water for cooking, drinking, for bathing . . . and for other business there's a hole at the edge of—"

"I get the picture," Second Assistant cut in quickly. Resigned, he lowered pen to paper again. "Okay, tell me about your dripping."

"My wife comes from a wealthy, important family," the man began. "And I . . . well, I told you. I'm a pepper farmer. The only reason I could marry her is because her father died back in the spring. Got himself squished. Freak accident: big stone terrace collapsed while he was underneath it. Terrible, terrible tragedy. But . . ." he trailed off, and when he spoke again there was a canny note in his voice. "I can't deny that things worked out well for me because of it." On the other end of the line, Second Assistant frowned. "Once he was gone, there was no one to object to my marrying his daughter," the man continued, "and we inherited the plot of land where I farm now and the old house that came along with the property. Well, what used to be a house, anyway— about half of it burned down at some point, and what was left was full of old garbage from squatters. And when I started rebuilding it, I found the bones."

"*Bones?* What kind of bones?" said Second Assistant, scribbling furiously. Now *this* was more like it.

"I'm pretty sure they were human, but I guess it could've also been some kind of big monkey. A lot of it was missing, see. The head wasn't there; neither was half an arm. I think the body had been sitting out for some time and some dogs had gotten to it.

"Now, out here, in the hills, we're not afraid of our dead. We know how to deal with them without having to hire fancy city conjurers—no offense, mister," he added with a chuckle. "So I just gathered up what was left of the skeleton, gave them what I thought was a proper burial out in the woods, and burned incense and some spirit money. Just to be safe, I made an offering in the corner where I found it too. And a year later, after I had finished building the new house, I made sure to put a little altar in the same spot. Didn't have any trouble at all, didn't see or hear anything funny, so I assumed that that was the end of the story. Until a few weeks ago, when the dripping began . . .

"Just that *plip, plip, plip* sound in the night. That's how it started. I was in bed, trying to fall asleep, and I heard it coming from the direction of the window. Water dripping slow and steady onto the floor. I lay there, listening for a while, and when I was sure I wasn't imagining the sound, I sat up and got out of bed to go over to the window for a look. But the moment my feet touched the ground, it stopped. No sign of wetness, no leaks, no puddles. I thought it was odd but went back to bed and heard nothing for the rest of the night.

"Two days later it was back. During the day. As if it was *bolder*, you know? As if it had just been testing the place out before, and now it was more comfortable. I heard the sound coming from the kitchen, that same, slow *drip, drip*—but again, not a trace of water. My wife was with me this time. We both stood there, listening carefully, and finally decided that it was coming from one corner near the kitchen door. And the moment we went over to investigate, the dripping suddenly stopped and then began in the *other* corner. It was taunting us!"

"Sir, you're talking as if you think this sound is . . . is *conscious*."

The man considered this quietly for a moment. "I do," he admitted at last. "I don't think that it's alive, necessarily, but I think that it's . . . I think that it *thinks*. Somehow. I don't know if it's a ghost, I don't know if it means to harm us, I don't know what it is. But what I suspect is that it wants me to believe I'm going insane. It wants us all to. Lately it's been trying something new: it waits for everyone in the house to be together—my wife, my mother, and me, at suppertime, usually—and then begins dripping for just one of us. Whoever hears the sound doesn't know whether or not they're imagining it, and the other two aren't sure either. I don't want to go crazy, and I'm worried I might be halfway there. Please . . . please let me speak with the Fortune Teller."

Second Assistant tilted backward on his stool to look out the door and into the coffee shop outside; at the moment, the Fortune Teller was in the middle of what seemed to be a very heated argument over a yellow card, and Second Assistant decided it would be better not to interrupt. He doubted that his boss would be interested in taking the case anyway—it was a straightforward, benign haunting. A more expensive assortment of fresh fruit on the altars should do the trick, and if that didn't take care of it, burnt offerings of paper decorated to resemble objects that the particular spirit might be in need of in the afterlife. In this case, perhaps a mop and a bucket.

"I'm sorry," began Second Assistant drily, "He's currently in another consultation. Why don't you just leave your number with me, and later I'll—"

"Okay," interrupted the man sharply. "I can tell that you're trying to get rid of me. But you just tell him this: my wife's family name is Ma. Your boss knows the name. He's got history with the family. You tell him we're the Mas from Ia Kare and he'll come."

"Icky-what?" Second Assistant frowned. Weirdest name of a town he'd ever heard. It sounded more like a sneeze than an actual word.

"Ee-yah Kah-ray," the man sounded out slowly for him. "Bastard-ized Viet form of the old hill tribe name of the place. No one knows what it really means anymore."

"Eeeeeee-curry," said Second Assistant, writing it out on his note-pad. When he glanced up again, he saw that out in the café, the Fortune Teller had turned away from the television and was looking back at him curiously from beneath the brim of his lucky hat—a Stetson too large for his head that he always wore for his rituals and for watching soccer games.

"What did you just say?" called the Fortune Teller, rising from his chair and walking toward their closet. First Assistant quickly stashed her magazine under the desk.

"There's a man on the line from—oh, here, just take it." Second Assistant handed the phone over.

"Yes?" said the Fortune Teller softly. And then, "Yes. Yes, I re-member. I see." His face darkened. "No, I didn't know that he had passed away." A long pause. "I will." And another. "We will. Thank you." The Fortune Teller hung up the phone and turned to both assis-tants. "Pack a bag and get the car ready," he told them, then returned to the soccer game just in time to see it end in a draw.

TWENTY-FOUR HOURS LATER, Second Assistant was in the Mas' kitchen, trying to light a fire in the already staggering heat. The bluish mountains they had driven over to get to Ia Kare had gotten his hopes up that the Central Highlands would be cooler than Saigon, but it turned out to be just as unbearable, only dustier. He had already sweat through various parts of·his shirt and down the back and sides of his neck, and his sweatiness prevented him from exuding the poised confidence that a professional ghost exterminator should possess. Unlike the rest of the house, the kitchen did not have electricity. Its walls were made of clay and palm fronds slapped over a bamboo-stake frame, the floor was dirt, and they cooked everything over coals using a three-legged cast-iron stand that was surely older than the war, and possibly predated the French. This complicated Second Assistant's task, which was to boil water with incense and secure the perimeter of the house from the spirits who would inevitably be drawn to the ritual that afternoon. There was still much to prepare before the actual ceremony began, and it was already noon. The Fortune Teller never worked after the sun went down. It was his only rule.

By the time that he managed to coax up a steady fire and bring the Mas' enormous kettle to a boil, Second Assistant had burned himself twice, and his face was now both sweaty and covered in soot. He lowered in three sticks of incense through the kettle's spout, and the scent of sandalwood began to permeate the kitchen. At first this was a welcome change from its earthy, burnt-rice musk, but it quickly became choking. Second Assistant wrapped an old rag around the kettle's handle and carried it outside to the edge of the garden, his legs already beginning to buckle and his arms shaking from its weight. Curls of perfumed steam rose up from the spout, causing him to sweat even more profusely.

He began at the family's well, which was an unwalled, circular pit with a fraying rope dangling down into damp, inky darkness. It was much larger and much less charming than Second Assistant (lifelong city dweller, unacquainted with wells) had been anticipating. Trying his best to move swiftly but unable to manage anything faster than a brisk waddle, he circled the entirety of the Mas' property, pouring out a thin stream of the hot water onto the ground as he went, and making sure to walk inside the protective ring he was making. Once, in the past, he had forgotten, unintentionally "locking" himself out of an exorcism. The perimeter was easy to follow because it was outlined by the crumbled remnants of a stone wall that had surrounded the house that stood here a century ago. When he arrived back at the well, he carefully connected the beginning and end of the ring.

Now completely soaked in sweat, Second Assistant returned the empty kettle to the kitchen. Even though First Assistant and the Fortune Teller were waiting for him to begin the rite, he decided to risk their annoyance and run back out to the well for a quick rinse before joining them. But in his haste, he plunged out the kitchen door without looking first and nearly plowed straight into Mr. Ma's mother—Bà, the small, benevolent-looking heap of wrinkles in plaid house pajamas he'd seen napping in a corner hammock earlier that afternoon. Luckily, Second Assistant's reflexes were fast enough that he managed to twist out of the way at the last second, swerving to one side and flapping his arms like a wounded stork. He landed on his tailbone in the dirt while four-foot-nine, eighty-seven-pound Bà remained upright and unscathed.

Bà did not appear to be startled. She did not gasp, or shriek, or laugh at the sight of Second Assistant sprawled on the ground. She did not even harrumph in displeasure. When Second Assistant gathered himself up and apologized politely for nearly knocking her over, she still said nothing. She offered no explanation as to why she had been loitering behind the kitchen. Second Assistant now noticed that in her arms she was holding a small dog.

The creature had short fur that was piebald white and orangey-brown and stuck up in clumps in different directions. Its snout was long and vulpine, and its tail was a feather duster. Second Assistant was studying the dog so intently because he had the curious sense that it was studying him back. It bore an expression that seemed distinctly uncanine. Second Assistant could have sworn that it was smirking at him. He apologized again, thinking that the old lady was just going deaf and hadn't heard him the first time. Again, he received no response. While the dog's eyes were still fixed on him in an unsettling kind of appraisal, the eyes of the woman were glazed over. She didn't

seem to be looking at him at all. The entire situation was now starting
to alarm Second Assistant, and he began to back away slowly from
both Bà and her pet. The elderly didn't really need a reason for loitering, he thought to himself, but he shivered, despite the sweat still pooling at his collarbone. Bà had not moved an inch since their encounter.
Second Assistant now decided against washing off, not wanting to linger in the garden with them. Because he was unwilling to go back in
through the kitchen door where they were standing, he had to walk all
around the property again and then enter the house by the front door.

Inside, Second Assistant joined First Assistant, the Fortune Teller,
and Mr. Ma in the living room, where they were kneeling on a woven
mat. He was informed upon entry by Mr. Ma that Mrs. Ma wouldn't be
able to join them because her stomach was still bothering her. Second
Assistant hadn't actually met the wife yet. His suspicions about this
family were steadily mounting. Never before had he heard of a husband taking his wife's family name when they married. Also, he was
certain that when they had first arrived that morning, Mr. Ma's excuse
for his wife's confinement to their bedroom was a migraine.

They faced the house's ancestral altar, which sat on a shelf above a
squat, ancient television with a wonky pair of antennae. On a good day,
Mr. Ma had told them, they could pick up three channels. This altar
was dedicated to an assortment of the recently deceased. The photographs clustered together were of varying size—the portrait of Mrs.
Ma's recently deceased father was the largest—and they were flanked
on both sides by tall red candles and matching blue-and-white vases
holding two-day-old chrysanthemums, newly droopy. A single sour-
sop, scaly and brownish green like a pangolin, balanced unsteadily on a
plate directly below.

"Much too symmetrical," the Fortune Teller mumbled to himself as
he studied the altar. "But also uneven." His behavior had been odder
than usual since leaving Saigon. He had not told his assistants why they
had needed to prepare for the Highlands in such a hurry, or explained
to them his own history with the place. Three or four times during the
overnight drive up, he had pulled the van (borrowed from Max) over

on the shoulder of the road, and then stepped out and stared intently into the rural nocturnal murk of a rice field or plantation or grove of lanky trees. He would remain there for several minutes, silently scanning the darkness, before getting back into the car and then continuing to drive. Second Assistant had been pretending to sleep the whole time.

The second altar—the altar for the bones—stood on the floor in a corner of the same room. This one was smaller—a box shrine, carved from splintery, dark wood and lit by a couple of battery-operated plastic candles—and haphazardly composed. It appeared that Mr. Ma had not known what to place in it and so had thrown together whatever was on hand. A ceramic figurine of a potbellied Chinese deity squatted next to a carved Buddha and one wobbly ornamental horse with a missing leg. There was a cup of ash and sand pricked with old incense stems, a dish bearing a small pyramid of tangerines, and both fresh and artificial flowers. The fake ones were cartoonish roses with dusty polyester petals and the real ones were chrysanthemums like those on the ancestral altar, but Second Assistant noticed that these ones looked conspicuously more pert.

The Fortune Teller was unlocking his briefcase, the only thing that he never asked his assistants to carry for him. It was a well-made bag— the leather was real, and of high quality, which was unusual, as the Fortune Teller was a notorious miser, only wearing the cheapest and most ill-fitting of clothes. First and Second Assistant both theorized that he had stolen the briefcase from a foreign businessman, for the initials J.F.A. were stamped in gold in one corner, and two of those letters did not exist in the Vietnamese alphabet.

The Fortune Teller rummaged around inside and pulled out a sheaf of papers covered in glyphs and diagrams that only he could read, then he turned to Second Assistant. "We're running behind schedule," he said briskly. "Is the perimeter sealed?"

"Yes," sighed Second Assistant.

"No gaps this time?"

"No gaps."

"Children and animals removed from the premises?"

Shit. The old woman's dog. "Yes," lied Second Assistant reflexively, though he could not stop himself from immediately breaking into a nervous sweat. It was fine though—he was already so sweaty no one would be able to tell the difference, and the Fortune Teller seemed too distracted to notice anyway. Second Assistant couldn't believe that he had been so stupid. It was crucial to always, always, *always* clear the kids and pets out of the site of the ceremony—spirits could take possession of their bodies too easily. But it was too late to start the house cleansing and protective circle over again. Sunset was too close. Second Assistant prayed that the old lady and her dog would stay in the garden and out of the way. He consoled himself with the thought that it wasn't wholly his fault—First Assistant should have reminded him.

"Then let's start, shall we? I will begin by establishing contact with your unwanted house guest. Assistants!" he summoned, clapping his hands once. First Assistant and sweating, shaking Second Assistant arranged themselves on their knees to either side of him. The Fortune Teller selected three incense sticks and lit them. He tilted his hand and let the flames lick nearly up to his knuckles for three seconds before shaking the sticks out so that they burned more slowly. He watched the smoke thoughtfully and then, keeping the sticks clamped lightly between his palms, began to trace symbols in the air and mutter indiscernibly under his breath.

The incense sticks were almost reduced to ash now. The air felt heavy, ready. The Fortune Teller laid the sticks at the foot of the floor altar—the bone altar.

"Spirit, are you here?" he intoned.

There was a double thump as both First and Second Assistant bent over and bowed, following his words, their palms striking the cement floor at the same time. It was important to show respect to a ghost in order to catch it. Then they sat up on their knees again.

"Who are you?"

Thump, thump. They dropped into the bow again. Then up.

"What do you want with this family?"

Thump, thump. And up.

"Where are you from?"

Thump, thump. And up.

"Why are you here?"

Thump, thump. And up.

"Why do you—" *THUMP.*

Both Second Assistant and the Fortune Teller turned and stared at First Assistant, who had bowed too soon. Neither could believe that she would make such a novice mistake. But as they were watching, she rose up and then immediately fell back into a bow with another thump. "Stop that!" hissed Second Assistant. The Fortune Teller was frowning. But First Assistant's eyes were closed. She did not notice them at all. She dropped forward again, but this time it couldn't be called a bow—her arms stayed at her sides as she fell forward and smacked her forehead against the floor. This thump was loud, more of a cracking sound, but with a sickening, squishy resonance. But, as if pulled by invisible strings, she jerked right back up onto her knees again, spine rigid, her arms still at her sides. Second Assistant had figured that First Assistant was hijacking the ceremony with one of her "trances" for the attention, but he was now beginning to worry. He had never seen her behave like this before. She beat her face against the floor again and again, down and up without rhythm, faster and faster like a piece of machinery ready to explode.

"Can't you do something?" cried Second Assistant to the Fortune Teller, embarrassed by the shrillness of his voice.

The Fortune Teller held up a hand to silence him. "It would be unwise to touch her," he said softly. But it was unbearable to watch. First Assistant's eyes were still closed, but her mouth had curled into a twitching grimace. A cut had opened on her forehead, but she still would not stop. Second Assistant turned around to look at Mr. Ma in the wild, desperate hope that he might step in and end the freakish display somehow. The farmer's face was horrified, but he remained motionless, and the awful smacking continued. Second Assistant couldn't take it anymore; he reached behind the Fortune Teller and seized First Assistant by the shoulder:

"Stop it! Just stop!" he shrieked. And at his touch, First Assistant went limp and flopped over onto her side.

It had been too easy. Neither one believed that it was actually over, and so they didn't dare make a sound. Second Assistant's hand remained frozen in the air where First Assistant's shoulder had been. The Fortune Teller alternated between wordless scowling at Second Assistant for disobeying his orders and worried glances at First Assistant on the floor. And in that hectic silence, the dripping finally started.

They all could hear it—the slow, clear *plip, plip,* just as Mr. Ma had described. Invisible water falling. The sound was coming from the front door, from behind them. While First Assistant remained slumped on the ground, the three men turned around and saw Mr. Ma's mother standing in the open doorway, the tiny orange-and-white dog still in her arms.

The dripping went on, languorously, as the group before the altar stared at the old woman by the door. Bà's eyes were no longer vacant and dully glazed over like they had been in the garden. They were mad and shining and darting wildly around the room, and she was clutching the dog to her chest too hard.

"She is here!" The old woman hissed suddenly, misting them with flecks of spit. "She is here, right now! Don't you see her?" The little dog made a muffled squeak as her grip on it tightened even further, and the sound of the dripping intensified, echoing off the walls, as if it were emanating from everywhere at once.

It was at this point that it seemed like the Fortune Teller had finally had enough and would bring an end to the chaos. He reached decisively for his briefcase. What action he was intending to take with it would remain a mystery though, because Mrs. Ma suddenly came bursting out of her bedroom, hair disheveled, one nightgown strap slipping down. She stumbled two paces toward them, leaned over and braced her hands against her knees, then with a great, phlegmy cough, she hacked up something dark and wet onto the floor. To Second Assistant it resembled a dead jellyfish, and he cringed at the squelch it made when it hit the concrete, before realizing that he had been able to hear it so clearly because the dripping sound had stopped. This did not comfort him as much as he thought it would.

Mrs. Ma remained doubled over, catching her breath. Her husband scrambled to his feet and rushed over to support her, but she brushed him off, and Mr. Ma had to hover anxiously behind her instead. After a minute she managed to straighten up again. "Hello," she said, feebly but still regally, tugging up the straps of her nightgown. "It's a pleasure to meet you, though I'm sorry it has to be under these circumstances." Second Assistant was struck by how oddly elegant she was; how out of place she seemed in this remote, tin-roofed shack. Her hands were pale, gracefully shaped, and tastefully manicured, the wrists exquisitely avian. These were not hands that hacked fish to bits with a cleaver or slit chicken throats or whatever it was that people usually did out in the countryside.

Mrs. Ma wiped the corner of her mouth with one of her lovely hands and then faltered when she looked down at the black, slimy thing on the ground. "I—I don't know what . . . how I . . ." She looked like she might be sick again.

The Fortune Teller rose. "It's nothing to worry about," he said soothingly as he walked toward her. "We've seen this sort of thing many times." Second Assistant, still hovering over First Assistant's unconscious body, knew that this was a lie. When he reached Mrs. Ma, the Fortune Teller faltered. He lifted his hand toward her head, as if to pat her hair, and then decided against it and made as if to take one of her hands instead. But he didn't end up doing that either; his outstretched arm just hovered in the air between them, like he was afraid to touch her. Eventually the Fortune Teller's fingers wilted back into his palm and he let the arm fall to his side. "Are you well?" he asked her quietly, peering intently at the woman's face in the same way that Second Assistant had observed him staring into the black, arborous wilderness from the side of the road.

"I'm sorry. I'll put her back in her room," said Mr. Ma, coming over and taking hold of his wife's shoulder. Second Assistant saw Mrs. Ma's body slacken perceptibly when his hand—craggy from sun damage, the nail of the thumb grown intentionally long and slightly pointy—made contact with her skin. The strap of her nightgown slid down again, but she did not bother to straighten it. "I don't know what's wrong with her," Mr. Ma said. "Or with my mother."

At this, he, the Fortune Teller, and Second Assistant all looked back at the doorway, only to find that Bà had slipped away unnoticed while they had all been preoccupied with Mrs. Ma.

"Oh dear," sighed the Fortune Teller. "Well, I'm sure she can't have gone too far." His usual briskness had returned. "Yes, why don't you help your wife lie down, and then we'll figure out where your mother has gone." Mr. Ma led Mrs. Ma back toward the bedroom. When they were out of sight, the Fortune Teller turned to Second Assistant. "My briefcase! Get my briefcase!" he hissed.

Second Assistant glanced down at First Assistant, reluctant to leave her side.

"She'll be fine," said the Fortune Teller. "She'll come around in another minute or so." While Second Assistant retrieved the bag, he crouched down to examine whatever it was that Mrs. Ma had regurgitated.

"What is it? Ectoplasm?" Second Assistant asked. He handed the Fortune Teller his briefcase and then peered over his shoulder to see. He immediately gagged. It was a thick wad of human hair. Long, black, soaking wet hair.

The Fortune Teller rummaged around in his briefcase and pulled out a plastic bag, into which he deposited the hair clump. It was difficult to get all the strands inside—they kept escaping and clinging to the Fortune Teller's wrist, leaving behind little ropes of slime.

Disgusted, Second Assistant went to go stand by the door and get some fresh air. The heat was still smothering, but he could feel his head clearing as he breathed. The land, starting at his toes and stretching out unbroken by any other buildings until the mold-colored mountains began in the distance, was drought parched and red brown and made him feel as though they were all trapped inside a giant clay pot. He scanned the empty road and mummified pepper fields for any sign of the insane old woman. The whole situation was making him very uneasy. He complained about his job, he knew, but he actually enjoyed it most of the time. He didn't mind the truly frightening parts—belligerent poltergeists hurling chairs across the room and apparitions of flame were fairly normal occurrences at peak haunting season. There were proper protocols for dealing with those ghosts—they had clear causes, and so they had clear solutions. But the wrongness of this house was undefined and therefore unsettling to him. Right now, all he wanted to do was toss the Fortune Teller and catatonic First Assistant into the van and drive back to Saigon immediately. And truthfully, he wanted to throw beautiful Mrs. Ma in the back of the van and steal her away from this wasteland as well.

First Assistant was catatonic no longer. Inside, she sat up abruptly with a huge, gulping, respiratory cymbal crash of a breath. Second Assistant hurried to her side. A beat later, the Fortune Teller strolled over to check on her too, the bag of hair swinging from one hand and his briefcase in the other. First Assistant patted the bleeding, purplish lump that had formed on her forehead. "What happened?" she asked groggily.

"Oh good, you're up," said the Fortune Teller, clapping her on the shoulder and almost knocking her over again. "We have just over four hours left before dark. I need to go have a look at those bones in the woods, and while I do that, *you*," he said to Second Assistant, punctuating it with a shake of the hair bag, "are going to go out and find her."

"Bà?" asked Second Assistant.

"No, that fucking dog."

Second Assistant laughed at first, thinking it was a joke, before he realized that the Fortune Teller was serious. "How do we know that it's the dog?" he asked.

The Fortune Teller raised his eyebrows at Second Assistant under the brim of his cowboy hat. "Have you ever seen a normal dog with eyes like that? Help the old woman if you can, but what matters most is getting that animal back. Here," he said, removing his hat and placing it on First Assistant's head to hide her lump. "You, in the meantime," he said to her, "will stay here and guard the lady of the house. We'll all reconvene before sunset." The Fortune Teller checked his watch, and the fear that Second Assistant saw sparking briefly across his face was just as unsettling as everything else he had witnessed in Ia Kare that day.

BÀ HAD NOT BEEN in the garden. She had not been anywhere in the house. Second Assistant had even crawled under the bed while Mrs. Ma was sleeping on it to see if the old woman was hiding underneath. Where she could have possibly gone Second Assistant did not know, but the Fortune Teller had made it very clear that it was his responsibility to recover the dog, as it had been his fault to begin with. So while his boss and Mr. Ma headed down the road to find and exhume the bones in the woods, Second Assistant set off in the opposite direction.

He didn't know how he should even begin looking for them, and he had no idea what he would do if he found them either. Optimistically, he had brought along an old rice sack to stash the dog in if he did catch it, but now he felt even more foolish as he shambled aimlessly down the dirt road with it clutched in one hand, like a budget boogeyman in the kind of story told to frighten bad children into obedience—"Listen to your parents and don't stray too far from home, or the Rice Sack Man will catch you and throw you into his bag!"

Second Assistant had been a good child. And he had grown up in the city, in a compound of cement cubes in District 4. So his parents had not told him stories about ghosts and ghouls and shapeshifters, but they did warn him to stay away from the men who shot up heroin by the smelly canal that ran through their neighborhood and a woman who sold lottery tickets on the corner. That was his earliest memory of fear—that woman. Her legs had gotten blown up by either the Americans or the Viet Cong—he couldn't remember which. She parked her wheelchair on the sidewalk every day, her lottery tickets fanned out across the patchwork blanket she kept folded across her lap, the ends of her trousers dangling empty below or knotted above the knees. But it wasn't her disability that frightened him, it was her face. The woman was always immaculately powdered and rouged. Her eyebrows were tattooed on, thin and perilously arched and blue-black, and above them were feathery Madame Nhu bangs, with each hair sprayed perfectly in place. She rimmed her eyes with thick black lines, both the inner and outer corners flicked out into little wings, and wore lipstick the color of dried blood. She sat there all day in the Saigon sun, still and silent, unlike the other ticket sellers who yelled and prodded and poked at you to buy. But she watched everyone who came down the street, eyes swiveling in their black kohl diamonds as she tracked their movements while a half smile curled on her lips. And it was the feeling of those eyes following you, and that inexplicable smile on her painted face, like a kabuki mask come to life, which gave young Second Assistant the shivers and were why he would always cross the street to avoid her. It was unkind of him, he realized when he was older, but he used to believe that she was a witch, even though he didn't know the first thing about witches, having never heard the stories. Sometimes he wondered if the woman was part of the reason he had signed up to work for the Fortune Teller in the first place. He had never told his boss about it, but he often thought of her. His parents had moved to a new house when he was sixteen, and he had never seen her again. If she was not dead, she had to be ancient.

He had now been walking for almost twenty minutes through the wastes of Ia Kare and there was still no sign of Mr. Ma's mother. It was time for a new tactic.

"Hello?" he called out to the empty ochre landscape, a little weakly. He cleared his throat and tried again. Embarrassment was no help in finding them, so he did his best to suppress it. "Hello! Bà, if you're here, please come out! Perhaps we can talk? I just want to see if you're all right!" His voice echoed off the rocks.

It was useless. She wasn't here. Maybe she had done the smart thing and taken the opportunity to escape from this Highland hellhole.

Second Assistant sighed. Not knowing what else he should do, he spread out his rice sack on the rocky ground by the side of the road, sat on it, and quietly despaired.

. .

"THIS IS WHAT WE KNOW SO FAR ABOUT THE SPIRIT," THE FORTUNE
Teller said, pausing on the side of the road to light a cigarette. "One: it
targets women, or finds women easier to control——you observed that
my female assistant, your wife, and your mother were the ones affected,
yes? My suspicion is that it has housed itself within the body of your
mother's dog while it continues to gain strength. It's a young spirit, I
believe. It doesn't realize the extent of its power yet. But this brings me
to number two: it is learning. Quickly."

"I'll happily get rid of the dog," said Mr. Ma. "Never liked that little
mongrel. Do you think my wife and your assistant are safe back at the
house? Has your assistant recovered enough?"

The Fortune Teller checked the position of the sun. It was the second time he had checked in the past five minutes. "How long until we
reach the woods?"

"Shouldn't be much farther now. Another ten minutes, perhaps."

"No harm will come to your wife, I promise. I have taken precau-
tionary measures to ensure that my assistant will not be possessed
again. She was left an assortment of protective devices." The Fortune
Teller hoped that Mr. Ma was buying it; the only protective device he
had left with Second Assistant was his lucky hat. He needed to change
the subject. "Do you watch the Premier League?"

"The what?"

"Soccer! English soccer!" cried the Fortune Teller, aghast. Mr. Ma
shook his head. "Your late father-in-law was a Chelsea supporter, if I
remember correctly."

"I don't really know anything about sports," said Mr. Ma blandly.

BY THE TIME THAT the Fortune Teller had finished his first cigarette
and lit a second, the edge of the town's old rubber plantation was visible, a dark line of trees waiting for them where the orange road abruptly
ended. The Fortune Teller paused. "When you said that you buried the

bones in a forest," he said with a twisted smile, "I'll admit that I hoped it wasn't this one in particular."

"You didn't know where we were going?" asked Mr. Ma. "But I thought you would recognize the road."

The Fortune Teller shook his head. "Nineteen eighty-six was a long time ago."

Looking at it made the Fortune Teller feel seasick. When the rubber trees were first planted, sixty-odd years earlier, they had been in tidy lines, but since the departure of the French they had been growing un-tended. Each tree was now feral-branched and tilting in a different di-rection, but their original rows were still discernible, and this created a mildly nauseating visual effect. It did not help that their trunks were helixed with dark, scabbed-over knife grooves from the bygone days of latex harvesting. This sometimes made it seem as if the rubber trees were wiggling.

Mr. Ma approached one and ran a hand up the lumpy spiral of its scar. "But there's nothing to be afraid of during the day. You know that. The little nasties that live in here are all down in their burrows and won't wake up until after dark," he said, locating a soft spot in the bark and then slicing into it with a long thumbnail. "But why would it matter? You're not scared of them—the last time you were here, you were in the forest overnight. I heard the story. Or a version of it." A slight blush spread over his face, and he waited for it to fade before he continued. "My wife never told me what happened when she disap-peared in here, when she was a girl. She can't; she's too . . . *fragile*. I've only asked her about it once. She said it's like there's a fog cover-ing her memories of that time in the forest and the two years that fol-lowed it. She can only remember little pieces of her life before age seventeen." He was trying his very hardest to sound nonchalant, but his fingernail was digging into the tree with savage intensity. "To be honest, I was excited when the noises in the house started, happy even, because it finally gave me an excuse to meet the man who'd saved her. I thought, *Maybe now I'll find out the truth. I'll find out why she's like this.*" He pulled his nail out and then leaned in closer to examine the cut he had made. After a moment he straightened back up. "No milk," he said. "It's too old. And the trees don't run in the afternoon anyway."

The Fortune Teller chose his words carefully. "I will say this once, and then I won't speak of it again: I can't tell you what happened here in 1986. This is both out of respect for your wife and because I'm not entirely certain what happened that night. Don't ask me to tell you why that is. I understand your curiosity. I do, Ma, I do. But I urge you to stop wondering about it. Instead, be content in knowing that many years ago, your wife came out of this forest alive. Be grateful that she is yours, and be mindful of the fact that were it not for that night, she probably would be someone else's." The Fortune Teller now approached the rubber tree and made a scratch in the bark next to Mr. Ma's gouging. "I saved her," he said softly, "But I've never been sure that I didn't cause her more harm in the process. I've come back to atone—that's partially why I agreed to help you get rid of your house spirit—but I'm starting to suspect that the forest has its own idea of what atonement entails, and it's different from mine. Look—"

A semeny dribble of latex had appeared in the Fortune Teller's cut. "You see?" he said, drawing back and wiping his hand on his pants. "These trees don't follow a schedule. They don't abide by human rules. Nothing in this haunted place does. Why else would it be abandoned? Why else would they let all this land sit here and turn into a snakes' nest, instead of tearing it down and planting another coffee field? You should always be wary of it, whether or not the sun is up." He took a pull on his waning cigarette and searched Mr. Ma's face for anger or disappointment.

The man's expression was even, though his cheeks were flushed. When he spoke again, he did not address what the Fortune Teller had said. "You should put that out before we go in," he said quietly, indicating the Fortune Teller's cigarette. "It's been a very, very dry season, and fires start easily."

The Fortune Teller licked his thumb and forefinger and pinched the cigarette out between them with an almost inaudible hiss. Because of the heat, he had left his jacket back at the house, which meant that he did not have a pocket in which to stash the butt for later. So instead, he rolled it up inside the cuff of his left shirtsleeve.

He looked down the warped row of trees before him, straining his eyes to see past the point where it all became a brown-green blur. He could feel the forest thinking. It was a twenty-hectare botanical mind, alive and warped, dangerous things nestled deep in its roots. A collection of tainted memories growing out of the earth, just at the edge of the town that was trying to forget them. The Fortune Teller felt something stirring at the part where his stomach met his sternum. He closed his eyes and he was in all of the forests he had ever known. He was a little boy, lost and frightened, running through cool, green pines. He was a uniformed young man, holding a gun in a sweaty southern mangrove fen. He was a middle-aged man striding cavalierly toward this very rubber plantation twenty-five years ago, thinking that he was coming to save another lost child. And he was an old man standing before it again now, wondering if this time he would not reemerge from the trees. In his lifetime, the Fortune Teller had never gone into a forest and come out fully intact afterward.

Mr. Ma cleared his throat, unspooling the Fortune Teller from his reveries. "Shall we?" he asked.

The Fortune Teller opened his eyes gave him a wan smile. "I guess I'm ready."

The men began picking their way carefully through the yellowing, shin-high grass. Behind them, the first tree was still weeping one long, white trickle from the slit the Fortune Teller had made.

"I REMEMBER THAT I buried the bones beneath a crooked tree about half a mile in," said Mr. Ma. "It's near this little hut I built, where I store some things—just my shovels and an ax or two, because I go out here to cut wood sometimes."

The Fortune Teller frowned. "You don't get frightened coming out here? I didn't think that many people ventured out into the rubber trees."

"I never come after dark. Haven't had any unlucky encounters yet."

They did not appear to be following a marked path; every so often Mr. Ma would pause, crouch to examine a root or a stick, and then take a sharp turn.

"My grandparents actually worked here, you know," said Mr. Ma. "Back when it was still a plantation. Came here in . . . oh . . . '51? '52, maybe? And barely made it out alive. They told me it was like a nightmare—the two Frenchmen who owned the place worked them like animals, everyone got dysentery, everyone got malaria, my grandmother almost lost a hand. They were lucky that the place went belly-up after only a few years. So that's why I don't mind coming out here—this dirt and these trees belong to me, because my ancestors bought it with their blood. Aha," he said suddenly, voice brightening. "I can see the little hut through the trees—it's just over there, sir. Not much farther now."

The Fortune Teller saw something dark protruding from a root crevice and drew in his breath sharply. Mr. Ma followed his line of vision. "Just an old collecting cup," he said, prodding it with a sandaled foot.

As they approached the wooden structure in the trees, it became clear to the Fortune Teller that it was not just a tiny shed, as Mr. Ma had led him to believe. It was larger than the Mas' house's kitchen, to start, and was constructed carefully, out of smooth, even wood planks. It had a padlocked door and a roof made of a sheet of corrugated tin, but no windows. The Fortune Teller cocked his head, listening, and furrowed his brow.

"Do I hear . . . birds?" he asked, puzzled.

"Let me show you," said Mr. Ma, removing a key from his pocket.

The door swung open easily, letting in enough light that the Fortune Teller could see what the cabin contained: a small cot, unmade, with a rumpled blanket, and next to it, an old-fashioned lantern. What was most remarkable were the birdcages hanging from the ceiling—there must have been at least eight of them, in a wide array of shapes, each one elaborately carved. From the cages came the little chirps, the whistles and low warbles that the Fortune Teller had heard from outside. In here, in that murky light, surrounded on all sides by the birds with their avian murmurs and the oppressive smell from the rotting fruit in their cages and the chalky splatters of their shit covering the cabin's dirt floor, he felt like he was suffocating. "What is this place?" he asked, exhaling heavily.

Mr. Ma leaned against the doorframe. "I told you—it's my shed."

"Does your wife know about it?"

Mr. Ma's silence was sufficient answer.

The Fortune Teller looked at the cot on the floor, and the two rolls of toilet paper beside it. "You're shitting in the woods? You're sleeping here? You *are* coming out here after dark. Have you lost your mind?"

Mr. Ma sighed and peered into the birdcage closest to him. "This is my red-whiskered bulbul. She eats small bananas, mostly. Sometimes I'll bring her a mango."

"I'm not really very interested in birds, Ma . . ."

But Mr. Ma was already moving on to the next cage. "This is my smaller bush lark." He would not make eye contact with the Fortune Teller and he was speaking more quickly than usual. "She likes seeds better than bananas. The larger bush lark is over in that corner, there. Next to my pair of swallows. It's been difficult at home these past months, sir. My wife's mind was never quite the same after she was lost in these woods all those years ago. I know her mother only let me marry her because no other man would, but I've never once complained! She'd been getting better though. *I* was making her better! I was making her *good*. Then the dripping started, and she fell apart all over again. Now, swallows are useful to have around. They eat mosquitoes, you see."

He peered into the cage, pursed his lips, and made a few audibly wet air kisses at the birds before continuing.

"She hears the noises all the time—times when I can't hear them. She hates the birds. *Hates* them! One night she tried to open their cages and shoo them all away. Lucky I caught her. I brought them out here and keep them locked inside so they'll be safe. I sleep here sometimes too, to keep them company. This is my house. My own house! I didn't inherit it, and I built it on earth where nothing had ever stood before. It belongs to only me.

"You see, I knew it was never going to be easy for her to share a simple farmer's life with me, but I didn't know that she came from a family of leeches! Old Ma's brothers divided up his fortune between themselves—they don't care about my poor, sweet, mad darling. All we were given was the shack and the pepper field. There's no one but me to care for her now. I brought my mother to come live with us, so that she could help me look after her, but now the dripping's made her go just as crazy as my wife. I'm the only sane one left!"

The Fortune Teller now doubted this very much. He sank onto the cot with a sigh. He was not sure how to proceed and didn't know which he wanted more: a cigarette or for a breeze to come through the door. "What kind of bird do you have in there?" he said, changing the subject to buy himself more time, and pointed to the smallest cage.

Mr. Ma beamed with pride and walked over to the corner where it hung. "That's my little girl—my green bee-eater. It's tough to find bees for her to eat, but I'll bring her flies, spiders, a baggie of ants, or even buy some berries if it seems like she's getting bored with the bugs, or . . ." he trailed off abruptly and sharply into silence.

"Ma? Are you all right?" It was hard to make out the features of his face in the cabin's poor lighting.

"She's dead," Mr. Ma said, his voice breaking. He lifted the cage's door and gently removed the green bee-eater. The bird was about the size of an avocado but seemed smaller cradled in his large, weathered palms. "Take her," he said to the Fortune Teller. "Feel how little she is. Look how beautiful. Take her out into the light and see." Concerned that refusing would only upset the man further, the Fortune Teller reluctantly took the dead bird from Mr. Ma, rose, and walked over to the doorway. He had to admit, it was a lovely creature, perhaps even more so now that it was dead—the feathers jade green at its breast and back, amber at the top of its head, a slash of blue at the throat, and the undersides of its wings the exact shade of orange brown as the Ia Kare dust.

"I'll get the shovels," the Fortune Teller heard Mr. Ma say somewhere behind him, and he murmured something in assent before returning to his examination of the bee-eater. He did not like the bird's eyes, he decided. They were still open, and they were red—bright red—perfectly round, with a slight film over the corneas. They looked like poisonous berries. They were much too red. He was staring at the eyes so intently, he never even heard Mr. Ma coming up behind him. The red eyes were the last thing he saw before he was hit on the back of the head with a shovel and the world turned inky black.

WHEN THE FORTUNE TELLER regained consciousness, his hands and feet were bound, and he was propped up against a tree. As his eyes struggled to adjust to the darkness, he groaned. "Ma?" he croaked. His mouth tasted dry and vinegary and his head was throbbing. He licked his lips and tried again. "Ma!"

He heard a sigh from somewhere in the forest behind him but couldn't turn his head. "Is that you, Ma?"

"I'm not Ma!" the sigher, whose voice belonged unmistakably to Ma, called back.

"Well, who are you, then?" the Fortune Teller said, leaning back against his tree and closing his eyes.

Ma choked back what sounded suspiciously like a sob. "I am no one from a nothing family!"

"So are most of us, Ma."

"Don't call me that anymore!" He was crying now, the Fortune Teller could tell. "I was never one of them, and I was a fool to believe that I could be. I married the insane daughter, I changed my name to theirs, for years I broke my back working their pepper fields, and I'm still nothing to them! Do you know what the family calls me behind my back?"

"No, what do the Mas call you?"

"Don't even say their name!" he hissed. His voice was quivering. "The Field Rat. It was my wife's father's nickname for me, and even after I married into the family they refused to call me anything else. I'm still the Field Rat, but now I'm 'Field Rat Ma.'"

"Well, that's not so bad," the Fortune Teller said brightly. "Would you prefer that I called you 'Field Rat' too? Seeing as you don't like 'Ma' anymore?"

"Don't. Say. That. Name!" Field Rat Ma shrieked, bursting forward from the trees to finally face the Fortune Teller. "It won't matter what you call me for much longer. Look to your left!"

The Fortune Teller turned his aching head and squinted at the ground. He could make out a small, raised mound of earth beside him, porcupined with the remains of old incense. The Fortune Teller smiled. "I see we've finally made it to the bones." He could see the Field Rat's teeth through the darkness as the man grinned.

"I've decided to give it a sacrifice. That's what they always want, isn't it? The old ghosts? Papers, boiled chickens, altars, perfumed sticks—none of that is any use to them. The only thing they ever really want is blood. So I'm going to give them you. And then the dripping will stop, my wife's mind will return to her, we will both change our names to Nguyen—to *my* name—and she will finally give me children, and then we will have the life we were supposed to."

"My," said the Fortune Teller, "that's quite a lot riding on one sacrifice. How are you going to kill me, then?"

The grin widened. "Why would I go to the trouble of killing you myself when we're in a forest full of snakes? Now, don't go anywhere," he said with a snicker, "I'll be back in a moment. I have a little bit of bait. You'll see." He suddenly retreated back into the trees, leaving the Fortune Teller to tug halfheartedly at the ropes around his wrists and ankles. Field Rat Ma was only gone for two minutes. And when he returned, he was holding a burlap sack in one hand. There was a strong, damp odor and a muffled thumping coming from within. "Hush now, hush!" Field Rat scolded the bag, before he thwacked it against the ground hard, twice. The thumping ceased. "Don't worry; they're only stunned, so they won't go far, but they've still got enough wiggle left in them to seem attractive enough to eat," he said, before emptying the contents over the Fortune Teller's head.

Two dozen toads, now mildly concussed, came spilling out of the sack, tumbling off of the Fortune Teller's shoulders and arms and thighs and making slapping sounds wherever they made contact with his skin. The Fortune Teller shuddered and closed his eyes as they flopped over him; he hated amphibians. A few toads struggled to crawl away across the pine needles; most lay in the spot where they fell, waving their warty brown limbs in the air.

"Dinner time!" trilled Field Rat, giddy with spite. "I'm afraid that this is where I leave you, sir. Your sacrifice is very meaningful to me, and my wife and I will never forget you." He rolled up the empty sack.

"Ma——" the Fortune Teller said, without opening his eyes. "Field Rat, Nguyen, whoever you want to be—do an old man one last favor and let me have a cigarette. Or just let me finish my leftover half from earlier." The Fortune Teller could hear the Field Rat pacing, agitated, but it was too dark for him to make out the expression on the man's face, and he was grateful, for it meant that he couldn't be seen either. "Oh, come on now," he pleaded, trying to make his voice sound as pathetic as possible. "I'm covered in toads. My death is already slithering toward me through the trees. Don't I deserve one last smoke?"

"If I untie you, you'll attack me with something," protested the Field Rat. In the darkness, the Fortune Teller heard him trip over something that made a clanging metallic sound when his foot made contact. "See?" cried the Field Rat, "There's old bottles and things lying around. You'll find a weapon!"

"Of course I'm not asking you to untie me—unroll my left sleeve and you'll find the cigarette. Just light it for me, will you? I'm not foolish enough to try and fight you—I'm seventy-five years old!"

Quickly, and with shoulders braced in case of a surprise attack, Field Rat Ma rolled down the sleeve and pulled out a crumpled segment of one of the Fortune Teller's hand-rolled cigarettes.

"And the lighter's in my pants pocket."

They were both taken by surprise when the tiny orange flame sparked to life and they could suddenly see each other again. They stared at each other—Field Rat Ma's eyes wide and too round, black pupils surrounded by whites surrounded by dark circles from a lack of sleep, and the Fortune Teller's eyes almost indiscernible from the wrinkles they were buried in.

Field Rat Ma averted his gaze first. "Hurry up," he muttered, tilting the cigarette to the Fortune Teller's lips and holding it there while the old man took a long, greedy puff. Then the Fortune Teller sighed, leaned back against the tree, and closed his eyes. An unusual, pinkish smoke rose from the end of the cigarette, and its scent seemed off. "This some sort of special mix?" Field Rat Ma asked, and the Fortune Teller could hear the raised eyebrow in his voice.

"You could say that."

"Well, it stinks." Field Rat Ma coughed and then straightened up.

"Hey, not so fast." The Fortune Teller tugged on his pants leg.

Field Rat Ma rolled his eyes and bent down to let him take another drag.

"So, I suppose this is how it ends for us, isn't it, old friend?" murmured the Fortune Teller drowsily, patting his belly.

"We're not friends!" scoffed Field Rat Ma. He nudged an escaping toad back toward the Fortune Teller with a foot. "What is it about them?" he sighed. "About their blood, that makes it so special."

"The toads?" asked the Fortune Teller. Field Rat Ma didn't notice when his mouth did not close completely.

"No, you demented old bat, not the toads, my wife's family. They were rich when the French were here, and they were rich when the French were gone. They were rich when the Americans were here, and they were rich when the Americans were gone too." His voice grew soft. "Wasn't that the reason we fought those wars in the first place? So that people like them would become like us? Well?"

He turned to look over at the Fortune Teller, who appeared to have lost consciousness. He was slumped forward; the ropes binding him to the rubber tree were pulled taut. His white head lolled against his chest. Field Rat Ma shook his arm. "Hey! Old man! You can't die yet—the cobras have to kill you!" He shook him again, harder, and the Fortune Teller's head flopped backward. Field Rat Ma gave a frightened squeal and jettisoned himself away from him, dropping the burning cigarette into the dry undergrowth.

The Fortune Teller's mouth was not there anymore. Neither were his nose and cheeks. The whole lower half of his face had caved inward; a sinkhole beneath two sad eyes. And then the smoke—thick, brick colored, choking—began to billow out rapidly, engulfing them both before Field Rat Ma had the chance to fully process the last thing that he would ever see. It was the Fortune Teller's final kindness.

The Field Rat twisted and thrashed, thinking he was fighting a creature concealed by the smoke. He did not realize that the smoke itself was the creature. In the red miasma surrounding him, a darker red opened. It closed over his head and torso and the Field Rat was half a man. Then the smoke swallowed, and he was nothing.

. .

THE SUN WAS BEGINNING TO SINK, AND FIRST ASSISTANT, STILL alone in the Mas' living room, knew it meant that something had gone very, very wrong. Mrs. Ma, her ward, had been asleep since the Fortune Teller and Mr. Ma and Second Assistant had left, hours ago, so First Assistant hadn't had much to do in regard to protecting her. She had spent most of the afternoon reclining in a hammock in the corner of the living room. The lump on her forehead was now the color and size of a ripe lychee, and she was still wearing the Fortune Teller's hat. She thought that it looked much better on her than it did him, though it did smell a little. She made a note to remember to send it out with the rest of his laundry for cleaning when they got back to Saigon. He wasn't paying her nearly enough for the extra hours she put in doing things that a spouse ought to. Once, First Assistant had asked him if he was lonely, having never taken a wife. The Fortune Teller had laughed loudly and then, bafflingly, pointed at his stomach and replied that he was never alone. First Assistant hadn't bothered trying to talk to him about his personal life after that. Perhaps his off-putting sense of humor was part of the reason he had never found anyone willing to marry him.

Matrimony and her own husbandlessness were never far from First Assistant's mind—unmarried at twenty-eight, she was standing on the high, crumbling ledge that overlooked spinsterhood. Her mother, who had wed at seventeen, always began their weekly phone calls by reminding First Assistant that her eggs were shriveling up, before launching into her usual reproaches about her unnatural employment—she was certain that the ghost-hunting business was really some sort of front, and that her daughter was actually a prostitute.

No, it was a more nuanced exchange than that. She was a *vessel*. That was what the Fortune Teller reminded her whenever she invariably started to question herself after one of her mother's phone calls. She had learned to accept over the years that the invisible cosmic strings that fastened oneself to one's body were tied a little too loosely in her case, allowing occasional, postcorporeal visitors. But she had never been able to understand what exactly happened to her during these times when her body was not her own. She never had any memory of the *occupations*. It was all just black until she woke up again. Where did she go? Did she stay in there, squished into a corner of her own mind while someone else took control? Was she hovering, unmoored, somewhere in the vicinity of her body but outside it? Or was it as she feared, and she actually took the spirit's place during the time that it took hers—in other words, that she temporarily died whenever they were performing a ceremony. The Fortune Teller had never been able to explain it in a satisfactory way. He would tell her to stop trying to make sense of the process through physical terms, but First Assistant didn't see how else one was supposed to understand a body.

The first time it happened, she had been at her grandmother's funeral. Nine-year-old First Assistant, bored and drowsy in a corner, had nodded off and then woken up a few minutes later on the floor in the middle of the room, where she was told that she had been complaining loudly in her late grandmother's voice about all the things that were wrong with the ceremony and scolding an aunt about a cooking pot she had borrowed three years ago and never returned.

By her fifteenth birthday, First Assistant had played host to half a dozen other deceased relatives and the occasional neighbor. Her mother admitted that there was something supernatural at play, and that it wasn't just an extended prank or an unusual form of epilepsy, only after the girl was possessed by a great-uncle who had died during the war, long before she was born, and during the trance rattled off the flamboyant, unusual profanities that he himself had coined, all in his thick Ha Tinh accent. The Fortune Teller was called.

He had been slightly less wrinkled thirteen years ago, but in all other ways the same: behatted, perpetually distracted, wreathed in a tobacco cloud. First Assistant remembered peering at him through the upstairs window of their house, down a quiet alley in Phu Nhuan, as he knocked on the door, and feeling slightly disappointed. He was far from imposing in his shabby suit, and there was no aura of power about him, no presence indicating that he was someone who possessed the secrets of the world of the dead. He looked like one of the delivery men she would see napping on their motorbikes between shifts, with their legs sprawling open and their heads balanced on the handlebars with a folded newspaper for a pillow.

She recalled her mother drawing the curtains and muttering under her breath about how the neighbors would see the "black magic" and gossip about the family even more than they already did. The Fortune Teller had begun removing equipment from his briefcase (like the Fortune Teller, it too was a little less battered thirteen years ago) and setting it up on their coffee table—there were small bags of dried herbs and unnaturally colored powders, a vial containing a viscous red liquid, sticks of incense, candles with runes carved into the wax, a buffalo horn, sheets of parchment paper covered in writing so minuscule that the words looked like fleas on the page, a knife, and one giant, gnarled root that still had dirt clinging to its fibers. First Assistant, in her blue school uniform, had gone pale imagining the procedures that were to come, and her mother had felt queasy and gone into the kitchen to make tea. Once she'd left the room, the Fortune Teller had looked at the terrified teenager and laughed.

"Oh, don't worry about all this," he said, indicating the objects spread on the table before them. "They're all for show. Props. Just some oddities I found while tidying up the other day that I thought I'd bring along. Because there's nothing I can do to fix you. But I didn't want to show up empty-handed. Image is everything in this business." He'd grinned. "Now, let's go over some important things before your mother comes back. I said I couldn't fix you, and that's true; you will never be able to stop the ghosts from coming in, but you *can* make it more difficult for them. Obviously, steer clear of cemeteries and funerals. Avoid the recently bereaved, because their loved ones are still loitering around. You've mostly been dealing with dead relatives, correct? Within the next few years it'll start being the spirits of strangers too, so be prepared for that. I'm going to give you these . . ." Here the Fortune Teller had gone digging around in his pockets and pulled out a small envelope folded out of red cellophane. Inside she could see what appeared to just be scraps of paper of varying sizes.

First Assistant had been skeptical, but the Fortune Teller reassured her. "No, no, this one isn't from my attic—this one is real. Don't open it. Keep it in your pocket at all times if possible. It might help. But really, why do you want to stop them? The spirits, I mean. I understand that they can choose very inconvenient times to come, but it's a gift, to be the way you are. If you decide, someday, that you'd like to do more with your talent and not just try to hide it from your neighbors, I hope that you might consider coming to work for me." He scribbled an address onto the back of one of the illegible papers and handed it to her along with the little red envelope. "Now, I think we should make your 'exorcism' a little more convincing." He tossed a couple of the little powder bags in her direction. "Why don't you smear some of that on yourself? That'll be a nice touch. And then when your mother returns, we can all go outside and set the root on fire."

He hadn't charged them very much, so First Assistant never felt too guilty about their deception. And his advice, for the most part, had worked; she feigned headaches or cramps to get out of going to funerals and wore the little red envelope on a string around her neck, under her clothes. There were only two more incidents, and both times it was Grandma again—both times with more complaints. Sometimes, however, she would feel a kind of tingling sensation, a buzzing that began at the top of her head before moving down to the base of her neck, and wonder if it was, figuratively speaking, a spirit jiggling the doorknob.

First Assistant attended a fairly well-known university in Saigon, received a degree in accounting, and was promptly employed by an electricity company. She purchased seven different pencil skirts and matching blouses, one for each day of the week, and wore her favorite set on her first morning on the job. But when she arrived at the office, she paused and felt the familiar scratch of the red envelope against her sternum. She turned and hailed a taxi. She removed the envelope from its string around her neck and tore it open, sending most of the little bits of paper, whatever they were, spinning away in the breeze. She uncrumpled the old address paper from the corner of her wallet where she had kept it all these years and gave it to the cab driver. Fifteen minutes later, she was in front of Café Max.

FIRST ASSISTANT ROCKED IN her hammock in the Mas' house, listening to the relentless hum of cicadas in the twilight. Her head itched a bit. She took off the Fortune Teller's hat to inspect it for lice, but it was now too dark to really see, and she was too comfortable to get up and find the light.

Sometimes she did genuinely think that she would grow old alone, like the Fortune Teller. Her friends had stopped setting her up with their handsome cousins and coworkers after a disastrous dinner date three months ago, when she had been possessed at the sushi restaurant where they were eating by the spirit of the man's late mother, who told him he was better off getting back together with the ex-girlfriend he was still in love with. First Assistant now had to take her chances with men she met on the internet. More than half of her online messages were from Westerners, but First Assistant didn't respond to those, knowing that her English wasn't good enough to tell the foreigners with fetishes apart from the ones without them. The cheap dates took her out for afternoon coffee, the ones who hoped she would be an easy lay took her out for evening coffee at cafés conveniently located next to room-by-the-hour motels, the old-fashioned ones took her for mung bean and coconut pudding, and the ones who wanted to show off but weren't really rich took her for Korean barbecue but showed up early and ordered for the both of them so that First Assistant couldn't ask for expensive cuts of beef. Apart from this, First Assistant viewed the men as generally indistinguishable from one another but didn't feel guilty about it, because she was certain that they used far worse rubrics on her and the other women they dated.

This was First Assistant's secret foolish wish: that if she had to be plagued by spirits, they could at least advise her on her love life. The midmeal intrusion of her date's mother had been embarrassing, but the more First Assistant thought about it, the more she was grateful for all the time it had saved them. For all of the pointless future sushi dinners and unenthusiastic fondling and the eventual breakup she had been spared. Why couldn't other ghosts chime in like that on all of her blind dates, albeit in a less aggressive manner? Just whispering discreetly into her ear—a little bit of romantic insider trading, that's all she was asking for—to let her know whether or not the man had any real potential. The dead knew. They could easily say to her, "This one isn't ready for a commitment." Or "This one has four different girlfriends and is stealing from two of them." They didn't even need to go into that much detail; First Assistant would be perfectly happy with a succinct "No, he's not the one. No, it's not him either—"

"It's me," came a voice from behind her in the dark. "Don't be frightened."

Too late for that—First Assistant was so startled by the sound that she tumbled backward out of the hammock. From the ground, she looked up and saw that the voice was Mrs. Ma's. Only her periphery was visible in the half dark—she was dressed in some sort of bizarrely floaty, full-length white outfit, and the effect was uncomfortably spectral.

"I'm so sorry! Let me help you up," said Mrs. Ma. A light flicked on, and First Assistant winced at the sudden brightness. She now saw that for some reason, the woman was clad in a Western-style wedding dress that gushed lace at its hem. "I thought it would be less of a shock if I announced myself first instead of just turning on the light," Mrs. Ma explained.

First Assistant just blinked in confusion, still sprawled on the floor with one foot tangled in the hammock's netting. This woman bore little resemblance to the frail, hair-vomiting recluse she had met earlier this afternoon—she was serene and self-possessed, radiating a cool power despite wearing a rabid meringue of a gown. Mrs. Ma floated across the tiles to her, and when she reached out her hands, First Assistant took them and allowed herself to be pulled up to her feet, even though she was perfectly capable of getting up on her own. While she was shaking her foot free of the hammock, Mrs. Ma suddenly crouched down again.

"Your hat!" she exclaimed. She retrieved it from where it had rolled and then placed it back on First Assistant's head. First Assistant hadn't realized how tall Mrs. Ma was—nearly the same height as the Fortune Teller. "It suits you," Mrs. Ma said to First Assistant. Then, "Oops!—" The oversized Stetson had slipped forward over First Assistant's eyes. Both women quickly reached to readjust it at the same time. First Assistant noticed herself noticing when their fingers brushed briefly.

"Thank you," she said as the brim lifted and Mrs. Ma's smile appeared in front of her once more. She gestured to Mrs. Ma's gown. "I feel a little underdressed."

Mrs. Ma laughed and shook her head. "Your outfit is perfect," she said. (Untrue; First Assistant was wearing a baggy orange boiler suit. There had been a sale at a store that sold uniforms for electrical linemen, and the Fortune Teller had purchased one for each of them, thinking it would make the Saigon Spirit Eradication Co. appear more professional, but he and Second Assistant never bothered to wear theirs.) "This dress is absurd, but it's the nicest thing I own, and it's the only thing I have that my husband didn't buy for me, so I didn't want to leave it behind with him."

It took several beats for First Assistant to put together what this meant. "Oh! So . . . so you're . . ." she stammered.

"Yes. I'm going to get away from Ia Kare," said Mrs. Ma. "And I'm going to get away from him. I'm scared that you'll think I'm crazy when I tell you this, but today I heard a voice." She steadied her breath before continuing, "I heard it twice. The first time was this afternoon, while you were all out here performing the ceremony. I was lying in my room, and I heard it say—I heard *her* say—'It's time for you to go.' I could hear her in my ears, but it was like she was speaking to me from inside my own skull."

"What did her voice sound like?" asked First Assistant. "Was it familiar?"

"I'd never heard it before. A woman. But with a voice that was low and . . . and sort of like rocks being crunched together. A crackly voice. But not a frightening voice. Immediately after she said it I felt sick to my stomach, and that was when I ran out here and I . . ." Mrs. Ma trailed off and looked at the spot where she had disgorged the hair clod. "I told myself that I had imagined her. But then, just now when I was in the room, I heard her again. That raspy voice from nowhere, clearer and more real than anything. She said, 'It's time for you to go. Go now, and go away from the trees.' And I am going to listen to her.

"You don't have a reason to trust me—you and I don't really know each other, after all, we've just been thrown together by the same ghost—but I think that we might be similar," said Mrs. Ma to First Assistant. "We're the ones that the strange things happen *to*. We are the ones who feel them, but we're never allowed to be the ones who control them. But now that's changing." She held First Assistant's gaze. "I think that I've been waiting here for the past twenty-four years to hear someone tell me that I'm free to leave. And now that someone finally has, I don't know why I couldn't just say it to myself all along. So, will you help me? And will you go with me?"

First Assistant hesitated. She did not make decisions without the Fortune Teller. She did not summon or control. She was the vessel. She was the possessed. But just because she was the vessel did not mean that she could not be brave, and even now she could remember the sensation of the red envelope scratching between her breasts, and how good it had felt when she finally ripped it open. The car keys were already in her hand.

"Come on," she said. "I hope that all two hundred pounds of your dress will be able to fit inside our van." She'd said this hoping to make Mrs. Ma laugh again; First Assistant had noticed the warning sheen of tears in her eyes. She was rewarded with a light chuckle.

"My mother was the one who picked out this beast for me," Mrs. Ma said, contorting the protrusions of tulle on her hips in order to fit through the doorframe. "I think it was her way of apologizing for not being able to protect me better. That's why I can't leave it behind. She really thought it was so glamorous." Mrs. Ma looked at First Assistant and now gave her a true smile, with all of her immaculate teeth. "There's a pair of fingerless gloves somewhere that match it, but I didn't think I needed to bring those too."

I will help you, and I will go with you, First Assistant thought to herself. *I think that I would go with you anywhere, probably.* "Don't worry," she said. "If my mother had gotten the chance to pick a wedding dress for me, I'm sure it would have been even worse."

"Ah, wait," said Mrs. Ma suddenly, squeezing herself back into the house. "There's one last thing I forgot." She walked across the room to the ancestral altar, her pale train flowing behind her, and stood up on her tiptoes. She plucked the portrait of her father from the shelf. "The voice didn't tell me to do this," she said, before smashing it on the ground. Then she picked her way delicately past the broken glass, over to where First Assistant was waiting for her.

· ·

SECOND ASSISTANT DID NOT REALIZE THAT HE HAD FALLEN asleep until he woke up and found himself looking at the stars. They were the first thing he saw when he opened his eyes, and they were magnificent—he had never seen so many, or seen them so clearly, before. While he was sleeping, he had wriggled himself beneath the rice sack so that it covered his chest like a little blanket. The Fortune Teller would be furious at him, he knew, but somehow he wasn't worried. The stars comforted him. He banished thoughts of his employer and his unfinished task from his mind and snuggled tighter in the dirt, clutching his rice sack. He should move out to the countryside, he thought. Learn how to be a pepper farmer. How hard could it possibly be? He smiled peacefully to himself. The smile faded when he suddenly smelled smoke.

Second Assistant sat up in alarm. He had to get back to the house. But when he tried to stand, he found that his legs had become inexplicably heavy. He could not even bend his knees. He pushed up as hard as he could with his arms, trying to raise his body, but it was as though his bottom half was now made of lead, and he could not lift it more than two inches off the ground. "What's wrong with me?" he grumbled. Then his eyes widened and he clutched a hand to his throat. Even though his mouth had been moving, his words had not produced a sound. Panicking, Second Assistant opened his mouth again and tried to yell, but he could only expel a hoarse wind. His voice, like his legs, had left him. He slapped his thighs in frustration and realized with horror that even his hand striking his leg had not produced a sound. He had become a ghost without dying. Or perhaps he had died and just hadn't known. Second Assistant began to cry, noiselessly.

On the road before him, an opaque, ruddy shroud of smoke began to drift into his blurry line of vision. Second Assistant wiped his eyes. It was not really behaving like smoke—it moved more like fog, creeping in from the direction of the house in the distance, staying low to the ground—but it smelled of burning, so he did not know what else it could be. It did not disperse; it seemed to be gathering instead, rolling in and then lingering like a lumpy reddish blanket, just above the surface of the dirt road.

The smoke was looking at him. It had no visible eyes, but Second Assistant knew that it could see, and knew that it saw him. He knew this in his body, in the terror sending cracks running through him like footfall on thin ice.

It left the road and began moving slowly in his direction, slinking over the stubbly ground. Unable to run, unable to have the dignity of even yelling, Second Assistant could do nothing but attempt to conceal himself behind the rice sack and wait for the end. He tried to think of the things he had loved: his parents, his grandfather, his motorbike; the bright green color of his favorite bridge, Cầu Mong; the smell of Café Max. But all he could see was the lottery woman in her chair, her makeup-enameled face and her fistful of tickets.

The end came. Darkness gobbled up his vision, and then there was a crumpling in his ears, and then it was not the end after all, because he heard the sound of an engine puttering to a stop followed by the sound of himself screaming, screaming, loudly and in his true voice at last. He realized that his eyes were closed, so he opened them and saw First Assistant standing above him. The smoke was gone, and it felt so good to be back in command of his vocal cords that he raised his shrieking half an octave just because he could.

"Hush!" First Assistant clamped a hand over his mouth until his screams had subsided to whimpers. "We have to go," she said gently. "The forest is burning. Look."

Second Assistant rose to his feet with what felt like glorious ease after his ordeal. He squinted at the spot in the distance that First Assistant was pointing to—there was a smoggy orange glow above the horizon.

He turned back around to face the road. Their van was idling in the spot where he had imagined the smoke. Second Assistant blinked and shook his head. He abandoned his rice sack in the underbrush and made his way on slightly shaky feet over to the car with First Assistant.

"Boss, boss, let's get away from this place," he begged, climbing into the back seat. "Please, let's hurry." The figure in the driver's seat turned around. "Mrs. Ma?!"

Mrs. Ma drummed her lovely fingers on the steering wheel. "We had to leave in a hurry and couldn't wait for your boss to come back. It was time for us to go. We hope he'll find us later." First Assistant slid into the passenger seat next to her, and the two women exchanged a smile which Second Assistant could not interpret and did not trust.

"Shall we?" First Assistant asked Mrs. Ma softly. Second Assistant saw that she was still wearing the Fortune Teller's hat, and now Mrs. Ma was wearing a frothy white wedding dress. Why were they having a fucking costume party? And where was the Fortune Teller? Mrs. Ma put the van into gear, and Second Assistant, feeling strangely like a child again, petulant when his parents were keeping secrets, swiveled in his seat to look out the back window at the dark country rolling away behind them.

As the van bumped along the road, Second Assistant was surprised to find that he was having trouble keeping his eyes open. He didn't know how he could possibly sleep after the nightmare he had just experienced, but he curled up on his side like a cat and managed to doze, until he was suddenly awakened by the startled cries of First Assistant. Mrs. Ma braked so sharply that Second Assistant was hurled against the back of the driver's seat. The vehicle went skidding sideways over pebbles and sent up a red nebula of dust before finally coming to a shuddering halt.

"Did we hit it?" whispered First Assistant, while Second Assistant picked himself up off the van floor. Mrs. Ma said nothing but unbuckled her seatbelt quickly and threw open her door, First Assistant following close behind. Second Assistant squinted through the windshield at the crouching figure caught in the beam of the headlights. He didn't realize at first that it was human—it was hard to see with all the dust, and he mistook the Fortune Teller's distended jaw, which was dangling open nearly to the ground, for a tail or long proboscis or fifth limb.

The Fortune Teller was down on all fours. What remained identifiable of the upper half of his face was bruised, and he was glazed unevenly with a wet, sticky film that had plastered his thin hair to his scalp and collected umber patches of dirt. His eyes were wide open but did not seem to register the two women approaching him. Even from inside the van, Second Assistant could hear the low, horrible moans that he was emitting from his gorge of a mouth.

"Help us carry him to the car!" yelled First Assistant, banging her fist on the hood. Mrs. Ma took a corner of the wedding dress and wiped away some of the slime from the Fortune Teller's forehead. Second Assistant opened the van's side door and scurried over to them, unable to stop his knees from shaking.

"Have you ever seen something like this before?" he whispered to First Assistant. She shook her head and began lifting the Fortune Teller by his armpits. Second Assistant hesitated for a moment before lacing his hands beneath his boss's stomach and hoisting. Together they shuffled back around to the side of the van, with Mrs. Ma cradling the end of his mouth to keep it from dragging on the ground. They laid him gently down on the car floor and made sure his toes and his chin were clear of the door before sliding it shut. Mrs. Ma restarted the engine, and they set off down the road again in fraught silence.

Second Assistant sat rigidly in his seat, hyperaware of the Fortune Teller's buckled form by his feet but determined not to look down until either daylight broke or they reached Saigon. The moaning grew softer. Gradually, Second Assistant realized that the sounds were changing too; the Fortune Teller was trying to form words. Second Assistant couldn't resist anymore, and he glanced down. The mouth had retracted nearly to its normal shape but was still too stretched out for the lips to meet when the Fortune Teller moved them.

"Briefcase?" asked Second Assistant, attempting to guess what he was saying from the few vowels he could make out. "Are you trying to ask for your briefcase?"

"He took it with him when he went with Mr. Ma," said First Assistant from the front seat. Second Assistant had noticed that she'd removed the hat when they discovered the Fortune Teller in the road, but she had since returned it to her head.

The Fortune Teller's eyes would not focus on any of the other people in the car. Instead, they darted around as if following an invisible fly inside the van. The mouth had continued shrinking, and his top and bottom lip could now touch, but the words were still undecipherable.

"It's just gibberish," said Second Assistant, swallowing back a sob. "It sounds like he's trying to speak goddamn French." He could see that the Fortune Teller's breaths were now slowing. Second Assistant counted between them. Seven seconds apart. Twelve seconds. He reached out and touched the Fortune Teller's cheek, which had become the shape he knew once more. Fifteen seconds, and they were shallow, with a wet rattle beneath them. Twenty seconds. He stopped counting and tried to commit the Fortune Teller's face to memory for the day in the future when he would need it—when his time really came, when the smoke or something like it finally got him, and he would have to think of what he had loved.

. .

HOURS LATER, JUST BEFORE DAWN, SOMETHING STIRRED IN *the well in the garden. From within it there came the creaking of rope, the sound of fingers scrabbling at dirt, and then Bà heaved herself up and out over the edge. Her movements were slack and unnatural, as if her body were a rubber glove flopping loosely on a too-small hand. Her eyes were blank and glassy. In the garden, she removed the little dog from where it had been tucked safely inside her pajama top and clumsily settled it into the crook of one arm like an infant. Then, with lurching, arrhythmic steps, Bà began to walk.*

The dog lifted its head and sniffed, then buried its face back down in the old woman's elbow. The fire in the rubber plantation had burned itself out by now, but there was still ash in the air. Bà did not blink. Her feet turned down the road, taking them toward the highway.

Bà and the dog had only been chilled from hiding in the well, and they were barely damp. But two paces behind them, something was following, leaving a wet trail in the dirt. It could not be seen itself—only the water that dripped from it, pockmarking the thirsty earth in its wake.

WINNIE HAD BEGUN TO BELIEVE THAT SHE WOULD get away with pretending to teach for the entire semester. Between her fake classes, she crept around the academy like a mangrove crab, hiding from her boss and her other colleagues and generally managing to squirm out of most human interactions. But one Friday afternoon toward the end of her third month in Vietnam, when Winnie had finished for the day and was preparing to sneak off into the sunset, Mrs. Cook tapped her on the shoulder and informed her that Mr. Quy would be taking all of his staff out that evening for a team-building dinner—a semiannual event.

"Don't worry," said Mrs. Cook, "We'll all share a taxi." The color drained from Winnie's face, and she wondered if Mrs. Cook could read her thoughts—she had been formulating a plan where she would get in a taxi by herself and pretend later that the driver had gotten lost on the way to the restaurant. "We're *really* going to get to know each other tonight," she continued. To Winnie, this was the worst of threats. She had not eaten a meal with another person since her ill-fated hot pot with Dr. Sang six weeks earlier and feared that this one would be exponentially worse.

Mr. Quy had chosen a stately two-story seafood restaurant near the

District 5 / District 10 border. The motorbike parking attendants out front all wore uniforms, and the only beer cans visible on tables were Heinekens or Tigers. The entrance was lined with bubbling glass tanks of fish and eels and lobsters and various other forms of marine life; it was an interactive menu for diners, who could appraise the specimens on display and then select which ones they wanted steamed or grilled or deep-fried. It was the kind of semiglamorous place that Winnie would typically only gawk at from across the street while she ate side-walk noodles.

She spent the taxi ride over sandwiched between the Cooks, listening to them smugly discuss how well their lessons had gone that day, with Mrs. Cook making particularly pointed comments about how produc-tive her students were. When they pulled up at the restaurant Winnie tripped on the curb in her haste to escape from them. Mr. Quy and some of the other Achievement! staff were already occupying a long table on the second floor; to Winnie's relief, it was clear that her boss had begun imbibing much earlier that day and was not in a state where he would be able to accurately differentiate his foreigners. Still, Winnie wedged her way into an inaccessible corner seat that was as far from him as possible (and put half a table between herself and the Cooks), where she would be partially concealed behind a container of chopsticks. As soon as the Friday teachers joined them, Mr. Quy summoned a waitress and or-dered a round of Tigers for the whole table. When it was gently pointed out to him that they had already received a new round only a few min-utes ago, he instructed them to all chug their just-opened beers in order make way for the next ones. The team-building dinner at Achievement!, it seemed, was just an excuse for school-sanctioned drunkenness, which suited Winnie just fine. She gladly accepted a glass and drained it, let-ting the alcohol soothe her Cook-frayed nerves.

The seat next to her was occupied by a Vietnamese staff member she didn't know. He was struggling with the last swigs of his own beer, and he glanced at Winnie's empty glass with admiration. "Why are you hiding out here?" he said to her once he had finally finished. "You should be sitting with Boss Quy, drinking him under the table."

He looked like he was a few years older than Winnie, and he was handsome in a sloppy and slightly vulnerable way. There was a small rice noodle on the collar of his dress shirt that had probably been stuck there since lunchtime, because it had gone all brittle. His hair was a touch too shaggy and he kept tucking and re-tucking it behind one ear. He was a little rabbity in the teeth, a little delicate in the chin, and his eyes were uncommonly gibbous and wide-set—a little bit carp-like. Winnie wasn't sure yet whether she found them disarming or disconcerting. "I'm Long," he said, extending a hand. "And you're Ngoan, aren't you?"

Ngoan. There she was again. Winnie had been reaching out her own hand and froze midway when she heard the name. She couldn't stop her face from registering her dismay at Ngoan's reappearance.

Long's face fell. "Oh no," he said quickly. "Did I get it wrong?"

Winnie found her voice in the back of her throat. "No, no, I was just surprised—I didn't think that anyone here knew my Vietnamese name. I go by 'Winnie' though."

Long was visibly relieved. Winnie realized that what she found unnerving about his eyes was that they were just too readable.

"I'm not a teacher; I'm in charge of the office," he explained. "I had to make a copy of your passport photo page when they hired you, which is how I recognized you. I'm sorry if that's creepy. And I'm sorry for not knowing your real name. Here"—the new round of beer was being distributed, and Long reached across the table and intercepted two cans. He poured one into Winnie's glass first, and then one into his own—"an apology toast. It's very nice to meet you, Winnie." They clinked glasses, and Winnie threw hers back quickly, trying to remember what her passport photo looked like and whether or not she should be embarrassed that Long had seen it.

Her passport. She set the half-drunk beer back on the table, a thought slowly dawning on her. "Oh shit!" Winnie said out loud. And then she surprised herself by bursting into laughter.

"What is it?" asked Long.

"My ninety-day visa! It's running out in . . ." She counted quickly in her head. "Two days! I have to go to the border to get restamped!" She was laughing so hard that her lungs were cramping. "Oh god, I'm going to have to take a bus to Cambodia tomorrow morning!"

"That doesn't seem very funny," said Long, but he started to laugh along with her, because it would be impolite to let her keep going by herself. Then Winnie realized that she had been in Vietnam for eighty-eight days and this was her first time laughing with another human being, and this made her feel so truly lonely that her laughter abruptly died. Luckily, the temporary cure for both the loneliness and her embarrassment about it was in the glass in front of her. Winnie finished her second beer almost as quickly as she had the first, with Long doing a better job of matching her pace this time. Because all the plates of food on the table were beyond the reach of Winnie's chopsticks, he grabbed half a dozen charred pink skewers of shrimp for her and deposited them on her plate like a spiky bouquet.

"Eat," said Long. "And look, about your visa—why don't I just drive you? The buses are terrible and make the trip take twice as long. I have a motorbike. It's only an hour and a half to the Cambodian border."

"That's too nice a thing to do for someone you don't know," Winnie said bluntly, tearing off a shrimp head.

"It really isn't. Besides, it's my job to make sure that your paperwork stays in order. What would your students do if you got kicked out of the country for overstaying your visa?"

"I don't think they'd really mind," muttered Winnie.

"What was that?"

"I said, 'I think that you're really kind.'" She inhaled nervously and then laughed. "Okay. Yes. Please drive me to Cambodia tomorrow. But let me pay for your gas, at least."

Long grinned. "Deal. And now that we've settled how to keep you from getting deported, we can focus on the job at hand," he said, reaching for two more Tigers from the table's constantly replenishing supply. "Drinking our way through the academy's budget. I take care of all of the accounts. Tuition is higher this year, and if we don't use up the extra money, it'll just end up in the pockets of Thầy Quy or the neighborhood police chief, one way or another." He smiled and raised his glass.

Winnie knew she should be wary of getting too friendly with Long. She found him likable, and probably still would have even if she were not drunk and getting progressively drunker by the minute, but this very fact made her nervous. When he wasn't pouring her more beer, he was trying to load up her plate for her, launching quick strikes on the communal dishes like a bird of prey, swooping in with his chopsticks to retrieve various little morsels for her: a tangle of water spinach, some rubbery pieces of steamed conch, a chunk of pearly flesh flaked off the side of a snapper. Long struck Winnie as the kind of person who needed to be constantly tending to someone, or else he wouldn't know what to do with himself.

She wondered if he was always this attentive to foreign teachers at first. Whether this was his routine. Whether the others had all rebuffed him and that was the reason he had turned his attention to Winnie now. She knew she was not pretty enough to warrant it otherwise. Winnie looked across the table at Dao (who, like all good Vietnamese girls, and unlike Winnie, had put a large chunk of ice into her glass so that it would water down the beer as it melted) and squinted her eyes in order to blur her features. They did look a bit similar when they were fuzzy. The girl she was looking at could have been Winnie. Though, Winnie supposed, she could have been most girls with dark hair. "Hey, Long," Winnie asked.

"Hmm?" He was looking across the table at Dao too, but was he looking at her because Winnie was, or because Dao was pretty?

"Do you think you would recognize me anywhere?"

Long laughed. "What kind of question is that?"

"I mean, if you saw me, would you know it was *me*?"

Long laughed. "Yes, Winnie. If I saw you, I would know it was you."

"Wrong," said Winnie. There was beer sloshed down the front of her brown sack dress. She did not recall spilling it on herself. "People don't notice me when I don't want them to. I'm like the geckos that can change their skin, and so people walk right past without seeing them on the wall. Or like one of those brown tree moths that look exactly like bark."

"I don't think you're a gecko," said Long, gently. "Or a tree moth. But I *do* think you should drink some water and think about heading home soon. We're going to Cambodia tomorrow, remember?"

"I'm sorry," said Winnie. "I don't know what I was trying to say."

"You were saying that you want me to notice you. And I'm glad that you do." He smiled, but Winnie frowned; she was sure that she hadn't said anything of the sort. Long poured her a glass of water and nudged it toward her. "I have to leave now," he said. "Will you be able to get home on your own?"

Winnie looked around; the dinner had ended without her noticing. The Vietnamese teachers were digging out their motorbike keys, and the foreign ones were finding their purses and jackets. Mr. Quy had fallen asleep across three chairs, and two of the staff were frantically discussing how to politely rouse him.

"Of course I will," snorted Winnie, too drunk to keep the indignation from her voice.

Long hesitated, his eyes searching hers. It was time to stand—everyone at the table was now getting up, including Mr. Quy, aided by both of the Alexes—but Winnie had to wait until Long's back was turned because she didn't want him to see her legs wobble. "Okay" was all he said when he finally did speak.

Winnie wondered if she had upset him. Maybe he wouldn't want to drive her to the border anymore. It didn't matter. She would just take the bus to Cambodia. She would bring a bánh mì and finish the crime novel she was reading— Detective Kusakawa was about to catch his serial killer. It would be a pleasant day and provide an eight-hour escape from her great-aunt's house.

When the dinner party began splitting into departing factions at the door, Winnie did not get in a taxi to go home. She allowed herself to get swept from the restaurant to Karaoke 666 next door, along with the rest of the staff who weren't drunk enough yet and wanted to cap off their night by screaming ballads from the '90s in an air-conditioned room with strobe lights. Long and Dao had left the restaurant in the same taxi, which Winnie wished she had been too drunk to notice. Maybe they were just going back to the school, where their respective motorbikes were parked. Maybe Long just happened to live near Da Kao too.

Karaoke 666 had four levels, each with five private rooms. As they walked down the hallway, Winnie could hear snatches of drunken wailing over throbbing techno beats. Every so often she would get on her tiptoes and peer in through the clear glass panel in the door at the people inside. Two separate birthday parties were being held on the first floor: one, a room of twentysomethings in clubbing attire, and two doors over, a full sixteen-member family with both sets of grandparents in attendance and half a dozen small children dancing around with cake-smeared faces. One of the second-floor rooms was occupied solely by two women who were standing barefoot on top of their table and belting into a shared microphone with delirious joy. There were a dozen green-uniformed policemen in the first room of the third floor, and like the Achievement! employees, they also appeared to be in the middle of their own office bonding bacchanal. They wore identical semifrozen expressions of carefully crafted enthusiasm as they sat in a row and clapped along to a thumping bass line while one of them solemnly warbled a pop song that Winnie half recognized.

The teachers were given the room next to the policemen. The enormous glass table at the center of the room was already furnished with two cases of beer, an ice bucket and a dozen glasses, an assortment of shrimp-flavored chips, and a fruit plate (with, Winnie noted with displeasure, a stingy mango ration). The remaining Achievement! crew spilled inside, the Vietnamese teachers pouncing on the remote immediately and cuing up their favorite numbers, the Western ones heading straight for the snacks. Winnie grabbed a beer for herself and a few slices of something hard and tart and green from the fruit tray before positioning herself in a corner again, beneath a speaker. She had no intention of singing but had come along because she wanted to be drunker, and she wanted to see if the Cooks would try to sing in Vietnamese. She could now feel comfortably invisible in the group, because everybody was enjoying themselves too much to notice her at their periphery. Winnie was just an extra clinking-glass sound, another blurry face in the background to support their intoxicated narrative of a good time. Of course, the Cooks were a different matter—after they managed to wrestle the microphones away from the Vietnamese teachers and perform a cloying V-pop duet, they pressed the remote control on Winnie, insisting that she do a song.

Winnie knew that it would be easier to hide than to argue, so she scrolled through the available English songs, added "Jingle Bells" to the list of cued tracks, and then excused herself to the restroom, lying that she would be back in time to sing it.

She stepped back out into the hallway and peeked into the room of the singing policemen. Someone had instigated a toast, and now the twelve of them were performing the complicated dance of having to clink glasses with every single member of the party. The next room, past the policemen's, was not currently occupied by a drinking party, but one of the karaoke attendants was curled up on a section of its padded seats, napping.

Winnie finally ambled into the women's bathroom and was confronted by her own face, disheveled and bleary-eyed, in the mirror above the sink. Her reflection winked at her, and she giggled. She made her way to the last stall, pushed open the door, and discovered a policeman sitting on the toilet, holding his head in his hands.

"I'm not pooping; I'm just hiding," he said, without looking up, and Winnie saw that his pants were indeed still on. There was such abject misery in his voice that she was hesitant to leave him.

"Are you okay?" she asked, hovering in the doorway.

The policeman finally raised his head. He did not look okay. Even with her own blurry vision, Winnie could see that his pupils were too dilated and that he was having trouble focusing on her. They were narrow eyes, catlike crescents perched atop high cheekbones on a milk-tea-complexioned face that was not, Winnie thought to herself with a nervous swallow, unhandsome. His hair had fallen down over his forehead and his green hat had somehow ended up in the bucket of flushing water positioned next to the toilet. "What's that accent—are you an American?" he asked. "What's your name?"

"Winnie."

"Binhie."

"Winnie."

"Binhie, I am incredibly fucked up. Earlier tonight I took something, because I needed a way to get through group karaoke but I don't like beer, and in the beginning it felt amazing but now I can't move and I think I am also hallucinating. Were you just in the hallway? Was it full of snakes?"

Winnie's level of intoxication was such that she devoted a full twenty seconds to trying to remember whether or not there had been any hallway snakes. "No," she finally replied.

"Oh god, that's a relief. Please help me get up." He extended his arms, palms facing down, Frankenstein style. Winnie entered the stall and took hold of his hands, but she had underestimated both her own drunkenness and the wetness of the floor; when she tried pulling him to his feet, she slipped and accidentally stepped into the flushing bucket while trying to regain her balance. Her shriek of surprise echoed around the bathroom stall, and she splashed cold water everywhere while getting her foot out, making the floor tiles even slipperier than before and promptly causing her to fall again. This time she landed in a compromising position between the policeman's knees.

"I'm sorry," she said from the ground, but she didn't make another attempt to get up, because she knew that she would keep slipping. She realized that she was still holding the policeman's hands and quickly dropped them and looked for something else to occupy her fingers with. Her soggy sneaker was making her foot cold, so she took it off and tried to wring some of the water out.

"If you take off one, you should just take off the other," advised the policeman.

Winnie shrugged, swiveled around on the wet tile, and tugged off the left shoe as well.

The policeman reached down and yanked Winnie back up onto his lap by the armpits. "Your dress is all wet too," he said, rolling the hem up her thighs and then struggling to get it farther. Winnie shifted her weight from side to side, helping him work the damp linen free from where it had gotten stuck beneath her haunches. She hooked her legs behind the base of the toilet to stabilize herself and, when she shifted her thighs, felt the policeman stiffen in his ugly olive trousers. His efforts to free her from the dress were growing more frantic; when he finally managed to yank it off over her head, he bundled it up in exasperation and threw it into the flushing bucket with his hat.

"No!" protested Winnie, "Why would you do that?!" But the policeman just pulled her mouth down onto his. His lips were trembling a little, which surprised Winnie. She kept her eyes open.

"You taste like crab," he murmured when they paused for air. "Did you have crab for dinner?"

"I think there was some crab in my soup?" She cupped a hand under his chin to attempt to refocus his attention on kissing, but the policeman had more questions.

"What else did you eat?" he demanded.

Winnie sighed and struggled to remember. "A lot of grilled shrimp."

"Mmm," he said, and gave an encouraging nibble to her lower lip. "What else?"

"Snails. *Rau muống* with garlic. Fried noodles." The policeman moved his mouth from her jaw to the hollow behind her ear to the lobe. "Fish wrapped in rice paper. Crispy squid." He moved from her earlobe to her neck, from her neck to her collarbone. The kisses were becoming progressively rougher and less trembly the longer she went on. "Clams with peanuts. Clams with green onions. A salmon cheek!" Winnie's voice went up sharply; the policeman had worked his fingers under the elastic band of her panties. She tightened her leg grip on the toilet and pressed herself against his hand. His breath caught in his throat with a lusty little hiccup and he bent down and took her left breast in his mouth. But just then, the sound of laughter from a passing group in the hallway outside floated in through an air vent and they both froze.

When the laughers were gone, the policeman indecorously spat out Winnie's boob and then straightened up. "We have to hurry or someone will catch us," he said. "Lie down on the floor."

"I don't want to be fucked on a bathroom floor!"

"But you were sitting on it earlier! What's the difference?"

Winnie ignored this and carefully eased herself up off his lap. She managed to stand successfully without slipping, but she leaned herself against the bathroom door just to be safe. The policeman tipped his head back and shamelessly surveyed the small, beige allotment of her body. In her nondescript nude bra and underwear, Winnie thought, she must have blended in nearly perfectly with the taupe bathroom stall. The few other mixes that Winnie knew back home tended to divvy up the extremities of their parents' Eastern and Western heritage, their hair either jet or auburn, their complexion either dark or milky and blue veined like gourmet cheese, their eyes almond shaped or their cheeks freckle dusted, their forearms hairless or the bridges of their noses high, but Winnie had been dealt the muddy ambiguity of the middle; she had turned out sort of brownish all over, with broad features that could be written off at a glance as belonging to a number of ethnicities. The policeman was still staring at her, and Winnie felt herself redden. "What?" she snapped. "Too chubby? Too dark? Whatever it is, I don't care—I've heard it all from my great-aunt already."

He looked hurt. "Of course not. I was just thinking that you have the perfect number of heads." He put a hand on the metal toilet paper dispenser for support and pulled himself to his feet. "Where do you live? Can we go there?"

Winnie stuffed her feet into her damp sneakers and then remembered that her dress was still in the flush bucket. "Shit," she said, reaching around the policeman to fish it out. She retrieved his hat from the water for him too. While she was bent over, she felt his hand graze her bottom.

"No. No tail," he muttered to himself. "All girl."

Even through her alcohol haze this struck Winnie as odd, but not odd enough to make her stop and reconsider taking the policeman back to her great-aunt's house with her. She wrung her dress out as much as she could before putting it back on, but it was still cold and squelchy and horrible on her skin. Winnie's teeth started chattering, and the delirious policeman gave her a concerned look. "Here! Keep your head warm!" he said, and chivalrously covered her wet head with his even wetter hat.

SHE LEFT A HAZARDOUS TRAIL of water down the hallways of the karaoke emporium as the two of them stumbled their way out to the street together. And she completely drenched the back seat of the taxi they took back to District 11, the driver silently fuming at the fact that he couldn't kick a policeman out of his cab. She was still soaking when they reached her great-aunt's house and left incriminating drip marks up the staircase to her shoebox of a room.

Winnie closed her door and peeled the dress off, letting it drop onto the tile floor with a satisfying slapping sound. She finally freed herself from her damp underwear as well, balling up the panties and nubby bra and tossing them into a corner. "Come here," she called to the policeman, lowering herself down to her bed on the floor and wriggling underneath the blanket.

He had left his shoes downstairs at the front door and was standing in his olive socks by the balcony, looking out at the hospital next door. There was enough light coming in through the window from a nearby streetlamp for Winnie to see that he was crying silently.

"Hey," she said softly, and this time he turned to her. She beckoned, and he got down on all fours and came crawling to her over the blanket, still in his uniform.

"Will you let me do something?" the policeman asked, his voice throaty, pleading. Winnie nodded.

He found his way under the blanket with her, and then he brusquely flipped Winnie so that she was facing away from him. He ran his fingers through her hair, and a syrupy warmth began spreading up her thighs. Anticipation arched her back. She waited for him to move his hands further down her body, to slide himself out of his trousers, to yank her ponytail and bite her neck, for something—for anything—to happen. But the policeman just kept playing with her hair. It took Winnie two more minutes to realize that this was all he had wanted to do to her. As she continued to lie there, her desire-propelled engines grinding to a halt, she realized that he wasn't just playing with her hair—he was combing it out with his fingers, picking through the knots like some sort of large, sad baboon. "Thank you," he whispered. He did not take off his clothes, but he did gently tug out Winnie's hair elastic to get at her tangles. After a while she started to find it strangely soothing. She closed her eyes, and when she opened them again it was morning and there was a face peering in at her from the doorway.

It was one of the cousins. The one with the bangs. Winnie didn't remember what had transpired between leaving the seafood restaurant and going to sleep until she noticed the policeman's hat lying on the floor a few feet away. She groaned and turned very, very slowly—as if her hangover headache wasn't an inevitability but a sleeping beast that she could elude if she just kept quiet and didn't make any sudden movements—to the snoring figure in the bed next to her.

"There's another man waiting downstairs for you," said the cousin with a nasty little smirk that took Winnie by surprise; until now, she hadn't thought that the girls' personality spectrums were wide enough to include malice. "Better hurry up; Auntie is talking to him. She wants to know about his *intentions* with you." She then decisively woke up Winnie's hangover headache by shutting the door intentionally loudly, but not quite loud enough that Winnie could complain that she had slammed it.

"Hey!" Winnie shook the policeman's shoulder. "You have to leave!"

The policeman rolled onto his back and blinked up at the ceiling. He turned to Winnie, and she was startled by how unfocused his eyes still were, their glassiness stark in the morning sunlight. "Hello. Who are you?" he asked, with blithe, unconcerned curiosity. He was not blinking.

"I'm Winnie," she said. "What are you even *on*?"

"I think it's mostly PCP and ecstasy mixed with cobra spit. Are you an American?" he asked. "Did we fuck?" He gave her a bleary smile. "I only know one other American, and I hate him."

"I'm sorry, but you really have to go," said Winnie. "And you'll have to jump out the window into the alley, because I can't let my great-aunt see you. It's not very high off the ground though."

"Don't be sorry; it's better if I sneak out," he said, rising obediently to his feet and wobbling over to her balcony. "It'll throw off the smoke monsters that have been following me."

"The what?" Winnie said before she could stop herself. She instantly regretted prolonging their dalliance by a moment more.

The policeman swung his legs over the balcony railing. "The smoke monsters. I finally got to see them last night, but they've been after me for ages. I think they were just invisible before. They're probably waiting to catch me at the door right now. But they'll never expect me to sneak out the window!" With a wild chuckle he let go. His landing in the alley below was both quieter and more graceful than Winnie had anticipated. As she watched the policeman stumble away toward the main street in his sock feet, she felt strangely melancholy. He had forgotten to take his hat.

BY THE TIME THAT Winnie managed to dress and make it down the stairs, her hangover was in full and brilliant bloom.

Poor Long had spent forty-five minutes sitting on an unpadded wooden sofa while Winnie's great-aunt sat across from him and glared and a badly dubbed Korean soap opera played on the television on a crucifix-covered shelf behind his head at full blast. When Winnie finally appeared downstairs, Long glumly held out a plastic takeaway cup of iced coffee that he had brought for her. "All the ice has melted by now.

I'm sorry," he said, struggling to speak over the television. "But it's still drinkable, and the *cơm tấm* shouldn't be too cold." With his other hand, he gestured to the Styrofoam rice box next to him on the uncomfortable sofa, tied up neatly in a plastic bag. Winnie could smell the grilled pork inside, and it made her insides turn. "This place does the best fried eggs!" Long continued eagerly. "A little greasy, but not too much. The perfect breakfast for the morning after a late night out when you're a bit"—he paused and glanced over at Winnie's great-aunt—*"tired."* He was still extending the cup of watery coffee out to her.

Winnie was too "tired" to be polite. "I don't really feel like eating or drinking anything right now."

Flustered, Long set the coffee down next to the takeaway box. His fingers had left ghostly streaks in the film of condensation on the plastic. "Sure! Of course!" he said, attempting to sound unfazed but coming across as slightly manic. "No problem! Sure! Do you want to just get on the road, then?"

Winnie nodded and headed for the door. She had succeeded in avoiding eye contact with her great-aunt so far and was hoping to get out of the house without it happening.

"Wait!" Long called after her, "Don't you want a jacket?" He was wearing an oversized navy rain slicker that, on his slim frame, made him look oddly childlike.

"Is it supposed to rain today?"

"Well, it always *might* rain, so you should be prepared, but what I meant was, don't you want a jacket to protect your arms from the sun?"

"I'll be fine," said Winnie, distracted. She had just noticed that the policeman's shiny black shoes were lined up in the most conspicuous location in the middle of the doorway. Winnie made sure that she stepped nonchalantly over them on her way outside, but she knew that there was no way they had gone unseen by her great-aunt. Or by Long.

Long said nothing about them though. His bike, parked in the gated concrete entryway to the house, was a slightly scuffed white Suzuki. "How did you know where I lived?" Winnie asked.

Long gave her a puzzled look as he buckled his helmet. "You gave me your address last night at dinner," he said. "Don't you remember? We agreed that I should come over around midmorning?" Winnie shook her head. The conversation had probably occurred after beer number six. Long handed her his extra helmet. "It's my fault—I should have called before I left to double-check that the plan was still on. Or to make sure you knew that there was a plan." He smiled sheepishly.

Long opened the seat of the Suzuki and took another old raincoat out of the storage compartment next to the gas tank. It was identical to the one that he was currently wearing, only bigger and baggier. "Please put it on," he said. "If you sit out on the back of the bike in that little dress for an hour, the sun will cook you. And the border police will think you're a backpacker if you wear short sleeves, and they'll try and get an extra bribe out of you."

This persuaded Winnie. She took the jacket from Long and zipped it up. The bottom of it rustled around her kneecaps, lower than the hem of the potato-colored linen dress she was wearing, and its sleeves ended four limp nylon inches past her fingertips.

Once she had the raincoat on, Long gave her his first real smile of the morning. "If the wind gets too rough and hurts your hands while we're driving, you can stick them into my jacket pockets," he said, a bit slyly, starting the motorbike.

They drove northwest from Saigon. The ride was not particularly scenic; the city did not fade gently into rice paddy—it just stretched itself out into an endless chain of dusty roadside coffee shops and gas stations and phone stores and stray dogs chasing each other. The wind did start to hurt once the slow crawl of the city traffic fed into the highway and trucks and buses started whipping past them. But Winnie curled her hands up protectively in her gigantic sleeves and kept them crossed over her chest.

When they approached the border, vehicles were funneled off into different inspection zones, and Winnie had to dismount and make her way to the checkpoint on foot. As she watched the border police moving between motorbikes and Phnom Penh–bound tour buses and trucks full of livestock, an insane kernel of fear began growing in her mind;

she started scanning the features of each man in a green uniform, paranoid that, in the unluckiest coincidence in the world, one of them would be her drug-addled policeman from last night.

The longer she waited in line (behind several dozen backpackers in loose souvenir tank tops who were all much less sweaty than she was in her raincoat), the more irrationally convinced she became that he was there somewhere. When it was finally Winnie's turn to get called up to passport control, she fully expected to find him wielding the exit stamp behind the tall desk. But her stamper ended up being a woman, who had to tell Winnie sharply to stop turning her head and looking over her shoulder during the process. After scrutinizing the face of every policeman during the time that it took her to exit Vietnam, enter Cambodia, walk fifteen yards, make a U-turn, and promptly exit Cambodia again, Winnie was able to admit to herself that he was probably not among them. However, during this process she had also determined that she could not really remember what her policeman's face had looked like to begin with. She did not know whether or not she hoped he had forgotten hers too.

She rejoined Long back in Vietnam, where he had parked the motorbike beside a curb to wait.

"They let us keep you?" he asked.

Winnie managed a smile and waved her blue passport. "For at least another ninety days."

On the drive back, they stopped for a drink at a little café by a roundabout on the outskirts of Saigon. Winnie ordered a fresh coconut, and Long ordered a glass of hot tea, the cheapest item on the menu, which Winnie knew he had only done because she told him when they arrived that she wanted to pick up the check. They still hadn't recovered the ease that they'd had with each other at the restaurant last night, and Winnie derailed both of Long's initial attempts at conversation. (He had tried asking her first about her students and then about what she had done after dinner the night before.)

He ventured a third time. "How do you like living with your great-aunt?"

Winnie had finished drinking the coconut juice and was trying to chisel out the flesh inside with a long metal spoon. "She's very religious. She was a nun for a while. At a convent in Da Lat," she said with a shrug. This seemed to answer his question without actually answering it.

"Is it just you two and that one cousin I met this morning?"

"There's another cousin too."

"Oh?"

Winnie didn't respond. She knew Long was too polite to ask outright whether it was a male or a female cousin. She did not need to confirm his suspicions about the shoes in the doorway for him.

"Well," he went on, after a beat, "if you ever do need to escape, Jeff mentioned not too long ago that he and Anna are looking to rent out the spare bedroom in their apartment."

Winnie snorted. She would die before she moved in with the Cooks. An uncomfortable silence settled between the two of them again. "What kind of apartment do you live in?" she asked, in an effort to be more forthcoming, but then she wished she hadn't, because she worried that Long now thought she was angling to move in with him instead.

"Actually, it's a house, not an apartment."

"Oh, so you have . . . roommates? Or . . . *a* roommate?"

"I live by myself." Long held her gaze coolly when he said this.

"How can you afford that?" She realized too late that this might be rude.

"Well, it's a very tiny house in a very bad neighborhood. It's more like a third of a house." Long paused and gave her a wry smile. "And the rent is so cheap because it's supposedly haunted. My landlord couldn't find anyone else willing to live there."

Winnie raised her eyebrows. "Have you seen anything? You know . . ."

Long shook his head. "Nothing in the two years since I moved in. My landlord told me a few stories from people who tried renting the place before me—ghost ladies crawling out of the bedroom walls, strange cold spots in the house, blood coming out the bathtub faucet, that kind of hokey stuff." Long laughed, but Winnie felt herself tingling all over.

"You don't believe in ghosts?" she asked.

"Of course not. They're just stories that people tell themselves to try and make the horrific shit that actually happens in the world seem less frightening in comparison." Long grinned. "I never even imagined that I'd be able to live in a place with a real bathtub. I'm so happy to have one, I don't care what comes out of its faucet. But it's only been water so far. Very brown water—my landlord messed up the plumbing because he dug up the floors to see if there were any bodies buried under the house that were causing the hauntings. That's probably another reason why the house is so cheap. No weird cold spots either—I wouldn't mind a few of those; the house is old, and it's always too hot. And I'm certain that there haven't been any mysterious women in my bedroom walls lately."

Was this intentionally suggestive? Winnie couldn't tell; Long's eyes were averted. "What are you scared of, then," she asked, "if you're not scared of ghosts?"

Long looked up. He had been furtively slipping a blue 20,000đ note out of his pocket, and he now passed it to the café owner, too quick for Winnie to stop him. He brushed off her protests. "I never said I wasn't scared of them, just that I don't believe in them."

Winnie considered the logic of this and found it faulty. "If you're scared of them, then part of you has to believe in them," she said. "You only fear them because you think that they're at least possible."

"No," he countered amiably. "I can find the idea of them scary, even if they're not real."

"I didn't think that Vietnamese people who didn't believe in ghosts were real. But you exist. So ghosts probably do too." She was still annoyed that he hadn't let her pay for their drinks, but it finally felt like they were almost friends again, as if the morning hadn't happened.

"All right. What about you, then?" laughed Long.

"Oh, I'm the opposite of you," said Winnie. "I believe in ghosts, but I'm not afraid of them."

"I think the only real thing I'm afraid of is my older brother," Long said quietly, after a beat. But immediately after the words left his mouth, he seemed startled to have spoken them aloud. Those too-readable eyes could not hide the fact that he regretted having done so. Winnie could see him trying to retreat now, somewhere behind them—shutting a small window, fastening its latch, drawing the blinds, turning off the lights. She didn't know what memory he was trying to hide from, but she was desperate to get him to come back out.

"There was this woman I met under a tree at a temple one time," she said quickly. "And this is silly, but I was so scared of her face!" Winnie's laugh was pinched and artificial. Long did not join in.

"Oh?" he said absently. It was clear that he wasn't going to leave the place he had withdrawn to.

"And then she sold me a fake lottery ticket. It's so embarrassing, look at this . . ." Winnie reached into her purse and took it out to show him, but Long had risen to his feet.

"Let's head back to the city now." He began walking toward the motorbike without waiting for his change from the café owner, or for Winnie.

Abashed, Winnie quickly stuffed the ticket into her pocket and hurried after him.

THE TWENTY MINUTES IT took to get back to her great-aunt's somehow felt even longer and more awkward than the three hours that had preceded them. When Long dropped her off in front of her house, Winnie was so eager to end the journey and get inside that she forgot to take her lottery ticket out of the pocket of his raincoat when she handed it back to him. It would be there to greet the next girl who had the privilege of borrowing Long's jacket. After he had already driven off, when she finally realized that she had left it behind, Winnie felt like howling. She didn't know why she was so fixated on the stupid ticket, but she couldn't shake the distressing notion that while it was in Long's possession, she could not be wholly herself again, or ever be completely rid of him.

That night her air conditioner was acting up and she spent the long hours lying sweaty and sleepless on the floor in her underpants, imagining Long's house as a Russian nesting doll that cracked apart to reveal his motorbike, the motorbike seat opening to reveal the raincoat, the raincoat pocket unzipping to reveal the ticket.

At some point in the early morning, utterly exhausted but still unable to fall asleep, she got up and put on the policeman's hat. She sniffed it before placing it on her head; its most prominent scent was artificial coconut, from some kind of strong soap or shampoo, but there was a trace of skin musk at the back of it, where the hat would have touched the nape of his neck. Winnie thought that she would probably have more luck trying to identify the policeman by his neck smell than by his face. It wasn't a comforting scent, and the hat was stiff and still a bit damp from its long soak the night before, but for some reason, once she was wearing it, Winnie was able to close her eyes and sleep until morning.

On Monday morning she went to the academy as usual but took particular care to drastically speed up when she passed by the head office so that, on the off chance that Long's desk faced the hallway and he happened to look up as she walked by, Winnie would be just a human-shaped blur.

Unstructured English Conversation Time elapsed uneventfully. Winnie thought that her students seemed more cheerful than usual— she wouldn't remember until later that it was because it was the end of the semester, and after today they would be done with Winnie for good. After class was over and her students had fled forever, Winnie made her way, as usual, to the back of the room to collect what the creepy doodling boys had left. She always peeked at the drawings, curious to see the vulgarities that their sixteen-year-old minds had dreamed up.

Today their canvases had been the worksheets on the English names of fruits and vegetables. The usual genitalia, etc., were affixed to cheerful illustrations of apples and broccoli, and Winnie was half-amused/half-horrified by one banana that had been turned into a many-phallused monstrosity. She flipped to the next worksheet and then frowned because she realized that she was looking at a drawing of herself.

It was unlabeled, but Winnie had no doubt that the face on the page was hers. The likeness was too uncanny, the level of skill with which it had been depicted too high for the resemblance to have been accidental. This sketch wasn't like the others—there was nothing sexual about it—but it was still disquieting. Winnie's unsmiling face stared back at her from the center of the worksheet, surrounded by striated whorls of her hair, which snaked out of her head in all directions to cover the entire page, concealing everything except for her face and her neck with thick, crosshatched tresses. Whoever had done the drawing had dug the pen in so ferociously that the ballpoint had torn through the paper in several spots. So much ink had been used that the worksheet weighed twice as much as the others. With a little trickle of unease, Winnie thought of the faces of the doodling boys who sat here. She could picture them clearly: five boys, each of whom always left behind one creepy drawing apiece. All semester long, Winnie had collected and thrown out five sheets of paper at the end of each class from the back of the room. Exactly five; never any more or any less. Today she was holding six in her hand.

Winnie ripped it in half. She ripped the halves in half again. It still wasn't good enough. She shredded it into the smallest pieces she could manage. Then, holding them tightly in her fist, she went to the bathroom and flushed the scraps of paper Winnie down the toilet, banishing her to the Saigon sewers.

APTAIN TAN PHAN HAD NOT SLEPT WELL IN ALMOST A month. He would wake up three, four, five times a night to find his entire body covered in sweat and his skin prickling with an itch of unknown origin. His sleeping pills did nothing. He could take five or six of them and he would still jerk awake a few hours later and then be unable to sleep again. His nightmares were pill-proof. He knew it was bad dreams that were waking him up, but he never could remember what they were about, just that he had had them. The worst part was that whenever he had the dreams, Tan would . . . well, not *scream*, exactly—it was closer to moaning. In fact, he could almost be certain that they were actually words. He knew this because the noises he made in his sleep were so loud, he would wake himself up. And in that fleeting moment just before he smashed head-on into consciousness and sat straight up in bed, Tan would hear himself, but could never quite grasp what it was he had been trying to say.

He wanted very badly to lay his head down on his desk and doze. The slants of mid-March sunlight coming in through the bars of his window were warm, and the bustle of the vegetable market outside his District 10 precinct was gentle this time of afternoon, even soothing. Tan's eyelids drooped. No! To keep himself alert he shook his head from side to side with such vigor that his cheeks flapped. Better. Tan gave a cursory pat to his hair, checking if any strands had been shaken out of place. Everything seemed intact, but just to be safe he took out a container of hair gel from his bottom drawer and slicked on an extra coconut-scented glob around each temple.

During his training at the academy, Tan had worked hard to ingratiate himself with the correct officers and so, after graduation, managed to get away with doing only ten months of the requisite year and a half on traffic duty. It had still been a miserable time, spent sweating in a peach-colored uniform at a roundabout in My Tho, blowing a small whistle and being ignored by the old women bicycling on the wrong side of the road. After the ten months were up, Tan was given an olive uniform and his first star and stationed at an Immigrations booth with a stamp at Tan Son Nhat Airport.

Tan's superiors were impressed by his knack for turning a blind eye at the right moment, particularly when it was done on their behalf, and so after a year at the airport he was made a lieutenant and assigned to an easy paper-pushing gig at a station in District 5. The pay was more than adequate and he even had his own little desk, but Tan was a man of greater ambitions. He had saved up enough of his airport bribes to always lose when he played cards with his captains and major, but he made sure to demonstrate enough skill that they felt pleased with themselves when they won. He quickly became a favorite, and so when the precinct in District 10 was in need of a new captain, he found himself with a promotion and a third yellow star. The area's large population of poor university students meant that Tan rarely had to deal with anything more serious than drunken brawling and petty theft. His office was private and well lit, his desk was spacious enough to store all of his hair products, and he received his groceries for free from the market ladies next door in exchange for generously overlooking their expired vendor's licenses. Tan was very content. He did not know why he couldn't sleep.

A junior officer named Khoa rapped on his door. "Sir? Sir?"

Tan sighed, patted his hair once more, and then put on his hat. He had become fanatical about his hat since losing his old one six months earlier; he never let it out of his sight. He rose to let the boy in. Normally he would invite Khoa to stay for a glass or two of rice wine from the bottle he kept in a different desk drawer, entertaining his subordinate's fawning behavior as penance for his own apple-polishing past. However, when Tan saw how the boy's face was drained of color and his hands—clutching a sheet of thick, cream-colored paper of a quality much higher than anything kept in the precinct—were shaking, he snatched the note and shooed Khoa from the office immediately. It was vague and brief, and it came from Colonel Khoi. Captain Tan was to report to him without delay. Tan swallowed hard. He was going to receive another promotion; he was certain of it. He'd only met the colonel once before, at a card game, but must have made an impression on him somehow. Perhaps word had gotten out about his invaluable work investigating a university drug ring (two first-years at a polytechnic college busted for dealing marijuana—Tan had proudly planted the evidence himself).

AS THE CHIEF OF the district, the colonel worked a few blocks down from the station in a converted French colonial villa. A small one, admittedly, but still magnificent, with high ceilings and a spiral staircase and a veranda with showy blue tiles.

Truly important buildings were always distinguished by the number and size of Ho Chi Minh busts displayed on the premises. In the colonel's waiting room alone there were two, of bronze, positioned at either end of the room atop tall cabinets. Tan looked from one to the other, back and forth, to pass the time. He wondered if he should try growing a beard. It might make him look distinctive and stately, befitting District 10's youngest major.

It was nearly two-thirty by the time Colonel Khoi returned, flanked by several lieutenants, back from a long lunch banquet and noticeably red. "Ah—the captain! Here already?" the colonel thundered, and Tan tried not to wrinkle his nose at the sour lager aroma that came blasting

out. "Come in! Come in!" The lieutenants slunk away to another corner of the villa—probably to nap off the beers, Tan thought enviously,
remembering how very, very tired he was.

There was another bronze bust of Uncle Ho in the colonel's private
office, along with a large oil painting of him in a jungle with his devoted
revolutionaries. Colonel Khoi sank back in his chair behind his desk
and flicked on his computer. He studied Tan with slightly bleary eyes
and then snorted loudly to dislodge some phlegm. Then he scowled at
the computer, which was taking a long time to come to life, and he
jiggled the mouse around impatiently. He turned to Tan again. "I've
got some important news for you, Phan . . ."

Tan leaned forward in his chair. His feet and palms were sweating.
The muscles of his cheeks twitched, poised to break into a gracious
smile at the news.

"We have reason to believe that someone may be trying to kill you.
Well, kill you or seriously harm you. Why are you smiling? This isn't
good news."

Cursing inwardly, Tan adjusted his face to express appropriate
alarm.

"Early this morning an officer was attacked out in District 2. He was
driving home at around—oh look, the briefing's right there." Colonel
Khoi waved his hand toward the stack of papers at the corner of the
desk nearest to Tan. "It's the top one. Yes, that's it. You read it—it's all
explained in there."

This was certainly not the news that Tan had anticipated, and he
was trying very hard to swallow the potent mix of rage and embarrassment and anxiety that he was experiencing simultaneously. "Three-
thirty A.M., morning of March the eighteenth, 2011," he read aloud
from the paper, "the victim, *Phan Quang Tan*—that's my name!"

"Yes, you both have the same name," said the colonel, staring at his
computer screen and clicking the mouse intently. "It'll make sense
later. Keep reading."

"The victim, Phan Quang Tan—Sergeant, Binh Thanh District,
Ward 26—was assaulted shortly after crossing the bridge into District 2.

The Sergeant recalls that he saw a woman in the middle of the road, possibly in her early twenties. Long, dark hair, but no other distinctive features that he can remember. It appeared that she was in distress and waving him over. When Sergeant Phan stopped his bike to offer his assistance, he claims . . ." Tan paused and frowned. "He claims the woman 'flew' at him, seized him by the throat, and held him above the ground. The woman possessed extraordinary strength and what the Sergeant refers to as 'claws.' He recalls that when the woman looked at his face, she first seemed surprised, and then angry, and dug her 'claws' further into the skin of his neck and shouted, 'Who are you?' in a voice the Sergeant describes as low and hoarse. He could not answer at first because her grip on his throat was too tight; he was consequently dropped onto the ground and then stated his name for her.

" 'Well you're not the *right* Tan Phan,' she said to the Sergeant. 'But I am going to leave you alive so that you can pass on a message for me. Tell him that I'm coming for him, and . . . and . . ."

Tan gulped. " 'Tell him not to worry, because he will get to sleep soon.' Sergeant Phan says that the woman then leapt over the edge of the bridge and into the river, but states that he did not hear the splash of her landing, and that when he looked over the side himself, he saw nothing in the water. The sergeant was able to drive himself to a hospital in District 2. No broken bones; minor blood loss from unusual-looking cuts on the neck. This morning he relayed the full account of the attack to his superiors." He put the paper back onto the desk.

"There are currently five men with the full name 'Phan Quang Tan' who are policemen in the Ho Chi Minh City metropolitan area," said Colonel Khoi, without taking his eyes from his computer screen. Tan, who had assumed that the colonel was working on some important document, now saw that he had been playing *Minesweeper* this whole time. "You and the injured sergeant, two privates—one of them in District 12 and the other one in 9—and a lieutenant in Thu Duc. After the attack on their sergeant, the guys in Binh Thanh ran a quick check on the rest of you and discovered that the Tan Phan in Thu Duc had been reported missing by his wife three days ago. There's no evidence yet that indicates these two events are related, apart from the shared names, but we were told to inform the rest of you so that you can take any precautions you feel necessary. So. Now you've been warned. Be careful."

"And that's it?" Tan wailed, fingers knotting his hair. "Just 'be careful'?"

The colonel had set off a bomb in the game and he shoved the mouse away, annoyed. "What were you expecting, Phan? A bodyguard? We don't have any video footage, just some scratches and a story from a guy who was drunk at the time—he was on his way home from a bar. And the colleagues of the missing lieutenant said he has a mistress and a second family out in Chau Doc, so he's probably just there. But if you're worried, you can go talk to the sergeant if you like. He's still in the hospital."

"Thank you for the warning, sir," Tan muttered. "I'll see myself out."

Colonel Khoi watched as he left the office. "Creep," he muttered to himself as the door closed, and then he snorted again. It was clear that the phlegm wasn't going to stay down, so he opened up the window behind his desk and hacked a clam-shaped splatter out into the garden.

TAN RARELY VENTURED ACROSS the Saigon River and into District 2. It was a confusing place for him—part slum, part haven for expats, part suburb for wealthy Vietnamese who wanted to live like expats, and the parts at the seams where they met and bled into each other. The hospital was located along one of the seams. To get there, Tan first had to drive through an enclave of tasteful modern villas with curly-haired Eurasian children playing in the front yards or riding bicycles up and down their driveways. Tan snickered at the helmets and kneepads they wore. The illusion of safety was an invention of the West.

Even though this hospital was painted a friendly butter yellow and its steps weren't overrun with weeping or bleeding people like the hospitals in the cluster of central districts, the grim atmosphere and aroma of hot antiseptic were the same. Loitering by the fence outside were half a dozen unemployed men waiting to hire themselves out to family members of the very ill who needed to briefly leave the hospital. The rented men would take their place at the bedside for an hour or two to make sure the patient didn't die of neglect by the overtaxed nurses.

Because he was a policeman, despite not being a high-ranking one, Sergeant Phan had been given a cot next to a window in a room with only two other patients. He must have been on the mend, because he was drinking a can of 333 beer and eating a pack of dried mackerel snacks when Tan walked in. There were three empty, crunched up cans lining the windowsill next to him already, and several more unopened ones waiting in a bag of ice beneath the cot.

"It's the captain!" the sergeant slurred, saluting him with his beer and then taking a swill. His neck was swathed in gauze and medical tape. He scooched over to make room for Tan on the cot. "Have a beer. Consolation prize for having to be in the Tan Phan Club. Most of the other ones already stopped by this morning—they were both pretty spooked too, if that makes you feel any better."

"Sergeant," Tan said, "I've read your description of the woman who attacked you in the initial report—early twenties-ish, long black hair—but are there any other, more specific details you might be able to tell me about her? Anything at all?"

The sergeant leaned back against his pillow. "She's not a woman, Captain. I mean, she's got the body of a normal-looking girl, but there's something inside there that's not human. She picked me up by the neck, with *one* hand, and threw me onto the ground. Like I was a doll! And she had claws!"

"Did you actually see claws?" Tan asked coolly. "Couldn't they have been those stick-on artificial nails that girls wear? My girlfriend poked me in the eye with hers once."

"They were real claws! I felt them! You want to see?" the sergeant asked, fingering the edge of his bandage. Tan nodded.

Wincing a little as the tape pulled loose from his skin with a sucking noise, the sergeant unrolled the white cloth. The cuts were stark and pink, just beginning to scab in places. Two sets of four parallel lines running down his neck. They were not shallow.

"No stick-on nails made those," said the sergeant, patting the bandage back in place. "Hurt like a motherfucker. But it's not so bad anymore. I could've been discharged already, but the time off is nice." He tossed back the rest of his 333. "Look," said the sergeant to Tan, "I don't know much about this kind of thing. The creepy shit. Monsters. Demons. Whatever. My folks do—they're Delta people, the real superstitious kind of hicks—and I used to laugh at them whenever they'd lecture me about, like, the twenty-eight different species of water ghost." He paused to open a new beer and took a long, noisy swallow. "Not anymore. After I leave the hospital I'm going straight to the closest pagoda and loading up on all the protective junk I can find." He appeared thoughtful for a moment, then solemn. He gave Tan a surprisingly sober look. "It's you, isn't it?" he said. "You're the real Tan Phan she's after. I'm sorry."

"How could you possibly know that?" Tan snapped, feeling sweat prickle at the nape of his neck.

A blush crept up the sergeant's face, spreading from his bandages to his eyebrows. "There was another thing she said to me. I left it out of the report, because I wasn't sure if I'd misheard. It didn't make sense to me. I mean, none of what happened made *any* sense, but . . ." He looked at Tan for a reaction before continuing. "Okay, what she really said at the end, before she ran away, was: 'You can tell *Cat-Eyes* that his *Bé Lì* is coming for him.' And when I saw you and, well . . . your eyes . . . I put it together . . ."

Bé Lì. Cat-Eyes. How did he feel, hearing their nicknames for each other after all these years? Tan asked himself. Not struck with terror. No, it was more like he was deflating slowly. Or sinking backward into something soft and dark. His eyes had always been narrow, with a feline upturn at the corners. And even as a child, she had always been a little cruel. *Cat-Eyes. Kitten. Kitty.* The names had done the double duty of mocking his appearance and emasculating him, and they had stuck. Bé Lì—"bad girl"—wasn't even really a nickname. It was what Binh had always been, and so it was what she had always been called. Old memories, down in the secret recesses of his mind where they had long been confined, began to tug at their moorings.

The sergeant was babbling, still embarrassed. "I think you're a very handsome guy! I wouldn't've told you the whole cat-eyes thing, but I felt like I had to, because I think that maybe you should be worried. She was just so *angry*. That's the only other thing I remember about her. She was angry, and you could feel it just, like, beaming out of her." He looked askance at Tan. "I don't want to be rude, but you must've done something *bad* to piss her off that much, Captain."

Tan rose from the cot and smoothed the wrinkles out of his trousers. He couldn't lose any more time here. He needed protection if she was really back.

"I can give you the phone number of someone who might be able to help!" called out the sergeant. "There's a company I've heard of just for this kind of thing—*unnatural* problems. The Saigon Spirits of something or another. I was told by the friend of a friend of . . ." But Tan had already left. He nearly bumped into a young, white-clad nurse outside in the waiting room. Tan glared at her, certain that she was smirking at him underneath the surgical mask covering most of her face.

TAN CROSSED THE THU THIEM BRIDGE back into Binh Thanh and then pulled his bike over to the curb and took out his phone—an old, calculator-sized Nokia. While Tan did own an expensive smartphone, he usually kept it at home, because he was worried about it being stolen. He switched SIM cards and brought out the fancy one when he needed to impress people, but secretly he preferred the Nokia, because it was so much easier to use. *Can we meet?* He typed with sweaty fingers, and as he pressed Send, he prayed fervently that the number still worked. He loitered on the side of the road for five minutes while he waited for a response, leaning on his handlebars, and was just starting to feel sleepy again when out of the blue he shivered. He jerked upright and glanced over his shoulder; the street seemed exceedingly unsuspicious. Traffic, muggy heat, some scraggly ginkgo trees, a woman sorting through garbage in the gutter, a man trying to sell old junk to tourists from a tarp spread out on the corner. Tan started the bike quickly, and set off down a random side street.

He tried his hardest to drive aimlessly but didn't really have the knack for it, and he just ended up first following one canal, and then another. When the road running alongside the second one ended, Tan couldn't choose between turning left or right, so he decided to stop at the coffee shop on the corner. He parked his bike and took a seat inside, at the table farthest from the café's television. There were still no new messages on his phone. Tan ordered and then quickly drank two coffees, one iced and one hot, and then hesitated over whether or not to order a third. Now that he knew who was behind his nightmares, though he had no idea how she was doing it, he had decided that he would stop sleeping completely. At least while he tried to figure out how close she was to killing him. And until he could manage to get his hands on something a bit more potent, caffeine would have to do. Tan's phone buzzed suddenly on the table and he pounced on it, blood whooshing to his temples and his heart pounding. When he saw that it was only a message from his girlfriend (*Miss u hubby! See u 4 dinner!*) he slammed the phone back down and almost knocked over his empty glasses. He jiggled a leg irritably, then ordered a Red Bull and was given a can of a Chinese knockoff brand called Angry Cow.

As Tan sipped it, he stared at two women seated a few tables in front of him. They were clearly a couple—he could tell by the way they were leaning against each other without noticing it, a natural gravitational pull. Tan resented them because they seemed unfairly happy. The woman on the right was slightly older and had the daintiest, palest wrists he had ever seen. The one on the left was wearing an unusual, broad-brimmed cowboy hat. Tan narrowed his eyes. There was something familiar about that hat. Another old memory was stirring at the back of his brain. But before he could latch on to it fully, his phone buzzed again. Tan reached for it wearily, prepared for another saccha-rine text from Tram-Anh, whom he kept meaning to dump though he never got around to it. Then his heart leapt—it was not from Tram-Anh, it was from *him*. All it read was: *The ᴢoo. 16:00.*

Tan summoned a waitress and paid. He left the café and drove off in such a hurry he didn't realize that he had left his kickstand down until he was already five minutes down the road. By now he had forgotten the woman in the hat completely.

TAN FOUND NO PLACE more depressing in the entire city than the Saigon Zoo. The animals were all dead eyed and bony and kept in filthy cement enclosures. He had visited more cheerful looking District 12 slums. Why the doctor had chosen to meet him there instead of one of the nightclubs he owned was a mystery to Tan.

He walked past a pit containing three malnourished tigers. One of them was gnawing listlessly on a log, and the other two were slumped against a wall. Next was an exhibit of scab-covered monkeys, observed through the bars of their cage with horror by two German tourists. Across from the monkeys, a group of children threw rambutan rinds from a plastic bag at a cowering Malayan porcupine.

It took him fifteen minutes of wandering before he finally spotted the profile he was searching for by the elephant ghetto, slouched against the railing and texting at warp speed.

"Captain," said Dr. Sang, snapping his phone shut. "Good to see you again."

"Thank you for meeting me," said Tan through gritted teeth. Even though the doctor's accent was nearly imperceptible, and his grammar was perfect, Tan could never stop a part of himself from bristling when-ever he heard the doctor's *Việt kiều* Vietnamese. The diaspora-tinged flourishes of his vocabulary. The way he always used the pretentious, pre-'75 words for "airport" and "opera house." The quintessentially capitalist manner in which he moved his lips.

"Don't worry, I'm always looking for an excuse to stop by the zoo.

This is my favorite place in Saigon," said the doctor, gesturing at the skinny elephants. "Let's go look at the hippos, and then we can discuss whatever it is that's on your mind."

Tan made sure to maintain two and a half paces behind him as they walked, partially out of respect for his former boss but primarily because the doctor was someone you never wanted to let out of your sight.

They were not going in the direction of the hippos, he realized, slightly too late. The doctor was heading for the reptile house. Tan began to sweat and drag his feet.

"Keep up, Captain," the doctor said cheerfully, without turning around. Tan scowled. The bastard knew exactly what he was doing. "I thought you might like to visit an old friend of yours." He gave a chilly, carefully meted-out three-syllable laugh.

It appeared that the reptiles were suffering from a housing shortage. Several dozen crocodiles were crowded into a single enclosure. There were at least eight pythons living in the same cage, heaped on top of one another like a clumsy serving of noodles, scaly bellies squashed up against the glass. Across from them, tortoises were being forced to share quarters with a species of acid-green tree viper.

His old friend, at the end of the hall of snakes, was the only one with the luxury of a cage all to itself. INDOCHINESE SPITTING COBRA, DAK LAK PROVINCE (POLYCEPHALIC), read the brass plate at the bottom. Its long body lay in sloppy, slate-colored coils in one corner of the cage, which was decorated with a lonely branch and a decorative cactus. The snake looked so harmless now, behind that glass. It was like visiting a prison to see the man who had murdered your family. *You. I remember you perfectly,* Tan thought to himself. *I took you from your home. And you took something even more precious from me. Now here we both are, two years later, meeting each other once again.* That time in the Highlands seemed ludicrous, laughable, now. It didn't seem possible that it had been his life once. Tan pressed his palms against the glass. This cobra wasn't pretty like some of the others had been, with their skin pearly white, or bangled with black. But this one had two heads.

"Species with the mutation don't often live this long," said the doctor, without taking his eyes off of the vivarium. "One of the heads will try to attack or eat the other."

"Did you ever make any more of it? The, um . . . the *stuff*?" Tan finished prudishly, unable to make his mouth form the word "drugs."

"No," said the doctor flatly. "The cobras were difficult to milk, the pills were wildly expensive to produce, and they sold terribly." He paused and then added, a little wistfully, "I still think it was worth it, just for the novelty of the thing, but the exercise wasn't rewarding enough to bear repeating."

Deep in the sunless, silty backwaters of his mind, a part of Tan laughed. *Of course it wasn't worth it*, it called softly from the darkness. *None of it was worth it. It will never be.* A vision came to him, unbidden, of removing his uniform piece by piece and then throwing himself into the tiger pen. He had to scrunch his eyes shut and shake his head hard to knock the image loose and make it go away.

When he opened his eyes again, the doctor's expression had turned sly. "From what I've heard, the effects of the pills were not particularly enjoyable. But you were still tempted enough to try it, weren't you, Captain?" Tan's throat tightened. "The Worm told me that you purchased some pills from him a few months ago."

Tan blinked several times and contemplated lying and saying that he'd bought them for friends. "I was just curious," he finally admitted. "I don't remember anything that happened that night, or the morning after, so I can't really say whether I enjoyed it or not. I took one "—this was untrue; he had taken three—"and the next thing I know, I'm sitting in the shower in my apartment and eighteen hours have passed and my hat and my shoes are gone."

"Yes," said the doctor, "That seemed to be fairly common, from what we heard."

"Missing shoes?"

"Missing *time*, Captain. People said they'd had blackouts and temporary amnesia. But I don't think that was the only reason for the poor sales. Backpackers are just less reckless nowadays. Their drugs are boring. They're all huffing nitrous oxide out of cute balloons in clubs, and they don't want their MDMA laced with cobra toxins." He gave an exasperated shrug. "Seven years ago, they would have gone wild for it. But of course, seven years ago I didn't have any friends in the police who could catch snakes in bulk for me." He bestowed a swift and conspiratorial smile upon Tan, and Tan could only bear it for a moment before turning away and pretending to be fascinated by the cactus in the cobra's vivarium so that he wouldn't have to respond.

"Whatever happened to the other eight snakes?" Tan suddenly wondered aloud.

"I wasn't sure what to do with them once we had extracted their venom. Several wealthy Chinese businessmen expressed interest in purchasing them."

"As exotic pets?"

"What? No, to eat," snorted the doctor. "But I thought that would be inhumane. So I set them free."

Tan felt a premonitory chill. "You let them out in the countryside?"

The doctor grinned. "I let them out here!"

Tan's eyes darted frantically around at the dense hedges lining the zoo paths and the other potentially snake-concealing bushery nearby.

The doctor roared with laughter. "Why would I want to release them at the zoo? Let me see if I remember . . . I dropped one cobra down an open manhole out in District 6. Then I left one on the lawn of one of the big banks on Vo Van Kiet Street. I made sure to take the flashiest looking snake out to Thao Dien—I thought it suited the new megamalls and fancy boutiques and cocktail bars there. And I let one go near the water park in District 11."

"You really don't need to tell me about every single one," Tan limply protested, but the doctor spoke over him and kept going:

"The largest went to an abandoned construction site in Thu Duc. I released another one by the little river between District 4 and District 7, and I stuck one in the branches of a tree at a Phu Nhuan monastery. The last one I left in a bush next to the airport before a flight to Singapore." He counted quickly on his fingers. "Yes, that's all eight. To my

surprise, I've never heard anything on the news about someone encountering one. Not once in almost two years! I guess the snakes have
just adapted to city life." He looked at the expression of dismayed in-
credulity on Tan's face. "What, you're not actually afraid of running
into one, are you, Captain?" he scoffed. "Why would you be—you're
an expert at capturing them!"

The doctor now turned to the cobra with two heads. "I knew this
one wasn't cut out for the streets of Saigon," he said ruefully. "So I
donated it to my friends at the zoo in exchange for the brief use of their
crocodiles."

He left a pause for Tan to ask him what he had used them for—Tan
kept his lips pressed together tightly; he was confident that the crocodiles had been deployed for an appalling purpose and had no wish to
learn the specifics—and when the question did not come, the doctor
proceeded, visibly disappointed: "So, Captain. What was it that you
wanted to talk to me about?"

Tan carefully considered how to phrase his request in a way that
sounded sane and vague and erudite. "I need protection," he said.
"From a dangerous individual."

The doctor looked intrigued. "Is it one of those Hai Phong machete
boys? Or the gang that peddles Japanese meth?"

"No, no. The individual in question . . . is not, corporeally speaking . . . tangible . . . at this present moment."

"Captain, it's admirable that you're exercising your vocabulary, but
you're also annoying me. Who is it?"

"It's a ghost!" Tan's voice rose sharply, approaching the territory
of a squeal. He coughed and then dropped it to a panicked whisper:
"An angry ghost. She's coming to get me."

The doctor patted Tan's arm gently. The palms of his hands were
silky soft. He was a man who had never held a shovel in his life. "How
did you think that I could possibly be of any help with this?" he said.
"Do I look like a shaman? Hmm? Do I look like I perform exorcisms
in my nightclub basements? Tell me!"

Tan had been a fool, asking for his help. "No," he said quietly.

"No what?"

"No, you don't look like you perform exorcisms in your nightclub basements."

The doctor laughed at Tan's reddening face. "Oh, Captain, you're so cute. This is why I like you so much. You haven't turned out nearly as helpful as I'd hoped you would, but I like you anyway. That's why you're still here but Douglas was cut into little pieces and fed to the crocodiles." Tan gave him a jittery fake smile. He had known that the doctor wouldn't be able to resist bragging. Part of him had always wondered about the fate of Douglas, the Australian smuggler they had worked with.

"He liked to beat his Vietnamese mistresses," said the doctor. "He used to boast about it. Said they were so small that it was funny if they tried to fight back. And he always took nude photos of the girls to blackmail them with later. When one of them went to the police with a broken arm, they laughed her out of the station and told her she deserved it for fucking a foreigner."

"Oh." Tan was not sure how to respond. "I mean, I'm sure it was . . . I didn't need to know the, the reason . . ."

"Of course," interrupted the doctor, "We would have still needed to get rid of him even if he hadn't been a monster. I just wouldn't have enjoyed it as much. But regardless," he concluded, "if you're really asking me to help you fight an angry spirit, I will be of less use to you than your colleagues were to Douglas's ex-girlfriend."

Tan was not angry. Nothing good ever came from getting angry at the doctor. He resorted to plan B instead. "If you can't protect me, could you at least get me something that can stop me from sleeping? It's important that I don't sleep."

The doctor raised his eyebrows. "Something . . . pharmaceutical?"

"Exactly."

"I'll ask the Worm to sort something out for you," said the doctor, flicking open his phone like a switchblade and typing with one hand. "He handles most of that end for me these days. The club keeps me busy, and I've started a new side gig finding Vietnamese wives for Korean men." He shot Tan a smile that was as reptilian as any creature in the cages surrounding them. "If you know any girls who might be interested, send them my way. Rural ones if possible, and under twenty-five—they need to be a bit . . . *malleable*. Can't be harder than catching cobras, right?" His phone was buzzing. "The Worm will be at my smaller club tonight after ten," he said. "You know the one—just down the street from here. He'll have something for you. And don't worry—it's on me."

Tan nodded. He did not thank him, because he knew that there was going to be a catch, and that whatever it was would be made apparent before too long. In its cage, the snake raised its heads an inch, and then flopped back down.

"I've read that having two brains affects the motor skills," said the doctor.

"That's why it was the easiest one to bag—it kept going in circles." That was what Binh had told him.

The doctor stretched his arms and then looked down at his watch. "I hope that you're going about this ghost thing the right way, because it really looks like you could use *more* sleep, if anything. Think it over. Pepto?" He had taken out his little pink bottle from his jacket. "Suit yourself," he said when Tan shook his head, then tilted two into the palm of his hand and swallowed them. "I have to leave now; wait for ten minutes before following. I'll need you to sign off on a bit of visa paperwork for me—the passports will be on your desk on Monday."

Ah, thought Tan. *There you are, catch.*

IT WAS THE MIDDLE of rush hour when he left. Tan tried to reroute his drive home to avoid some of the worst traffic but still ended up trapped at the large roundabout where Districts 10, 3, 5, and 1 intersected, stuck in a hot, fume-choked, slowly-clogging-toilet swirl of traffic. It was haunted in addition to being over-congested—two thousand bodies from a failed nineteenth-century uprising were buried in a mass grave somewhere underneath it. Tan blamed the ghosts for the

traffic. When he was finally able to break free of the traffic circle, he
sped over the bridge to District 4 with his olive trousers flapping against
his ankles in the wind, headed for home.

DISTRICT 4 WAS WEDGE-SHAPED, surrounded on all sides by river,
and its demographics were a mix of young professionals who had
moved away from the center of Saigon to escape rising rents, and past-
their-prime gangsters. These were pedestrian goons, the kind with sad
facial hair, who only trafficked in soft drugs and domestic prostitutes,
and who were several rungs below the doctor in the world of contem-
porary Vietnamese thuggery.

Tan rented a room in a hive of small apartments down an alley behind a pagoda. The entire neighborhood smelled like incense, which
was pleasant, but the noisy predawn chanting of the monks was not.
Each apartment in the complex was identical, and every door had a
built-in, translucent acrylic panel at eye level. Though most of the ten-
ants had taped newspaper or cardboard over their little windows, gaps
were inevitable. Everyone had a habit of spying on their neighbors, and
all were aware that they were spied on in turn.

The three boys living on the second floor were all students. Two of
them attended the law school and the third was studying painting at the
academy of fine arts. One of the law students was rarely home, and the
other spent all his time on his computer playing an elaborate online
game about intergalactic warfare. It was the young painter, Vung, who
was the only one worth secretly watching. He was usually up until the
early hours of the morning, attacking his canvases or staring at them
despondently, brushes flung in a corner in frustration, and he appeared
to subsist entirely on cigarettes. For unknown reasons, Vung was quite
fond of Tan and would treat the policeman to private viewings of his
work when the mood struck him. That afternoon it did.

"Older brother! Hey! Older brother ơi!" Vung poked his head out
and called to Tan when he heard him in the hallway. "Come and see
what I've been working on!"

Though he didn't possess an eye for art, Tan could appreciate the nude portraits that the painter did of his various girlfriends, so he strolled over for a look.

"Any new cases?" Vung asked as Tan slipped off his shoes and entered the room. He liked imagining that Tan was some sort of hardboiled detective, and Tan usually didn't mind encouraging him. But today he was not in the mood to be playful. The painter could sense this, so he dropped the subject. "It's right over here." He gestured grandly to a painting propped up against the wall on the far side of the room and ran over to fetch it.

"Well, what do you think?" Vung turned, smiling eagerly, the canvas in his hand. Then his smile fell when he saw Tan's face. "*Anh* Tan, are you okay?"

Tan's face had gone completely gray. "Who is that?" he spluttered, once he had found his voice. "Who is that woman?"

Vung hugged the painting defensively, trying to hide his disappointment at Tan's reaction. "It's a girl I saw in a dream. I liked her, so I painted her."

Tan could barely hear him. He was transfixed by the eyes on the canvas. Undone by them. It was Binh. Her face, her impish smile, her unruly hair, pointy chin, full lips, small forehead with a widow's peak. "Tell me the dream," he whispered, unable to look away from her for even a moment. He was filled at once with ecstasy at seeing the face he had yearned after for so long and utter terror from knowing that she was trying to kill him.

"Well, it was a weird dream, and I had it three or four times," said Vung, cheered by Tan's apparent new interest. "That's how I remembered her face well enough to paint it. They were those kinds of dreams where you don't think you're really dreaming, you know? Because everything seems so normal. The dream would start with me right here, just working, nothing out of place, nothing strange, and then I'd look up, and the girl was standing in the room. The first time I had the dream, I was scared when I saw her there all of a sudden. But then she told me not to be afraid, and said that she was in the wrong room."

"And?" Tan had realized that he was now shaking slightly.

"Well . . . I woke up. That was it. It was short and strange and it stuck with me. The other dreams were all like that too."

"The girl would show up and say she was in the wrong room each time?"

"Well, it changed a little bit each time, I guess. She would always appear out of nowhere, and then one time she asked if she could watch me work. And then another time she told me that I should try painting her. So that's when I started."

"Nothing else?"

Vung shook his head. "Nope. She really didn't say much. But it's a beautiful face, right? I had no choice but to paint her." Suddenly he grinned. "That reminds me: I saw your girl walking past on her way up to your place about an hour ago. She was carrying a *lot* of grocery bags."

Shit. Tram-Anh. Tan groaned. He had completely forgotten about her text. She was upstairs now, cooking something bland and nutritious for dinner and cleaning the apartment and snooping around on his laptop. And then she would want to stay over, which meant nine minutes of insipid intercourse followed by three hours of cuddling, he realized disconsolately. Tan needed to get rid of her if he was going to be at the doctor's club tonight.

Tan dragged himself up the stairs to the third floor, to his door at the end of the hallway. He leaned against it miserably, listening to the sound of clanging pot lids coming from inside. He screwed his eyes shut and kept them that way until he could summon up Binh's face in his mind again. He held her there, etched behind his eyelids, until he suddenly worried that his neighbors were watching him from behind their doors. Tan sighed, opened his eyes, and went inside.

He could tell that Tram-Anh was angry with him when she didn't immediately turn around to greet him as he walked in. She kept her back to him while she hacked an onion apart with a cleaver. Tan cringed. If he tried to apologize without knowing why, exactly, she was upset, it would only make her angrier. So instead he silently took a seat at his small table and waited while Tram-Anh diced vegetables and smashed his pots and pans around with increasing frenzy. The longer Tan sat, the worse his mood grew. He did not feel anything remotely near the realm of love for Tram-Anh, and in fact, he secretly doubted that she actually liked him very much either. She was his barnacle. A girl with a symmetrical face and decent teeth from a village in an insignificant, mosquito-bitten corner of the south who thought her only chance at happiness was marriage, and so at seventeen she had come to the city and immediately latched on to Tan. He could admit it was his fault that the relationship had begun in the first place—she was too young for him, but he had been flattered by the attention, and he had been sure that once she'd lived in Saigon for a few months and the city had gotten its depraved hooks into her she would lose interest, distracted by younger, better-looking guys with flashier bikes and moneyed families. But it had been two years now, and she was still coming around and cooking dinner and dropping hints about which banquet halls she thought would make good wedding venues.

Tram-Anh worked at a phone store and shared a room in a boarding house with two unmarried female colleagues. They all wore each other's clothes and brought home magazine clippings of designer shoes and purses that they would tape up on the wall and then try to find cheap replicas of at night markets. Tan had made the mistake of coming to visit her there once, and the two other girls had cooed and tittered over him while Tram-Anh held his hand and made possessive half jokes. She tried to model as much of her life as possible after the girls she saw in the popular Korean soap operas she devoured—her pouts; her exaggerated cutesiness; her hair, dyed an orange-brown and cut into bangs that looked like they had been trimmed around an upside-down phở bowl, her slightly wooden kisses. In fact, she was probably an ideal candidate for the doctor's new bride-trafficking business. Every six weeks or so she would take the long and dusty bus ride down to her village to visit her parents. Each time she would beg Tan to come along, each time he would refuse, and they would fight and she would cry and he would hope that this would be the time she would finally decide to break up with him. And then when she returned to the city, she inevitably forgave him and came over and cooked him dinner like tonight.

It was finished. Tram-Anh began banging platters on the table in front of Tan, then two bowls and two pairs of chopsticks, practically throwing his at him. Finally, she slammed down the rice pot so hard it made the other plates jump and the fish sauce in its dipping bowls slosh over the sides, and then she took her seat across from Tan and wordlessly began to serve him dinner even though she was trembling with what he correctly assumed was rage.

Dinner was boiled pork, scrambled eggs with slivers of bitter melon, and a soup full of green bits that floated atop it like algae in a pond. Country food. Wifely food. Tan and Tram-Anh began to chew in tormented silence. Tram-Anh would not look up at him from her bowl. They kept this up for five minutes before she started to sniffle, and Tan saw a tear fall into her soup and could not control himself anymore. He hurled his chopsticks onto the tile floor. One of them splintered as it bounced, and the other rolled underneath the refrigerator. Tan was fond of his chopsticks and regretted breaking them, but it felt so good to lose his temper. Tram-Anh snapped her head up, startled, to look at him, and her eyes were red-rimmed.

"Well?" Tan snarled at her. "Tell me what's bothering you. I'm sick of this game."

Tram-Anh leapt up from the table and stormed into Tan's bedroom. He thought she might slam the door closed and stay in there all night, which she had done on several occasions, but instead she returned a moment later with something balled up in her fist.

"Explain these," she hissed, opening her hand and thrusting it in Tan's face.

Several strands of long hair were unkinking on her palm. They were unmistakably female, but they were black, not the artificial orange of Tram-Anh's hair. "Who is she?" Tram-Anh's lips were quivering. "These were on your pillow."

It was impossible. Impossible. Tan's mind raced. He was not, he regretted, sleeping with anyone else. He did not have a cleaning lady. Perhaps there was the slim chance that a girl on the street had been driving past him, had caught a few strands on one of his buttons or a helmet strap . . . but no, no, he would have noticed that. How would they have gotten onto his pillow? He had made his bed this morning, and he had not been back since. No. It was her. She had finally found the right room. He smiled cruelly.

"They're my lover's," he said coolly, and enjoyed watching Tram-Anh's face crumple. "My old girlfriend. Binh."

"You're lying!" Tram-Anh was not very pretty when she cried, Tan thought. "That's not true! You told me she died in a traffic accident!" she whimpered.

"There was never any accident," said Tan, which was the truth. "And now Binh is back. So you'll have to leave." This was also true. His face felt hot, felt irradiated, but he did not have any sense of shame at causing the poor girl pain. This was new and thrilling. The neighbors were probably pressed up against their walls listening. Still, he could not stop himself. "I hate your cooking!" he yelled. "Fucking you is like having sex with an almost dead fish! You just lie there and twitch! The makeup that you wear to cover your acne scars doesn't match your skin, and it's so obvious!" Tan was running out of insults. "And you do not and will never look Korean!" he concluded, then stopped and panted.

Tram-Anh bared her teeth unintentionally as she wept, and her eyes were so puffy they resembled cowrie shells. Her sobs were guttural, little seal barks.

"Just get out! Get out now!" Tan banged the table. Tram-Anh screamed, grabbed her jacket and handbag from the counter, and then ran from the apartment, hiding her face with her jacket. She had forgotten her shoes in the corner by the door. Tan picked them up and tossed them out of the apartment's bathroom window into the pagoda's courtyard. They were thick-heeled foam sandals, and he heard them bounce when they hit the concrete. Then he returned to the kitchen and crawled around on his knees on the floor, looking for the hairs.

"Bé Lì?" he whispered. "Are you here? Can you hear me?" There was no reply from anywhere in the empty apartment. He swept his hands across the floor underneath the table but only felt dust. And then, because he was already on the ground, Tan decided that he would do pushups to help keep himself energized until it was time to go to the club. He did thirty, got too sweaty, and then took off his uniform and did twenty more. In high school Tan had been a kickboxer. He rose to his feet and tried to resurrect some of his old moves from training—jabbing and uppercutting the air in his fraying underpants. The kitchen wasn't large enough for kicking, he discovered, after he roundhoused a table leg and sent Tram-Anh's bitter melon splattering. Tan didn't bother to pick it up. He went into the bathroom, ran a freezing cold shower, and made himself stay under the jet of water until his skin had gone numb. He rinsed all the gel out of his hair and then lathered it up with Tram-Anh's fancy honey-locust-bean-infused shampoo, delighted that he could now use as much as he wanted (he had only stolen the occasional, stealthy squirt before). Tan was proud of his upper body, which he considered to be fairly well sculpted. He had always been the strongest one in his family—more muscular than both his younger brother and their father (even before the late Duc Phan had drunk himself soft and flabby). His legs, though, were chicken skinny and bore two scars: one down by the ankle, courtesy of his father, and one by the knee from Binh and a broken bottle. His cock resembled a steamed fish cake—on the small side, yes, but not laughably small, he thought. He was convinced that his brother's had to be smaller, simply on account of Long being the shorter and skinnier sibling, but as he hadn't seen his brother naked since their prepubescent years, he couldn't be completely sure. This still bothered him. His eyes, of course, were squinty and catlike.

Tan toweled himself dry and then reapplied his hair gel with great precision. Being out in the world without his uniform made him nervous, so most of the casual wear he bought tended to be olive too. He selected from his closet one of the several dress shirts he owned in the color, and a pair of jeans. He could sense the eyes behind doors following him, the held breaths, as he strode down the narrow hallways of the apartment building, and it made him feel strangely powerful.

Tan figured he had three hours to fill up with eating, which would not be a problem for him. He parked his bike in front of his favorite neighborhood snail shop and greedily eyed the tubs piled with assorted mollusks, more gleaming and beautiful than gemstones. He ordered carelessly, and he ordered too much: A dish of paddy snails in a lemongrass soup, with rubbery flesh that squeaked as he chewed. A dish of ice-cream-cone-shaped mud creepers in coconut sauce. A dish of blood cockles with tamarind. A dish of crab claws encrusted in chili salt. Tan didn't order beer, both because he didn't like its taste and because he wanted to leave as much room as possible on his table for plates. He hunched over them possessively, barely taking the time to breathe or spit shells onto the sidewalk between bites. He didn't notice the girl with the long hair in the corner until he had already crunched through half his plate of crab.

To be precise, he noticed what she was eating before he actually noticed the girl. She had ordered a snail porridge, and his eyes followed it with envy as it was brought over to her. Tan was tempted to call for a bowl of his own but was beginning to feel full and wasn't sure if he could fit the *cháo* into his stomach on top of everything else that was swimming in there. He observed her doctoring it, first dropping in a sensible amount of chili paste and swirling it into a thin orange spiral, then dusting the top with shredded herbs and onion. He watched as she raised her first spoonful up to her mouth—one hand cupped protectively beneath it to shield the loose white smock she was wearing from spills—and then he lingered on her face even after she had set the spoon down again. There was something a bit odd, something vaguely foreign about the features. Something from elsewhere. He couldn't identify what it was exactly—the width of the nose, or in the reddish undertones of the hair, though perhaps it was all just an effect of the snail shop lighting. She could have Khmer blood, or Hmong blood, or a drop of French. But the longer he looked at her the less sure he became until, when he looked at faces of the other people in the restaurant, they all resembled people from elsewhere too. He focused his attention back on sucking the chili salt off his crab legs. He did not notice the small brown-and-white dog, because it was lying on the ground between the girl's feet, batting an empty shell around with one paw, with something like boredom.

To kill a little more time, Tan made some perfunctory small talk with an aging gangster at the table next to him whose saggy chest skin was crawling with faded indigo tattoos of slack-jawed dragons. Tan accepted a beer from him and drank it while trying not to grimace. Eventually he gave in and ordered a snail porridge of his own but could only finish half of it because the hard, convex curve of his belly was straining his shirt buttons. The long-haired girl's table was empty now—she had left without his noticing. Tan stifled a yawn and then, for the second time that day, felt an inexplicable shiver right at the base of his neck. Slowly, Tan turned on his stool in every direction and checked his surroundings. He even looked up, fearful for a minute that the vengeful ghost of Binh would be dangling above him like a bat. She was not, and he was embarrassed by his paranoia. The street was much too crowded. She would not come for him here.

"Your mouth," sighed the photographer. "Could you please try making it less . . . scary?"

In response, Binh contorted her smile to include more teeth. The photographer, who had endured nearly five minutes of scowls and manic grins and crossed eyes that only grew worse when he tried to politely correct them, now ran out of patience. He threw up his hands and turned to Tan and Long. "If your friend doesn't make a normal face for me, I'm kicking all you delinquents out of my shop."

Tan, who was preparing to submit his application for the police academy, was the only one who had actually needed an ID photo taken today, but Binh had insisted that she and Long both accompany him to Ea Sup from Ia Kare. The two of them had shopping to do in town anyway—that afternoon, all of the year nines would be going on an end of the semester overnight camping trip to a lake in Ea Wy, and because Binh had the lowest grades and the most absences in the class, she had been tasked with purchasing drinks for the trip. Because Long had the highest grades, all he had been asked to do was make sure that Binh only used the school budget on nonalcoholic beverages.

"I'm sorry, sir! I've never been in front of a camera before! Am I doing it wrong?" chirped Binh innocently, spinning on the seat of her

stool and flashing the photographer her most congenial and ordinary
of smiles over her shoulder.

"Bé Lì," snapped Tan in the policeman voice that Long sometimes
caught him practicing when he thought he was alone in the house. "Just
let him take it! You're the one who wanted a photo, anyway."

"I'm only doing it for you, so that you'll have a picture of me to put
up next to your bunk next year." Her grin veered wicked once more.
Tan was not able to stop himself from blushing. She was wearing a
voluminous white button-up that the photographer provided for clients whose shirts did not comply with the government guidelines for
collars. It draped over her like a wedding tent, and its ends covered her
knees. "How did you even find a shirt this big, sir?" she asked, swiveling back around to the photographer. "Did you inherit it from some
Americans?"

From the back wall where he was watching, Long chuckled. He and
Tan had looked absurd when they had donned the enormous shirt for
their own photos (Binh had forced Long to get a set taken too), but
somehow their Binh was beautiful in it, even while grimacing in nine
different ways to annoy the photographer. He had laughed softly, but
Binh still heard him. She looked up and gave him a small, appreciative
smirk, and the photographer, sensing that this was his only moment,
clicked.

"You're done!" said the triumphant photographer. "I'm done! Get
out of my shop!"

Shaking her head at her own defeat, Binh slid off of the stool and
wiggled out of the giant shirt.

"We'll be back in an hour to pick up the photos," Long said politely
as the three of them were herded out the door.

"Not with her!" said the photographer. "Don't bring her. I never
want to see that face again."

IT WAS LUNCHTIME. The trio piled onto the Honda that Tan had
borrowed from one of his year-eleven classmates. Binh sat jackknifed

at the front, her bony knees drawn up toward her chest and her feet balancing against the neck of the bike. Tan was in the middle, and Long was clinging on to the back. He wriggled his sneakers up onto the Honda's foot pegs next to Tan's and wrapped his arms around his brother's torso.

"What are you doing?" growled Tan, trying to shake free of his grasp.

Long grinned at the back of his brother's neck and held on tighter. "Why can't I *ôm* my own *anh*?" he protested innocently. "I don't want to fall off." Truthfully, he was doing it because Tan was steering, and his arms were therefore around Binh. Long's touch was to remind him that he was still there too.

His brother was clearly aggravated, which meant that it was working. "After my first year of physical training at the academy," Tan declared, "I'm going to be too big to ride with three people. I'll have too much muscle to fit on the bike."

At this, both Long and Binh snorted with laugher—Binh so hard that she nearly fell over—sandwiching Tan with joint mockery. "Did you hear that, Long? Our kitten thinks he's going to turn into a tiger!"

"Just you wait," said Tan. "Just both of you wait and see." But Long could tell from his voice that he was smiling too. They were still three, though they were stretched.

EVER SINCE THE FIRST TIME they had been allowed to drive into Ea Sup on their own, when Tan turned thirteen and Binh and Long were eleven, they had developed a routine. They would buy a takeaway box of *nem nướng* with extra dipping sauce and bring it to the reservoir, where they would eat while watching the old men fish, and then when they had finished, they would climb down to the water's edge and use the empty skewers from their grilled meatballs to try and spear eels.

"I don't know why your class doesn't just go to this lake to camp," said Tan, in between bites of pork. "It's bigger than the one in Ea Wy."

"But this one smells like fish and gasoline," Long said as he crunched a peanut-sauce-soaked cucumber. "And the lake in Ea Wy is closer."

Next to him, Binh raised her eyebrows. "It's more haunted too," she said. "People are always accidentally falling in and drowning. I don't know why Lady Huong decided that everyone should go spend the night there. The water ghosts are going to eat someone. Hopefully it'll be her." Huong was their class president, and Binh's facetious nickname and dislike for her were due to her wealthy family; like nearly half of all of Ia Kare, Huong's father was employed by the Ma family's pepper company. But while most of their classmates' parents worked in the Mas' fields, Huong's dad was their head of accounting.

Whenever Binh mentioned something involving the supernatural, Tan and Long would promptly attempt to steer the conversation away from it. This was perhaps the only way in which the brothers behaved like allies. There was a tacit agreement between them to never, ever bring up the incident in the graveyard, and to avoid all topics that might possibly lead to it—the dead, the undead, the pass in nearby Chu Dreh that was haunted by French soldiers, a spirit-possessed neighbor who had spent a full week speaking in tongues and eating nothing but bananas before abruptly returning to normal with no memory of it, the water ghosts of Ea Wy, the disappearance and rescue of the Ma daughter under mysterious circumstances back in the eighties, anything involving funerals. They didn't even like talking about their own grandmother, because some suspicious Ia Kareians had started a rumor about her being a witch after she stopped leaving their house.

"We should go to the market," said Long quickly. "We're supposed to meet the group in front of the school gates at four."

He had not been expecting Binh to nod in agreement. "You're right," she said. "There's lots to do." He was so surprised that his hand, which had been bringing a rice paper roll up to his mouth, froze midway, causing him to drip onto himself.

"Pig," said Binh. She suddenly reached out and grabbed Long by the wrist, pulled his arm toward her, then, with one feral swipe of her tongue, lapped up the golden streak of sauce herself. She looked up at him and grinned, her face just centimeters from his skin, before she released the arm. Long stood up in mock disgust so that she wouldn't see that he had goosebumps.

"What's wrong with you?" he laughed, keeping the fluster from his voice. He wanted to look at Tan and see what his reaction was, but that would have given him away.

"I marked you!" said Binh, following him to her feet. "I got sad thinking about Tan going away to Saigon, so I'm making sure that you won't be able to leave me too."

Long looked down at the gleaming slug trail of saliva on his arm. "Of course I won't," he said.

"Yes he will," Tan finally said. "He's too good at school. Unless he cracks his skull open sometime in the next two years, they're going to be throwing scholarships at him." It was a compliment, but he was looking at Long as if he wanted to be the one to do the skull cracking.

Binh had climbed back on the motorbike. "He won't," she said. "Long, we'll drop you off so you can pick up the photos while we go ahead to the market; you can meet us there." She saw him opening his mouth to argue that he was supposed to go shopping with her and held up her hand to stop him. "Don't you dare say it. I don't need a money supervisor. If you say it, I will push you into this lake."

Back onto the Honda they squeezed. When they arrived at the print shop, Long dismounted. "Give me some money," he said to Tan. "I don't have enough to pay for all three sets."

Tan wiggled his wallet out of his pocket and tossed it to him with a pleased little sneer of superiority before driving off with Binh.

When Long entered the shop, the photographer scowled up at him from the counter and slid him a plastic bag that contained four surly Tans, four uneasy Longs, and four grinning Binhs. A 2x2 Binh was at the top of the pile. "Your brother's friend could be so pretty," said the photographer, shaking his head, "if she just learned how to control herself."

Long bristled. "She's my friend too," he said, and opened Tan's wallet so he could pay for the pictures and leave quickly. As he was counting out the bills, his thumb touched something harder than money. His eyes flicked downward. Tucked into the billfold, there was an unopened condom. Without thinking, Long took it out and dropped it into the bottom of his own knapsack. He was stopping it from happening, he told himself. But he did not let himself dwell upon what it was he was stopping.

When he arrived at the market, the photos stowed safely inside his knapsack along with the stolen condom, he sensed that something was not right. He saw Tan and he saw the bike and he saw Binh, but he did not see the three liters of Coca-Cola or the twenty-four water bottles that she had been instructed to buy. Instead, Binh was holding a plucked chicken in a bag, a bundle of coals, and a plastic sack of clear liquid that Long could guess was rice wine.

"What have you done?" he groaned.

"I couldn't stop her," Tan said, though he didn't sound as if he had tried very hard.

"Change of plans," announced Binh. "We're going to the beach."

None of them had ever been farther east than the national highway, or traveled more than forty miles from Ia Kare, or even knew how to swim, but Binh did not seem concerned by this, or any of the other objections that Long raised.

"The plan is perfect!" she said.

(The plan was foolish. It was not even a real plan.)

"We don't need a map. If we just drive in the opposite direction of the road to the Cambodian border, we'll get to the sea eventually. It can't be more than, what, five hours? Eight hours? Ten at most if there are a lot of mountains? We already have a motorbike!"

(But it did not belong to them, and they were supposed to be returning it to Tan's friend later that afternoon.)

"And we already have an excuse for where we're supposed to be tonight. We'll reach the ocean by dark, have a barbecue, sleep on the shore, go for a swim at dawn, and be back here by lunchtime tomorrow."

(What would happen when the rest of the class realized that they weren't coming?)

"Besides, I can't return this chicken now."

(That you bought with the school's money!)

"I didn't spend all of it! The change is in here—" She tossed Long the small tamarind-candy tin that she carried her things around in instead of a wallet. "Look," she said, irritated by his reluctance, "do you really want to go to a small, haunted lake with two dozen people we can't stand, just to have a Coke and a sapodilla and a bad sandwich and sing group songs about the Fatherland, and definitely get eaten by mosquitoes and possibly also get eaten by ghosts? If you think it would be more fun, you can still go with them." She gave her head a canny tilt. "Besides, Lady Huong will miss you if you don't go. Everyone knows she has a crush on you." Long blushed furiously. "You can take the two-thirty bus back home from here and still make it, and Cadet Kitten and I will just go to the beach on our own."

She and Long both knew that he had no choice.

THE FIRST PROBLEM THEY encountered was that they could not figure out which way Cambodia was in order to drive away from it. They spent ten minutes arguing about it while going in circles at the roundabout in Ea Kiet, then chose the wrong road and didn't realize for another fifteen. When they finally found the correct route, they were only able to drive for another hour before they encountered problem two: the rain.

The sky did not warn them; one minute they were dry and the sun was warm without burning and Long was watching the black filaments of Binh's hair blowing backward in the wind and thinking that perhaps this had not been a bad idea after all. The next, his entire body and everything he could see of the world was wet, the unpaved road was turning into brick-colored sludge, Binh's hair was plastered to her face, and Long remembered that this was a terrible idea.

"Pull over!" yelled Binh as Tan struggled to keep the bike upright. The road had become the texture of warm margarine. Tan swerved and had to stick out a leg to prevent the confluence of motorbike and mud.

Binh jumped to safety, clutching the bag with the chicken to her chest like it was an infant. Long tumbled off and managed to save his knapsack from hitting the ground but not the rest of him. The impact didn't hurt—he just sank into warm, mineral squelch, and for a long moment he lay back and surrendered to it, closing his eyes and letting the rain strike his face. The ground smelled like goat hide and blood, like gasoline and fertilizer and sugarcane.

When he picked his body up again, his entire back half was coated orange. He waddled over to the side of the road to join Tan and Binh, who were crouching down even though there was nothing to crouch under, because it felt better than just standing. Long stepped out of his shoes and then clumsily wiggled out of his jeans, draping them over the motorbike, mud side up, to rinse them in the downpour. Shivering in his underwear, he swore to never leave home without a raincoat again for the rest of his life. As he squatted down and wrapped his arms around his thighs to hide them, Binh jokingly wolf-whistled, and even Tan, pushing the dripping hair back from his face, gave his rare real laugh—the one where he wasn't trying to keep his voice low and policemanly or his eyes from vanishing into slivers.

Long would try and picture it later—the three of them, rain soaked on the side of the road in a place that was even more of a nowhere than the nowhere they were from, Binh cradling her chicken, Tan still a person that he could recognize, his own scrawny, pantsless fifteen-year-old self—and wonder how they could have ever been so happy.

WHEN THE RAIN FINALLY STOPPED, the sodden trio set off once more. Long tied his wet jeans to his knapsack so that they could flap behind him like a flag and dry while they drove, his bare legs broiling in the restored afternoon sun.

They got lost again, but because there were so few markers and road signs, by the time they began to suspect that they were going the wrong way, it was much too late. When they tried to ask for directions to the beach they were met with shrugs and blank stares. In places like these, towns that were so small they had numbers instead of names, no one went to the ocean. No one ever went anywhere. The raw chicken was starting to smell, the motorbike was running low on fuel, and sunset was approaching. Long's jeans were dry but had hardened to a crispy and uncomfortable texture that hurt his skin when he put them back on.

"We're just going around in circles," lamented Binh. "We've been driving toward those mountains in the distance for ages, but they never get any closer. I've seen those exact same cows three times."

"You don't know that for sure. All cows are identical," Tan said halfheartedly. He had slowed them to a crawl now, driving as if the bike itself was dejected because it knew that they were not going to make it.

"It's this place," said Binh, her voice just loud enough for Long to hear it over the engine and just loud enough for him to detect a note of genuine despair in it that he had never heard before. "It's this land. We're lost and going around and around because it wants to keep me here. It's never going to let me leave."

The raw hem of the evening was now beginning to descend. When they spotted a section of hill that was covered in large, flat boulders, smooth and not too far from the road and free of the kind of shrub that snakes liked to hide in, they finally decided that it was time to stop.

"At least we have the chicken," said Long, trying to comfort Binh. "And the coal stayed dry. We're still having a barbecue, even if we're not at the beach." He was concerned by how uncharacteristically defeated she seemed.

But she started to cheer up once Tan had gotten the fire started; she ripped a hole in the corner of the rice wine bag with her teeth and began to suck from it. While Tan constructed a makeshift rotisserie out of some sticks and a coat hanger that Binh had pinched from the market back in Ea Sup, she and Long passed the bag back and forth between them. By the time the stars came out, Binh had achieved a level of tipsiness that made up for the joviality she had started the trip with and then lost.

"Take out my wallet," Binh said to Long. "There's a deck of cards in there."

He retrieved them from the tamarind tin and dealt them each thirteen. They played three practice rounds of *tiến lên* together while Tan finished fortifying the chicken. It didn't matter—once Long dealt Tan in, they both lost to him every time. Eventually, Binh got fed up with it and started periodically snatching cards out of his hands and tossing them into the fire to try to get him to lose. Tan still managed to win anyway.

"This isn't fun anymore!" she finally said, flinging her cards away in frustration. "You're too good! Do something else you're good at instead and fix my hair for me." She yanked an old elastic—clearly on its last legs—from the end of what had been her attempt at a braid and then handed it to Tan, who dutifully assumed his position behind her.

Even Long had to admit that his brother's fingers were impressively deft as they smoothed and unsnarled the Binh nest without the aid of a brush and then began to neatly replait. "Why *are* you so good at that?" he wondered aloud. He had never asked him before.

Only a fluctuating third of Tan's face was visible in the firelight, and it was orange. "Because of Dad," he said. "You were too young, so you don't remember, but he used to make hammocks. Not string ones—the real kind, made out of tree fibers or some shit. He learned how from *Ông Nội*." Addressing Binh, he explained, "Our dad's dad was originally from some island down south." He tied off the braid he had made but let his fingers rest on her hair for a moment longer. "When I was seven, he sometimes used to let me help him with the twisting if he was too drunk. He always said that I inherited his hands." All three of them fell silent at the mention of the late Duc Phan's hands. Duc Phan's hands were the reason that Long and Tan's mother only wore long sleeves. Duc Phan's hands, drunk and clumsy with a lighter, were the reason that half of their house had burned down ten years ago. Duc Phan's hands had finally done Duc Phan himself in for good when Long was twelve and Tan was fourteen.

Binh reached behind her head and gave a light squeeze to one of Tan's inherited hands. There was an ugly part of Long that wondered if Tan had made the story up, had brought their father up, for this exact purpose. "But at least you know that there was one good thing in what you got from him. My aunt and uncle always tell me that I inherited nothing but evil from my parents, but that they will keep praying for my soul even though I am a child of *irredeemable sin!*" she said, mimicking the intonation of a fanatical preacher. All Long and Tan knew about Binh's aunt and uncle was that they had adopted her when she was an infant and were staunch Christians.

By now, the chicken's transformation into charbroiled succulence was nearly complete. Tan basted the bird with the tiny pouch of chili lemongrass oil that had accompanied it and Binh squeezed the last drops of the rice wine into her mouth. Long gathered up the deck of cards and packed them away in the tamarind tin. As he was unzipping his knapsack to stow it once more, Binh suddenly remembered the pictures they had taken.

"Show me my photo!" she demanded excitedly.

Long drew one of the Binh 2x2s from their protective sheath and handed it to her, careful to hold it by the edges so he wouldn't get prints on her face.

Binh took it from him without bothering to do the same. She brought her face down to examine its own miniature reproduction and stared at it for a whole minute without saying anything. Finally, she lifted her head again, and with a smile, she abruptly flicked the little photograph into the fire.

It was deeply upsetting to Long to watch the little Binh blacken at the edges and then burn away into nothing but a pencil-shaving-sized curl of ash and a plume of smelly, chemical smoke. "Why would you do that?" he said. "That was you! And that was . . . that was money!"

"I didn't like that she was trapped inside it," said Binh. "I was letting her out."

"Oh, she's just drunk," said Tan, taking the chicken off of the coals. "And you're drunk too. Don't breathe in those fumes, Binh. You probably poisoned the meat with it."

The three of them were so hungry that they ripped into the chicken without letting it cool. Tan went straight for the tail and then worked free the fatty strips of the inner thighs. Long tried to tear a whole leg off for himself but the meat was too slick and his fingertips too sensitive—the blackened chicken claw burned him when he grabbed it—so he settled for stripping off little pieces of skin and lowering them into his mouth. Binh separated the chicken's head from its body with a cartilaginous crack and began to gnaw off the rubbery neck flesh. In less than ten minutes, they had eaten the bird down to its skeleton, and then they sat back and licked the grease from their fingers in the dying light of the coals.

Long, still in the comfortable stage of intoxicated wobbliness, lay back to look at the stars. Somewhere behind him, Binh announced that she was going to find a place to pee, and he heard the light slap of bare feet on smooth stone moving away from them. He wished that he had gone to piss too—he felt uncomfortable whenever he was alone with his brother. Binh was the only thing that made being around each other bearable, but Binh was the reason that they had begun to feel themselves branching apart in the first place. Driving was all right because they didn't have to talk, but he and Tan tried to avoid all other scenarios where it was just the two of them. If the situation was inescapable, they would spend it in silence. But here, unexpectedly, Long heard Tan's voice in the dark:

"She's not yours."

"Huh?" Long started to raise his head, but Tan's hand shot out and pushed it firmly back down again, just enough that his molars clacked together when he hit the rock but not so hard that it stung.

"*Shhh.* Don't move. She's not yours, because you have everything already."

"Tan, I don't—"

"*Shhh.*" Tan's fingers were still pressing down on Long's forehead, except for his thumb, which was stroking the side of Long's temple in an almost comically tender way. "You turned out smart. You'll get to do anything that you like. You were too little when Daddy was still around, so he never hit you. You already got to be the lucky one. So you don't get to have her too." Tan now moved his hand from Long's head to his forearm and ran his finger over the spot where, nine hours ago, Binh had licked away the spilled sauce from his nem nướng.

He drew his hand away as they heard the patter of Binh's feet approaching once more.

"Binh, all that junk you threw into the fire did something to the chicken!" Tan yelled over to her. "My stomach doesn't feel good!"

"I think you're actually right!" she called back cheerfully, voice echoing across the rocks. "I just took a *really* weird shit!"

Tan turned back to Long, and there was no trace of his earlier menace. He reached over and gave Long's stomach a little pat. "Good luck," he said with a laugh. "It's probably coming for you too."

Still lying on his back, still a little afraid to open his mouth, Long wondered if he was much drunker than he'd thought and had only imagined everything that had just happened with Tan.

The fire was dead, and they each claimed a spot on the rock to sprawl out on. Tan fell asleep instantly and started snoring, but Binh shifted positions for nearly an hour, until her breaths slowed and her own snores—softer, raspier—began too. Long had not moved from his initial spot by the fire. He wasn't sure if he was asleep or awake. He felt asleep, but his eyes seemed to be open, because he was looking across the rock at the lumpy indication of shadows that composed Binh's body. Was he dreaming? He never dreamed. But how else could he explain what he saw next?

She was still unconscious, but her mouth had fallen open slightly, and at one of its corners, something was forming that looked like a drip of blood, or a tiny ember on her lips. It was such a vivid, burning scarlet that Long could see it even in the dark. As he watched, the red bead grew longer, but instead of trickling onto the ground, it began to rise into the air, like a thin, glowing ribbon of smoke uncoiling from her body. For some reason, Long did not feel afraid, even as it continued to stretch itself skyward and then, when there was at least a meter of it floating in the air, the rest of Binh slowly began rising too. Long wondered if he should get up and grab hold of her, to keep her from drifting away into the night. But when sleeping Binh had reached a height of about a foot, she just hovered there, above the rock. The end of her long braid still rested on the ground, like a black umbilical cord. Her hands were folded over her stomach. Her brow was furrowed. The sky had now lightened enough for Long to see it. This was why he was so certain he was not dreaming.

Long opened his eyes. It was morning. Binh was kneeling in front of the ashes and burying their chicken carcass, and Tan was doing sit-ups. The act of eye opening indicated that they had been shut; he had been asleep after all. Of course it had been a dream. Still, he could not stop himself from going over to the spot where Binh had been sleeping and circling it, unsure of what kind of evidence he was searching for, but trying to find it anyway. He stared at her lips when she wasn't looking, secretly pleased to have an excuse to do so.

None of them needed to say it out loud. They silently climbed down the hill, and Tan wheeled the motorbike out of the bushes where they had hidden it and turned it back to face the way they had come. Binh did not climb on immediately. She stood in the road, her hands balled into fists, staring in the opposite direction, over the dusty ochre immensity and at the mountains in the distance that they had never reached. Long could not see her face, but he could read her fury in the rigid way she held her back. Part of him feared that she was going to start running down the road, determined to make it to the sea even if she had to go by foot. Another part of him wished that she would do it, just to save him from having to witness the look of disappointment on her face when she turned around. But Binh did not let him see it; when she finally turned away from the mountains and walked back to Tan and Long and the motorbike, she hid her face behind her hair.

They began to drive. At the back of the seat, Long let his arms dangle down by his sides. When the motorbike ran out of fuel two miles from the nearest town, they tried all pushing in unison at first, and then took turns. Every so often, Long glanced hopefully up at the sky.

WINNIE MANAGED TO AVOID FOOD POISONING UNTIL her one-hundredth day in Saigon, when her reckless consumption of tap water and diet of cloudy gray mystery broth from sidewalk carts finally caught up with her. Fortunately, the first wave struck while she was at one of the big chain coffee shops on Cach Mang Thang 8, so she was able to commandeer their spacious lavatory for an hour, recover slightly, and then take a motorbike taxi back to the Cooks' District 1 apartment before the second, more serious wave arrived.

The Cooks' smugness would end up being the worst part of the forty-eight hours of intestinal torment that awaited Winnie. She had moved in with them less than a week earlier and was already regretting her decision. Now that they were her roommates in addition to being her coworkers, there was nowhere that Winnie was ever truly safe from them. Her private bathroom was the only place in the house that was reliably Cook-proof, and for this reason, Winnie almost enjoyed being forced to spend a night shackled to the toilet. But by morning her insides had temporarily run dry, and she crawled to her bedroom to take a break from shuddering on the bathroom tiles and shudder more comfortably beneath her blanket instead. And almost immediately, Mrs. Cook arrived to gloat.

The door to Winnie's bedroom was slightly misaligned, and so it never shut completely. When Mrs. Cook knocked lightly, it swung wide open, hinges snickering. She had brought Winnie a pot of hot green tea, which Winnie found surprisingly thoughtful, but her smile was far too wide to be sympathetic.

"Was it street fruit?" Mrs. Cook asked cheerfully. "You can't eat street fruit in the city—everyone knows it's farmed in feces. Besides, it can't compare to the produce you get in the countryside. Have I ever told you about the coconuts Jeff and I had on our homestay in the Mekong Delta? They were beyond am-*aaaa*-zing," she said, leaning on the word's second syllable so hard that it creaked.

Yes, thought Winnie emphatically, *repeatedly*. But at the moment she was still too queasy to open her mouth and reply.

"They grew right outside our window," Mrs. Cook continued dreamily. "We could lean over the balcony and pick them from the trees ourselves. . . . Of course, we always made sure to disinfect them before digging in!"

The Cooks were prolific disinfectors. Wherever they went, they carried at least two packs of Lysol wipes to attack any surface they encountered that did not meet their standards. On Tuesday and Thursday mornings, their housekeeper, Bà Khanh, cleaned the apartment, and after she left, the Cooks would spend another hour revacuuming and scrubbing everything. They brushed their teeth with bottled water and did not allow any beverage that had been in contact with a Vietnamese ice cube to pass their lips. Sometimes Winnie wondered if the Cooks had only agreed to let her move in because they thought of her as a kind of giant mystery germ that they were eager to sanitize. They had not been very effective so far; Winnie's inherent untidiness, which would flare up periodically while she was living at her great-aunt's house, had immediately erupted into full-blown filthiness at the Cooks', perhaps in response to the sterility of the rest of the household.

As Mrs. Cook continued to linger in the doorway, her gaze gradually shifted from Winnie to the mess that surrounded her. Mrs. Cook's smile faded. Dirty clothes trailed across the floor like discarded skins.

All the sheets had been kicked off the bed, but books, candy and tampon wrappers, scrunched-up coffee shop receipts, and shed hairs shared the bare mattress with Winnie and her swaddling blanket. One of her feet was visible, and its sole was blackened with old dirt. Several pairs of hand-washed cotton panties were strung up to dry across the window, which overlooked the street.

"Well," said Mrs. Cook, her lip twitching slightly. "You'll let us know if there's anything we can do to help you feel better." Then she swished away with the pot of tea, which, an embarrassed Winnie now realized, had never been intended for her.

Over the next few days, both Cooks sprang more unannounced visits on Winnie to propose their theories about what had gotten her sick. Mr. Cook asked her with a straight face whether she had gone swimming in the Saigon River. He didn't seem to fully believe her when she replied that she hadn't, and then he asked if she had gone swimming in a public fountain. On another morning, Mrs. Cook brought Winnie her own personal dustpan and tiny broom and suggested that doing a gentle activity like cleaning her room might make her stomach feel better.

When Winnie's appetite finally returned on the fifth morning, she immediately went out and purchased 200,000đ worth of street fruit from the vendors nearby—ripe mangoes and lychees and mangosteens with eczemic purple rinds that seeped milky nectar from the cracks—and then ate all of it in one sitting, straight from the bag at the kitchen table, in full, defiant view of the horrified Cooks.

WINNIE HADN'T KNOWN WHERE else to go when, two days after her very un-Catholic overnight visit from the policeman, her great-aunt had informed Winnie that she and her compromised American morals would be better suited living elsewhere. To hasten her move, a crucifix had appeared in the hallway outside Winnie's room the very next morning, and whenever Winnie was in the house during the daytime, her great-aunt would put on a videocassette recording of the papal inauguration of Benedict XVI and play it on a loop at full volume on the downstairs television. Winnie was already feeling on edge from finding her strange, doodled likeness in her classroom, and the constant, crackly background of Latin chants and cheering Vatican crowds rattled her even further. And to do their part in helping drive her out of the house, her two cousins had started sneaking into her room when she wasn't there and moving things around. While Winnie hadn't actually witnessed either of them doing it, she knew that there was no one else it could have been; she always kept her windows locked, and her great-aunt's bad knees prevented her from going up to the second floor.

The cousins only played small, strange pranks—none of Winnie's possessions went missing during those last three days she spent in that house—but they got under her skin. There seemed to be no logic to them. One day she returned home and there was a two-inch gray heap on the floor next to her bed that she was able to determine were ashes by sniffing. And the next afternoon, all of her books had been rearranged. The following morning, she woke after a night of poor sleep and troublingly vivid nightmares to discover that her bedroom floor was wet. It appeared that they had sloshed water in under her door.

On what would be her last afternoon at her great-aunt's, she entered her room and was greeted by the policeman's shoes dangling inches away from her face, strung up by their laces from her ceiling fan. Winnie wasn't able to stop herself from shrieking, and the cousins even had the audacity to come running in to check on her when they heard the screams and then pretend to be surprised when they saw the hanging shoes. That night, Winnie composed one of her rare emails to her mother, announcing that she had decided to move in with some new friends. Just to be safe, she added that her great-aunt seemed to be going senile (. . . *So if Dad hears any weird stories from her, just disregard* . . .) and packed her suitcase. At three in the morning, unable to sleep, she had crept downstairs to the kitchen. She found her great-aunt's poultry shears in a drawer, sawed off her long hair into an uneven bob that ended just past her ears, and then pushed her severed ponytail down into the bottom of the trash can. Another fresh start.

THE COOKS' APARTMENT BUILDING was within walking distance of Achievement!, as well as a large, Western grocery store, two Korean barbecue restaurants, and several more language academies. Both of the apartments beneath the Cooks' were also rented by foreigners; there was a family from Singapore on the first floor and two American teachers who worked at one of the other nearby schools on the second. There was a security guard stationed in the building's motorbike garage, and three intimidating-looking cameras mounted above the door, but Winnie had peered inside the guard's booth one afternoon while he was on a smoke break and seen that the surveillance monitor wasn't actually plugged in—the system had been set up just for show. The street outside the building was lined with poinciana trees that were old and umbrella-branched and thick with scarlet flowers that were a shade of red so saturated the color looked like it might drip off the petals.

Nearly everything inside the Cooks' apartment was white though: white walls and white Formica countertops and cabinets, glistening white floor tiles that reminded Winnie of her childhood dentist's office, white glass globes on the ceiling discharging hard white light, a white pleather sofa that made high-pitched alarm squeals if Winnie tried to sit on it. Goji, the Cooks' one-eyed rescue mutt, slept on a white cushion that always managed to remain spotless. Goji himself, however, ruined the Cooks' color scheme by being tan—he was roughly the color and shape of a sturdy leather ottoman—and Winnie liked to imagine that this deeply bothered the Cooks. He was still the cleanest dog she had ever met; she assumed that this was because he spent the majority of his time asleep. Twice a day, Mr. Cook took him out into the walled courtyard behind their building, where he would saunter around in circles for three minutes and then deposit a pile of droppings in the corner of his choosing. Despite his limited exposure to the elements, Goji still received a weekly bath, and his fancy imported dog shampoo and conditioner smelled so good that Winnie occasionally washed her own hair with it. She always saved him the bones from her meals, keeping them stashed in her purse until the Cooks went out. Once they were gone, Goji would crunch them in the kitchen contentedly. Winnie knew how to locate the particular spot of taut, peachy belly that made his left hind leg twitch with rapture when scratched, and Goji gave her plenty of slobbery, appreciative licks in return, but he could never be the pet that Winnie longed for, and each of them knew that they did not really belong to the other. They were just cellmates.

Even on the days when they weren't teaching, the Cooks were up early. First, they shared a pot of herbal tea—neither of them drank coffee, and they often expressed their concern about Winnie's rate of caffeine consumption—and then they made spinach/banana/mango smoothies out of the unblemished, plastic-wrapped produce they bought at the Western grocery store. Every morning Winnie was awakened by the sound of their breakfast being blended, fell back into a shallow half sleep, and then woke up again twenty minutes later when it was Goji's turn to eat and the chicken-flavored pebbles of his organic dog food cascaded noisily into his metal bowl.

After breakfast, if it was a day on which they taught, the Cooks would don their matching helmets and long-sleeved overshirts with built-in UV ray protection and bicycle five minutes down the road to the academy. The mornings when they didn't have to work, Mrs. Cook took a taxi to a yoga studio out in District 7, and Mr. Cook composed new posts for their blog or edited photos. At noon they would meet for veggie burgers at their favorite spot, a gastropub owned by an American chef friend who had once been featured on a Vietnamese cooking show. The Cooks only ever ordered veggie burgers and never ate the side salads that came with them; they didn't trust the lettuce. Winnie knew all this because every time they ate there, without fail, the Cooks would come home and tell her about their semifamous friend's restaurant and its untrustworthy salad. After lunch, they sometimes liked to spend their free afternoons at a rooftop hotel pool, but they went to swim laps, not sun themselves in lounge chairs like the wealthy international guests who observed the Cooks' aquatic exertions over the rims of their daiquiris. Occasionally, however, the Cooks did indulge in a sensible evening tipple at a District 2 wine bar before they returned to the apartment to work on lesson plans. And if they weren't preparing for class, they were mapping out a potential cycling trip around Laos, or finding a new orphanage to volunteer at, or attending the weddings of their former students, or video chatting with their families back in America, which they made a point of doing every Sunday evening without fail. They always ended their calls by hoisting Goji by his wattled armpits and dangling him in front of the webcam so that the elderly Cook parents in Oregon could babble at him; "Who's a good boy? Who's a good boy?! Is it our Goji-Goji-Goo-Goo? Are you being a good boy for Mommy and Daddy?"

Mrs. Cook would respond, on the dog's behalf, "Me! Me! I'm a good boy! I'm the *best* boy! I never pee in the house!" in a special "Goji" voice she had developed: an ignoble, Elmo-esque squeal that they thought was delightful and Winnie found insulting. She was certain that if he could speak, Goji would have the stately wheeze of a Vietnamese Don Corleone. She now made sure that she was out of the apartment on Sundays, both to avoid overhearing this embarrassing weekly exchange and to prevent herself from thinking guiltily of her own parents in Maryland.

EVEN THOUGH HER NEW floor mattress at the Cooks' apartment had cushy Western springs and was twice as thick and twice as comfortable as her old one, which had been made out of a hard and unyielding pink foam that felt like she was lying on a giant brick of Spam, Winnie was not sleeping. Since leaving her great-aunt's house, she had been plagued by insomnia and did not know why. Sometimes at three in the morning she would tiptoe into the kitchen and tug gently on Goji's white leather collar, trying to convince him to come back to her room so she could snuggle up against his warm, hairy bulk. She wanted to believe that sleep was something she could osmose, that if she only held him tight enough it would cross between their skins and into her own body. Goji never came with her though. He would just crack open the lid of his one working eye to gaze apologetically at her before resuming his canine snores.

On good nights, Winnie managed to glean five nonconsecutive hours of a shallow and unsatisfying slumber. But those nights were rare. Usually, Winnie was wide awake between midnight and dawn and passed the time by staring at the street below the apartment. Her room did not have its own balcony, just one window outfitted with a cage-like lattice designed to keep out burglars. When the afternoon sun came through at the right angle it created shadowy tessellations on her bed, and Winnie would lie down and position herself so that the scales of light would be cast onto her own skin. After dark, she climbed up and perched motionless on the sill for hours with her legs poking out through the bars, until her lower half went numb. She liked the feeling of having nothing beneath her feet while she was three stories high. It allowed her to pretend for a moment that she was no longer a girl, just a hovering, discorporate displacement of night sky. Safely concealed by the treetops, she could clock the nocturnal comings and goings of the trash collectors and grilled-squid carts and irresponsible, drunk revelers driving home from bars, occasionally wobbling off the road and crashing into a utility pole.

She also kept track of all the dogs who lived on her street: the coddled Pekingese that was carried inside a handbag and never allowed to touch the ground; a pair of toy poodles with dyed pink fur and an extensive wardrobe of toddler's clothing; a wealthy neighbor's pedigree Siberian husky, which he seemed to own mostly for show—the Saigon heat was too much for the poor creature, and in the middle of the night Winnie could hear it howling in its apartment. And then there were the local strays, rangy and keen jawed and encrusted with ticks. Winnie could not help but feel a certain affinity with them because they were all mixed breeds, like she was, and dirty like she was too. Still, if she encountered one outside during the day, especially the dingo-sized ones with slavering gums, she would cross the street to avoid it. But in the middle of the night she watched lovingly from her window as they

loped down the quiet road and rooted for food in the garbage and
humped each other in the fuzzy yellow glow of the streetlights. Winnie
gave secret names to all of them. When a dog disappeared, as all strays
inevitably did in the city, she hoped beyond reason that it was because
they had found their own set of Cooks to adopt them and not because
they had been eaten.

Only when Winnie was at her most desperate—two or three full
nights in a row spent wide awake at her window, eyes bloodshot and
twitching, and with an ache that lingered in her teeth, her kneecaps, her
scalp—did she take out the policeman's hat. Winnie had thrown his
shoes into the alley dumpster behind her great-aunt's house when she
moved out, but the contraband hat came with her, wrapped in one of
her dresses and hidden at the bottom of her suitcase. It was now the
sole inhabitant of her bedroom closet, where she kept it tucked carefully away in a plastic bag; all her other clothes lived in piles on the
floor.

The hat was one of her only ways to effectively court sleep now.
She would cover her face with it like it was a gas mask and inhale slowly,
breathing in the fading scent until she could remember the sensation of
his fingers in her hair and her heartbeat began to slow and her eyelids
felt heavy and she finally slipped away. She didn't wear it on her head
anymore out of fear that it would be colonized by her own scent, and
she limited its use, convinced that it would lose its soporific potency if
employed too often. The other option was spending two dollars on a
750 ml bottle of nearly undrinkable Vietnamese vodka from the convenience store and then taking grimacing sips until succumbing to the
alcohol's dizzy approximation of drowsiness, which she found herself
turning to more and more often as the sleepless weeks wore on.

However, there was a part of her that did not actually want her paranoid windowsill night sickness cured. In some ways, Winnie preferred
it to sleeping, because when she did fall soundly asleep on hat nights,
she would have nightmares. They were always disturbing and often
about the Cooks, whom she could not even escape while unconscious—
recurring dreams in which she was walking Goji down the street on a

leash, but he was a perverse human-dog hybrid with a canine head on the naked body of Mr. Cook on all fours; or where Mrs. Cook chased Winnie through an endless, grid-like forest; or where they both tried to burn her alive. Between these dreams and her increasingly unhinged late-night ideations, Winnie's mind was filled with as much garbage as her room. She saw herself as a haven for all the filth, large and small, literal and figurative, that had been banished from the rest of the Cooks' abode and now had nowhere else to go but her room—where it accumulated as dust and fingernail clippings and period stains and regiments of ants seeking old bánh mì crumbs, and her brain—where it landed as spores and shot out thin, burrowing roots deep into her soft matter.

Her mess had eaten away the Cooks' patience. A few weeks after the food poisoning, Mr. Cook finally asked Winnie outright why she wasn't letting Bà Khanh in to do her job. Winnie told him that she didn't feel comfortable with other people touching her things, but the truth was that it was the housekeeper who refused to set foot in Winnie's room. Bà Khanh hated her, and Winnie had never been able to figure out why. On Winnie's first Tuesday in the apartment, Bà Khanh had shown up as usual with her broom and bucket of bleach. She'd tidied the living room and scrubbed the kitchen and swept the hallway, and then she approached Winnie's room. Winnie, who had been expecting her, left the door slightly ajar and positioned herself in a spot where she thought she would be out of the way while the housekeeper worked. However, when the old woman arrived at her door and put her hand out to push it open farther, she jerked backward violently the moment she touched the wood, as though suddenly repelled by an invisible force. Winnie would replay the bizarre moment in her head later—it made no sense, but she was certain that it was what she had seen. She had hurried over to check on the housekeeper and was relieved when she saw that the woman was unharmed, though pale and clearly distressed. But when Winnie proceeded to introduce herself in Vietnamese, Bà Khanh hadn't responded. She hadn't even been able to make eye contact with Winnie; she just muttered something indiscernible and fled with her cleaning supplies. Since that morning she had treated Winnie's corner of the apartment as if it were infected with a highly communicable disease. If she happened to run into Winnie out in a common area like the hallway or kitchen, Bà Khanh would immediately drop what she was doing and go find a different place to wait— usually the bathroom or the Cooks' balcony—until Winnie retreated back into her room.

Winnie began making sure that on Tuesdays and Thursdays she was out of the house before the cleaner arrived. She wondered if Bà Khanh just disliked her because she was American, even though Winnie had seen that she was always cordial to the Cooks. Perhaps it wasn't Americans that she loathed but race mixing. Winnie told herself that this was what it was, and chose to overlook the worrying implications of the fact that she found comfort in this explanation. But she couldn't suppress the nagging sense that there was something else behind Bà Khanh's abnormal behavior with her; each time she encountered the cleaner, Winnie saw undisguised fear in the woman's face, sparking briefly in her eyes like twin highway flares.

WINNIE'S DAY DID NOT begin with herbal tea or green smoothies. After the Cooks' breakfast commotion in the kitchen wrenched her from a flimsy postdawn drowse, she continued to lie facedown, unwilling to concede defeat to the morning and sit up, and unable to muster the energy to do it even if she wanted to. Winnie had to remove herself from the bed by performing a slow horizontal creep across the mattress, scooching sideways on her belly in microscopic increments over the course of an hour and a half until she finally tipped over the edge, onto the floor, and the cool smack of the tile provided the motivation to get to her feet.

The Cooks' enormous master bathroom was the same flossed enamel white as the rest of the apartment, and it boasted a double sink, a bidet, and a Western-style tub that Winnie was wildly jealous of. Winnie's bathroom, in contrast, was small enough that she could stand in the middle of it, stretch out her arms to either side, and touch the door and far wall at the same time. She hated the coffin-sized shower stall with echoing glass walls. She hated the old drain, hated how it was always clogging, hated that every morning she had to twirl soggy bungs of coiled hair out of it like forkfuls of spaghetti. "How can there be so much of you?" she would groan at it as she crouched in five murky inches of backed-up water, digging up slimy strands that seemed to self-replicate and double in length, like tapeworms. She did not know how her hair could wreak the kind of plumbing havoc that it did, now that it was so short.

She lacked the confidence and gamine cheekbones necessary to make the haircut look like it had been a deliberate style choice and not the result of a garment factory accident, but Winnie was pleased by how unbecoming it was on her. In conjunction with her body-obfuscating sack dresses, the raggedy monk hair had the effect of rendering her sexless, and therefore invisible. Strangers either reflexively averted their eyes from her or just looked straight through her. She was frequently bumped into on the street, and afterward, instead of apologizing, the person who had walked into her would blink with confusion at Winnie, as if shocked to see someone standing where they were certain no one had been before. The haircut made it impossible for her to continue trying to avoid scrutiny by feebly cosplaying Dao this semester, but it didn't really matter, because she had ended up making herself transparent all on her own.

Even Winnie couldn't look at Winnie. When she stood in front of the bathroom mirror, she wasn't able to maintain eye contact for more than a few seconds with her own reflection. If she tried, her gaze would automatically slither over to the dark spots at the mirror's edge where its backing was rotting away. In the shower, she took pains to touch herself as little as possible while washing, because coming into contact with the naked borders of her body made her feel anxious and a little bit sick. She would only skim herself with a bar of soap, using it as a protective barrier between her fingertips and the rest of her skin. Shampooing was a swift and perfunctory three-movement sequence. Shaving was better. The clinical scratch of the razor bore no resemblance to the sensation of flesh, so she could disconnect herself almost entirely from the process and pretend that the blade was moving of its own accord.

She would exit the shower only marginally cleaner than she had entered it, then quickly shroud herself in one of her dresses without toweling off first, wet stains blooming over the fabric. It did not matter, because the sun would barbecue her dry within minutes of being outside.

The security guard never looked up when Winnie passed by his booth in the motorbike garage. He spent his days holed up inside it playing *Snake* on his archaic ingot of a Nokia and rarely lifted his head from the phone. On her way out the building, Winnie would always peek over his shoulder to check his score and marvel at how quickly his thumbs were moving. And when she stepped outside she would pretend that she was the snake in her own real-life version of the game: winding her way slowly around the streets, stopping periodically to ingest whatever she happened to cross paths with—bowls of soup, fried sesame doughnuts, plastic bags of mangoes chili-tinted a radioactive orange—with an invisible tail dragging along on the sidewalk behind her, growing longer and longer with each bite. She walked in zigzags, making sharp turns wherever she could, careful not to loop back onto the path she'd made. She theorized that because Saigon was so vast and mazelike and perpetually expanding, she could probably play forever, endlessly threading through the kinks and rivulets of the city without ever meeting her own tail.

She wasted her daylight hours carefully. Coffee first, always. Lingering for as long as she liked in the shop, secure in the knowledge that no one had taken enough notice of her in the first place to be annoyed at how long she was occupying a seat. Then there was walking to stay awake, punctuated by eating to stay awake. When she remembered to, she massaged her face, which was permanently puffy from the lack of sleep, dragging the heels of her hands across her forehead and down her cheekbones to drain them. Her skin always felt too tight, like there was a woolly extra layer beneath it. At some point in the afternoon she would return to the apartment and attempt to nap. Sometimes she man-aged it, and sometimes she just lay drowsily on the mattress in the sun, luxuriating in a Cook-free environment. She fed bones to Goji, and curled up on the floor next to him while he snored on his cushion, pre-tending that they were both cuddling together instead of merely lying down adjacently. Then more coffee, then an hour idling in the park across the street from a Korean barbecue restaurant, alternating be-tween reading her books and studying the young couples who sat in the restaurant's window booths. She had single-handedly exhausted the local supply of Japanese crime fiction, so she had moved on to romance novels from the late nineties, which seemed to make up the bulk of Sai-gon's secondhand English literature. Their plotlines all began to run together in her sleep-deprived brain, and she would forget whether she was reading about a secret marquis or a beefy but taciturn ranch hand or a high-powered Manhattan attorney with a broken heart or a plucky bridesmaid who would eventually end up with her friend's fiancé.

If it was a Tuesday, Thursday, Saturday, or Sunday, she would buy a sugarcane juice and then head to a nearby roundabout to drink it and watch sunset turn the smoggy sky above the traffic into scrambled egg. She would loiter on a curb until dark, eat more soup if she was hungry, and then slink back to the Cooks' apartment. But if it was a Monday or a Wednesday or a Friday, she would buy two energy drinks from the convenience store and begin making her way to the academy.

The adult night course she taught ran from seven to nine P.M. She could not prove it, but Winnie was convinced that it was Mrs. Cook who had proposed to Mr. Quy that Winnie teach the night classes, and that this was her vigilante justice for Winnie's wanton duty-shirking the prior semester. There was nothing that Anna Cook hated more than having her nighttime ritual of showering, meditating, and situating her-self in bed by nine-thirty being thrown off; she would consider it the cruelest of punishments to teach an evening class that always started late and ran over. Perhaps she had also gleefully been anticipating that as the youngest staff member, Winnie would find it awkward to teach the old-est student age group. But Winnie actually preferred her adult students to last semester's group of teenagers with their withering stares, latent horniness, and phone charms of obscure cartoon characters.

Everyone in her new class was in their thirties or forties. Most of them were employees of hotels or restaurants or other businesses where they already interacted regularly with foreigners, and they had signed up for the course to improve their language skills and seek promotions. A few of the younger ones were in different lines of work but hoped to transition into jobs in tourism.

Her students did not seem fazed by Winnie's unteacherly demeanor—her peculiar haircut, the dark circles beneath her eyes, her general colorlessness. Most of them had sussed out immediately that she was a poor educator but a potentially useful reservoir of knowledge about the proclivities of Westerners. Every evening began with an interrogation about American food, slang, dating habits, and the meanings of pop song lyrics, each answered question only Hydra-spawning more questions. This conveniently ate up most of the class period for Winnie, who needed to perform a more convincing pantomime of teaching this semester, now that she had a proportionate rent to pay (at her great-aunt's house, Winnie's room had cost her fifty-five dollars a month) and couldn't risk her only source of income. She made sure to write her students' unfamiliar vocabulary—*loaded nachos, booty call, Obamacare*—on the blackboard small enough that it would be illegible to somebody catching a glimpse of it from the hallway. She didn't need Mr. Quy to find out that she was feeding the class a diet of junk-food English. Even her students could barely read her tiny handwriting, and every time that Winnie raised her chalk there was an accompanying chorus of squeaks as they inched their desks forward en masse. By nine P.M. they usually had migrated a full two feet closer to the front of the room.

SHE STILL HADN'T SEEN or spoken to Long. Not since their awkward trip to the Cambodian border, which had now been four weeks ago. Since she had been exiled to the adult night course, Winnie arrived at the academy after Long had already left the office for the day, and she assumed that he hadn't reached out by phone because he felt as embarrassed about the visa run as she did.

One evening after class, on her way out of the building, she carelessly swept a hand through her mailbox without looking, expecting to find it empty, as it always was. But this time she sucked in her breath sharply and recoiled. Papercut. Popping her bleeding finger into her mouth to suck, she reached in again warily with her other hand and pulled out a folded sheet of paper. Long must have written her a letter. Something in her chest felt like it was in danger of toppling sideways. Winnie quickly uncreased the paper. Her insides righted themselves. No, he hadn't. It was an invitation to a going-away party the following week. Dao was going back to the States.

ALL OF THE ACHIEVEMENT! staff had been invited, as well as Dao's students. Mr. Quy himself ordered the cake and went in person to pick it up from the bakery: an imposing six-layer edifice of vanilla sponge, spackled together with a nearly indestructible pink meringue icing and fortified with decorative spears of mango and carved kiwi halves. Dao broke two plastic knives trying to saw through it before she finally succeeded. Because he had been so focused on getting the cake, Mr. Quy had completely forgotten about providing drinks for the party. After a desperate last-minute scavenger hunt around the office cupboards, he delivered a meager assemblage of beverages: five cans of unrefrigerated beer (three of them from his personal desk stash), a bottle of Dr. Thanh herbal tea, and two orange sodas left over from someone else's farewell party four years ago. Dao's twenty students gamely split the sodas among themselves, each one taking a microsip and then passing it on. They had pooled their money to buy her an album full of photographs of themselves and a pair of fake Chanel earrings. Several of them openly wept when they presented the gifts to her.

No one would weep for Winnie the day she finally vanished from the sunless halls of the academy. She knew this already, and she did not

begrudge Dao all of the pomp and displays of emotion that her departure merited. Truthfully, Winnie wasn't even paying much attention to
it. Songs were performed, speeches were given, slices of the terrible-
tasting cake were distributed and then discreetly disposed of, and Winnie barely noticed. She spent the whole afternoon lurking in a corner,
hogging one of the room-temperature lagers to herself and stewing
over the fact that Long hadn't shown up. She had considered skipping
the party because she was sure that he would be there, but ended up
coming for the same reason. She wondered whether she mattered
enough to him that he would purposefully avoid her. Her entire body
pricked up each time she felt a new person enter the room, and each
time, when they turned out not to be Long, she couldn't tell whether
her stomach was deflating with relief or disappointment.

The party abruptly began to wind down in the late afternoon, after
one of the teachers decided to crack into the two ripe durians they had
brought to share with the group. They did it next to an open window,
but the smell was still too much for about half the guests in attendance,
who cleared out quickly. Winnie, durian lover, hung around to receive
a lobe of the fruit (a truly perfect piece, she noted with admiration—
flesh that was the color of sunshine and the exact shape, quiver, and
heft of a raw kidney) before drifting along with Dao and the rest of
foreign staff to the bars in District 1 for the after-party.

Dao had chosen the backpacker quarter instead of somewhere quieter, hipper, and expattier in 2 or 7, she told them, because it was where
she had spent her very first night out in Vietnam a year and a half ago,
and so she wanted it to be the site of her last one too.

They were among the first of the evening's roisterers to arrive;
there was still an hour left before sunset and Bui Vien was uncharacteristically empty. It was Winnie's first time witnessing the street
unthronged, and she was unnerved by the sight of all its naked asphalt. Its topography was unrecognizable without the chaos of booze-
bucketeers, panhandlers, pickpockets, irritable sausage vendors, and
Western men of a certain age who kept to the corners with their arms
around the shoulders of much younger Vietnamese companions.

The teachers had no problem finding a sidewalk table that could accommodate the six of them (the Cooks had returned to the apartment for a liver-friendly night of lesson planning instead). Dao ordered everybody cocktails that were a menacing shade of electric blue. The drink tasted like Tiger Balm and pineapple juice, but no one knew what it actually contained, apart from vodka. In seven hours' time, when she vomited hers up into a potted plant, Winnie would discover that the cocktail took on an even more alarming turquoise phosphorescence in its semidigested afterlife.

She ended up wedged on a stool between the two Alexes. Dutch Alex was to her right, texting his wife fabricated excuses about why he would be home late, and American Alex was to her left. Although he was not the oldest one there, American Alex predated them all and thus considered himself to be the old guard of the academy. And because there was no one remaining who had known him when he first arrived ten years earlier, he attempted to cultivate a kind of louche mystique, deftly avoiding any questions about his pre-Asia life, only disclosing that he had moved to Vietnam after college and hadn't found a convincing reason to leave yet. He wore tight black jeans every day, claiming that he had grown immune to the climate after so many years in Saigon, but always left his shirts unbuttoned to the mid chest. He only ever sat backward in chairs, and the stories he told in the teachers' lounge were either about various bar girls he'd dated, road-tripping around Cambodia "before it got too safe," or the time he'd let a drunken monk tattoo his back. But on multiple occasions, Winnie had caught him rolling up his pantlegs to air out his overheating calves when he didn't think anyone was watching. She guessed that he was really a well-behaved boy from someplace like Michigan who was still here because he liked teaching and took the work seriously; otherwise he wouldn't have lasted a full decade.

American Alex had taken a small clothbound notebook and a pen out of his bag. He cleared his throat and tapped on the side of a vodka pail with his pen like he was about to give a toast at a wedding. "As you all know," he announced, once he had everyone's attention, "in order to give Dao a proper sendoff, we must perform our most sacred of Achievement! traditions: the Final Snack List!" This was met with laughter from Dao, groans from Nikhil and the blond teacher whose name, Winnie had recently learned, was Susan, and applause from Dutch Alex. Winnie kept her face carefully expressionless, because she had no idea what the Final Snack List was or what her reaction to it should be.

American Alex affected the waggish posturing and elocution of a game-show host. "Our contestant today is Dao 'The Devourer' Huynh!" he crowed. "She hails from Washington, D.C., can crush a *bánh mì ốp la* in under a minute, and last year she broke the office microwave by trying to make flan in it! Dao is abandoning us to go to law school, but while she might have aced her LSATs, how will she score tonight, on an even harder test? Contestant Dao! Are! You! *Ready!*" Dao gave him a nod and an acquiescent wiggle. She was already flushed from the blue drink. "There are eight questions, and at least twelve possible points. At the end, if there is any additional quote-unquote 'weird' Vietnamese food item you have consumed that was not on the list and you think is worthy of extra points, you may submit it to the jury"—American Alex indicated the rest of the teachers at the table— "for consideration. Let's kick things off with the easiest one: during your time here, have you, Contestant Dao, eaten . . . an embryonic duck egg?"

"Of course," Dao laughed. "Everybody drink!"

"Contestant Dao, this is a serious assessment, not a drinking game!" They all drank anyway, and American Alex put a tally mark in his notebook. "Question two: insects. One point for crickets or grasshoppers, two for scorpions or spiders." A brief argument ensued: Nikhil protested that scorpions and spiders were arachnids, not insects, and American Alex countered that nobody cared.

"How many points for fried coconut worms?" Dao interrupted with a grin, ending the dispute. Everyone else at the table shuddered.

"Oof. You definitely get two points for coconut worms," said American Alex.

"Hey, hey! I get three—I've had crickets."

American Alex duly recorded her cricket point in the notebook as well. "Next, and this one's the big one: dog meat?"

Dao's smile faltered. "Okay. It was one time. I got invited to dinner by some friends of friends while I was visiting Hue. I didn't know what we were going to eat until I was already there, and then I was afraid it would be rude if I didn't—"

American Alex held up a hand. "The Final Snack List does not judge, and explanations are unnecessary. Question four: rat meat?"

"Gross. No."

"Snake meat is next, and I'll just go ahead and give you the point for that because I *personally* witnessed you eat cobra when we were in Hanoi last summer," said American Alex, adding the check mark. Dao smiled, but it was a little lopsided. And upon seeing that smile, Winnie realized—with the same mild and half-guilty titillation of catching a glimpse of something embarrassing on the television screen of a stranger through the unshuttered windows of their house—that Dao and American Alex had slept together. And Dao either regretted it or regretted that it had stopped.

American Alex had oozed seamlessly back into his game-show act without any similar facial displays of emotional complexity, so Winnie guessed that it was the latter, and that Alex had been the one who ended things. "Contestant Dao, there are only three questions left and you are still at six points—let's see if you can make up some ground with these last ones. Question eight: have you eaten a sea turtle?"

Dao sighed and sipped from her bucket. "No."

"Question nine: lizard? Any kind of lizard?"

"No."

Sunset had transpired without Winnie noticing, and she suddenly realized that the sidewalk tables around her had filled with bodies when she wasn't looking. The air smelled like charcoal. Somewhere close behind her, she could hear the first accidentally dropped beer bottle of the night smashing on asphalt. And on the other side of the street, two different techno songs blasted from neighboring bars and competed for dominance over their respective sound systems. The sky was indigo, Dao's black hair under the streetlight—true black, not Winnie's swampy brown black—was indigo, the drink-tinted inner edges of American Alex's lips were indigo. "Ladies and gentlemen," he said with a grin that flashed blue teeth as well, "We have come to the last question of the Final Snack List, and this one is for five whole points!" He drummed dramatically on the table. "Cat meat! Have! You! Eaten it!"

Dao threw her hands up in a gesture that encompassed repulsion, confusion, and resignation all at once. "No! Why is that even on the list—Vietnamese people don't eat cats!"

But American Alex brandished a jubilant finger back at her. "Oh yes you do! In 2008, our dear friend and former Achievement! teacher, David—South African David—"

"Whatever happened to South African David?" mused Susan from the other side of the table.

"He moved to Yangon and got married," said American Alex. "Anyway, during a road trip, David accidentally ended up at a festival in some far-fucking-flung village up by the Chinese border, where he was fed a cat stew. He was too drunk to remember the name of the town, but that cat was seared into his memory; it was the most horrific thing he had ever put into his mouth . . ." American Alex trailed off momentarily and stared into the middle distance, thinking about cat stew with all the wistfulness he hadn't shown moments earlier toward Dao, before continuing: "Ever since, cat has become the holy grail of the freaky meats. Contestant Dao, you finish with six points, and your name and score will join those of our former colleagues in the official Final Snack List record book. Six points isn't terrible by any means, but I think we were all expecting a stronger showing from you!"

Again, that not-quite-smile from Dao, which she quickly converted to faux outrage. "Alex!" She slapped him jokingly on the forearm, but her hand lingered too long when it made contact with Alex's skin, and Winnie knew that she had been waiting for an opportunity to touch him. "That's so racist! You think I've been out here eating dogs and rats and cats just because I'm Asian?" Dao snorted, hoisting her bucket and struggling to find her mouth with the straw. She set it back down, sloshing some of the drink onto herself in the process. Then, without warning, she turned her head and stared directly at Winnie.

Please no, thought Winnie. But Dao's lips were already beginning to form the W.

"Winnie! You're, like, Filipino right? Do you eat cats?"

It was the first time that Winnie had heard Dao say her name. She wondered if it was her first time even uttering it out loud. The word had fallen awkwardly from her mouth coated in a slimy, caul-like new-ness that wasn't an effect of the alcohol. Was the fact that Dao didn't know she was also Vietnamese a success, wondered Winnie, proof that she had achieved the invisibility she'd sought these past months? Now the entire table was turning to look at her. Winnie told herself to just flick out a harmless nonanswer and redirect the conversation. But she was so unused to the feeling of this many eyes focusing on her—being in front of the classroom didn't have the same effect; her students never really *looked* at her when they looked at her—that it blistered. She had succeeded in opening her mouth, but nothing was coming out of it, and now an uncomfortable amount of time had passed. Winnie was con-vinced that the stares had intensified. She pleaded with herself to at least laugh if she couldn't manage words, but instead she imagined her skin turning into bubbly brown pork cracklings under their gazes. Her fat rendering and dripping down the legs of her plastic stool. Her hair singeing and shriveling and burning away completely.

It was American Alex who snapped Winnie out of her roast-pig trance and saved her from having to answer Dao. "Wait! Stop!" He waved his hands frantically in front of Winnie's face. "You can't tell us! You're not a contestant yet! Don't spoil it!"

"Oh, whatever," slurred Dao. "Cute haircut, by the way," she added to Winnie before turning back to the others and launching a case in favor of a wholly unnecessary second round of buckets.

THE NIGHT UNRAVELED FROM there in predictable ways. The group debated whether to go to karaoke or to a nightclub next, were unable to come to an agreement, and ended up just lingering on at their table, hailing a fried-corn vendor rolling past with a wok cart. They all shared a single order, leaning over each other to scoop kernels from a carton at the center of the table with minuscule trowel-shaped spoons. Winnie was careful to take only one bite for every three that the other teachers did, calculating that this would draw the least amount of attention to her; either eating too much or not eating at all would be a noticeable offense. Little wet scabs of scallion clung to the crannies of her mouth, and she resisted the urge to swipe them free with a finger. She still hadn't fully recovered from Dao speaking to her, and her shame at her own disproportionate reaction. The unquiet energies it had unleashed were growing steadily louder inside her, like dissonant notes being played on a pipe organ located somewhere at the base of her spine, an invisible foot slowly mashing down on all its pedals.

After Dutch Alex accidentally knocked over a parked motorbike while trying to find a dark street corner to pee, the other, marginally less inebriated teachers phoned his wife, and ten minutes later she arrived in a taxi to retrieve him. The remaining five finished their corn while they watched the evening's regular lineup of street performers: first there was the man with an amplifier strapped to the back of his bicycle who sang ballads and circulated through the crowds with a fistful of stale candies for sale; then the pair of fire breathers who looked no older than fifteen, armed with old Sprite bottles full of kerosene; and finally the man who took a live snake, small and jade green and pencil thin, fed it up one of his nostrils, and then pulled it back out of his mouth. ("Jesus," muttered Susan, wobbling to her feet and hailing a taxi for herself. "When the snake-nose man shows up you know it's time to leave.") This performance prompted American Alex to regale the remaining three teachers with a story about the English friend of a French friend of a different English friend who had tried a club drug made from cobra venom. ("He said it was the best night of his life and gave him the wildest fucking high!" said American Alex, unable to keep the jealousy from his voice. "But it's basically impossible to buy anymore."

Nikhil snorted. "Bullshit. If it actually existed, someone would have died by now and we'd have heard about it.") Then a girl standing on the curb three feet from their table got her purse snatched by two men on a motorbike, and this was what finally prompted them to abandon their table and taxi over to a nightclub by the river.

The ambience of the club, with its membrane-pink walls under hazy aquatic lighting, cavernous ceilings held up by exposed, rib-like joists, and pervasive saline aroma from the many sweaty bodies inside, suggested the interior anatomy of a whale. As soon as they entered, Alex recognized the Vietnamese DJ as one of his prior conquests and immediately split from the group to go flirt with her, too eager to even feign coyness by going to get a drink first. Winnie watched Dao's smile collapse as he wended his way toward the DJ booth. She could read every successive thought that knit itself across Dao's brow as if they were her own: Dao—beautiful Dao, thin Dao, bilingual, law-school-bound, beloved Dao—comparing herself to this nameless girl and trying to identify the symptom of her own Americanness that made her undesirable to Alex. Was it her field hockey calves, Winnie knew Dao was asking herself, or the time she had publicly declared a preference for ketchup over chili sauce? Her pride regarding her orthodontically straightened teeth? The inability of her larynx to wrap itself around the word *"Anh"* for him in the same way that the other girl could, even if Vietnamese had been her first language too?

Winnie watched Dao wait for five minutes to elapse and then go outside to cry. She waited two more before following.

Dao had found a secluded spot and was sitting on the curved rim of a large, cement planter holding a dwarf palm. In another three hours, this would be the planter that Winnie threw up into. Dao was dabbing her mascara smears with a folded tissue triangle and didn't notice Winnie quietly approach and then loom over her shoulder with the sinister demeanor of a sweaty club vampire.

What Winnie wanted to say to Dao was this: One day, years in the future, he will play such an insignificant role in your memories of Vietnam that when you think back to this night, you will be able to recall the exact blue hue of your bucket cocktail but you will not even remember his name. He will be so insignificant that forgetting his name will only cause you to feel a mild annoyance at your own forgetfulness, and you won't even relish having proof of how fleeting his hold on your heart had truly been. He will be so insignificant that proof will be superfluous. Somewhere inside you, you already know this—if not in your heart or your brain, maybe in your marrow.

But Winnie did not say this. By now she was far too drunk to find the words she needed. She couldn't hear herself think; the pipe organ in her bones was reaching its crescendo, and she could feel all of her body's windows rattling from the sound. And now, whistling over it, the refrain of Dao's earlier "Winnie! You're, like, Filipino right? Do you eat cats?" looped inanely in her head, its needle-in-eardrum, microphone-feedback shrillness intensifying each time it repeated.

When she finally spoke, Winnie thought at first that she was yelling to make herself heard over the noise inside her. But the words came out calm, barely louder than a whisper: "No, I'm not; I'm just like you. And no." Winnie spoke directly into Dao's ear, and in alarm, Dao dropped her tissue and threw herself off the planter edge. She should have announced her presence earlier and in a less creepy way, Winnie realized in retrospect. Dao was clearly relieved to see that she had been surprised by Winnie and not an unfamiliar English-speaking pervert but still kept her distance when she replied.

"Oh. Hi. Sorry, what did you say?"

"The questions you asked me. Those are my answers: No, I'm not; I'm just like you. And no, I don't eat them. That's all."

Poor Dao, who had no idea what Winnie was talking about, only blinked. But Winnie was too relieved to be embarrassed; the instrument in her body had gone abruptly, blessedly silent, the notes cut off mid vibration, leaving her feeling taut and dangly on the inside. She was no longer a pipe organ; she was some sort of drum now, all hollowness and stretched skin. With a giggle, she slapped herself on the belly, pretending it was a bongo. Then she turned away from the confused Dao, knowing she would never see her again, and pushed the doors of the club back open. Still drumming, she plunged inside once more, picking up the rhythm of the song that American Alex's DJ was playing and reproducing it on her own flesh. She met with no resistance when she entered the crowd. She did not have to grapple her way in or dodge any limbs; she was accepted seamlessly, like water. She started dancing.

No one who met Winnie or beheld her lizard-like way of scuttling through the world would suspect that she was a person who could dance, or one who even enjoyed it. But here in the whale belly, with three hundred other people in strobe-light-stippled darkness, she had shed her ungainly body. Together they had become a shapeshifting superbeast, all churning as one. Winnie swayed in bass-propelled ecstasy. This was insomnia well spent. It was even better than counting the night dogs from her window perch. She had never felt more invisible. It was possible that she had never felt happier.

Hours passed, and Winnie hadn't realized how much time had elapsed until she was abruptly snapped back into her own body by the sight of American Alex. The internal currents of the crowd swirled her past him. He was off to the side, detached from the superbeast but now very much attached to the DJ, who had bequeathed her headphones to someone else.

Winnie broke loose and hovered in the shadows near the couple, thinking of Dao wiping tears away outside and regretting not having said something to comfort her. She had the chance to try and make amends now. There was an unchaperoned drink on a nearby table, and Winnie sailed over to it. In a single movement, as smoothly as if it had been choreographed, the drink was in her hand. She stole a sip of it for herself—it tasted like her own recklessness—and then poured the rest down American Alex's back. By the time he noticed and swung around, hoping for a fight that would become a better story when he told it later, she had already been safely absorbed back into the crowd.

BOYS WEREN'T USUALLY SENT AWAY TO THE *ÉCOLE* UNTIL they were at least eight years old. Jean-François was only seven and a half when he went, but large for his age, which was one of the reasons he was permitted to go early. He took after his father, a Khmer, originally from the deep, sticky reaches of the South, who was tall and broad shouldered and the rich umber color of a swamp eel. Or at least this was what Nounou, his mother's Vietnamese housekeeper back in Saigon, had told him. Jean-François had never actually met his father. While the Auffrets had been Catholic enough to keep and raise a mixed bastard, they weren't as forgiving toward the man who had seduced their daughter and sired the child, and so one day Jean-François's father was bundled onto a boat headed for the prison camp on Con Son Island and was never heard from again.

Growing up, the boy had seen his mother regularly. On most afternoons, if he behaved himself, he was allowed into the main house to take tea with her on the grand blue-tiled veranda, and then at bedtime she would cross the garden to the small quarters he shared with Nounou at the far edge of the compound and give him a papery goodnight kiss on the forehead. But his memories of her had started leaching away almost immediately after he left home, and later, whenever he tried to recall what she looked like, he could only conjure up the haziest of images. It was Nounou whose round Nghe An face would always haunt him with preternatural clarity. For nearly all of the long hours of those Saigon days he had belonged to the housekeeper. She was the one who kept him fed and washed, his toenails trimmed, and his hair parted neatly down the center. The one who scolded him when he threw rocks into the family koi pond, taught him to sleep with a knife beneath his pillow to keep away ghosts, and took care of him when he was sick, which was often. This was the second reason that he was sent to the école young. Jean-François, despite being tall and strong and rambunctious for his age, frequently suffered from crippling stomachaches of unknown origin and mysterious fevers that lingered for weeks before clearing up on their own, and his doctors thought the cooler mountain climate of Dalat would be beneficial for his health. Nounou had not wanted him to go. She didn't trust French doctors and believed that most, if not all, ailments could be cured by either drinking a saucer of fish sauce or taking a very hot bath, and so whenever his stomach was acting up she would stick him in the tub and scrub him raw. For the rest of his life, Jean-François would have regular nightmares in which Nounou drowned him, or the bathwater filled with blood, or fish, or both, or his skin sloughed off with her washcloth, revealing something fibrous and golden and sticky like mango flesh underneath.

But the third and most pressing reason for Jean-François's early enrollment was that by 1942 the old order of Saigon had been upended. France was preoccupied with the war in Europe, the Japanese now occupied all of Indochina, and the emperor was off hunting tigers in the Highlands. No one was quite sure what the governor-general was up to, or whether they should be more afraid of the Viet Minh or the Caodaists. Dalat was safer than the city, and the prescient Auffrets wanted the boy left in the responsible hands of the école, should the family need to make a speedy exit from the colony in the near future. Arrangements were made. A suitcase was packed, and for his going-away present the boy's mother gave him a boxy leather briefcase bearing his initials in gold—J.F.A.—just like the one his grandfather carried. Nounou had rolled her eyes at it, saying that schoolboys carried satchels, not briefcases, and that he would be made fun of. Jean-François was put on an early morning train. It was the first time in his life he had ever been anywhere on his own, and he relished it. He dozed off, and when he awoke hours later, the unkempt bougainvillea outside his window had become tall, dark pines, and the air seeping in at the latch was clammy-cold to his unaccustomed southern lungs.

Father Thaddée was waiting with the école's oat-colored Peugeot 402 when the train came shrieking into Dalat station. He wore a tweed sports coat over his cassock and was hopping from foot to foot to keep warm in the mountain chill.

"*Bienvenue,*" he said to Jean-François, opening the car door. His once crisp Auvergne vowels had gone sloppy after nearly a decade in the colonies. "At school it is expected that you will speak only French, so we may as well start now." Impatient to get out of the cold, he ushered Jean-François inside the vehicle quickly and tossed the boy's luggage onto the crumbling leather seat beside him. Then he slid into the front, wrangled the Peugeot into gear, and guided it out onto the narrow road. The city's nightly mist was encroaching early, already marshaling around the trees behind the station. "You will be happy here, Jean-François," the priest called over his shoulder brightly. "You are going to be with other boys who are just like you."

The ailing Peugeot threw itself at each of the five different hills it scaled or circled en route to the school with admirable vigor and a fearsome rattling sound from its engine. Jean-François clenched the handle of his briefcase so hard his knuckles turned white, certain that at any moment they would go careening into a gulch. The crowded markets and narrow termite-nest houses of the Vietnamese neighborhoods gave way to the pale, cuspate, evenly spaced villas of the French, which in turn gave way to farmland with piney wilderness at the edges. It was growing darker and foggier, and twice Jean-François thought he saw strange red lights winking out in the distant trees, but he could not ask Father Thaddée about them, because he did not want to distract the priest from driving or reveal how poor his French actually was. At home he had spoken a mangled Vietnamese-French dialect of his own design, which his mother had found charming.

The school was perched on a hilltop at the end of one last twisty climb. They spluttered to a stop before a squat building of whitewashed concrete; through the car window Jean-François could make out two identical structures beyond it. Their pale edges were hazy and almost appeared to glow in the mist, which was now so thick that when he stepped out of the car, he could barely see the outline of his own feet below him in the grass.

THE FIRST OF THE white buildings was the dormitory, where Jean-François and the three dozen other métis boys slept on metal cots that lined the walls of one long, low-ceilinged room. Another held the dining hall and the private quarters of their instructors, the priests. The third building contained the chapel and the classrooms where the boys received lessons on mathematics, history, and French grammar and literature in the mornings. Afternoons were reserved for their religious studies or for military exercises out on the grassy expanse behind the classrooms. Boys of ten and older were given wooden guns and sent crawling on their bellies over the field while a stocky man in a uniform they called the commandant barked formations at them. Jean-François and the others too young for the drills were stuck marching and saluting instead. In their short navy uniforms and carefully angled berets, knees high and backs straight, they stomped back and forth across the hilltop and around and around the perimeter of the school, alternating which boy had to carry the tricolor.

Mealtimes were also considered an important part of their education; they were only allowed French cuisine, prepared by two cooks from Madagui who had been trained at a restaurant in Marseilles. Sometimes the older boys would look down glumly at their plates and wistfully recount what they had eaten before the war had started: roast beef, glossy terrines, shellfish shipped in from Nha Trang, a different pastry every night. However, even their current, frugal menu was exhaustingly rich to Jean-François. They were fed gratins, sausages, heavy stews, sheets of ham, forearm-sized omelets, more kinds of cassoulet than he could keep track of. Jean-François was unused to so much dairy in his diet and had been too nervous to eat anything but bread during his first few days in Dalat. Consequently, he was unable to shit for a week. Boys who misbehaved were usually given a lash across the hands or buttocks with a leather strap, but after the priests discovered Jean-François's particular aversion to butter they used it to punish him whenever he fought with the other boys or turned in sloppy work. They would place a fat, frozen pat in his mouth and make him stand in a corner until it dissolved. If Jean-François gagged or tried swallowing it to end the ordeal more quickly he was given another tablespoon. Afterward he was not permitted to wash it down with water.

He was the only one whose French heritage was matrilineal. All of the other boys had Vietnamese mothers and European fathers, most of whom were in the military. They had developed a complex, unspoken ranking system among themselves: beady eyes or freckles placed you at the very bottom. Wavy hair was prized, but only if it wasn't too frizzy. Small teeth were good; hairy legs were bad. They weren't sure whether Jean-François's French mother placed him higher or lower on their scale. His height was a plus. So was his scrappy streak—he tended to settle his disagreements with other boys by brawling, which they deemed a hot-blooded, Gallic trait. He lost points for his complexion, which was dark and uneven, but made up for it with his nose, which was dainty, and his eyes, which were large and framed by dramatic lashes. Eventually it was decided that he fell somewhere in the middle.

Jean-François turned ten on the seventh of March 1945. In his three years at the école he had grown ganglier. His hair had darkened slightly. As his old doctors had predicted, the mountain climate had improved his health—he now suffered from his inexplicable stomach spasms only rarely. Nearly all of his permanent teeth had come in, and they were shaping up to be some of the straightest in the school, which significantly improved his position in the boys' rankings. In their Saturday soccer games he was the best goalkeeper, and he once kicked the ball so hard into the face of another student, Michaux, that it had broken the boy's nose. Father Auguste, who refereed, had punished Jean-François by not allowing him to attend a special ballroom dance lesson with the girls who went to school at the Domaine de Marie convent down the road. Jean-François had secretly been relieved because he found both nuns and teenage girls terrifying.

After his first year he had stopped wondering whether his mother was coming to visit, or why she hadn't sent for him at Christmas or Easter like some of the other boys' parents had. She had written him a long, formal letter once, most of which he was unable to decipher save for "I hope your French has improved!" and "With love, your mother." Jean-François put very little effort into his academics. He was always at the bottom of his class in reading, writing, and history, and his teachers—and Jean-François himself—assumed that his best hope was a future in the military.

"Don't worry, Auffret," Father Phuoc would say whenever he handed back Jean-François's flunked grammar tests. "Soldiers don't need to know the conditional tense."

The only subject he showed interest in was religion, but Father Benoît suspected the boy was more taken with the various elements of pageantry in the mass—the candles, the smoking censers, the kneeling, the flinging of holy water—than he was concerned with actual worship.

Two days after his birthday, Jean-François was one of six boys selected for the school's bimonthly mountain excursion to Lang Biang Mountain to practice navigation and wilderness skills. At breakfast his name was called, along with Batandier, Petit, Grisolet, Lauriac, and Dufour. They quickly fetched their marching berets and lined up outside to wait for the commandant's truck to arrive from the army base north of the city.

Jean-François liked Batandier, a narrow-faced eleven-year-old whose father owned several textile mills outside of Tourane. They were usually seated near each other in class because of where their names fell in the alphabet, and, like him, Batandier preferred to use Vietnamese whenever he could get away with it. He spoke with a heavy

Central Coast accent and knew more curse words in either language than any other boy at the school.

Petit and Lauriac were both fourteen and newly cynical, long legged and smirking and Saigonese. Jean-François did not know them very well. Dufour was ten and unpopular because he had a habit of nibbling off his fingernails and leaving their sharp little sickles scattered around the dormitory floors. Grisolet was a quiet and studious fifteen-year-old who planned to enter the seminary in Can Tho after the école. He was a quarter Algerian. The other boys used to mock him for this until the day they overheard Father Auguste make a snide remark about Grisolet's heritage, and after that the teasing stopped. The boys never wanted to be on the same side as the priests.

The six boys bounced up and down in the back of the green truck as it rumbled over the rough dirt road to Lang Biang. They played a game where they would try to stand for as long as they could until either they toppled over or the commandant turned around in the front seat and yelled at them. When they arrived at the outpost at the foot of the mountain they were already a little bit bruised and tired from too much laughing, and the mood quickly turned somber when they stepped out of the truck and saw a small group of bored-looking Japanese soldiers swatting away midges beneath the awning of the wooden lean-to.

"Don't worry about them," said the commandant, not altogether convincingly. "Their war isn't going very well, so they have nothing better to do than hang around here and try to seem important. I'll go speak to them—Capitaine Foucher will be in charge of you." He strode off toward the soldiers, boots squeaking in the dewy grass.

The boys wanted to watch, but Capitaine Foucher, their other mountain guide that day, led them around to the other side of the truck, where he handed out equipment and lectured them on safety. They each received a knife and a knapsack containing a canteen of water, a box of matches, a small bundle of fatwood, a length of rope, and a ham sandwich. Grisolet was put in charge of the map because he was the oldest, and Dufour was given the compass because it occupied his hands and kept him from biting his nails.

"It is easy to get distracted by the natural beauty of Lang Biang," Capitaine Foucher began to recite wearily. He had not wanted to do wilderness training with the boys today; there were far more important things for them to worry about, as the unexpected and unwelcome presence of the Japanese demonstrated. "However, you must always pay close attention to your surroundings! You will be perfectly safe as long as you—"

"Are there tigers?" interrupted Lauriac.

"There haven't been tigers in this part of Lang Biang for many years," said Foucher. "They hunted them all back in the twenties."

"Bastien's dad knew someone who was killed by tigers," said Petit. "When they went looking for the body the next day they could only find his feet, because the tigers didn't want to eat his boots."

"And what about snakes?" Dufour asked, sending a noisy ripple of alarm through all the boys.

Capitaine Foucher had to bang his pistol against the truck like a gavel to get them to quiet down. "There aren't any venomous snakes at this altitude. Not outside of the North." This was not strictly true— banded kraits were known to turn up occasionally in the forests around Dankia to the northeast, but they were nocturnal, and Foucher didn't see any sense in worrying the boys unnecessarily. "The only animals that might pose any danger to you out there are wild boars, which can be territorial. I doubt you'll run into any, but if you do and they seem aggressive, just climb a nearby tree and wait for them to leave." Foucher glanced over at the commandant, who had taken out his hip flask and was plying the Japanese soldiers with vodka. He sighed. "Well, let's not waste the daylight."

They set off single file on a path through the bunchgrass that would lead them into the forest and partway up the mountain. There, Capitaine Foucher would leave them, and the boys would navigate on their own through another two kilometers of terrain to meet him and the truck at a designated spot. When they stepped into the trees and everything abruptly became cool and dim and damp, Jean-François had the uneasy thought that they had all been swallowed.

The light seemed to behave differently in the forest. It shimmered off surfaces he normally didn't think of as being reflective: tree bark and soil, the rough canvas of the boys' knapsacks, the goose-pimpled skin above their chilled knees. And it looked greenish even when it wasn't being diffused through leaves, as if that was simply the true color of the light. After an hour of walking, the route became steeper and the boys' breathing grew labored. There was no wind, but Grisolet observed a cluster of purple asters swaying back and forth to one side of the path. He wasn't sure whether the prospect of the flowers moving on their own or the thought of an animal hidden within them was more alarming. Lauriac kicked a clod of moss absentmindedly but then got nervous and gently set it back in place on the ground. Whenever the boys heard birdsong, they could not agree on which direction it was coming from.

At half past one they stopped on top of a large, flat slab of rock to eat their sandwiches. Capitaine Foucher gave a long and rambling talk on compass reading, poisonous mushrooms, and the importance of not falling into the waterfall they would be shortly approaching. He showed them how to set and splint a broken bone using tree branches and a neckerchief, and then they paired off to practice building fires.

"This is boring," Batandier whispered to Jean-François in Vietnamese once they were out of sight and earshot of the others. They were supposed to be searching for dry kindling but were dangling their sore legs off the rock ledge. Jean-François nodded even though he wasn't bored at all. The forest was so beautiful that he felt giddy and a bit ill at the same time. Before today he had never seen a fern, and the perfect emerald coils of their young fronds were so alien and lovely they made his stomach twist.

"Do you know what would be funny?" said Batandier suddenly. "If you went missing."

"What do you mean?" asked Jean-François.

"Let's frighten Foucher!" Batandier flashed a devious little smile. "After he leaves, you slip off and hide somewhere. The rest of us will keep going, and when we get out of the woods we'll tell him that you got lost. I'll say you were right behind me one minute, and the next you were just gone."

"The commandant and Foucher aren't going to believe that."

"We'll put on a good act for the two of them. Pretend to be really shaken up. Petit knows how to fake-cry."

"And then what happens?"

"And then they come back in here looking for you! And you'll be ready for them. Imagine it: they find you lying on the ground with your eyes closed, just like this." Batandier flopped backward on the rock and threw one arm over his face and the other out to the side. He gave two exaggerated twitches and then lay still. Jean-François giggled. "And when they go to wake you up," Batandier continued, still on his back, "you pretend you're sick. Moan and groan and wiggle around like a fish." He demonstrated.

"What do I say when they ask me what happened?" asked Jean-François.

Batandier sat up and mulled it over. Then he cracked another wolfish grin. "Tell them you ate some berries you saw growing on a bush off the path. Weird red berries that made you feel so sick you had to lie down."

"I'll say I ate the berries because I thought they looked like *so ri*, but then I started throwing up so bad I couldn't yell for help!" Jean-François was starting to warm to the plan.

"Don't say that—then they'll wonder where the vomit is. Just say you ate some berries, you got dizzy and lay down, and it's the last thing you remember before they found you. You have to keep the lie simple for it to work."

"Why don't you be the one who gets lost instead? You're better at this than me."

"And that's why I need to be the one who tells them you're missing. You'd cave in two minutes."

Jean-François fiddled with his matchbook. "What if they don't see me because I'm on the ground? What if they walk right past me?"

"They won't—I'll be there too. They'll have to take me along so I can guide them back to where I remember seeing you last. Oh, please do it! Just imagine how funny the older boys will think it is when we tell them later! And if you do it I'll give you two of the cigarettes I stole from Father Thaddée this morning," wheedled Batandier.

Jean-François didn't really need any convincing to go along with Batandier's scheme; he had been sold from the start, but not because he thought it would be funny. There was a part of him that wanted the forest all to himself. He wanted to be alone in this place, just to know what it felt like. "Okay, I'll do it," he said, and was pleased that his voice didn't tremble. He took out one of his matches and tried to strike it against the rock, but it broke in half.

According to the map, the trek that the boys would complete on their own was fairly uncomplicated. After reaching the waterfall up ahead, they would follow its stream downhill for most of the remaining route. Capitaine Foucher inspected the boys' fires and deemed them all unsatisfactory in some way. Then he made sure they were properly extinguished, warned the boys once again about falling into the waterfall, and then strode off down the slope and back toward the outpost. From the rock, Jean-François, Batandier, Petit, Lauriac, Grisolet, and Dufour watched him grow smaller between the trees, and once he had vanished from sight completely, they released the roar of joy they had been holding in.

No one made the decision to start running—the boys all seemed to take off at once in a collective, spur-of-the-moment frenzy. Their tired legs felt brand new. They sprinted in a pack all the way to the waterfall, knapsacks bouncing, knee socks slipping down to their ankles, startled thrushes fleeing at their footsteps. Grisolet ran with the rolled-up map clenched in one fist and held aloft like a spear. Dufour's beret fell off, and when he stooped to pick it up he tripped Batandier; they both tumbled to the ground but were moving so fast that they just rolled over and back onto their feet and kept going, unfazed by their scraped palms and dirt-caked shorts. The boys' panting was so noisy it echoed off of the tree trunks; their ribs felt ready to snap through their skin. They were close to the waterfall now and could hear the wet radio-static hiss of its spray, and this made them sprint even faster. With the savage, sinister thing that had been awakened inside them now singing in their blood, they imagined what it would be like to keep running, right over the edge of the fall, feet treading the air until they struck the water below. But when they felt cold mist on their faces and the stones beneath their boots turned slippery and unforgiving, one by one they slowed to a halt. Jean-François was the last to stop, mere feet from the overhang. He leaned forward to peer over the edge and blanched when he saw the shallowness of the pool at the bottom and the jagged rocks studding its surface.

The boys did not meet one another's eyes while they caught their breath. Cautiously, wordlessly, they made their way down the stepped formation of mossy boulders that flanked the waterfall and did not break their silence until they had reached the base. Although they were supposed to be navigating their way out of the forest without the help of a trail, they could clearly see a path to one side of the gully that had been trampled into the dirt by the boys of the école on previous excursions. They read their classmates' names and assorted dirty words in French and Vietnamese carved into the trunks of camphor trees. These traces of the world outside the forest conjured the memories of their whitewashed classrooms, their snoring dorm mates, the priests' knuckle-rappings, and shook from the six boys the last vestiges of their mania. They resumed their chatter and stomped along merrily beside the stream for half a mile. It felt so natural to Jean-François when he and Batandier started trailing behind the pack that he didn't even register that it was happening until the others were already twenty paces ahead. The path had started to curve away from the stream and was now more difficult to make out, its edges eaten up by ferns and unruly vines and thickets of wild mint. Though it was still the middle of the afternoon, the mountain sun had already grown weaker.

Batandier stopped at an imperial-looking pine that grew in the middle of their trail. From his knapsack he dug out the stolen cigarettes, and then held them out to Jean-François with a grin. "This is the spot," he said. "Wait right beside this tree. And make sure you put on a good show when we come back to find you!" Batandier's speaking voice hadn't dropped yet, but his laugh was starting to deepen already, and for the rest of his life Jean-François would recall the sound of it when he smelled pine resin. "See you in about an hour, Auffret!" Batandier winked at him, and then jogged off to join the others.

He tossed his knapsack onto the ground and sat down beside it to wait. The earth was cool and damp beneath his khaki-clad bottom, and he let himself flop backward and roll in the mossy undergrowth like a buffalo wallowing in a mudhole. He dug his fingers down into the soft dirt at the foot of the tree and then brought his hands to his face and luxuriated in the scent: soil, sap, decay. He tried to recline against its trunk using his beret as a pillow, but the bark was still too rough through the thin wool. Then he took out his two remaining matches and coughed his way through Father Thaddée's cigarettes. He had never smoked before and was planning to have one and save the other for later, but the first cigarette tasted so awful that he thought it must have gone bad, like an old apple. He lit the second one immediately after, hoping it would erase the taste of the first, and was disappointed when it turned out to be equally unpleasant. He sighed, bored already, and looked up at the sky, unaware that in Saigon and Hanoi, in Hai Phong and Hue, and outside the white gates of Governor-General Decoux's summer villa ten miles south of this very mountain, the Japanese had finally launched their coup.

Capitaine Foucher and the commandant would not be coming back for him. At that very moment they were frantically trying to wrangle Batandier, Grisolet, Petit, Lauriac, and Dufour into the back of the truck and were far too distracted to bother counting them. When Dufour tried to interrupt the capitaine to tell him that Jean-François was missing, he received a sharp smack across the face, and none of the other boys dared to say anything afterward. The truck sped away from Lang Biang, dislodging chunks of the dirt road as it took the curves too quickly, sending them showering down the mountainside. They reached the école as it was being evacuated. By the time a tearful

Batandier managed to inform the priests that one of them had been left behind in the forest, it was already too late.

Jean-François grew uneasy after the first hour. After two, his unease turned to panic. He had paid very little attention to Capitaine Foucher's navigation instructions, and in the fading daylight, out of matches and without the map, he did not trust himself to get out of the woods on his own. After three hours, panic yielded to resignation, and as the sky turned the jellied blue-black color of a century egg, Jean-François took his knife out of his knapsack and braced himself against his tree for the night, shaking.

A chill, moist wind stirred the pine needles at his feet. Jean-François bit the insides of his cheeks to silence his chattering teeth—the noise was too loud in the dark. His hearing had sharpened in response to the loss of light. Before sunset the hum of distant cicadas had been soothing; now it was excruciating to listen to. Even the sound of his own cautious breathing was abrasive to his ears.

When the smoke came for him, he heard it before he saw or smelled it. It made a smothered rustling noise as it moved through the trees, snapping dry twigs and pushing low branches out of its way. At first, Jean-François's heart leapt at the thought that his teachers had finally come to save him, but he quickly realized that the sound he was hearing could not be made by human feet. As it drew closer, he gripped his knife and imagined tigers, giant pythons, wild boars with sharpened tusks. When it finally came into view, dense and low, glowing slightly, he saw that it was no living thing but a formless, copper-colored cloud. It had no discernible source, and even though the wind had picked up and was bending back the branches of the nearby trees, the smoke was somehow able to flow against it. Its smell was acrid but slightly sweet, like burning honey. As Jean-François watched, it condensed, oscillating in place and growing thicker and redder, and when it was about two large quilts' worth of choking, opaque mass, it crept once again over the ground toward the boy. Its edges spread wide and curved back in to form a circle around him.

When the smoke was within arm's reach, Jean-François lashed out, kicking and punching and slashing with the knife, but his boots and fist and blade met no resistance. Wherever the boy tried to strike it, the smoke simply dissipated. Jean-François had never run from a fight before in his life, but now he fled. Abandoning his knapsack by the old pine, he tore off into the darkness. The smoke waited a beat and then followed. Jean-François had sprinted in the wrong direction, so he would not have made it out of the forest in any case, but he was suddenly wracked with the worst stomach spasms he'd ever experienced in his life. It felt as though all of the pain he had been spared during his years of good health in Dalat was now catching up to him at once. He dropped his knife and clutched his abdomen, digging his fingers into the tender muscle as if hoping to find and tear out his stomach to make the throbbing stop. He staggered on for another twelve yards before falling to his knees in a copse of feathery young casuarina trees. The smoke overcame him then, and as it enveloped Jean-François the pain ceased, for which he was thankful. Filaments of it snaked up the boy's nostrils and flowed into his lungs. Red wisps of it wrapped around his wrists and ankles, tugging him down onto the grass and binding him in place. Two thick tentacles reached up for his mouth and began prying it open as far as it would go. Jean-François screamed. Then the smoke wrenched, and his jaws were torn clear apart. His face gaped open like the shell of a steamed clam, and all of the smoke poured down his throat, silencing him, filling his stomach like seawater and wrapping itself around the soft sacks of his organs, trickling out into every limb, to each extremity. It threaded itself through the kinks of his intestines and wreathed around his eyeballs in their sockets.

Jean-François was conscious the whole time. He lay there, gaping, waiting for the thing to kill him, but the minutes dragged on and he remained very much alive. While he experienced no pain, he could still feel grass itching the backs of his legs and was surprised by how much this could annoy him even in the midst of everything else that was happening. Jean-François tried to distract himself from the itch. He thought about what the others were eating for dinner at the école. He wondered if he would still be able to play soccer with a broken mouth. It never occurred to him to try praying.

The smoke contracted again, slowly packing itself into a warm, dense mass at the base of his spine about the size of a dumpling. The tendrils of smoke that had been restraining his arms and legs now released their hold, slithering up over his limbs and down his throat to join the rest of itself, like fishing line being reeled in. He had the unmistakable sensation of the smoke *settling* inside him, like a dog walking around in circles before finally curling up and going to sleep. And only then did Jean-François's split jaw finally begin to close, the bottom half slowly drawing back into place on its own. After it rehinged, he cautiously lifted his hands to touch his cheeks. The skin felt smooth and seamless, unchanged. Jean-François coughed and briefly tasted cinders in his mouth, and then rose to his feet slowly, afraid of disturbing the creature he now contained.

But there was no need for him to worry—moving into its new home had exhausted the smoke, and for now it was content to lie dormant. In the ensuing years of chaos, Jean-François would come to know all its habits and its proclivities—what woke it, what summoned it, what appeased it—though he would never be able to figure out what it was that it truly wanted with him. Later, when he learned about the beheadings in Lang Son, or about Father Thaddée and Father Auguste, who were gunned down near the Cambodian border while trying to flee in the Peugeot, or about the prison camp outside Hue where Capitaine Foucher spent five months dribbling away his insides with acute dysentery, or the bamboo cage where the commandant was kept while he was interrogated, or about the lucky boys of the école who were sent to new Japanese-language schools in Saigon, or the unlucky ones who weren't and were never heard from again, Jean-François would wonder if it had been the smoke that had saved him. For now, though, Jean-François staggered off through the trees, in the right direction this time, and emerged in a country that had been as irreversibly transfigured as his own flesh.

Bà never left Dak Lak. Her feet gave out just before they reached the Lam Dong border, their soles shredded to bloody confetti. She took one last, jerking, mechanical step and then collapsed on the side of the road, four miles from the province of her birth. The dog continued walking south alone.

IN DA LAT, a group of American backpackers waited on the steps of the night market for their shuttle bus. Over the past thirty-six hours they had hiked Lang Biang, seen four different waterfalls, and spent twelve dollars each to drink coffee made from beans that had been passed through the digestive tracts of palm civets. While they waited, one of them scrolled through a Southeast Asia eco-travel blog on their phone while two others chipped dried mud off their trekking boots. The remaining two were watching the orange-and-white dog. It was sleeping at the bottom of the stairs on top of a heap of small, sticky bones—the remnants of the quail carcasses it had scavenged from a barbecue cart and gnawed clean.

"Look, it's dreaming!" said one of the girls to the other. "It's so cute." The little dog was on its back with its four legs in the air, twitching.

"What if we adopted it?" said her friend, who was wearing a thick woolen hat that she had purchased from a market stall, more out of boredom than coldness. "It looks homeless and hungry and I'm sure the hostel wouldn't mind."

"But what would we do with it when we go to Laos?" said the first girl.

The girl in the hat didn't reply. She was still looking at the sleeping dog, but now she was frowning slightly. The dog's twitching had been growing more extreme and convulsive. And the girl didn't know how to explain it, but there was something wrong with the air around the dog; it was as if it were being warped by the little body.

Her friend had now noticed it too. As they watched, a dark puddle appeared beneath the dog and began spreading outward from it in thin, hair-like rivulets.

They were grateful when their shuttle arrived at that moment, saving them from having to admit to each other that they did not want to adopt an incontinent dog with seizures.

EMBARRASSINGLY, THERE WAS A PART OF WINNIE THAT HAD secretly imagined herself becoming a better teacher after Dao's departure. As if, in her absence, Winnie would automatically become the good one, and the academy would hire an inferior new demi-Winnie to occupy the space she had held before. But unfortunately, in the weeks that followed, Winnie continued to be herself.

She did start to give homework though. The same single assignment at the end of each class: "Write five sentences." After the long question-and-answer session about American slang, her students would take turns reading aloud what they'd written at home. This took care of the remainder of the class period, sometimes with a spare five minutes to fill with rote pronunciation exercises. Winnie told them to interpret the homework however they liked. Some of the students wrote simple lists about their likes and dislikes, and others used the assignment as a sort of diary, cataloguing the various banalities in their lives that had transpired since the last class. Winnie even made occasional appearances in them on days when they were feeling less inspired. ("Teacher Winnie is American." "My teacher wears one dress every day." "Our American teacher does not smile a lot.")

The only student that Winnie actively disliked was Hai, a squirrelly man in his early thirties. Every Monday and Wednesday and Friday evening, Hai arrived for class at 6:50, and then, because the rest of the group didn't begin trickling in until quarter past seven, he would sit alone in the room for twenty-five minutes and stare gloomily at the wall while he fiddled with the wrinkled grocery bag full of pens that he always brought with him.

While his clothes were normal—unremarkable outfits of slacks and polo shirts—he wore three long strands of kumquat-sized wooden beads around his neck, one of them with a dangling carved Buddha, and when he wasn't fidgeting with his pens he was nervously twisting the beads in his fingers and accidentally clacking them against his desk or each other. He usually had a sheen of perspiration on his neck and forehead that was unwarranted given the power of the Achievement! air-conditioning system. There was something contagious about his twitchy energy, and if Winnie watched him for too long, she would start feeling anxious and sweaty herself.

She dreaded when it was Hai's turn to read his homework assignments out loud. While her students' fragmented English generally lent their sentences a kind of loose jocularity, there were sometimes flecks of darkness scattered around the edges of what they wrote—allusions to illness, to husbands with bad tempers, to elderly parents and motorbike accidents and theft. Hints in wobbly English about lives in the kinds of neighborhoods that Winnie would never venture into, however far removed she might consider herself from the Cooks and their veggie-burger-yoga-expat stratum. But Hai always outperformed his peers in darkness. His work was incessantly creepy in tone, with subject matter that tended to verge on the hallucinatory.

The first session that the students had shared their homework, nearly all of them had read a variation of the same five-sentence introduction off their sheets of paper: "My name is _____. I am __ years old. I have __ children. I work at _____. I like to study English."

But when it was his turn, Hai cleared his throat and then recited from memory: "My old boss was die. That night his mouth, open so big. I can see the red cloud. Is the red cloud the truth?" Then he looked down at the final sentence in his notebook and frowned, reassessing it upon rereading. Eventually he mumbled out a halfhearted "I like to study English," instead of what was written on the page.

All of the other students burst into applause, but their positive reaction seemed to make him even more melancholy. He just clutched his pen and stared into space with his mouth set in a hard, cheerless line.

After the period ended, he waited for the rest of the class to clear out before he slouched up to Winnie's desk and nervously handed her a piece of notebook paper, its margins scalloped with the translucent half prints of his sweaty thumbs. He had written a long list of Vietnamese terms that he needed assistance translating into English, and Winnie reluctantly agreed to help him, even as she quickly scanned the words and was alarmed to see that they included "exorcism," "ghost," and "demon possession."

Armed with his new vocabulary, Hai's homework only grew more disturbing and less coherent over the following weeks.

"In my old job, I find the ghost. Everything is so nice before we go to the mountains village. My old colleague have demon possess her inside. After, I do not like sleep. Sometimes, I see the red smoke in my dream."

"My old boss with the mouth too big, he was die inside the car. At Saigon, my colleague tells for everyone, 'He is die because he is the old man.' It is the lie! He is die because there is the ghost. As well, maybe he is die because I cannot find the dog. So I only want to make a good tour guide now. This week I write too many sentence. I am sorry my Teacher Winnie."

He always appeared to be deeply anguished when he read his work aloud and was often shaking perceptibly. At the end of class, if he didn't have another list of words to give to Winnie for translation, he would shoot up out of his seat and sprint from the room with his rustling pen bag clenched in one fist.

AS SHE APPROACHED HER sixth month in Saigon, Winnie could feel herself beginning to crumble at the edges. Her eyes had little red veins

in them all the time. She was accidentally walking into walls and starting to be less careful about when she stepped off sidewalks into traffic.
The morning she went to renew her visa again at the Cambodian
crossing point, she drank nearly a quarter of a bottle of vodka before
climbing on the bus, hoping that it would let her sleep for the duration
of the ride and prevent her from thinking about the trip three months
ago, with Long. It worked too well—at the border, after all the other
passengers disembarked, the driver had to come shake her awake in her
seat, scolding her as she finally stumbled off the bus. Later, unsteady
on her feet in the foreign passport line, she tripped face-first into the
hiking backpack of the man ahead of her, hitting a tooth against the
aggressively sleek metal water bottle clipped to its side. The backpack's owner paused his conversation with his friends, about driving
motorbikes from Phnom Penh to Battambang, turned to look at Winnie with equal parts concern and annoyance, but then he decided to
ignore her. After she had her Vietnamese exit stamp, Winnie drunk-
enly contemplated just continuing to walk. Going on into Cambodia
and starting fresh there, with only her passport and straw purse containing her phone, the remainder of the vodka, and a romance novel
set primarily on a rugged Irish cliffside. She could do it, she told herself. She could leave behind all the evidence of her failed, lonely life in
Saigon—leave her dirty room at the Cooks', leave the academy and
her students, who could learn how to correctly pronounce "burrito"
from a better American. Leave Long too, though there was nothing
between Long and herself to even leave in the first place. This time,
she could become the kind of person who drove to Battambang with
friends.

Winnie's feet turned her back toward Vietnam. She didn't think her
karaoke bathroom policeman was the one who stamped her back in,
but she still searched his face when he handed her passport back, to see
if there was any half-buried recognition there. There wasn't, but he
could smell the alcohol on her and wrinkled his nose with distaste.

HER SLEEPLESSNESS WAS STARTING to do funny things to her English. At home, sometimes the Cooks would say something to Winnie, something perfectly normal, something they always said ("Hi, Win, just wanted to ask you—Goji's stool has been a little chalky lately. You haven't been giving him human food by any chance, have you?" "You'll never believe this: today we saw an *actual rat* run out of the kitchen at Gabe and Trinh's restaurant. Never eating there again!" "Listen, Win, Anna made extra smoothie this morning, so help yourself to leftovers in the fridge—everyone needs a mineral boost sometimes!"), and Winnie would be unable to parse what she had heard. The words just rolled off her brain like drops of rain on a waxy lotus leaf. Other times, she would see their mouths make words ("Winnie, we think it might be a good idea for you to talk to someone about what's going on with you."), but her mind would replace what they had said with a Hai-homework sentence about demons and red clouds, or a line from a romance novel, or a string of her students' mind-numbing vocabulary demands. It was as if all of Winnie's English had been loaded carelessly in a washing machine, and now the colors were bleeding.

"My old boss with the mouth too big, he is lose his bag when the night he was die. It has contents of his papers and also of some hairs . . ."

Humblebrag, catfishing, bikini body, friends with benefits.

An email from her parents she already knew she was not going to respond to, accompanied by a photo of her middle brother's pink beach ball of a four-month-old—*Hi Ngoan, your dad and I hope you are having fun on your big adventure! I'm sorry things didn't work out at Bà Cô's house, but we're so happy you're making friends!*

Ridin' dirty, Brangelina, happy hour.

". . . My colleague tell to us, this is secret. She is now lovers with the wife of the mountains villager man! Maybe, I am jealous a little. The mountains villager man, I believe he is die also."

You still haven't sent us your new phone number.

Werewolf, chicken nuggets, auto-tune, thigh gap.

A vivid dream where Winnie was two feet tall and Mrs. Cook picked her up by her tiny arms and said, "Who's a good girl? Who's a good girl? Is it Winnie? Are you being a good girl for Mommy and Daddy?" and Mr. Cook waved a dog treat in her face.

We'd love to hear from you more often.

```
Ronan could resist no longer. Lady Catherine's
auburn hair danced in the wild wind as he drew
her to his sinewy chest, his manhood throbbing
like the waves of the North Atlantic against
the Kerry cliffs.
```

Attaching a sweet photo of Hien and Elliot's new baby—you have another nephew! When you can, let us know the next time you're planning on coming home.

Cannonball, breaststroke, doggy paddle, belly flop.

Love, Mom

ONE NIGHT AFTER CLASS, Hai came up to her desk and asked Winnie if she was all right. He then offered her one of his beaded necklaces, saying that they were for protection.

Winnie smiled, holding back tears. She thanked him for his offer but declined. Then she left the academy and hailed a cab instead of returning to the Cooks' apartment to sit on the windowsill and get through ten sentences of *The Lord of Ballyduff.* The last time she had felt happy, or free, had been in the club at Dao's farewell party. She could find that feeling again, and she didn't need anyone else. She was going to seize it tonight. In her bones, the organ played a warning note.

Back to Bui Vien first. Two beers to start—cans of something cold from a convenience store she stopped into after exiting the cab, too easy for her to toss back in the heat—temporarily granting her a brazenness and a charm that no one would be able to tell was phony, because no one was sober here. The rattle of that inner instrument was already dampened. It was late enough and the sidewalks sufficiently full that there was no longer any distinction made between tables, so Winnie inserted herself among the ranks of the drunk backpackers. She was clinking glasses, and then she was eating skewers of chili-salt pork on a street corner while the world spun. She was taking an offered cigarette even though she did not smoke. She was squatting to pee in the forgiving shadows of a parking lot, warding off sweaty elbows in a nightclub she didn't remember agreeing to go to, and then there were shots, and fingers fumbling at the hem of her linen sack, and then she was vomiting off the back of a motorbike, and then there was nothing, nothing.

WHEN SHE OPENED HER EYES, a man's face was gazing curiously down at her.

Winnie gave a hoarse little shout, which resurrected the taste of the previous night's cigarettes and liquor. "I'm sorry," she squawked, just to be on the safe side, though she didn't yet remember if she had done anything wrong. Or know exactly where she was. She was lying on one side. Her arm hurt. Her cheek was resting on something scratchy. She sniffed, smelled vomit, and prayed that it did not belong to her despite the damning, familiar evidence of a stomach that felt squeezed empty and a tongue that was coated with a yeasty scum. She slowly pushed herself up to a seated position and saw that she was on a sofa in a windowless room she did not recognize. It turned out that the scratchy material beneath her face had been a graphite-colored suit jacket in ultrashiny, possibly flammable polyester.

"I'm glad you're awake. I am the Worm, you are in my nightclub, and that is my jacket." The Worm was indeed wearing its matching shiny trousers. "A few hours ago, you asked if you could use it as a pillow and told me that you were just going to take a five-minute nap. We didn't want to disturb you," he continued with a wry smile, but then his expression suddenly grew sober. "Do you remember anything from last night?" he asked Winnie.

She frowned. This was when the greasy bits of the night before should have conjured themselves up, providing her with a loose outline of the evening's events. But now she discovered, with the same, vertigo-like lurch of walking down a staircase in the dark, anticipating one more step but abruptly meeting the floor instead, that she recalled nothing. "No," she coughed.

The Worm watched Winnie's face carefully. "It's likely that something was slipped into your drink," he said.

Winnie tried once again to dip into her memories and still came up empty. She looked down at her left arm for the first time, wondering why it was so sore, and saw that there was a ring of dark, splotchy bruises on her forearm and lower biceps, like squashed grapes on her skin. A thought occurred to her. She took her right hand and arranged her fingers over one of the bruise clusters to test her theory. Each of them nearly corresponded with one of the grape marks. He had grabbed her here. She moved her hand up to the next cluster. And here. "Who was it?" she asked, wondering if she might lie back down on the coat again. It was making her dizzy, trying to piece together a story with only the clues on her skin. She felt like there were two wires she needed to connect, and if she could only get them to touch, it would all make sense, but they kept missing each other.

The Worm shrugged. "Just some asshole with quick hands," he said. "You can buy the drugs anywhere. I— Oh no." He had noticed Winnie starting to slump sideways again and quickly intervened, steadying her. He retrieved his suit jacket, shook out some of the wrinkles, and gave the jacket a surreptitious sniff. Then he helped Winnie rise unsteadily to her feet. "No more naps; this is a dance club, not a hostel," he gently scolded.

With a bitter ache, Winnie realized that this was probably the longest night's sleep she'd had in weeks.

"Listen," said the Worm. "My boss and I reviewed the footage from the security cameras ourselves, but it wasn't very helpful. We're probably never going to find them."

"Them?" Winnie's skin crawled.

"And even if we did," he smoothly continued over her, "what could we do? You're fine."

"I'm fine," repeated Winnie softly.

"Nothing really serious happened, did it? This was a bit of a scare, but it doesn't have to be a big deal. If you can't even remember it anyway, then what's the harm?" He had pulled out his wallet. "Now, if you go out, turn right, and keep walking for about ten minutes, there's a *bánh ướt* cart right in front of the zoo. Best shrimp cakes in all of Saigon. Why don't you go and get some breakfast and put all this behind you?" He pressed a crisp 500,000₫ bill into Winnie's hand while she tilted her head back to keep her tears in. "Our treat."

BECAUSE SHE DID NOT know what else to do, Winnie went. The two *bánh ướt* women eyed her coldly from behind their cart as they prepared a serving of flabby rice-noodle sheets for her, served heaped up like a pile of damp Kleenex with the famous shrimp cake on top, then drenched in sweetened fish sauce. To Winnie's shame, when they handed her the plate, both of them physically leaned away from her. Winnie knew how badly she smelled and suspected that she looked even worse. They made her pay before eating, worried that she would try to skip out on the bill. Winnie found a stool as far away from them as she could. As she ate, she overheard the noodle ladies settling the bill of a Vietnamese customer, and realized that they had overcharged her by 5,000₫.

Winnie did not think that she felt angry. It was nothing. It was the equivalent of a quarter. But she watched herself quietly take a handful of chopsticks out of the communal basket on the table, break them in half one by one, and drop them onto the ground. *Crack, crack, crack.* She heard the sound each one made as it snapped, but she could not feel them in her hands. Then she rose and left before they could see what she had done.

Because the zoo was there, and because the morning was still cool, Winnie bought a ticket and went in.

She was dizzy again and the shrimp cake was not sitting well with her. Her arm was throbbing, but she refused to let herself look down at the marks on it. The morning light leaching in through the branches of the dipterocarp trees lining the path was tinted bluish at its edges. She heard the little scrabble of rat feet in the bushes, and birds whose calls sounded uncomfortably like human screaming. What had her body done in those hours she could not remember? She had the troubling notion that she was going to start screaming soon too.

She passed an enclosure that appeared to house an extraordinary number of crocodiles and then turned and entered the snake house because it seemed empty. The building was designed like a nautilus, or perhaps like a coiled serpent itself—one long, spiraling hallway. The squeezers were first. Burmese python. Reticulated python. Indian rock python. Winnie read each plaque as she passed but did not spend too long studying the cages' inhabitants. She guessed that the snakes were arranged in order of venomousness. What would be at the center? Pit vipers next. Malayan pit viper. Sumatran pit viper. Tonkin pit viper. Bornean palm pit viper. Every place, it seemed, had their own pit viper. Banded krait. Many-banded krait. Splendid krait. The body of the splendid krait was covered in blue-black markings the exact same shade as Winnie's bruises. That made her the splendid Winnie. Chinese cobra. Monocled cobra. She was almost at the center now. Mandalay cobra. King cobra. And there, in the final vivarium at the end of the hallway, the Indochinese spitting cobra.

"Well, what's so special about you?" she muttered to herself. Then the snake raised its second head. "Oh god!" yelled Winnie, stumbling backward.

Winnie would have described the expression on the snake's face as offended were this not a preposterous notion. She wondered if she was only imagining it; if this was just a hallucination from the last of whatever she had been dosed with as it left her system. "I'm sorry," she said. "You startled me." If the snake was a hallucination, then it was permissible to speak to it. The Indochinese spitting cobra had now lifted itself nearly to her eye level, using a forked branch as a stepladder.

It was pressing itself up against the side of its tank. The slat-like ventral scales of its belly looked like Venetian blinds. Winnie approached the display again. She took a breath, held it for a moment, and as she exhaled, she reached out and placed her hand against the glass, right at the spot beneath the cleft of the two heads, where she imagined its heart was. Or hearts. She kept her eyes averted, and she was quivering, but she did not take her hand away. The snake did not move either. Winnie thought she could feel its body pulsing faintly through the pane. Or perhaps it was just her body's woozy receptors that were giving her the sensation that solids were not as solid as they should be. She pushed harder against the tank, almost believing that the barrier would yield to her, that with a slick pop she would emerge on the other side of the glass. The two-headed snake could take her place out here instead—she wanted to be the one inside the vivarium. She would be happy in there, with just her branch and her cactus and her clear walls. She wouldn't even mind the people who would come to gawk at her, because she was done with being invisible; invisible didn't work. Winnie pushed against the glass with all her strength. The bone at the base of her hand hurt. Finally, she pulled herself back from it.

"Oh, Winnie. What the fuck are you doing?" she laughed to herself, and her laughter tasted like smoke and bile. She needed to go. She needed to sober up. She needed to stop talking to the imaginary snake, which had slid back down the glass again and was leaning to one side like it was cocking its heads at her.

Winnie turned and she started to run. She ran back down the hallway, past the cobras and kraits and pit vipers and pythons. Past the happy Vietnamese children, whose trip to the zoo now featured the surprise appearance of a disheveled, sprinting foreigner. She ran back toward the entrance, pausing only for a few seconds to hack up her undigested shrimp cake into a bin just outside the gates, and then she wiped her mouth on a sleeve and started to run again.

She did not slow down until the sidewalk grew too narrow and crowded, congested by banana and pineapple and sesame donut vendors and drivers who were trying to circumvent red lights by climbing up from the street onto the pavement. And then Winnie finally stopped and leaned against a crumbling concrete wall and gasped for air. When she had recovered her breath, she decided that what she needed more than anything was coffee.

She beckoned to an idle motorbike taxi. When the driver pulled up beside the curb, she asked him what district he lived in.

"Six," he replied, handing her a spare helmet.

"Take me there, please," said Winnie, climbing up behind him.

The elderly *xe ôm* man looked scandalized. "To my house?" he choked.

"Oh, no. No, no, no. Just take me to whatever your favorite coffee shop is in District 6."

Relieved, he started his bike and they rattled off down the road.

The *xe ôm* man ended up selecting a coffee shop that he had clearly never set foot inside but assumed Winnie would like—the front of it was designed to look like a large, pink windmill, there was a white picket fence around the perimeter, and when Winnie looked in through the window she saw that instead of chairs, the shop's clientele (all teenaged girls) sat on tiny tuffets of peach velour. Winnie knew that she could not possibly besmirch a tuffet by depositing her hungover carcass on it, but the *xe ôm* man seemed so enthusiastic about the place when they pulled up that for his sake she pretended to go inside. After he had driven out of sight, she left as fast as she could and wandered down the street to find a coffee shop that seemed grubby enough for her this morning.

No one looked twice at her when she entered Café Max. It had wooden chairs and scuffed black-and-white checkerboard floor tiles and lazy flies circling uncovered cans of condensed milk. Winnie found an empty table between a group of old men yelling at a soccer match and two uniformed middle school students frantically copying each other's homework and glancing over in panic at a clock on the wall every few minutes. She ordered a hot coffee instead of an iced one because she wanted to watch it fall, drip by drip, through the little tin filter and into her glass. There was something soothing about the plipping sound it made. Winnie closed her eyes and pictured herself compressing everything she had experienced last night and this morning into a small, hard seed that she could bury inside herself. The dripping stopped; her coffee was finished brewing. She opened her eyes, set the filter aside, and used a dinky tin spoon to stir in the ribbon of condensed milk at the bottom of the glass. But after two sips Winnie felt vomity again; she got up too quickly, and her chair legs scraped against the floor with a noise that made her cringe.

"Bathroom?" she asked the mustachioed man unrumpling small notes at the cash register. He gestured down a back hallway. Winnie passed a storage room and a kitchen before rounding a corner and finding the toilet behind a sliding door—a little ceramic squatter with a green plastic bucket of flushing water. She leaned against the wall for five minutes while waiting to see whether or not she would throw up, and when she eventually decided that she didn't need to, she hiked up her dress and squatted to take a piss instead. When she stood back up she discovered that her pee was a disheartening egg-yolk hue and frowned down at it. Suddenly her nostrils flared. She leaned toward the toilet and sniffed; impossible as it sounded, her urine smelled like smoke. How many cigarettes had she smoked last night? Winnie quickly tilted in some water from the green bucket to flush it away. But the fumes were still there, stronger even, even after the pee was gone. Winnie panicked briefly, imagining that the coffee shop had started to go up in flames and she would burn to death in the toilet. But when she threw open the door and stepped out into the hallway, she realized the scent was much too faint, a fragrance that was somewhere between woodsmoke and incense and tobacco. It wasn't coming from her pee or from the front of the coffee shop but from farther down the hall. Winnie checked to make sure she was alone before starting toward what smelled like the source.

At the very end of the hallway there was a staircase that led to the second and third stories of the building, a small box altar in the alcove beneath the stairs, and across from it, a sliding glass door, half-open, leading to a walled-in patio. In the center of the patio there was a metal ash bucket leaking smoke, with little fingertips of flame just visible at its lip. Next to the bucket, reclining on a beach chair with a rusting metal frame, was a very old man smoking a cigarette.

He saw Winnie looking at him through the door before she could slink away. "Come in!" he called, crooking the index of his free hand at her. "You wouldn't happen to be half French, would you?" he added as she tentatively stepped out onto the patio.

Winnie shook her head. "Half American. My mom is Irish and Italian, I think?"

"Ah, so we're different mixes then," said the old man. "A pity. I haven't had anyone to speak French with for years. I never thought I'd miss it back when I was . . . Well, when I was younger. Whatever your blood, you can pull up a seat and then we'll get started." He gestured to a corner of the patio that held a terra-cotta planter of red and green chilies and a three-legged wooden stool.

Winnie obediently retrieved the stool and positioned it at what she hoped was a polite distance from the man. She did not know what else to do. He was barefoot and bareheaded, his nut-brown scalp bald and gleaming in the sunlight, and he wore dark dress pants that were a bit too short and exposed the skin at his ankles. He also had on a yellowing undershirt and an oversized black cardigan, despite the midmorning humidity. The clearest indicator of his Europeanness was the white beard covering most of his face, much bushier and more luxuriant than the ones she usually saw on Vietnamese men, who tended to cultivate wispy, Ho Chi Minh–esque chin whiskers. Apart from Dutch Alex's baby and herself, this old man was the only other mix she knew in this city. They made an odd trio.

"Beg your pardon, but what are we starting?" asked Winnie nervously.

The man grinned and extended his hand. "Jean-François Auffret, fortune teller, à votre service."

"Ngoan," said Winnie, reaching out her own. She didn't know why she had said it. It had flopped out of her mouth unintentionally. Maybe it was because she was afraid of lying to a fortune teller. Or maybe she just couldn't bear to be Winnie anymore right now.

They shook hands, but instead of letting Winnie's hand go after-ward, Monsieur Auffret flipped it over so that the palm was facing up. Then he abruptly started to squish the flesh on her fingers, scrunching the hand up and kneading her phalanges. Winnie suppressed a yelp.

"This is the old-fashioned way of reading it," he said, without re-leasing her hand. He prodded the meatier part of her palm, by the thumb, and pinched her wrist bone. "Not very popular anymore, but often more accurate than a birth chart. Hands can't lie. To be honest, I prefer this method. I don't have the head for numbers and stars any-more, now that I'm retired. Well, mostly retired. I still come back sometimes to do these little backyard readings because I have nothing else to do. It's much less exciting than you'd think, the part that comes after. I even grew this beard because I was so bored."

Monsieur Auffret flipped Winnie's hand back over to study the web of lines on each of her knuckles. Then he went over her fingernails one by one, tilting them in the weak sunlight, looking closely at the white spots or ridges on some. Finally, he folded Winnie's fingers closed over her own palm like an envelope and returned her hand to her. He reached over to tap the ash of his neglected cigarette out into his bucket. The corner of Winnie's mouth twitched nervously as the loose sleeve of his sweater dangled right above the fire. Then she blinked and she frowned—now the sleeve was *in* the fire, but somehow it wasn't burn-ing. It was as if the flames had parted around it, repelled by a magnetic force. Winnie shook her head. Just more hungover vision tricks.

Monsieur Auffret had returned his arm to the safety of the beach chair. "It's a confusing one," he said. "I can't get a whole picture for you—only half snatches. You will be moving somewhere new soon. And you will be going to the sea, but at the same time, you will never go to the sea again. I'm sorry if that seems like a riddle, but it's all that I could decipher. Watch what you eat and drink. Be very careful about what you put into your body."

"That advice would have been very useful about twelve hours ago," Winnie said with a pained half smile. She saw Monsieur Auffret's eyes take in the bruises on her arm for the first time. He did not ask her about them, and she was grateful. She did not want to know what he could read on the skin there.

"This is a stubborn hand," he finally continued, and his voice was gentle. "But its grip is weak. That is an unlucky combination. A hand that does not heed warnings. It insists on choosing for itself, but it does not choose wisely. Tell me, do you sleep well at night?"

"No," said Winnie.

"Ah. I thought so, but I could tell that from your face, not from your palm. Also, it is going to rain soon, but I know that from the tingling in my arthritic jaw. That will be 10,000đ for the reading, please."

Winnie took out her wallet and leafed through what remained of the money she had been given at the nightclub. She didn't have any bills smaller than a fifty. "Do you have change?" she asked him.

"Let me see," said Monsieur Auffret. He took Winnie's stack of đồng from her, and then promptly dropped all of it into his fire. She couldn't suppress a little squeak of surprise, and this made him laugh so hard the legs of his beach chair shook.

"Oh, I'm sure you've accidentally thrown away more American dollars than this in your lifetime," he hooted. "You didn't need any of it anyway. Now look—look at the smoke. I'm sending it up to the heavens to see if it can intercede on your behalf. That's the best use for it."

The flames in the bucket had gobbled up the plastic polymer notes, adding an acrid tang to the air and a murky umber hue to the smoke rising from it in intertwined coils.

Winnie wasn't sure how she should respond. "Thank you?" she offered, after a beat. Then it began to dawn on her: "I— I don't have enough money to pay for my coffee," she stuttered, only realizing it fully as the words left her mouth. "That was all that I had on me." She flashed her empty wallet at Monsieur Auffret.

"Here, give me one of those unlucky hands and help an old man out of his chair." He extended his bony arms, and Winnie gently steadied him while he rose. He pointed to the far corner of the walled-in patio; "It's not as high as you'd think," he said. "It's very climbable. And on the other side there's an alley—turn left and it'll take you past a meat market, and you can find your way home from there. Come on! Bring your stool." He padded across the concrete on his bare feet, Winnie trotting behind him obediently with the stool in her arms. She set it down beside the wall and then tested one foot on the seat, frowning as its legs wobbled. She had never been very coordinated, and the events of last night had made her limbs even less reliable than usual.

"Here," said Monsieur Auffret, bending into a half crouch and bracing himself against the wall. He laced his hands at chest level to form a makeshift rung and offered it to Winnie.

"But I'm heavy," she protested. "I don't want to hurt you!"

He grinned. "That's something to be proud of! It's the American milk you grew up drinking—you all have very dense bones! But don't worry, you can't hurt me."

Winnie climbed up onto the stool. When she stood on tiptoe her hands could just cup the edge of the wall. She wiped her hands dry of sweat on her dress and put them back up in position. "Ready?"

"Ready! Now, up and over!" said Monsieur Auffret.

It felt unforgivably rude to step on him, but Winnie had no other choice. She hefted her filthy-sneakered right foot up onto his hands and balanced herself on her left leg.

"One! Two! Three!" she counted quickly, and then launched herself from the stool, switching her weight to the foot in his hands. Her triceps quivered as she heaved herself up, and she hoped that he couldn't see her underwear from this angle. The rubber sole of her free left foot scrabbled for an instant before finding traction. One scratchy instant more, and the leg reached the top of the wall. She swung it over to the other side, intending to sit straddled there for a minute while she thanked Monsieur Auffret, but instead she lost her balance and tumbled backward, landing on alleyway concrete with a loud smack.

Her tailbone was stinging and the arm that she had stuck out to break her fall was scraped and oozing red from wrist to elbow. There was some gravel in it. It was the same arm that bore the bruises, and Winnie was almost glad that she had cut it, that there was a fresh injury supplanting the old one. Now she could tell herself that the bruise was just from the fall too. Gritting her teeth, she slowly got to her feet. It was strangely quiet in the narrow alley, and although she knew that it had to just be a trick of the light, the concrete wall seemed several feet higher from this side. It wasn't as sunny either—the alley was lined on both sides by other tall fences and the windowless brick backs of row houses. Winnie could no longer smell the smoke and ash from the old man's fire bucket.

"I'm okay!" she called, hoping he could hear her on the other side. She waited. "Thank you!" she yelled, louder this time. Her voice echoed off the surrounding walls, and she winced at how shrill it sounded. There was no response. Winnie couldn't remember which way was supposed to lead to the market. The alley was deserted to either side as far as she could see before it curved out of her line of vision. She wondered why there weren't any passing motorbikes, for this surely had to be a useful shortcut to somewhere. Eventually she decided to limp left, imagining that the distant, muffled buzz of traffic she heard was coming from that direction.

The alleyway gradually widened, and to her relief, Winnie caught sight of market stalls. After a few more steps she could smell hot blood. It was nearly ten now, most of the morning shoppers had already bought their groceries and gone, and so the idle vendors gossiped with each other or were engrossed in their cellphones. Winnie made her way down the row of stalls largely unnoticed. A whole hairy pig's face, stretched out wide and grinning on a wooden board alongside deconstructed pink stacks of its body, greeted her first. There were several other pork stands, and women who sold only the blood—congealed and sliced into lipstick-colored cakes—or the bones, or the fat. There were chickens and ducks across a wide spectrum: unhatched inside their speckled eggshells (they would be simmered and eaten late at night on street corners, their partially developed embryos sprinkled with pepper and scraped out with little spoons); squawking in wicker baskets on the ground; newly decapitated and twitching in plucking buckets; featherless and headless and on cutting boards. Some women sold bundles of herbs along with the meats they traditionally accompanied—basil and sawtoothed quills of culantro beside the marrow and knuckle bones destined for the phở pots, purple perilla and laksa leaves and lemongrass by the chickens.

The sky had grown darker without Winnie realizing, and the first raindrops landed on her bare shoulders just as she reached the end of the market. Winnie looked around at her new surroundings: the alley had opened out onto a broader and much more inhabited lane—there were storefronts and sidewalks and houses and motorbikes again. Drivers were pulling over to the side to take plastic ponchos out from under their seats, tugging them over helmeted heads and then billowing off down the road again. It had started drizzling steadily, but Winnie kept meandering onward. She didn't know where she was, she had no plan for getting back to the Cooks' apartment, and the pebbly cuts on her arm stung when the rain ran down it. Her wet dress was clinging crookedly to her thighs and breasts and armpits in unflattering ways, and she was shivering, but Winnie could feel her hangover washing away, and she imagined that she hadn't lost just her memories of last night but of everything that came before it as well. It was a full downpour now, and she was so wet that she saw no reason to stay on the sidewalk. She stepped down into the gutter and strode along, ankle deep, then midcalf deep. It was filthy; the rain had swept up all manner of blood and feathers and tiny bones from the meat market. But Winnie was filth too, wasn't she? She let her sneakers fill with brown water, laughing at the loud sloshing she made.

Something brushed against her leg. Winnie stopped laughing and looked down. Just a bit of plastic tubing, or an old toy, she told herself. But it hadn't felt like trash. It had felt alive. Winnie took two more difficult steps against the deluge. It touched her again, and Winnie knew that it was something long and smooth and scaled and muscly. Then she saw it ahead of her. Just a glimpse at first—a slick black body breaking the skin of the water, just like those dubiously grainy photos of the Loch Ness monster. It was weaving down the gutter. And Winnie followed it.

It never revealed its whole body to her, but she guessed that it was nearly six feet in length, based on the occasions when multiple curves of coil were visible simultaneously. Winnie did not keep track of where she was going. She just kept her eyes fixed on the rippling water in front of her. What was left of her rational inner voice insisted that this was another hallucination, that she was seeing snakes because she still had the zoo on her mind, but this did not stop her from continuing to trudge through sewage after her creature.

Because she could not look away from the gutter thing and risk losing it, Winnie did not notice that the downpour was letting up. A sudden beam of sunshine slicing through the clouds and illuminating the last gasp of raindrops caught her off guard. Winnie turned her gaze heavenward for a split second in surprise and, when she looked back down, saw the black shape wriggling down a storm drain, lost to her forever. Her last image of it was a speckled reptilian tail disappearing beneath the sidewalk.

She looked at her surroundings. The gutter guide had left her in a narrow alley. The houses here were small and old and seemed like they were a single stiff breeze away from all collapsing onto one another. Winnie pushed back several soaking strands of hair from her forehead, wiped her eyes, and squinted at a marigold-yellow house across from her that was so skinny it looked like it had been illegally built into the crevice between two other buildings. She recognized the white motorbike parked in front of it. And she recognized the man who was shaking the last of the raindrops off the two large jackets he had draped protectively over its seats and handlebars.

Winnie could not bring herself to call out to him. She wanted him to go back inside before he saw her dripping all over his alleyway.

But Long looked up. He saw her and he blinked. "Winnie?"

LONG WAS ONLY PLANNING ON BRINGING ONE BAG WITH HIM to Saigon in the morning and knew he didn't need much time to pack. So after helping his mother bundle up her unsold lychees at the market and washing their sticky juices from his arms, he decided to head straight to Fat Uncle's—the *quán nhậu* at the edge of town. As he approached the restaurant he saw Binh's battered Honda Super Cub parked at a crooked angle next to Tan's motorbike. This indicated that the two had arrived separately, which relieved Long, but also meant that Binh had shown up already drunk, which worried him anew. Since dropping out of school to work full-time in her family's cashew orchard, Binh had found herself with a surplus of long, solitary hours to spend in the trees with her uncle's old army canteen, which she had appropriated and kept filled with her own mixture of rice wine and sugarcane pulp.

She had been furious when Long told her he would be going to a university in Saigon instead of attending one in Dak Lak or Gia Lai or even Lam Dong. He would never admit it, but part of the reason that Long had ended up taking the scholarship in the city was so that he could see what Binh's reaction would be. When Tan had left for the police academy two years earlier, it had briefly been the happiest time in Long's life. He had been so sure that without his brother, he and Binh would become closer. That she would realize that she and Long had never really needed him. Instead, she had left high school a month into their new semester. She and Long only really saw each other when he came over with books for her to borrow or if she wanted a drinking buddy. Most of the time, she didn't.

So her reaction at his leaving had filled him with joy. Long would not have been able to bear it if she had been indifferent. Her anger meant everything to him. It felt almost life-sustaining. She refused to speak to him. For three weeks, whenever he came by the orchard with apology books for her, she disappeared into the high branches where he could not follow. His good soccer shoes mysteriously disappeared in the middle of the night, and a few days later he noticed canvas scraps and pieces of undigested rubber in the dung of his neighbor's pigs when he walked past the pen. But eventually she seemed to make peace with Long's departure. She was the one who had insisted on holding the going-away party tonight at Fat Uncle's.

BINH SPOTTED HIM AS he walked in and waved him over from the table in the back corner that she preferred. She hadn't changed out of her dirty work coveralls, and there was a tiny twig in her ponytail. Tan was seated across from her, looking sallow and dyspeptic in his green uniform—he had driven up to Ia Kare two days ago and would be taking Long back to Saigon with him in the morning, as Long had no motorbike of his own, and his motion sickness ruled out the bus.

"Look who else is here," Binh hissed to Long as he slid into the plastic chair next to her.

At first Long thought she was referring to the fact that there were two other women in Fat Uncle's tonight, which was an unusual occurrence. They were sharing a sarsaparilla soda and making uncomfortable conversation with each other while the boyfriends they were accompanying took shots of rice wine and ignored them.

But then Long realized that Binh was talking about Old Ma, the richest man in Ia Kare and second richest in the Ea Sup district, who was sitting a few tables away with a small group of workers from his pepper fields. Two crates of beer were stacked beside their table, and the empty bottles were lined up on the floor to make room for all of their plates of food. They were eating frog legs cooked in so much chili that Long's nostrils itched from across the room, rectangular cakes of fermented pork parceled up in banana leaves, and the roasted bones of something that might have been rabbit. Long tried to add up in his head how expensive it all must have been but wasn't exactly sure how much a crate of Saigon Red cost, because he had never bothered to look at the beer prices on the back of the menu, knowing he could not afford it. As usual, tonight Binh had ordered them Fat Uncle's musty home-brewed rice wine, steeped with roots that turned it the color of fish sauce and gave it a medicinal aftertaste. It was so cheap that it came served in old plastic water bottles with the labels scrubbed off. Tan, who disliked alcohol, was sipping from a carton of corn-flavored milk, his favorite drink and the beverage of choice for young children with stomachaches. Long saw that Tan had also already polished off half of their plate of fried rice, so he quickly spooned out a small bowlful for Binh and another for himself before it could all vanish.

"Not so fast," said Binh. "Drinks first! And as punishment for being late you have to do three." She grabbed Tan's untouched glass, lined it up next to hers and Long's, then poured out the shots and slid them over, only sloshing a little of the liquor onto the table in the process. Long downed them in rapid succession, trying not to breathe between glasses in order to delay the burning. He wasn't a very good drinker, but he did it for Binh. It was something the two of them shared that she and Tan did not.

She had turned her attention back to the Ma table. "Look at how uncomfortable they are. They don't want to *nhậu* with their boss—it's so awkward. They can't get too drunk, but they can't stay too sober either, or they'll offend him. They can't curse, they can't spit their bones out onto the floor . . ."

"Can't eat with their fingers," added Long, watching as one of the farmhands struggled to maintain his chopstick grip on a chili-slick frog leg. Another was making an ostentatious show of opening a new beer and pouring it into Mr. Ma's glass. The backs of his hands and neck were tanned to a deep brown shade nearly identical to that of the glass bottle.

Binh cackled under her breath. "I know they're getting a free dinner, but I feel sorry for them. All that the poor bastards want is to get drunk at home, in their underwear, in peace."

Tan was feeling left out, because his back was to the group of pepper farmers and he couldn't turn around to look at them without being too obvious. He took a gulp of his corn milk and wiped his mouth with his hand. "You're just jealous," he said to Binh.

Binh cocked her head dangerously. "What do you mean by that, Kitten?"

"It's more than etiquette," said Tan. "It's important. It's ritual. So they have to chew with their mouths closed for one night. So what? They know that it's what you do. It's not really about table manners, it's about respect. Order. Tradition. It's a man thing. *You* can't understand it because you're a girl, and so you're jealous." He took another smug sip of milk.

"Or maybe I actually understand it better than you, because *I* know how to drink and *you* can't hold your liquor," said Binh, knocking back another glass with a grin.

"He sort of creeps me out," Long said absently, his eyes still fixed on the craggy profile of Old Ma. "I know the stories about his daughter probably aren't true, but I always get . . . *shivery* if I see him around town."

"I heard a new one about her," said Binh, dropping her voice, and Long instantly regretted bringing up the subject and quickly tried to think of another one to change it to.

"No." Tan shook his head emphatically. "I don't want to hear it. I don't care."

Binh ignored him. "It's a good one. When the guy from the processing plant in Ea Drang came to pick up some bags from us we started talking. He has a cousin here whose son was at school around the same time as the Ma girl, but a few years younger. The kid didn't know her all that well, but he remembered when she went missing—he was eleven then."

"Then I'm sure he's *very* reliable," Tan muttered under his breath.

"He didn't see her again for two more years," continued Binh. "Until the midautumn festival they hold at the school. He said that he was in the back, trying to climb a fig tree to get a better view of the lantern parade, but he slipped down the trunk and then stumbled backward into the girl by accident. She was by herself—her parents had probably taken her out to watch the parade, and she must have gotten separated from them in the crowd. The boy said that he turned to her and apologized, and she just smiled at him. He didn't recognize her yet, but she made him uneasy, because she was scary thin and her clothes were fancy, but her hair was dirty, and her smile kept moving around her face."

Binh dropped her voice down to a whisper. "She said to him, 'Don't you remember me? I'm the girl who was lost. They thought that they had saved me, but they found me too late.' Then she brought her face right up to his, and she said: 'Because the many-headed serpent had changed me already.' The Ma girl smiled, and then . . ." Binh suddenly slammed her hands down. The keys to her motorbike jangled on the table and one of the empty shot glasses toppled over. "And then she flicked her tongue out of her mouth and it was forked!" Long jumped in his chair; Tan rolled his eyes. "And skinny and black and ten inches long! She tickled the tip of his nose with the pointy ends of it!" Binh made a V with the middle and index fingers of one hand and waggled them in Tan's face to demonstrate. "And then she just slurped the tongue back up into her mouth, like a big noodle. He ran away. Was too terrified to tell anyone about it for years."

"Ugh," said Long, shuddering.

"I'm sure your cashew man from Ea Drang was glad that he impressed you with his little story," smirked Tan. "Did he ask you for a quickie behind the pigpen afterward? Did you let him?"

"Oh, you're disgusting," said Binh.

"*You're* disgusting—look how dirty your nails are," said Tan, reaching across the table for her fingers and then holding them up for inspection. "How often are you bathing?"

"Another drink," Long said quickly, interrupting them. He poured out a glass for Binh and pushed it into the hand that Tan was touching.

"How many heads?" Binh pondered aloud, bringing the glass to her lips. "How many heads does it take to make a many-headed serpent? Two? Three? Twelve?"

"Oh my god, he's looking right at us!" hissed Long under his breath. "He must have heard you!"

Old Ma had turned all the way around in his chair and was staring at the trio in the corner. The workers at his table were all following suit. Tan, with his back safely to them, shrugged and reached his spoon out for more fried rice, while Long froze in place.

But Binh lifted her hand and gave Old Ma a debonair wave. "Respect," she said, flicking her gaze over to Tan. "Order. Tradition. Right? So, let's go!" She rose to her feet and slapped the back of Long's chair. He tried to shake his head no while making as little movement as possible, knowing that the other table was watching him, but finally stood up too. "Well, Kitten? Are you coming?" Binh picked up the bottle of rice wine in one hand and her keys in the other and then strode off across the restaurant, Long following nervously behind. Tan finished chewing before he joined them.

"Uncle!" Binh greeted Old Ma, slathering the politesse on thick enough to conceal her contempt. "It would be an honor to invite you to share a drink with us."

Old Ma sized Binh up, taking in the twig in her hair and the red mud on the soles of her boots but also the swell of her breasts in her coveralls. "Do I know your parents?" he asked. The deep wrinkles on his face looked like cracks in a dry rice paddy. Long had expected his voice to be sonorous and grand, like what a buffalo would sound like if it could speak. Instead it was reedy and a little hoarse.

"*I* don't even know my parents," laughed Binh. "I think they're both dead. I was adopted by my aunt and uncle when I was a baby."

"But these are Duc Phan's boys," said Old Ma, looking past her at Tan and Long now. "Your father and my late brother fought together. Put that away," he said, indicating the bottle of murky rice wine with distaste. "We'll toast your father's memory, but not with that garbage. Sit down here—make room for them, Field Rat!" Long did not want to drink with Old Ma, and he certainly did not want to drink to the memory of Duc Phan, but the man they called the Field Rat was already reluctantly scooting down to the end of the table, and a waiter had brought over three new chairs and three new sets of glasses, bowls, and chopsticks. Binh made herself comfortable in the seat beside Old Ma and tossed her motorbike keys down on the tabletop. Another one of the farmhands bent over to take new beers out of the crate, but Long, who was now the youngest at the table, deferentially knelt and retrieved them first. He served them carefully, topping up Old Ma's glass first and then moving counterclockwise around the table to fill those of the farmhands. He made sure to pour extra generously when he got to Tan and could feel his brother working to maintain an expression that did not reveal how much he disliked beer. Long gave himself and Binh slightly less than the others, because he was worried that she was getting drunk too quickly, but Old Ma himself snatched the bottle out of his hands and proceeded to fill their glasses to the brim.

"Shall we start with fifty percent?" he asked, making a slash with his finger halfway up the side of the glass.

"Oh, I couldn't possibly drink on an empty stomach," said Binh sweetly, with her eyebrows raised. Old Ma gave a wheezy chuckle and waved the waiter over again.

"Order whatever you like," he said to Binh. "This is a special occasion—it isn't every day a lady joins us and we get to drink to the memory of the great Duc Phan."

Binh didn't bother to look at the menu. "Beef."

"Two plates of fried beef topped with pickled onions," said Old Ma to the waiter. "And then some *bò lá lốt*." Long heard Tan's stomach burble. "Is that enough beef? In the meantime," he said, gesturing to their uneaten frog legs, "you'll have to help us make some room on the table. Field Rat, fill up her bowl for her."

Long felt sorry for Field Rat, who obligingly leaned over to serve Binh a pair of oily amphibian thighs and a chunk of blackened mystery flesh from the dish at the center of the table. His hair was still damp, and the skin on the back of his neck looked recently scrubbed. Long imagined that he had sped home after work to shower carefully and change into his good clothes before coming to drink with his boss. He wore jeans that looked tight and shiny and cheaply made, and a striped polo shirt that was too big; the sleeves of it came down past his elbows.

Binh speared the morsel of charred meat with her chopsticks and waved it aloft. "What's this?" she asked.

Old Ma grinned. "Dog. It's very good for women to eat, you know. Especially pregnant ones." He watched, with an expression that Long didn't like, as Binh gnawed the flesh off of the bone. "Are you able to drink now?" he said when she had finished swallowing.

Binh flicked her cleaned bone onto the floor and then picked up her beer. "Your men won't be coming into work tomorrow—they'll be too embarrassed that a girl outdrank them," she said, and they clinked glasses.

Their first toasts were predictable fare—they drank to the memory of Duc Phan, who had apparently saved a comrade's life in the jungles of Kon Tum, and to the good health of Binh's aunt and uncle, to Tan's continued success at the police academy, and to Long's university scholarship. With each one, half a beer was drained. One of the crates was emptied and cleared away by the waiter. The beef dishes arrived, and Long had to concentrate hard to keep from dropping his chopsticks or the meat onto the floor.

By the time the table was halfway through the second crate, the toasts that Old Ma proposed were growing more and more outlandish. They drank to Field Rat someday finding a wife who would put up with his overbearing mother, they drank to the lucky sixth toe on another farmhand's foot, they drank to Tan and Long encouraging their fat grandma to take up aerobics. Binh's language became saltier with each empty beer bottle that was retired to the ground, but her profanity only seemed to amuse Old Ma. Long found himself needing to grip the edge of the table to keep from feeling spinny. His brother's face had turned a magenta shade that contrasted horribly with his uniform— Tan was drunk despite the fact that since sitting down, he had been keeping his pint glass filled with ice and cupping it between his hot hands so it would melt faster and dilute the beer. Old Ma had wagered that if Tan could make it until Fat Uncle's closing time without needing to go throw up (as the six-toed farmhand had already done), he would put in a good word for him with the police captain he knew in Pleiku. Long wished that the bet was with him instead, because even though he was notorious for vomiting on the bus, he always kept everything down when he was drinking. He knew he shouldn't like Old Ma—the man had to be bad, there was no way that he could be so rich if he wasn't—but could not help but need his approval. He found himself constantly wishing for the man's attention to turn to him, and when it did, a warm mix of pride and gratitude at being noticed would wash over his whole body. It was the same kind of potent magnetic pull that Binh also possessed.

The restaurant was beginning to empty out. The two bored girls had left with their stumbling boyfriends a while ago. The six-toed farmhand could no longer hold himself up in his chair, and so one of the others had to take him home, apologizing profusely to Old Ma for not staying until the end of the night. When Binh stood up to go to the bathroom, her chair toppled onto its side. She kicked it out of the way instead of picking it up and walked to the toilets with one steadying hand held against the wall.

Old Ma himself rose and righted the fallen chair. "That girl is a savage," he chuckled, and Long loathed himself for laughing along with the others. Then Old Ma picked up her motorbike keys from the table and tossed them to Field Rat, who slipped them into his pants pocket. Tan, who had been bent over trying to sneakily breathe hot air onto the ice in his glass, did not notice, but Long saw, and turned to Old Ma, baffled. Old Ma held a finger up to his lips.

Binh sauntered back to the table. Her hair was all wet—she had clearly been splashing water on her face in the bathroom. "Uncle," she announced, "thank you for the food and the beer. But it's time for us to go now." She rested a hand on Long's shoulder, and he turned his head what he hoped was an imperceptible amount so that his chin could subtly graze her fingernails. "They have an early drive down to Saigon, and I want to go buy dried squid from Bà Ly around the corner before she closes her stall. It's the only thing that cures my hangovers." She reached around behind her bowl, expecting her fingers to meet her keys, and frowned when they did not. Quickly she patted down the pockets of her coveralls, and then she began to push aside every bowl on the table and look underneath each platter. Long watched Old Ma curb a smile starting at the edges of his wrinkled mouth.

"Should you really be driving in your condition?" asked Old Ma.

Binh blinked, and suddenly she seemed dangerously sober. "Who took them?" she said.

"I'm sure they've just fallen on the ground; Long, why don't you help her look for them?" He gave Long a perfectly bland smile, and Long found himself kneeling down beneath the table and going through the motions of rummaging through the empty bottles. His feet slipped on Binh's chewed-up bones. "If you can't find them, you can just come home with me," he heard Old Ma saying above him. "I'll have a new set for you made in the morning. I can give you a whole new motorbike, if that's easier. No? All right, how about this," he added cagily. "If you give one of us a kiss, you'll get your keys back." Long stared up at him from the floor. The old man's smile had widened slightly. "Anyone you like; you can pick one of your friends if you'd prefer. Just one sweet little kiss."

Binh looked from Tan to Long, from Long back to Tan. Long's heart sank. Her upper lip had curled up and was twitching. "Tell me where my fucking keys are," she snarled at Tan.

"I don't know what you did with them!" Tan bellowed back.

Binh picked up an empty bottle by the neck. "Tell me where they are." Everyone who still remained at Fat Uncle's was watching their table now.

"I told you that I don't know!"

She smashed the bottle against his knee. It did not bleed immediately—after the noise of the cracking glass and Tan's single, sharp cry, everyone at the table looked down and saw that his pants were torn, but that the leg seemed fine otherwise. There was a moment of stasis. And then, as they were watching, blood suddenly came seeping through the olive fabric, a scarlet patch like a handprint with long fingers stretching down his calf. Binh had dropped the jagged remains of the bottle onto the ground and was reaching for a new one.

"Wait! He has them!" cried Long from the ground, pointing to Field Rat. He could not bring himself to look at Old Ma, and so he met Binh's eyes instead. And for one terrifying instant she gazed at Long with an expression that was not rage but the kind of hollowness that he knew from his mother's face. He was relieved when anger replaced it once more and she turned to the Field Rat, her grip tightening on the bottle's neck.

"Do not strike him," said Old Ma calmly. "You've had your fun, and we've had ours. Now you're getting out of hand. You can do whatever you like to your friends, but you will not assault my workers. If you do, there will be consequences. Do you understand? Think of your aunt and uncle. Now, put down that bottle. Field Rat, stand up please."

Long half expected Binh to ignore him and attack the man anyway, but she slowly set the beer bottle down on the table.

"Very good. Your motorbike keys are in his right pants pocket. No, no!—don't *you* move, Field Rat. Just stand right there; she has to come and get them herself. Well, girl? What are you waiting for?" Binh shot him a look of pure poison and walked over to Field Rat, who waited with his arms slightly raised from his sides, a sloppy grin on his face.

Because his pants were so tight, she couldn't just quickly reach in and snatch out the keys. Binh had to wriggle her hand down into the pocket. Long could see the outline of each of her fingers through the thin, shiny denim. When she finally grabbed hold of the keys her hand got briefly stuck, and she had to tug several times before finally getting free. Field Rat snickered. Binh did not look at any of them again. She spat onto the table and then ran out of the restaurant with her head bowed. Long heard her engine revving shortly afterward.

"Binh." He breathed the word rather than saying it; his exhalation took the shape of her name. Forgetting that his brother's knee was bleeding all over the floor, no longer caring about the approval of Old Ma, Long stumbled out after her.

She was already gone, of course, and he stood in the street for a minute, wondering what he should do. He wobbled over to Bà Ly's squid stall and purchased two, asking the woman to just bag them up for him without grilling them first. He was convinced that if he could just find Binh and deliver the squid to her, she would forgive him.

Long searched for her in every tree in the cashew orchard. He walked around and around the cemetery, too drunk to be frightened, calling her name. When his feet grew too sore to keep going, he dragged himself over to the statue of the weeping woman and climbed the base. It had seemed so enormous when they were children, but now he could scale it with little effort in the dark. Clutching the squid bag in his teeth, he pulled himself up to the dead soldier and lay himself down across the stone body, assuming its pose. Then he waited. Sometime before dawn, Binh came blistering into the graveyard on foot, with Tan limping after her.

He was too far away to make out exactly what they were saying, but Long could hear dislocated strands of the argument echoing off of tombstones when they raised their voices.

". . . because I would *never* lie to you . . ."

". . . all along! . . . a fucking coward . . ."

". . . do you know how long I . . ."

". . . nothing! Nothing!" followed by pottery shattering against stone—it sounded like Binh had kicked a grave vase. Then they walked on in hostile silence, Tan lagging a few steps behind and struggling to keep up.

Their two angry shapes were drawing closer to the statue. They were almost at the cluster of graves where, twelve years ago, they had agreed to a wager with a monster in a hat. Suddenly, Tan sprinted forward to plant himself directly in Binh's path. Moonlight lacquered the dark blood on his knee. It daubed its pearlescence onto his hair, onto Binh's hair, onto the rounded toes of Binh's rubber boots. Long shrank away from it, clinging to the shadows in the lap of the statue, trying not to rustle the squid bag.

"So then hit me again!" Tan roared at Binh. "You can take out the other leg this time!"

Binh said nothing. Long counted eleven quick heartbeats swooshing against his chest as he watched her stand still and look at Tan. Then she reached up and pulled his head down to hers. Long would never forgive the moon for making him see Binh's face when she kissed him. He did not count it in heartbeats, but it was long enough that he knew there had been hunger in it. It was long enough that Tan's fingers found their way into her hair.

Binh broke away first, pushing Tan aside and then beginning to walk again.

"There. I did it," she said, without looking back at him. "I lost, and I did it, and now I never want to see you again."

"Binh."

"Don't follow me anymore. I'm going to go to the only place where you're too afraid to follow, and I'm going to stay in there until you're gone."

She had picked up speed now. She was running toward the rubber plantation. Tan could not match her pace, and he stopped anyway once he saw where she was going. "You can't!" he called, his voice cracking in a way that Long knew his brother was ashamed of. "It's not safe!" Binh never looked back. She entered the trees without hesitating. A flash of white boots and she was gone.

Tan stood at the edge of the forest and Long lay on the statue, neither of them moving. She had been right; they were too afraid to follow. Eventually Tan turned and began to walk back across the graveyard in the direction of their home.

Now you can run in and save her, Long told himself. *It could still be you.*

He climbed down from the statue, but he did not go into the rubber trees. He knew it had not been Binh's first time.

WHEN HE RETURNED TO the house Tan was asleep, his bloody pants on the ground beside the wooden bed. In the last of the wasting darkness, Long finally started packing. His small backpack only held three identical outfits, his paperwork, Binh's old tamarind tin—which she had forgotten to take back years ago and he had never returned—and the two dried squid. He finished as the sun rose, his mother awake with it. She picked Tan's pants up off the floor and brought them out back to wash them but did not ask Long what had happened. Long helped her load up her lychee baskets for market, and only after he had carried them out to the gate for her did she suddenly remember that he was leaving today, and she stood on tiptoe to kiss him goodbye on the forehead.

There was a bus heading south at six-thirty, and Long told himself that he deserved the motion sickness that awaited him. He took the broom from the corner and thumped it softly against the wall. After a pause he heard the same pattern tapped back to him from inside his grandmother's room. He smiled and then lifted his bag.

He did not wake Tan up to say goodbye. In a way this made things easier—what had happened at the restaurant, what they had each seen the other do. Something had finally broken completely, and its irreversibility was a relief from the years of painful stretching that had preceded it, from the agony of waiting for the snap.

When the bus rolled through downtown Ia Kare, it didn't come to a complete stop—it opened its doors and slowed down just enough for the passengers to run alongside it and then leap on board. Long's history of motion sickness on the local route was so storied that the bus attendant recognized him when he got on. He gave Long a plastic trash can to barf in instead of the usual plastic bag and made him promise to sit next to an open window.

The bus drove south all day and in the early evening, Saigon finally appeared like a gray smudge on the horizon.

N THE WINTER OF 1949, GASPARD VALENTIN RENAUD AND Jean-Pierre Courcoul, who originally hailed from Ivry-sur-Seine and a small village outside of Limoges, respectively, pooled the money that they had saved up over ten years spent working as guards in the Con Son penitentiary and used it to lease twenty hectares of brushland in the sparsely populated stretch between Ban Me Thuot and Pleiku, upon which they planned to plant rubber. Neither of them had ever worked in the agricultural sector before, let alone traveled north of Saigon, but Gaspard was confident that the Highlands were the ideal site for their enterprise. First of all, it was cheap, he had argued, after Jean-Pierre had expressed concerns about the suitability of the climate of Darlac, but it still lay beneath the 15th parallel, and the trees would be able to grow. This had been assured to him by an acquaintance who worked at the experimental forestry station at Trang-Bom. Additionally, the remoteness of the region also made it unlikely that the Viet Minh, who were currently occupied with destroying the rubber factories around Binh Duong, would set fire to it.

But the Montagnards! Jean-Pierre had protested. Did he not fear the tribespeople who lived in the hills? Their intended plantation lay at the intersection of indigenous Rhadé and Jarai territories, and Jean-

Pierre couldn't imagine that two Frenchmen would receive a very warm welcome from them.

That's the beauty of the thing, said Gaspard. The Montagnards actually prefer us to the ethnic Vietnamese! To them, the Annamites are deceitful invaders who are trying to take their land.

But are we not also taking their land? countered Jean-Pierre.

Gaspard shrugged dismissively. Well, perhaps. But at least we brought doctors, Jesus, and coffee along with us.

In the end, Jean-Pierre had agreed to go to the mountains, not because he trusted Gaspard's scheme but because, after a decade of being slowly steamed alive on an island a hundred kilometers southeast of the geographical ass of Vietnam, the scent of hot sea air had become fused in his mind with his memories of the prison camp and of what he had done there, and he never wanted to smell the ocean again for as long as he lived.

IN SAIGON, THEY TOOK out an additional loan; they would need to hire men to clear the land and then to water and graft and tend and stake and weed. They would need to hire even more to construct the compound where the latex would eventually be processed. Their farm would be small, but it would take several years for the trees to mature enough for tapping to begin, and Gaspard and Jean-Pierre knew that they would have to manage their money prudently. They headed north in a secondhand truck with seven hundred *Hevea brasiliensis* saplings tucked snugly in the back.

The first problem they encountered was that when they stopped in Dalat to spend the night after a long day of driving, Jean-Pierre did not want to leave. His eyes lit up when he saw the gabled villas, the men all wearing smart coats and scarves to fend off the mountain chill, the noble pines, the manicured rosebushes which only grew in this particular climate, the charming man-made lake around which couples strolled arm in arm, and he declared that he had been transported back home and wished to stay.

This is nothing like your home! Gaspard finally snapped, annoyed by Jean-Pierre's squeal of excitement upon spotting a Vietnamese man sipping a *chocolat chaud* while wearing a beret. Gaspard hadn't left Southeast Asia in the last fifteen years, so he was not even sure if he could correctly identify what home was or was not like anymore, but he could sense that Jean-Pierre's nostalgia was imperiling his rubber dreams. Besides, he added for spite, that man isn't drinking hot chocolate, he's drinking soy milk.

Jean-Pierre's face fell, and Gaspard switched tactics and tried to appeal to his sense of adventure instead. We didn't leave France and cross half the world just to find more France, he gently cajoled. We came here to see wild elephants! We didn't spend ten years being shat upon by gulls on Con Son to end up here in this . . . this . . . Potemkin Grenoble!—here he waved a hand up at the café terraces upon which Europeans nibbled ice cream made from the nonnative strawberries that flourished only in Dalat and nowhere else in the colonies—The city you're seeing isn't real, it's just a dream concocted by the homesick in order to console themselves. It's already fading. It's not going to outlast this war, but you and I will, my little *Jeanpi*. We are in search of something greater. Something that is more than a dream.

Gaspard did not even let them eat supper at the Hôtel du Parc that night, despite Jean-Pierre's pleading that if he could just eat a couple of real *gougères*, he would never complain about anything ever again.

I'm sorry, but it's much too dangerous, admonished Gaspard. If you taste one, you'll never leave. You must think of yourself as Odysseus and this as the land of the lotus eaters. The land of the gougère eaters! Ha!

He steered them to the Dalat night market instead for a meal of artichoke-and-pork-knuckle soup at a Vietnamese-run stall, telling Jean-Pierre that it was a fair compromise, because artichokes had been introduced by the French back at the turn of the century, which made the dish more or less European. Jean-Pierre could only nod silently and stare with glum resignation at the bones bobbing in his bowl.

IN THE MORNING, AFTER consulting their map and checking that the trees in the back were secure, they started off on the treacherous mountain road that would lead them northwest. Jean-Pierre took the first shift behind the wheel, because he was the more capable driver of the two and they would face many steep climbs and nauseating hairpin turns on the first leg of their journey. They had to stop three times to clear fallen rocks from the road, twice to dig their wheels out of mud, twice more because there was too much fog to see, and once when a herd of three dozen wild boars came thundering out of the forest and across their path. Every fifteen minutes, Gaspard would claim to see something moving in the trees that he thought was a tiger.

When the landscape finally began to flatten and the lush forests of the Lang Biang Plateau thinned out to a less voluptuous greenery, Jean-Pierre switched places with Gaspard, eager to study their new world more carefully through the passenger seat window. The colors of Dalat had been emerald and mint, mahogany and claret, peach pink and the milky blue white of a cataract. Here it was all scratchy saffrons and ochres and olives, with the occasional sapphire peep of a lake coming into view before the road dipped and it disappeared behind the trees once again, like a secret being slowly teased out.

As they approached Ban Me Thuot he began to see cultivated farmland again and, finally, villages, the houses clustered like small archipelagos in a sea of coffee or pepper fields. He smelled the first of the rubber plantations before he could see them—the burnt stench of distant smokehouses where sheets of coagulated latex spent days in drying chambers, carried by the wind across the fields and over to his window. Jean-Pierre frowned and pinched his nose shut.

When Gaspard smelled the smoke, he leaned out of the truck to inhale even more deeply. Drink it in, Jeanpi! he laughed. That's the scent of our new life!

The road took an unexpectedly sharp bend, and as they went around it the two men were suddenly confronted by a full and unobstructed view of the lake they had only glimpsed before. The sun on the water's surface had transformed it into a pool of molten gold, and the dark green silhouette of the mountain range they had traversed earlier that morning loomed in the background like the carcass of a collapsed dragon.

Gaspard slowed the truck and then killed the motor. They were alone; there wasn't another visible soul in all the surrounding miles of sun-soaked wildness. For several minutes, both men gazed at the scene in front of them with wordless awe. And then a cloud passed, the light flickered, and the water turned back into water. The spell had lifted, and Gaspard turned the key in the ignition. But they were both left feeling light-headed. It was as if they had been granted a quick taste of that wild and nameless thing that they had left France for as young men, momentarily distilled into sunlight on an unblemished landscape.

I'll bet you anything that we'll finally get to see our elephants here, whispered Gaspard reverently. This is the place that we've been searching for.

THERE WOULD BE AN ELEPHANT, it turned out, but she was ancient and foul tempered and the last of her kind left in the backwoods town where Gaspard and Jean-Pierre had decided to start their new lives. She was named Su-Su, after the wrinkly squash she resembled, and on their third morning in the Highlands, Gaspard and Jean-Pierre had awoken to the sound of her headbutting their truck.

Su-Su belonged to a Rhadé elder and, now that she was too old to work, was generally given free rein of the village. The children adored Su-Su even though she did not reciprocate their feelings, and they would parade behind her like rats following the Pied Piper while she wandered from house to house, stealing pumpkins from front gardens. They just made sure to always maintain a safe distance from her feet and tusks.

While Gaspard and Jean-Pierre were assessing the damage to the truck, they heard a voice—in French—call casually to them over the stone wall that surrounded their house:

Old Su-Su'll leave you alone if you bribe her. She likes bananas! You should always keep some handy. That's what I do.

The man said his name was Lejeune. Louis Lejeune. But everyone called him Louis "l'Anguille" because a giant eel had bitten off three of the toes on his left foot thirty years ago. (Never go swimming in the Dak Bla River! he cautioned Gaspard and Jean-Pierre, after they had invited him inside for tea.) Over the course of the morning, they learned that Louis l'Anguille had arrived on the shores of Cochinchina as a young soldier in 1908. Five years later, he found work as a civil servant in the newly established province of Kontum and traded Saigon for the Highlands. He had had malaria twice (Nasty little disease; turned my piss purple! was Louis l'Anguille's succinct take on it), and, under Sabatier's tenure as provincial administrator of Darlac (Randy old goat. Unbelievable moustache. Pointiest fucking thing I've ever seen), he had overseen the French construction of the network of roads in the region. Now, weathered and seven-toed and nearly sixty-six years of age, he owned a very large coffee plantation and spent his days straining his malaria-weakened kidneys with vast quantities of rice wine and then veering indiscriminately between angry drunk and affable drunk. He hadn't had a fellow compatriot for a neighbor in nearly four years, and invited Gaspard and Jean-Pierre over for dinner the following night.

I've got a local girl who does the cooking for me, he said. Very capable.

Can she make gougères? asked Jean-Pierre hopefully.

EVEN THOUGH LOUIS L'ANGUILLE was the only other Frenchman within a ten-kilometer radius, Gaspard was upset by his presence, as it spoiled the illusion that he and Jean-Pierre were the first foreigners to ever set foot on this virgin Highland soil. He had chosen to overlook the fact that the former inhabitants of the house where they were now living had clearly been French as well; if it wasn't obvious enough from the size of the place and the comparative luxury of its building materials (brick and decorative tile and painted plaster, as opposed to thatch and timber and bamboo), when they first moved in they had found a rattan sofa with two moldering silk cushions and the water-damaged remains of a Stendhal novel (*Armance*, sighed Gaspard with disappointment, picking it up too carelessly, tea-colored pages coming away from the spine in sheaves and falling to the floor before Jean-Pierre could catch them. I was hoping it would be *Le rouge et le noir* at least).

Jean-Pierre thought Gaspard's hostility toward their neighbor was unwise. He hadn't particularly liked Louis l'Anguille either, but it was obvious he held enough power here that if they did not stay on his good side, things would get difficult for them quickly. He would have thought that after ten years of working at a prison, Gaspard would have realized this too.

SADLY, LOUIS L'ANGUILLE'S COOK could not make gougères. Unlike in Dalat, with its herds of imported alpine cows happily cavorting around the temperate foothills of Lang Biang, there was no readily available dairy in the remote reaches of Darlac, apart from canned condensed milk. But she was as capable as Louis had advertised and prepared a dish for them that Jean-Pierre supposed bore some semblance to a lamb navarin, only made of goat instead of lamb and bamboo shoots instead of everything else and with the liberal addition of hot chilis that upon his first taste evoked the sensation of eating a spoonful of flaming gasoline but by the end of the meal he found almost pleasant—a good pain, like a sharp slap to the face when you were drunk, like a bite in the middle of a kiss.

The walls of Louis l'Anguille's dining room were decorated with the yellowing tusks of Su-Su's deceased kinfolk. The ivory of at least a dozen slain elephants was represented. Some tusks had been arranged into crisscross designs like macabre wainscoting, others jutted straight out of the plaster and had been repurposed into bottle racks for his rice wine. Gaspard spent the entire meal staring down into his stew to avoid having to look at them. But Louis's private museum included more than mere tusks. The taxidermied head of a water buffalo and the skull of a muntjac were mounted in the living room. The muntjac was particularly unsettling, with its long canines and unbranched, Mephistophelean antlers. From every angle, it appeared to be grinning at them. In the entryway, Gaspard and Jean-Pierre had been greeted by an albino cobra, which was slightly comical by comparison—the taxidermist had given it mismatched glass eyes and done such a lumpy stuffing job that its body resembled a stocking full of eggs. The snake had been arranged into an imposing, half-coiled, ready-to-strike position, but it listed heavily to one side and was propped up against an old wine bottle, which did not balance it very effectively but did make it look like a bit like a possessive drunk. These parts used to be crawling with cobras before we planted the coffee fields, Louis l'Anguille told them. Couldn't walk twenty meters without tripping over one. My men killed this spooky little bastard in this very spot when they were clearing away the brush to build the house. Thought it was only right to have him preserved and keep him around, since this was his home first. Even designed the place so that the entryway would be right where we found him!

He also boasted of owning a tiger skin rug that he kept in his bedroom, but because he did not invite them upstairs to look at it, Jean-Pierre doubted its legitimacy.

Louis waited until after dinner to show them the crown jewel of his collection. They moved out to the veranda to take coffee and dessert while overlooking a sunset-bloodied vista of coffee fields and the prickly shadowlands of uncleared bamboo and podocarpus forest. The air had cooled, and the gentle, jasmine-like fragrance of the small white flowers on the coffee bushes grew stronger as the light faded.

Louis's cook brought out a large, cyan-glazed dish in which poached lychees swam in cinnamon-scented syrup. While tasty, Jean-Pierre found it visually suggestive of a bowl of disintegrating eyeballs. Louis l'Anguille sighed while spooning himself a portion—This is the closest I can get to a *poire à la beaujolaise* out here. The girl knows how to skin and cook any fish, fowl, or hairy beastie imaginable, but she's no pastry chef. All she does is poached lychees, poached pineapple, poached jackfruit . . . she's even tried to poach a durian before.

Does she understand French? asked Jean-Pierre as the cook reached around him and deftly poured a stream of hot water over his coffee filter. When he spoke, she glanced over at him and shook her head. *Peculiar eyes on that one,* thought Jean-Pierre to himself. They were pale and slightly golden in color.

Gaspard laughed. I'd say that you do—you clearly understood him well enough, he said, addressing the girl directly. The girl aimed a smile at the floor that was demurely polite, but her eyes met his, and she regarded him without any shame. And you can understand what I'm saying to you right now, Gaspard continued, don't you?

She's a little polyglot, this one is, said Louis l'Anguille proudly. She's too shy to tell you, but she can understand French, Rhadé, and even a little Jarai. She doesn't talk very much, but a quiet woman suits me just fine. Isn't that right, Odile? The cook was no longer smiling. She gave him a cursory nod and retreated back into the house as quickly as she could with the hot kettle. Louis watched her leave before turning back to Jean-Pierre and Gaspard. I gave her that name, he said. Don't you think "Odile" fits her? He took a sip of coffee. Now, have a look at what I've brought out to show you, boys. My finest specimens are in here.

The book he produced was bound in dark leather. Jean-Pierre didn't know what he was looking at when he opened to the first page. It appeared to be blank. Then he saw that a pale, fine strand of hair, about twenty centimeters long, had been pasted vertically down the center of it, like a nearly undetectable crack in a plaster wall. In the bottom right-hand corner, printed neatly in blue ink: *Madeleine.*

Jean-Pierre looked up at Louis l'Anguille with confusion. It's chronological, said Louis, as if this would clarify things for Jean-Pierre.

It did not. Jean-Pierre turned to the next page. The hair glued to it was a dark copper, and so long that it had been folded in half to fit on the sheet of paper. *Camille,* read the blue letters in the corner.

Now, *she* was a real stunner, said Louis l'Anguille, voice oily from the rice wine he had poured into his coffee and the old lust creeping back up his throat. Make sure that he can see too! he directed Jean-Pierre, motioning to Gaspard.

The book was as thick as a chair cushion. Now beginning to feel uneasy, Jean-Pierre started to flip faster, reading the names but trying to ignore their corresponding strands of hair. *Jeanne. Marie-Sophie. Delphine. Caroline.*

Slower, slower! laughed Louis. Or I won't be able to keep up! This is how I keep my mind sharp in my old age—I'll know I'm ready to die when I can't put a face to the name anymore. He chuckled. Let's see . . . Jeanne had a perfect ass. Caroline was a screamer—nice big tits on her but even bigger lungs. He leaned over Jean-Pierre to turn the next page himself. Ah, little *Aurélie*, he sighed, caressing the strand with a finger. What a temper. She caught me trying to get a sample from her for the book. Tried to scratch my eyes out. Got the hair anyway. I always do, in the end.

Jean-Pierre glanced over at Gaspard, who wasn't even attempting to hide the disgust on his face. Keep going! said Louis, returning to his seat and slurping up a lychee.

The black hairs began a third of the way through. *Thi. Hoa. Lan. Cam. Tham. H'Ni. Nhung. H'Bia. Yen.* Some of the hairs were so long that they had been folded multiple times to fit, creating a dark sine wave against the white paper. The worst pages had the names written in quotation marks beneath a dark Asian hair, implying that Louis either hadn't known her real one or had chosen a different one for her, à la Odile: *"Lola," "Babette," "Mimi,"* and *"Gigi,"* and several women who had been given only initials—*X, V, A.* Jean-Pierre turned the pages robotically, trying to shut out Louis's commentary, the relentless recounting of what she had worn, the color of her nipples, how rough she had liked it, the things she had whispered in his ear, how far she could bend. Even though hearing it made him feel ill, he was still growing aroused despite himself, and he could tell from the poisonous expression on Louis's face that this was exactly what the man wanted.

He was relieved when it became too dark to read and he could shut the book with feigned regret, then begin making the standard polite murmurings about the lateness of the hour, and how he and Gaspard ought to be heading home.

Louis l'Anguille rang a small bell to summon Odile. Promise me that you'll both come back often, he said. Dine with me whenever you like. I can't tell you how happy I am to have you as my new neighbors. Odile appeared in the doorway, and Louis handed her his revolting catalogue of bedded women. Take this back upstairs, my good girl. Be careful with it! Once she was out of earshot he turned back to Gaspard and Jean-Pierre. I've got a blank page ready for her. Have to wait a bit though. He chuckled. Not quite ripe, you see. She's only just turned fifteen.

At this, Gaspard pushed his chair back from the table sharply and said that he was going to get their coats.

THEY WALKED BACK TO their house in the velvety dark. Frog song shimmered in the air around them. How could such a vile man be allowed to live in a place as pure and beautiful as this? said Gaspard quietly. It was the first time he had spoken since leaving Louis l'Anguille's. He doesn't belong here, he continued, his voice still soft but shaky with anger. He doesn't deserve beautiful things. The ground here should have swallowed him up the first time he stepped on it. The air should have . . . should have *dissolved* him into particles. The giant eel should have eaten all of him.

But didn't he bring coffee and Jesus and doctors? asked Jean-Pierre sardonically.

Don't be cruel, Jeanpi.

Jean-Pierre suspected that Gaspard's outrage was actually a thin screen for his guilt, even if he could not admit this to either Jean-Pierre or himself. Gaspard had slept with plenty of local girls. So had Jean-Pierre. On the island, there was no one else, unless you were fucking each other or the prisoners or the goats. Do you remember the handsome Khmer? Jean-Pierre asked Gaspard.

Of course, Gaspard replied. I was thinking of him the whole time we were looking at that book.

The handsome Khmer was back on Con Son in a cell that stank of rotting mussels, with murderers and captured revolutionaries for neighbors and a rotating roster of drunks, opium addicts, and other miscellaneous dregs of French society for guards. (Jean-Pierre included himself and Gaspard in the last category.) Neither of them could remember his real name, just that he'd picked the wrong French girl to accidentally impregnate and was now growing old in a prison because of it.

I think he actually loved her too, poor unlucky bastard, said Jean-Pierre. He had spent a lot of time wondering whether the absence of love would make incarceration easier to bear or harder. He still did not know the answer.

That night, as he was settling down to sleep, he had the sudden sensation that he was being watched. He wandered from end to end of their old house, leaning out each window and looking for eyes glowing in the Highland darkness beyond their gate, listening for a rustle, a footstep, a cough. There was nothing. He retraced his steps, this time checking the shadows in every room for potential intruders, human or otherwise. The western wing that had been the servants' quarters twenty years ago was now partially collapsed—anything could have crawled in through the rubble. Everywhere he went, he could feel something following him, always watching. Jean-Pierre hadn't checked on Gaspard yet. He quietly pushed the door to his friend's room open a finger's width and saw that he was snoring peacefully inside. And it was then that he sensed the invisible gaze lifting from him and fixing itself on the sleeping Gaspard instead. Jean-Pierre backed away, mostly sure that whatever the watcher was, it was harmless, but unable to shake the feeling that he had betrayed his friend by leading the thing to him.

He returned to his bed. When he finally closed his eyes, the pattern of phosphenes that crackled across the blackness inside his lids took the form of thin, bright hairs. Ghostly hairs made of light. Hundreds upon hundreds of them. A ten-thousand-strand mobius strip wound around the interior of Jean-Pierre's skull, spinning endlessly, each one whispering a name that he could not hear.

FOR THE FIRST YEARS, they were very nearly happy. The rubber trees took to the red soil and began shooting skyward. Jean-Pierre and Gaspard had no problem hiring workers—a steady stream of Vietnamese were leaving the North and resettling in the Highlands, and they were in need of jobs. The settlement grew. A new school was built, and then a clinic. The cemetery expanded. There were patches of guerrilla fighting to the north and west of them, but they were left untouched by the greater war around them. While they waited for their trees to reach the age when tapping could begin, Jean-Pierre and Gaspard made money by renting out their truck for construction jobs that in the past would have been given to Su-Su and her pachyderm colleagues, and occasionally driving cargo down to Ban Me Thuot. (Su-Su herself had passed peacefully in her sleep; Jean-Pierre and Gaspard occasionally brought bananas to place on her grave.) On one of his Ban Me trips, Jean-Pierre met a French schoolteacher—a young widow, complexion like a peach, tinkling laugh and charming Normandy accent—and they began sending letters to each other. Jean-Pierre did not tell her what he had done for a living before coming to Darlac. Over the course of a year and a half, he made three visits to the city to visit her. On his third trip, as they were strolling the grounds of the newly constructed Khai Doan Pagoda, she paused in the discreet shade provided by a ficus and looked up at him expectantly. Gaspard would surely kiss her, Jean-Pierre told himself, before he was finally able to bring his mouth down to hers.

In her next letter, she promised that she would move out to the countryside to be with him and they would be wed once the rubber plantation began production in the following year. She had also enclosed a small lock of her hair as a romantic keepsake, tied with a silk ribbon. When Jean-Pierre opened it, he flung it away from himself like a hot coal. He put it in a drawer and could never look at it again.

They were frequent guests at the house of Louis l'Anguille. Even though they despised themselves for it, they went over on a regular basis for dinner. They tolerated his wildly exaggerated anecdotes and lecherous reminiscences and the cruelty he displayed toward his workers; they took shot after shot of rice wine when he wanted them to be drunk with him, vomiting off of his veranda when necessary and then continuing; they even offered to rub his two-toed foot for him when rainy weather made it ache. Jean-Pierre did it because Louis had successfully purchased their loyalty; he had lent them the extra money they'd needed to repair their house and hired them for what were clearly made-up part-time administrative positions in his coffee business: charity while they waited for their own plantation to be ready. Gaspard did it because he had fallen hopelessly in love with Odile.

It wasn't worth it, Jean-Pierre would tell him. It wasn't worth playing sycophant to a man he loathed just for the opportunity to exchange four words and a handful of glances with her during their brief interactions while she ladled out portions of bizarre poached fruits. And although he could not admit this, Jean-Pierre was jealous of Odile. He disliked how easily and instantaneously Gaspard had proffered his heart to her, and truthfully, he suspected that there was also Highland witchery involved. It was those unnatural eyes.

He tried to find other ways to warn Gaspard instead. Remember the handsome Khmer! he told him. Going after the wrong woman gets you locked up, unless you're untouchable, like Louis. If you're lonely, I'll ask Marguerite to introduce you to one of her nice French teacher friends.

How could I be lonely—I have you, don't I? I'll always have you, Jeanpi. Gaspard would just say. Besides, I don't need more than four words and a handful of glances from her. I love her, but I don't have to have her. I just have to be near her. And that's enough.

Jean-Pierre was troubled by his friend's uncharacteristic sentimentality. Gaspard had never been one for maudlin declarations before. Louis l'Anguille had not mentioned his book again since their first dinner, and Gaspard and Jean-Pierre never asked him about it. Jean-Pierre knew that Gaspard would not be able to bear it if he ever discovered that the alleged page for Odile had been filled.

IN THE SPRING OF 1954, mere days after Jean-Pierre and Gaspard had successfully harvested the first of the latex from their young trees, the smoked sheets still draped over their drying racks, they learned that Dien Bien Phu had been overrun by the Viet Minh. The French had surrendered. Shortly after, Jean-Pierre received Marguerite's farewell letter, dated three weeks earlier and beginning: *My darling, by the time you read this, I will have already set sail for France . . .*

Are you going to leave too? he asked Louis over what would be one of the last of their dinners together. He had been disturbed by his own reaction to Marguerite's departure. He would have hoped that the end of a two-and-a-half-year relationship would make him feel more than relief.

Louis snorted into his plate of fish. Of course I'm not. This is all just a little tremor.

A seven-year tremor?

Trust me—you can't panic and toss away everything you've worked for, especially now that you've just started cutting your trees. Wait it out.

THEY DID, NERVOUSLY, for the next few weeks. And then they learned that there had been an ambush in Chu Dreh Pass, less than thirty kilometers away.

HE'S PACKING! GASPARD CRIED, running into the house and seizing Jean-Pierre by the shoulders. I've just seen him!

Who's packing? asked Jean-Pierre, even though he already knew the answer.

Who else do you think! That bastard Louis. He told us to wait it out, and now I've just seen him packing up all his fucking ivory.

How? Were you hiding in his bushes?

Gaspard ignored the question. He's leaving. And he's going to take her with him. He abruptly turned away from Jean-Pierre and punched the nearest wall, leaving bright dots of knuckle blood on the yellow paint. Then he tore out of the house again as quickly as he had entered. Jean-Pierre knew Gaspard had only hit the wall so that he could pretend afterward that the pain was the reason he was crying. He had seen his friend's eyes welling with tears before he had even formed the fist.

IT WAS FOR THE BEST, thought Jean-Pierre. Odile gone, Louis gone, Marguerite gone, everybody gone except for himself and Gaspard. Just the two of them once more. They had the truck—they could get out when the time came. Maybe they would go to Algeria. He was feeling remarkably, foolishly calm about the entire situation when Gaspard stumbled back in just before midnight, drunk and clutching something in a rucksack.

Jean-Pierre was alerted to his return by the clumsy clinking of glass against tile. He entered the kitchen to find Gaspard pouring petrol into an old bottle, spilling it all over himself and the floor in the process.

Gaspard gave him a wobbly smile when he saw him. Do you know what, Jeanpi? he said, wiping his fingers onto his shirtfront, He doesn't even have a tiger skin in his bedroom. Gaspard's speech was slightly slurred. He lied to us! There's no tiger, and the whole room smells like his pissing pot. Gaspard spat on the floor for emphasis. He tried to twist the cap back onto the bottle, then gave up after a struggle and handed it to Jean-Pierre. Help me, my old friend. His breath reeked of rice wine.

Jean-Pierre shut it for him. Where have you been? he asked—his second unnecessary question of the day.

Gaspard shook his head. He shoved the bottle of gasoline into his rucksack, where Jean-Pierre could hear it clank dully against something else inside. I can't save her, Gaspard said, his voice cracking. He closed his eyes to gather himself and took several shaky breaths. Okay, he said after a minute, opening them back up. Now I'm ready. Let's go! he said with forced brightness. He patted Jean-Pierre's arm and strode back out the door. At the road he made a right, heading in the direction of their plantation instead of Louis l'Anguille's house, which was a relief for Jean-Pierre.

But as Jean-Pierre was turning to follow him, he suddenly paused. He had felt it again—that old sensation of being watched, back for the first time in five years. Jean-Pierre swiveled his head to the left. He didn't see anything moving in the darkness, but he hadn't expected to.

Come on! Gaspard called. Jean-Pierre hurried after him, trying not to trip.

EVERY MORNING, WHEN HE and Gaspard walked together to the plantation, Jean-Pierre would experience a swell of pride as they rounded the bend and the neat, uniform rows of their trees came into view. He liked to think of them as their seven hundred leafy children. As they approached now, the wind picked up, making the dense tract of branches sway.

I snuck in, Gaspard finally admitted to him when they entered the trees. To Louis l'Anguille's house.

I know, said Jean-Pierre.

They walked in deeper. After fifteen long minutes, Gaspard turned to Jean-Pierre again: I wanted her to come with us. I wanted to free her from him. And she wouldn't go.

I know you did, old friend. I'm sure you tried your best.

Another fifteen minutes passed: I'm not a good man, Jeanpi.

Don't say that. That's not true.

It is. It *is*. I was never a good man to start with, and I'm the worse for thinking I was better than I am. I . . . I am not a man who deserves beautiful things. I'm not as bad as Louis, but I'm not good.

Well, said Jean-Pierre, if you're not good, then I'm not good either.

At this point, they had reached the very center of the property. Nothing but trees extending in all directions, and varying viscosities of darkness. Gaspard unbuckled his rucksack.

I can't save Odile, he said, but I can try and set the rest of them loose instead. He turned the bag upside down and the book of hairs tumbled out of it and onto the ground.

Did you see if she was in it? This was the first question Jean-Pierre had asked today that he did not already know the answer to.

Gaspard ripped the cap off of the gasoline bottle with his teeth and poured it out onto the book. It was too dark for Jean-Pierre to see that he was reserving half of it.

Stay back, Jeanpi, he said, producing a lighter from his pocket. Jean-Pierre took two steps away from the book. Gaspard gently nudged him back another meter. It was the tenderness of this gesture that finally began setting off the alarm bells in Jean-Pierre's head.

The noise of the gas igniting took him by surprise. It was a whooshing sound, like the wings of a colossal bird swooping down on them. The flame shot up in a ferocious column and then fell back, crackling as the book began turning black at the edges.

Awash in orange light, Gaspard lifted the bottle a final time. He stepped forward into the fire as he emptied the remains of it over his own head.

Jean-Pierre ran toward him, in vain. He flinched first at the sound of the giant wings flapping again, which was Gaspard and his gas-soaked clothes catching flame, and then once more at the smell that came afterward, immediate and overpowering. But when he followed Gaspard into the fire, he did it without hesitation. He did not have to have him. He just had to be near him. It was enough. The pain that he met was something he could have never imagined. He was red and he was orange and he was gold, and then he was white, white, white, white.

He wrapped his arms around Gaspard, placed his own head beside his friend's, and they held each other as they burned.

———

JUST BEFORE DAWN, THEIR workers arrived at the plantation. They did notice the strong scent of smoke but thought it was unremarkable. The air always smelled like smoke because of how the rubber was cured. Then two of them discovered the first cobra, coiled in the roots of a tree, long and thin and pale and dangerously camouflaged against the bark. Snakes of this kind had not been seen in the region for nearly twenty years. While they were discussing what they should do with it, a separate group of workers came running over to tell them that they had seen another cobra, a few rows over. Then, while they were all trying to process what was happening, they heard a disquieting rustling sound and looked up to see a large black snake gliding toward them over the dead leaves, its hood flared. They fled.

MEANWHILE, LOUIS L'ANGUILLE HAD spent his morning stumbling across his foggy coffee fields, swinging his cane savagely at every unlucky plant or worker in his path. He was still drunk from the night before and in a howling rage, beyond certain that Gaspard and Jean-Pierre were the ones who had robbed him, and heading for their house. When he did not find them there, he went to go hunt them down in the rubber trees instead. He had not yet gotten word that overnight, a vast colony of snakes had taken over the plantation. It briefly struck him as odd that no one was there working when he arrived, but he was too angry and inebriated to give it a second thought. Louis marched off into the trees, eel foot dragging behind him.

Occasionally he thought he saw something moving out of the corner of his eye, or heard a sound he couldn't place coming from behind a tree. Each time, he dismissed it, blaming the rice wine, which he had brewed himself. The rats had been bad last year—perhaps some droppings had gone into the vintage and this was a small side effect.

Louis only started to realize that something was not right when he reached the center of the trees. The stench of burnt human flesh was

overwhelming, but there was no sign of a charred body. He saw the pile
of ashes, still smoking, and shuffled over to inspect it.

As he approached, the ash heap moved. Louis knew he'd seen it—
this wasn't the wine playing tricks on his eyes. Down in that soft gray
mound, something had shifted. Had wriggled, even. Curious, Louis
leaned over and gave it a prod with his cane.

WHEN THEY FOUND HIM, four hours later, it was too late. He was on
the opposite end of the plantation from where he had entered it, the
side by the town cemetery. A funeral party noticed him propped up
against a tombstone, covered in orange dirt from having to crawl out of
the trees after his leg stopped working.

It was the right one that had been bitten. The limb had grown so
swollen that later, the coroner wouldn't be able tell how many puncture
marks there had actually been.

He was incoherent by the time he got to the clinic. Two heads was
what he kept saying. Two heads, two heads, over and over until his
mouth couldn't form the words anymore. It was the only thing they
could understand. Odile arrived just in time to see the moment when
his lungs gave out. She did not even try to hide her smile as they bundled him up and carried him away.

The dog had finally made it out of the mountains. It had taken months to cross Lam Dong and northern Dong Nai on foot. Its paw pads had callused to the texture of limestone, and its shits had turned to goo from a meager diet of wild berries with the occasional dead bird or squirrel. Now that it was in Binh Duong and moving through more populated areas, the route was easier and there was more to eat. However, the dog now had traffic to fear, as well as poachers and other, larger dogs. It preferred to travel at night, keeping to the trash-filled ruts running alongside the road where it wouldn't be seen.

In between the factory towns were rubber plantations twenty times the size of the haunted one in Ia Kare. These trees were regimented and snakeless and the scars in their bark were wet, but their air and soil still smelled of the same burning. One night, while the dog was walking past the rows of their mutilated trunks, it paused. It had heard something deep in the rubber. The dog sat down at the edge of the trees and waited for it to appear.

The smoke came darting from trunk to trunk like a flying squirrel. This one was a darker red, an overcast garnet. It was small and it was young and it was clumsy. It had not yet fed. When it sensed the warm body of the dog, its edges fluttered eagerly, like the bell of a jellyfish, and it squirted toward it through the trees. The dog cocked its head curiously but did not move.

The smoke tried to strike quickly, stretching into a thin, wine-colored ribbon and then wrapping one end of itself around the dog's leg and tightening. But the dog merely lifted its paw and lazily shook the smoke off.

The smoke contracted backward, startled. It looked more carefully at the dog then, and realized that it was already occupied. There was no more room—something else was inside. Disappointed, it drifted away through the trees to find itself a better body.

"THE MOUTH," SAID LONG. "COULD I HAVE YOUR MOUTH NOW, please?" His eyes were already scrunched up and he was proactively biting his bottom lip.

A bit presumptuous, Winnie thought to herself, but, ever consenting, she slid down below the quilt. She had known the request would come once the lights were turned off. Long only ever wanted the mouth. He was always polite when he asked, but he never looked at Winnie while she plied the soft cuttlefish of his penis for him, and he would not speak again until it was over. Winnie wondered if he was pretending to receive a blowjob from a ghost. After she had ingested a half-teaspoon of semen she would crawl upward again and resurface above the quilt, like some sort of marine reptile emerging after a swim. At that point Long would be able to look at her once more, and he would brush back the sweaty hair—now grown out nearly to shoulder length—that clung to her neck, and say, "Is there something I can do for you, Winnie?" and she would whisper *no*, then wait for him to fall asleep so that she could get out of bed and wander around his house.

The houses on either side of Long's were slightly newer constructions, four stories high and occupied by large multigenerational families with very young children and very old grandparents, whose coughs and yells Winnie could hear through the adjacent walls. But the building directly across from Long's was a restaurant, advertising "Dog Meat: Seven Ways" on a glowing sign. Its red letters were right at eye level with the small balcony outside his bedroom, along with a stock photo of sleeping golden retriever puppies that perhaps in America would have been used to advertise fabric softener instead. While Winnie knew that the dogs being eaten in seven ways were not fluffy designer puppies but the kind of strays she used to watch from her window at the Cooks' house, in a way this made her even sadder. This was not a country for mutts. Every day at sundown, the Dog Meat sign flickered to life with a buzzing sound like the stirring of a large, weary bee, welcoming the night's customers, and it tinged the whole bedroom red until three in the morning, when the restaurant closed and the drunk businessmen drove back home and the beer girls changed out of their heels and started sweeping discarded bones into piles on the sidewalk. Only then did the light go off. But Winnie would still be awake.

The house had two and a half floors for her nocturnal prowling. The half floor was the airless crawlspace beneath the roof. Winnie did not venture up there often, because it was about fifteen degrees hotter than the rest of the house and the lock to its sole window was stuck shut, but occasionally during the night she would get the urge to spend an hour crouched in it like some sort of attic ghoul.

The master bedroom and its balcony were directly below. Winnie's suitcase now lived underneath Long's bedframe. Her five dresses occupied a corner in his closet next to his week's worth of pressed slacks and identical Oxford button-downs, two pairs of knockoff A.C. Milan soccer shorts, a single pair of jeans, and a giant T-shirt from the University of Economics Ho Chi Minh City. Winnie sometimes borrowed the shirt to sleep in, as a kind of pantomime of intimacy.

At the other end of the hallway, the bathroom with its allegedly paranormal bathtub. It was small and old and high rimmed—an odd and mostly inconvenient luxury to have in place of the standard Vietnamese unwalled shower with a sloped floor and corner drain. But the beauty of bathing was that Winnie barely had to touch her own body to come out clean. When she was a child, there had been a game that she liked to play in the bath: Winnie would sink back in the tub and go slack, keeping her eyes open and unblinking, feeling her hair floating around her, and then she would let her jaw fall open and the water trickle into her mouth and throat. She would stay like that, imagining she was a corpse in a pond, until the pinching in her lungs became too much to bear and she coughed out the water and sat back up, spluttering to life. Now that she lived with Long, Winnie found herself returning to the game. She soaked until her edges were soft and pretended to drown three or four times until she was so light-headed that she didn't really feel her own fingers when she shampooed herself as an afterthought.

ACROSS FROM THE BATHROOM: a tiny spare bedroom where Long stored odds and ends, a few cardboard boxes that he had never gotten around to unpacking, and a pile of books he'd bought from the second-hand shops on Tran Nhan Ton Street.

Winnie had been delighted the first time she saw the pile; "I love the used book stalls here!" she told Long excitedly. "We could go together next time. Which of these are your favorites?" She'd started flipping through them, hoping that there would be a few in English, or anything accessible enough for her poor Vietnamese reading comprehension.

But Long had coughed awkwardly. "I'm not actually very into books," he said. "I got those a few years ago for a friend back home who reads. I used to buy a few random ones and mail them up every couple of months. But now we don't keep in touch anymore. You can pick out any you want and I'll donate the rest later."

As she scanned their titles more closely, it became clear to Winnie that the books had been selected without care—outdated military histories, a memoir, a cookbook, a water-damaged book of street photography.

Long saw Winnie's face fall and quickly added, "I can still take you to buy more sometime, if you'd like." He never had, and Winnie had never suggested it again.

On the ground floor was the kitchen, with its warped floor tiles over the spot where Long's landlord had tried to exhume the building's ghost, and a small alcove beneath the stairs with a toilet that had been rendered unusable after the landlord's body search had failed to do anything apart from damaging the house's already temperamental plumbing. In the square entryway, Winnie's sneakers were flung in a corner across from Long's neatly arranged work shoes, soccer shoes, casual shoes, and sandals. And past the shoes, just before the gated door, the spot where Long parked his motorbike. Inside its seat, the spare raincoat where Winnie's fake lottery ticket was still folded. She had taken his motorbike keys and checked for it the very first time that Long had left her unattended, the dog greeting her with its wagging tail and counterfeit number. But instead of taking the ticket back, she had folded it up again and left it inside the pocket. It felt like it belonged there, now.

ON THE DAY WINNIE had washed up to Long's house, bedraggled and bruised and bleeding down her arm, she had looked into his strange, ichthyoid eyes and identified the yearning there. She hated herself for it, but she could see that she was as close to perfect as she could ever be for him—a helpless girl, a shivering girl, a girl who needed saving, a girl brought to him by fate.

Winnie had waded over to him and collapsed in his arms. A calculated collapse—his arms were a touch weedy and Winnie could not fall with her full weight for fear that he would drop her, thus spoiling the dream she was trying to spin for him. She had been taken inside. She had let him run the hot water in his haunted tub for her, peeled off the wet dress before he left the bathroom and then tugged at his sleeve and asked him to stay when he chivalrously made to leave, sought out his mouth with hers when he leaned over to gently mop her with a washcloth. Later, in bed, when he asked softly, "Who hurt you, Winnie?" gently tracing the purple bruises and blood-crusted abrasions, she became hysterical for him. She sobbed against him but did not answer. The hysterics were the answer he really wanted anyway.

"I can't go back to the Cooks' apartment" was all she said, once she was done sobbing. "And I can't go back to that school." She buried her face in Long's chest so she couldn't see his face when he came to the conclusion she knew he would. She was not proud of what she did, but she knew that this was New Winnie, finally braiding her long, hard roots over the soft trunk of her former self, keeping her safe.

"Of course not," he said, and brushed his lips against her forehead. "You'll stay here, and I'll take care of you."

Long had given Winnie's notice to Mr. Quy on her behalf and brought home her final paycheck. "It just makes me sick when I see the two of them at the office," he said. "They even asked me how you were doing. Winnie, I have to tell somebody. I can at least get them fired."

"No, no, no," she replied. "I don't want the Cooks to be fired. I just want to forget about them. I want to forget about everything."

He had taken her key and gone over to the old apartment while both Cooks were teaching, then packed up Winnie's room for her and brought the suitcase with all of her belongings over to District 6. If he had been horrified by the mess, he hadn't said anything. Ah, no—not *all* of her belongings: when she opened her suitcase, the policeman's hat was missing. Either Long hadn't seen it or he had but thought it wasn't hers. And why would he, when it was wrapped in plastic and hidden away? But losing the hat was not a large price to pay, Winnie had to remind herself, for her lies and the new life she had used them to buy. Long was not even asking her to pay rent. All she had to do was become the Mouth for him when he asked her to. She needed to be a Grateful Mouth.

IT WASN'T THE COFFEE that had been keeping her awake. She now knew this definitively, because she no longer drank it but still couldn't sleep. During their first month, Long had spent every minute he wasn't working with Winnie. When he returned home from the academy in the evening, he would first present her with a snack (a frozen yogurt, a bag of seaweed-flavored potato chips, a plastic sack with a pineapple inside—a Grateful Mouth was always hungry) and then take her with him to meet his three old college roommates at Café Cúc, which was a coffee shop during the day and became a low-budget karaoke club after eight P.M. Winnie thought that Café Cúc must be struggling, because she had never seen any customers in it apart from their group. It had no air-conditioning, and its couches were stuffed with a synthetic foam so soggy that Long's friends could safely stub out their cigarettes on it where it poked out through the holes in the vinyl.

Like Long, the three friends were Saigon transplants from the countryside—two from the Delta, one from outside Hue—but they seemed to have been honed to sharper points by the city than he had. They all worked in restaurants and hotels, they wore their hair identically shorn at the sides, and they treated insulting each other as a competitive sport. They mocked Long for his job at the academy, for the way he dressed, for the preposterous concept of renting a whole two-and-a-half-story house for himself.

The first time Winnie had shown up with Long, the three of them had welcomed her with eager, carnivorous smiles. "Long's always liked foreigners," said one. He turned to Long. "Weren't you in love with that other teacher for a while, the pretty Việt kiều one who rejected you?"

"Which half is the American half?" another asked Winnie, looking pointedly from her head down to her legs, then back to her head again. The boys had all laughed then, so she did too.

She, like everybody else, had ordered an iced coffee, but she spent an hour sipping it with boredom while the four boys played cards, and their banter become increasingly hard to follow. None of the others had brought along a girlfriend or significant other, and Winnie neither knew how to play cards nor was well versed in the lexicon of male Vietnamese shit-talking.

On their drive home, Long asked Winnie not to order a coffee the next time they met his friends. "It's not really something that good girls do," he warned her. Winnie, thinking this was a joke, had laughed at first. "I'm serious," he said. "Polite Vietnamese girls don't drink coffee."

"Polite girls don't drink coffee in coffee shops?" Winnie asked sardonically. Long had turned around on his motorbike to frown at her.

"It's fine to drink coffee at home. But the next time we're out together, order a juice or a smoothie. My friends felt uncomfortable today because you were drinking coffee."

Winnie pressed her lips together hard and did not say anything until they arrived back at the house. She was sure his friends had been more uncomfortable with Winnie joining them at their special Manly Gambling Club in the first place than they were at the fact that she had ordered coffee. It didn't matter, she thought. Now that she had offended them, she wouldn't have to spend any more time with them. She felt relieved.

But the next evening, Long had taken her with him again. His three friends had looked up with obvious displeasure when they saw Winnie walk into Café Cúc, but they had benevolently tried to mask it. While she spent another hour sitting in silence, watching the boys play *tiến lên*, Winnie drank a winter melon tea, which had seemed like the most ladylike beverage on the menu because it came in a pale green can. Long had seemed pleased with her. Since that day, Winnie had given up coffee entirely.

When Winnie was there again the next day, they told her that she could at least make herself useful by tracking their scores. Winnie was oddly flattered, and she was pleased to have something to do. Unfortunately, she was not very good at it. The rounds moved too quickly for her to keep track of, she didn't understand the points system, the boys' card-flinging and insult-trading distracted her, and the pen that the owners of Café Cúc had let her borrow was running out of ink, which was not her fault but made things even more difficult. It was a disaster, and Long had ended up doing most of the math for her. Still, by the fifth or sixth time, Long's friends seemed to have resigned themselves to having Winnie as a new fixture at their gatherings, and by the second week she had almost gotten the hang of the scoring.

Sometimes after cards Long and his friends wanted to go drinking, and so they would drive over to Bia Hơi Baby, which served glasses of draft beer for 8,000đ and a variety of grilled or deep-fried dishes in an open building that looked like a garage. The first time she had gone with them, Winnie had assumed that girls who were too polite to drink coffee in public were also forbidden from drinking alcohol, but the rules were slightly more complicated for beer; Long made a point of boasting to his friends when they arrived that Winnie was able to hold her liquor, but he also whispered to her in English that she should stop after two glasses so that she could drive them home if he got too drunk. Winnie was not surprised when he drank eight. The beer was weak to begin with, and it was normal for Long to have three cans of Saigon Green with dinner.

It was difficult for Winnie to handle the bike, but she always managed to get them back to the house intact. One night, in a celebratory mood after winning at cards—a rare occurrence for Long—he had twelve beers and made her pull over by the river on the way home so he could pee. Midstream, he had started crooning twangy Vietnamese pop ballads down to the dead fish in the water. As she watched Long sing to the river, his hair flopping over his eyes, Winnie knew that while what she felt for him was not love, it was closer to it than she deserved.

NOW THAT SHE NO longer drank coffee, Winnie did not have any reason to leave the house on her own. The first day that Long reluctantly left her to go to work, she had gone out and tried to find Café Max again, attempting to replicate the sequence of meandering turns that had brought her there on that rainy afternoon. She successfully located the meat market alley, but no matter how many times she walked the length of it, she was unable to identify the café's back wall that she had climbed over, or locate the street with its front entrance.

The next day she hadn't left the house on her own at all. It was much easier than she thought it would be. She sat in the bathtub, she sat on the balcony, she nibbled at the least squishy member of a browning claw of bananas, she took an unsatisfying nap, and then Long was home again. *This must be how it feels to be Goji,* she thought. Two days later, she needed to go to the pharmacy. There was a deep, wet itch inside her ears that had been eluding her, and she was out of Q-tips. But when Winnie got to the gate, she hesitated. She did not feel like she was doing the hesitating; it was her feet that were refusing to move. They suddenly each weighed four hundred pounds. Winnie took a few careful breaths. "I am going to walk out this door," she said out loud, and willed herself to inch her right foot forward. It finally obeyed her. But it had taken her nearly two minutes to cross the threshold. The pharmacy was just around the corner, a walk that took less time than the act of leaving the house had, but Winnie felt utterly, inexplicably drained by the errand. She stumbled through the door in her haste to get back inside, nearly collapsing in the entryway. The warm rush of relief she felt flooding her body the moment she returned to the house was overwhelming.

Winnie had nowhere to go the next day, but she decided to get dressed and try to go somewhere, just to see what her feet would do. Once again, when she reached for the gate, she felt an irrational torpor take hold of her body, stronger than yesterday. She was physically unable to go out the door. In a small voice, she thought to herself: *The house does not want me to leave.* Then she had gone back up to bed.

When Long was at home, Winnie was released from whatever bound her. He could move freely in and out of the house, and he could take her with him. But during the day, when she was on her own, Winnie was not able to walk out the door. What surprised her the most was how little she minded her captivity. It was a good feeling to belong, and Winnie belonged to the house.

She began making excuses to get out of going to coffee with Long and his friends, saying that she was too tired, or that her ear itch was bothering her too much. (The itch was not a lie—it had come and gone since Winnie had moved in, and she could not figure out what was causing it. Twice, Long had taken her to see a doctor: the first time for an examination where nothing wrong was found with Winnie, and the second time, a few weeks later, to extract a Q-tip bud she had gotten stuck inside her ear canal while trying to go after the irritation on her own. Winnie was more careful when she poked herself now, but sometimes she thought about how nice it would be to take a sharp bamboo skewer and end the itch for good.) Enough time had passed that Long was no longer afraid to leave Winnie home alone in the evenings; he did not press her to come with him when she pleaded out.

WINNIE COULD NOT, HOWEVER, get out of going to Long's hometown with him for Lunar New Year.

"I can't leave you all alone for four days!" said Long. "I'd go crazy worrying about you. But I have to go home and visit my mother and grandmother. It's my turn to go up—my brother and I alternate Tết years so we won't have to see each other."

The brother whose mere mention had caused Long to fold in on himself like the leaf of a mimosa plant before. Winnie could tell that Long was being careful to keep his tone even, but one hand sprang up to touch his forehead when he said the word "brother," like an involuntary twitch.

Still, he continued smoothly. "The rest of my mom's family is dead. And we're not close to my late father's side. They're all down in the Delta anyway. Don't worry, I don't have to tell them about *us*," he said, sensing Winnie's reluctance and misinterpreting it as her being worried about what meeting his family would mean for their relationship. The truth was that Winnie did not want to leave the house. "I'll just say that you're my American friend from work, and that I didn't want you to be alone during the holidays. It'll be an awful trip, but I promise to make it up to you. Once we get back, I'll take you to the beach. How does that sound? We'll go to Vung Tau for a long weekend and eat grilled oysters and watch the sun rise over the ocean."

Vung Tau. Winnie knew that this was where her father had been evacuated from in 1975, the last place where he had touched Vietnamese soil. She had no desire to go there, but this wasn't because of its history, it was because she disliked the seaside in general. Growing up, Winnie's summer vacations had consisted solely of her parents taking her to Ocean City for five unhappy days in the beginning of August. It was the only place they had ever gone. Perhaps unfairly, this had instilled within Winnie a lifelong hatred of the beach. But she knew that there was nothing a good Grateful Mouth would want more than to meet Long's family, see where he grew up, and then be taken on a weekend getaway in Vung Tau. "I love grilled oysters," she said with a smile.

The night before they left, she lay awake in the empty bathtub, whispering apologies at the wall, telling the house that she was sorry for going.

WINNIE COULDN'T REMEMBER THE names of all the provinces they drove through on the thirteen-hour trip; she charted their progress by what was being grown alongside the road. For the first few hours it alternated between sugarcane fields and spindly rows of rubber trees. Then they turned onto a narrow mountain highway and the coffee plantations began. The asphalt at twistier passes was marked with rune-like squiggles of white paint, which took Winnie a long time to recognize as police outlines at accident sites. The coffee fields became tea fields, which gave way to unruly, uncultivated miles of thirsty brush and thickets of yellowy bamboo. When the pepper plantations began, Long called over his shoulder that they were getting closer.

Downtown Ia Kare was a small, dusty collection of low buildings, most of them painted brick with corrugated tin roofs, but some newer ones were made of concrete and tile. There was an empty gas station, a motorbike repair shop, and a stand selling chicken and rice where a woman was napping in a hammock. There were two coffee shops: one with a large sign outside that advertised FREE WI-FI and was full of

teenagers, and another directly across the street from it, without internet access, that was full of old men drinking rice wine. They drove past
a beauty salon featuring a poster in the front window of a platinum-
haired American boy band from the nineties, a shoe store whose inven-
tory consisted of only rubber sandals, and a store that appeared to sell
tombstones. Two men played chess beneath a leafless, witchy-branched
tamarind tree with shriveled brown pods, while a third man watched.
In a small park, stray dogs chased each other around manicured hedges
and tiled walkways flecked with sundried pellets of their own shit.

After passing the semi-enclosed concrete square of the Ia Kare central market, they turned onto an uneven orange-dirt road that took
them away from town and made Winnie feel seasick. Flocks of electric
yellow butterflies hovered along the edge of the road, and a few unlucky ones, fluttering directly in the path of the motorbike, turned into
smears of golden dust on Long's helmet and Winnie's sleeves. For a
time, the road ran alongside a cemetery. Within it there was a curious-
looking statue—an enormous one, great and black and hulking—but
Winnie couldn't tell what it was supposed to be because they passed by
so quickly.

The small brick house where Long's mother lived was so well camouflaged against the ochre fields and the orange dirt of the road that
Winnie didn't notice it when they pulled up in front, and she was confused as to why Long was stopping. Then her eyes adjusted and she
saw the figure of Mrs. Phan, clad in black, watching them from the
front window.

They were ushered into the front room. Winnie was told to make
herself comfortable on a wooden bed covered in rush matting that
buckled and made splintery squeaks when she sat on it. Her eyes did a
sweep across the room. At one end, an altar with a color photograph of
Long's late father in his army uniform. At the other, two geckos shimmering across the wall and disappearing into a crack. Mrs. Phan
brought out tea from the kitchen. She moved like her bones were too
heavy for her skin. She seemed neither perturbed nor intrigued by
Winnie. In fact, she didn't appear to feel any sort of way about her at

all. Her hair was entirely white, but her complexion was remarkably unlined and possessed a sort of blankness that Winnie found comforting. She asked Winnie twice if she wanted something to eat and gave a vacant smile when Winnie replied both times that she was fine with tea.

A sudden cadence of sharp taps came from behind the door in a corner.

"Oh, Grandma's up," said Long, and Mrs. Phan wordlessly rose to her feet and went to tend to her. "That's her room," he explained to Winnie. "She doesn't really leave it anymore. Would you like to freshen up before we eat dinner? The outhouse is in the yard, straight back toward the lychee grove after you go out the kitchen door."

Winnie did not meet the grandmother at all that first evening. She wondered if Long had gone into the side room to greet her while she was out back in the bathroom. If she was being kept secret from the old woman she didn't mind, but she was curious about what was going on behind that closed door. At dinnertime, Mrs. Phan spread out a simple meal for Winnie and Long on a woven floor mat—boiled quails' eggs, braised pork that fell apart into strings at the touch of chopsticks, pickled greens and sticky disks of rice cake—and then piled some of everything onto a dish and took it into the back room when the tapping started again.

Even though there was still another day before New Year's, that night there were early fireworks in the hills. Winnie and Long watched from the front yard, leaning against his motorbike. The fireworks were homemade, sporadic and weak. They were more noise than flash, and even then, they were nearly drowned out by the howling of all the local dogs. They were over quickly, and the hermetic countryside darkness descended over everything once more. Then the dogs quieted down and all that remained was a glottal chorus from miles of toads chirping in the surrounding fields.

Long slept in a hammock slung up in the kitchen, his mother retired to the room behind the door with the unseen grandmother, and Winnie was assigned the unforgiving wooden bed in the front room, beneath the translucent dome of an ornate mosquito net that unfolded like an old lace parasol. Winnie felt like a trapped spider, or a cake beneath a glass cover. She lay stiffly on her back to keep the bed planks from squeaking and anticipated a normal, sleepless night, perhaps a more uncomfortable one than usual. But miraculously—was it because of the pitch blackness of countryside or the soothing toad sounds?— Winnie was unconscious within minutes and remained that way until morning. But her excitement at waking up well rested for the first time in longer than she could remember was eclipsed by the dismay of dis- covering that her period had started. Winnie's menses were capricious; they adhered to no reliable schedule. She had brought tampons with her to Ia Kare, just to be safe, but had not been fully prepared for the plumbing and system of waste management at Long's house.

Long was still snoring in the kitchen hammock, even though his mother was already up and cooking, chopping garlic beneath him. Winnie slipped outside to the washroom, which was a separate wooden structure at the back of the house beside the outhouse. At the doorsill she traded her sneakers for the rubber showering sandals inside. Her feet were too big to fit inside the straps, so she had to balance on the balls of her feet on top of them while she crouched down to splash her- self clean with cold water from the wall faucet. When she was done she corked herself with a tampon, trying not to panic about how to dispose of it later. The previous night she had helped wash the dishes and ob- served that trash was collected in a small, clear plastic bag that was hung from a nail by the kitchen door. Winnie was too embarrassed to put the tampons in there for Long's mother to find.

They spent the morning in the cemetery cleaning the family grave. Mrs. Phan was in all black again, walking in her slow, painful way and holding a broom and some old rags. Long carried a bundle of long in- cense sticks in his arms and kept accidentally dropping them on the ground and then crouching clumsily to pick them up, usually dropping more in the process. Winnie had never seen him quite this nervous. Each time they crossed paths with another family in the cemetery he would practically jump out of his skin. Winnie had nothing to hold, and kept her empty hands folded somberly across her chest. The Ia

Kare graveyard looked like a spilled bag of sun-melted candies to her, all fading electric colors and warped, semifamiliar shapes. The stale, sweet smell from burning incense and rotting flowers was everywhere. As they walked by the large, dark statue Winnie had spotted on the drive in—it was a woman, she now saw—Long reached out a hand and lightly touched a carved fold of robe. Winnie twisted her neck and bent backward to try and see the face under her hat but couldn't make it out.

Together they swept and polished the tomb of Long's father. When Winnie's sweat dripped onto the grave she rubbed it in with her cloth and made the stone even shinier. Past the distant edge of the cemetery she could see a crooked hem of treetops stretching off beyond her line of vision. This in itself was not remarkable, but what caught Winnie's eye was that the trees were all blackened and charred. "What's that over there?" she asked Long, pointing. "What are all those dead trees?"

He looked up from plucking the weeds at the base of his father's tomb and frowned. "That's the old rubber plantation. I'll tell you some of the stories about it later, once we get out of here," he said, but Winnie could tell that he wouldn't. Long reached down and ripped out a clump of dry grass with unnecessary force. "God, I could use a beer," he muttered to himself.

THEY RETURNED HOME AND Mrs. Phan once again disappeared into the grandmother's room, this time bringing her tea. Long had purchased two cans of Saigon Green from a woman with a beverage cart at the cemetery gates and was noticeably less edgy after drinking one. After he finished the second he suggested to Winnie that they go for a walk.

Instead of going down the main road they went out the back door, past the outhouse and washroom and through his mother's twelve ly-chee trees. They reached a skinny dirt road, only about a foot wide, that marked the edge of the Phans' property, and then crossed over it and into a neighbor's grove of shaggy longans. Winnie could smell that they owned pigs long before the sty came into view.

The pig encampment was made from dark cement, long and rectangular and roofless, with a trough running along one side. There were about ten of them, and their odor was so strong that it seemed to distort and blur the air around their bodies. They were larger and darker and hairier than American pigs, and they examined Winnie with hungry, clever eyes.

"Don't try to pet them," said Long, even though Winnie wouldn't have dared. "They'll bite your hand off. Whenever I was bored as a kid I used to sneak over here and feed them. I would give them the worst things I could find and they would eat it all. Sticks and pencils. Dead rats. Every kind of garbage. My brother threw up in their feed trough once and they ate that too." He reached into his jacket pocket and took out a bag jiggling with leftover rice porridge from breakfast. Winnie knew most of it was hers—she hadn't been able to finish her bowl in the morning because she thought that *cháo* had the texture of hot glue. Growing up, it had been the sole Vietnamese dish that her father ever cooked for them, and only if someone in the house was sick. Winnie wished she could say that it tasted like her childhood, but if she tried eating it, all she could taste was the memory of stomach flu.

Long jiggled out the porridge into the trough, where it was slurped up by eager snouts and clung to long, porcine chin hairs. "I still feel guilty about it," he said, "so I always make sure to bring them something nice to eat whenever I'm back for Tết. Mom and Grandma don't care about any of the fancy gifts I bring back for them, but at least I can make the pigs happy."

After folding the empty porridge bag back up, Long checked to make sure that there was no one else around. "Winnie," he asked slyly, taking her hand and pulling her toward him, "Are you hungry at all?"

He had inadvertently smeared a little gray dab of rice gruel on her wrist. Winnie tried to ignore it. "Here?" she asked. "Are you sure the neighbors can't see?"

"I'm sure." He was leaning back against the cement wall. A Grateful Mouth was always hungry. Long closed his eyes and Winnie crouched down. She could hear the pigs' jaws grinding and the sound of their wet grunts. She could feel them watching her, even if Long wasn't.

AFTERWARD, THEY RETURNED TO the dirt road, and this time they turned to stroll down it, leaping aside into the brush whenever motorbikes laden with lumpy burlap sacks of coffee beans came puttering by. They walked for fifteen minutes, until they reached a grove of unfamiliar trees whose branches appeared to be sprouting red bell peppers.

"Do you know what these are?" asked Long, smiling. Winnie shook her head. Long found a long stick and whacked the closest tree with it until one of the fruits dropped to the ground. "It's a cashew!" he said, picking it up and handing it to her with a grin. "This one's not ripe yet, but do you see the little nub growing out at the end of the fruit? See the shape? That's the nut."

The cashew apple fit in Winnie's hand comfortably, like a grenade. She ran her thumb over the little embryo-shaped protuberance of the nut and thought smugly that the Cooks probably didn't know where cashews came from, before that smugness was replaced by guilt.

"This way," said Long, and walked farther into the orchard. He stopped at a sturdy-looking tree with branches that arced low, then hoisted himself into them effortlessly. It was clearly a tree he was familiar with, thought Winnie as she clambered up after him, skinning a knee in the process. Long tucked himself into a smooth L-shaped crook. His arm rested on the tree's trunk in the casually possessive way that some men liked to drape their hands on their girlfriends' thighs in public. Not Long though. It was not polite.

"This orchard actually belongs to the family of an old friend," said Long.

"That's nice. Are we going to visit him?" asked Winnie, picking little bits of bark from her knee.

"Ah, no. She's not here anymore."

Winnie looked up. "Where is she?" she asked, hoping that she sounded nonchalant, struggling to restrain the curiosity trying to claw its way into her voice.

Long patted his jacket pocket before he remembered that he had already finished his last beer back at the house. He shrugged. "I don't know. Maybe she moved to Pleiku. Maybe Hanoi. She didn't even tell her family that she was planning to leave. One day they just realized that she wasn't there anymore. I only heard about it from market ladies."

"Was she your book friend?" asked Winnie. Her curiosity had broken loose; it had made the question come out too high and too eager.

Long nodded slowly. "She was my book friend. She was my best friend. She and my brother and I were close, when we were all growing up." Long absently reached out and took hold of a low-hanging cashew, gently squeezing its little tan knob like it was a nipple. "But I haven't spoken to either of them in six years. Why?" he said, intercepting the question with a sad smile before it had fully formed on Winnie's lips, "Because I was stupid. We had a falling-out before I left for Saigon. It was small enough that I thought she would just forgive me when some time had passed, but it was big enough that I couldn't bring myself to apologize, because I felt too ashamed.

"So I waited instead. I wrote the occasional letter. I mailed her the books. She never wrote back. I didn't reach out to my brother, because I didn't really miss him at all. Maybe that's why I like you, Winnie. You moved to the other side of the world. You never talk about your family. They don't have a hold over you. You make me feel less guilty about how little I mind losing mine." Winnie opened her mouth. She would have told him that a part of her was always thirteen, watching her brothers and sisters and mother and father at her brother's graduation from the corner. Then she closed it again. Long was talking to her, but he was looking at a point past her head.

"In a way," he continued, "I'm happy she left. She had always talked about wanting to leave this place but never actually did it—because of money, or because she was more afraid of leaving than she let on.

"Now whenever I come home, after I visit my dad's grave, I'll come out here to visit this orchard. It's another cemetery for me. For my memories of her, maybe. For our friendship. For our old life."

This was a lie, thought Winnie, but without jealousy. He was not here to honor their friendship. He was here because he was still waiting and always would be.

THAT NIGHT THERE WERE bonfires in front of every house, distant orange smears of light in the dusk that Winnie and Long could see from Mrs. Phan's front yard. They did not make a fire of their own, but the wind carried the smell of smoke to them. Long sat in the grass and tugged Winnie down with him. His skin smelled like dust and beer. That afternoon he had driven over to the convenience store in town and bought an entire case of Saigon Green, and then made impressive headway with it during dinner. When midnight struck, scores of fireworks were set off all at once, and it sounded like the fabric of the sky was being ripped apart.

In the early hours of the morning, long after the explosions had stopped and the fires had all burned out and everyone else in the house was sleeping, Winnie slipped out from underneath her mosquito net. She crept outside and found her shoes. Then she felt her way through the lychee trees, tripping over roots in the dark. In her hands she held two used tampons that she had wrapped up in newspaper and kept hidden during the day. The pigs were not asleep. They were swaying by their trough, all reeking shadow and flashes of eye whites in the moonlight. Winnie tossed them the soggy tampon parcel and left when she heard chewing.

THE NEXT MORNING THERE was fresh fruit and incense for the family altar. More sticky green rice cakes for breakfast. Long had bought a lucky kumquat tree to place in the corner. Festive music was being piped over a loudspeaker in town, and the histrionics of electric bam-

boo flute reached them even out here. But it was still a skeletal Tết—
a Tết that was just going through the motions.

Winnie's New Year's present was that Long would be driving his
mother to the temple that morning and he had gently suggested to
Winnie that she might feel awkward if she came along—they would
see all of their neighbors, who would have questions about her.

When they were gone, Winnie crawled back beneath her mosquito
dome even though it wasn't necessary during the day—the ones she
needed to worry about only came out after dusk, she'd been told. She
allowed herself to slide into the pleasant kind of half doze where her
consciousness sagged just until the point where it felt like the hard surface of the bed was tilting gently underneath her. She didn't know how
long she had been laying there before she heard the tapping coming
from the grandmother's room. Winnie turned her head to look—the
door was cracked open about an inch and a half. The tapping was soft,
but insistent. It was an invitation. Winnie lifted the edge of her net and
rolled herself out. She padded barefoot across the concrete to the bedroom and then, using one finger, she pushed the wooden door open
wide enough to peep through.

Long's grandmother lounged in a wooden bed twice the size of the
one in the sitting room. She was a large woman, three-chinned and
bounteously berolled in flesh, wearing a purple pajama set. That such
an unapologetic abundance of female body existed in Ia Kare was as-
tonishing to Winnie. She had only seen women here like Long's
mother—gaunt, with deep cheek hollows that looked pecked out by
vultures. There were certainly fat men—she had noticed them in town,
their white undershirts rolled up all the way to the armpits to stay cool,
smooth brown guts puffed out and gleaming in the sun. But only they
were allowed to expose their bellies, or to even possess them; in their
world, Long's grandmother's extravagant size was an act of defiance.
Winnie could see that Long had inherited his peculiar eyes from her—
hers were almost identically wide set and bulging, but while his were
dark brown, hers were an unusual pale color, a yellowy gray, as if the
color had been seeped out of them, and they lacked the warmth of his.

Her wild hair was still more black than white; it was cropped to her shoulders and frizzed out in a triangle around her head.

"Girl," she said. In one hand she held an empty glass, in the other, a long, stripped lychee branch, which she used to deliver a dactylic series of whacks against the wall beside the bed. This solved the mystery of the tapping. "Girl—I've run out of tea." She stopped hitting the wall and now aimed the stick at a low table at the foot of the bed, where there was a dented tin thermos and more empty glasses with slimy shreds of old tea leaves clinging to their sides. Winnie pushed the door open just far enough to let herself in. "Not too much water; I want it to be strong," the old woman said, as Winnie poured out a luke-warm stream from the thermos into one of the glasses, unable to find a clean one, or any fresh tea leaves. When she brought it over, the grand-mother dropped her other glass down on the folds of the filthy quilt beside her before taking the new one. Winnie inched backward toward the door.

"Well," she said, sipping the watery tea, "tell me, do you think I seem well?"

Winnie realized she had been staring at her again and blushed. She leaned back lightly, resting in the gap between door and doorframe, wondering how she could escape. "Yes," she said, and it was true. Long's grandmother seemed to pulsate with an energy that made everything else in the room pallid and bland in comparison, including Winnie.

The old woman barked with laughter and spat a tea leaf out onto the wall. "You're wrong. I'm all rotten inside," she informed Winnie with relish. "If you sliced me open, black goo would ooze out. I'm full of poison. Full of pus. I'm dying. Would you like to know how I'm so sure that I'm dying?"

Winnie nodded because it seemed like it would be rude to do otherwise. The grandmother grinned. "Because I did it to myself. Do my eyes seem unusual to you, girl?"

It felt like another trick question. "Yes," Winnie said eventually. She had decided it would be best not to lie.

"That's because they are. I have a special sight. When I was twelve, my family sold me to a Frenchman like a farm animal, and every single night, before I went to sleep, I wished that I could climb out of my own body and run away. And then one night, after I made my same wish and closed my eyes, I figured out how to open my *other* set of eyes. And these eyes did not have to stay with my body, no, no. My other eyes can drift off my face and go wherever I want them to go. They watch whoever they want to watch, and no one can see them. While my body was sleeping, my other eyes would go out into the world. They saw nasty old Louis get up to all sorts of perverse things. They peeped in the windows of his neighbors—they liked to spy on the handsome Frenchman, but not that other one, not the boring one who was in love with the handsome one. They would see what kinds of creatures were sneaking around in the woods. They saw wondrous things. But there is a cost for the special sight. And it's the body that pays it. Every time I looked, a little more poison would trickle into me.

"My joints started to grow weak. Sometimes I wouldn't have the strength to stay on my feet all day long. I started swelling up. And then one day my legs stopped working. That's the wicked trick of the gift—the more I looked, the less I was able to move, but the less I was able to move, the more I needed to keep looking, to see what was lost to me. My body's been trapped in this room for years, but my eyes still go roaming every day and all night, whenever I want. My magic eyes have seen such awful things happen in this place. I saw what happened out in those rubber trees when it was still a plantation. And I saw as much of the war as any soldier. I saw what happened to the rich man's daughter when she was lost out in the trees, years later. I saw evil being committed by members of my own family tree." Grandmother emitted a guttural little chortle. "But the second wicked trick of these eyes is that the more I see, the less I care. I see such beastly things, yet I am never horrified anymore. The black goo inside me keeps me from feeling. But I still can't stop looking. And I won't stop until I'm dead."

Grandmother suddenly started to cough. She took her stick and thumped herself on the back with it, then spat out another tea leaf.

"Talking makes me tired; bring me a slice of rice cake, and then I'll tell you more."

Winnie nodded, backed out of the door, pulled it shut, and then turned around to see Long and his mother, back early from their social calls.

"Grandma was talking to you?" Long's eyes flashed alarm.

"I just got her fresh tea," said Winnie. "And she asked me to get her some *bánh tét.*"

Long looked relieved. "Mother will get it for her. And just ignore anything she said to you—Bà Nội is a little bit of a lunatic."

IN THE MIDDLE OF the night, after disposing of her tampons at the pigsty again, Winnie did not return to the house. Instead, she kept following the little dirt road, stumbling occasionally over tire ruts. Every few steps, she would pause and look around furtively, wondering where the eyes were.

The cemetery was somehow a friendlier and less frightening place at night, without the sun blistering the colors into distorted hues. The shapes of the stones softened in the cool dark, and the smell of incense, which draped thick and heavy over everything during the day when it was being burned, had dissipated. Stranger and more interesting scents were now allowed in: wood smoke from the bonfires in town, soil and the distant stink of pig on the wind, the metallic odor of the dry-season sky.

It felt like it took ages to cross the cemetery, but Winnie could not know for certain because there was no moon to help her keep track of time. When she passed by the statue at the center of the graveyard, something pale suddenly fluttered at the edge of her vision and her heart slammed against her chest. It was just a large bird, perched on the statue and rearranging its wings, Winnie realized, but her pace quickened anyway. When she finally reached the plantation she was slightly out of breath.

Winnie looked hard into the darkness between the rubber trees.

The air still had the faintest tang of charcoal. The trunks were scorched, blacker than the rest of the blackness surrounding them, but there were already thin new shoots growing out from them. Winnie closed her eyes. There was not much difference between the night and the inside of her own skull. She raised her arms above her head like branches. She tried to open her other set of eyes. From somewhere deep in the stomach of the forest, she heard a humming.

THE SKY HAD NOT lightened by the time she made it back to the house, but that was still no indication of what time it was; the dawn here was the kind that arrived without warning. It could have been hours away, or it could have been ready to erupt over the hills in a matter of minutes. She crept back inside, but before she could seal herself back underneath the mosquito dome, she heard tapping from the grandmother's room again—quiet this time, more of a gentle scratch than a tapping. She hesitated, knowing that Long's mother was asleep in the same room, but the scratching did not stop and so she tiptoed over and softly pushed the door open.

"Don't worry—she won't wake up." The mound of shadows and blankets called softly from the bed, and gestured with her stick at Long's mother snoring on the floor near where Winnie stood in the doorway. "She sleeps like a corpse. But you can stay where you are— I just wanted to tell you that I'm glad you didn't go into the forest."

It was true, then. She could leave her body. Winnie smiled, overcome with wonderment.

"Because my fool grandson didn't warn you, did he? Those trees are full of snakeys!"

The smile dropped off Winnie's face.

Grandmother threw her head back and cackled so hard the bed shook, but Long's mother continued sleeping, undisturbed. "They're why no one goes in the rubber-tree forest—it's full of them. *Rắn hổ mang*—you know that kind?"

Winnie shook her head, unfamiliar with the Vietnamese. Grandmother set her lychee stick down across her lap and then curved her hands around to the either side of her face to mime a cobra hood. She flicked her tongue in and out. "You know. The spitting ones. There are nests and nests of them in there. Some of them were barbecued when the forest burned, but still, snakeys everywhere! You can never kill them all. Only I can go in, with my special eyes, and not get bitten. You're lucky, stupid girl. Even though you're slow and you can't speak correctly and you never brought me my *bánh tét* like I asked, you can still marry my grandson if you want to." The grandmother used the stick to itch one of her feet. "It doesn't make one lick of difference to me, because I'll be dead before too long. This is all I wanted to say to you. You can go now."

BY MORNING, HER PERIOD was nearly gone. Winnie didn't have time to visit the pigs before she and Long drove back to Saigon, so she dug a shallow hole in the ground behind the washroom and buried her final tampon in it. She tried not to think about what would happen in a couple months, when the rains returned.

1981 DID NOT FEEL LIKE THE AFTERMATH, BUT IT DID not feel like a new beginning either. The Americans were gone, but they were still fighting the Chinese because of Cambodia. General Giap had resigned as minister of defense. The Central Highlands experienced an abnormal amount of precipitation in January. On the second day of the Lunar New Year, Old Ma's daughter, at nine and a half years old, had her first period and hid it from her family. Old Ma himself was still known just as "Ma," but there was early iron woven into his hair. While the subsidy years would not be his most prosperous era, he would still emerge from them having amassed a small fortune due to strategic political friendships and a thriving side career in the black market. Rural Ia Kare, whose inhabitants were desperate enough to murder each other over ration stamps for condensed milk, provided no opportunity for him to spend the money he was clandestinely accumulating. Therefore, every few months, Old Ma would descend from his perch in the hill country to play poker down in Nha Trang, at an illegal makeshift casino set up inside one of the hangars of an abandoned air base outside the city.

It was the local haunt of cadres in the know and the Russians they did business with. Old Ma was acquainted with most of the men who gathered there, and so he was instantly suspicious of the Fortune Teller, having never seen him before, when the man turned up with his brief-case one cerulean coastal evening, clothes rumpled and shoulder-length hair disheveled as if he had blown into the casino on a gust of anchovy-scented ocean wind.

Old Ma was very pleased, however, by the fact that he was able to immediately discern that their new guest was mixed race. It made him feel like he was a secret agent, a career he had always fantasized about. "French daddy in the army?" he said, a little too loudly, as he dropped into the seat across from him. "No need to ask what your mother did for a living, then, eh?" He lifted an eyebrow and made a crude hand gesture. "But you're a little dark for a halfie, aren't you?"

At this, the three other men at their table—a young and virulently mustachioed Vietnamese officer and two older Russian arms dealers, one wearing a suit the color of dishwater, the other one dressed for a spaghetti western, eyes obscured by the brim of a creamy white Stetson and toes stuffed into pointy boots of pimpled ostrich skin—started to snigger. The Fortune Teller chuckled gamely along with them through gritted teeth. "Yes, yes, you got me, you sniffed out the baguette crumbs in my veins, well done," he said, with convincing amiability, and then glanced down at the skin of his deeply tanned forearms. "Am I really that dark?" he muttered to himself. "Perhaps I should get a sun hat."

But Old Ma wasn't finished having his fun yet. "So, did Daddy die, or did he just leave you behind when he fucked off back to Paris?" he asked. "And if you're French, why haven't they picked you up and put you in a work camp somewhere?"

The Fortune Teller gave him a taut smile. "I never knew my father. And I have a certain ability that was useful enough to keep me out of trouble during the last few decades. I usually manage to end up where I need to be."

"Ability?"

"I'm a fortune teller."

But Old Ma's face was impassive. "What, so, you read palms?" he asked.

"Palms. Birth charts. Faces," said the Fortune Teller.

"Go ahead, then," said Old Ma, jutting his chin out so that the light-bulb dangling above their table could illuminate his face. His skin had the pallor and moist, flabby quality of a freshly steamed *bánh cuốn*. "Read mine."

"You have a wealthy nose," the Fortune Teller replied. It was excessively narrow, with cruel little nostrils that were positioned too high up and made every facial expression a sneer. "You have the chin of a gambler—I know, I know, not a particularly insightful thing to say to someone in a casino—but the curve is auspicious. You usually do quite well for yourself when you're here, don't you?" Old Ma acknowledged this with a little half nod and a pleased smile, which quickly faded when the Fortune Teller continued: "One of the nephews who works for you is skimming money. He's been doing it for years. You have a daughter. Your family name will end with her. She is more willful than you think, more reckless than you like to imagine, and one day you will lose her. You will outlive your younger brother, but your death will be far more gruesome, and it is going to be unexpected."

When Old Ma was furious, he turned even whiter and his nostrils contracted with rage instead of flaring. "And where exactly on my face do you think you read all that?" he hissed.

"In your ears," smiled the Fortune Teller.

"I can't stand men who think they're funny. I'm going to have you thrown into a ditch after I win all of your money," said Old Ma, snatching up the cards on the table in front of him.

The Fortune Teller proceeded to win every single hand that was dealt. He didn't have particularly good cards or seem to fully grasp the way the game worked or even appear pleased at the chips accumulating in front of him; the others all just kept receiving combinations that were so bad that they seemed to defy the laws of probability. The Russians were growing vocal in their displeasure, and their dealer even swapped their deck of cards with another table's to try and prove that it wasn't rigged.

"Enough," Old Ma finally said, tossing his truly useless three of hearts and six of diamonds to the side. "We don't know how you're cheating, but we're tired of it."

The Fortune Teller pushed his mound of chips back to the center of the table. "I don't need these," he said. "But it doesn't seem fair to win all those hands and then walk away with nothing." He reached across the table and lifted the hat from the Russian cowboy's head. "This, however, will do nicely. Oh yes. A perfect sun hat." The Russian was so stunned he did not even protest.

The Fortune Teller was now rummaging in his briefcase for something. "Here," he said to Old Ma, handing him a small card. "For when you lose her. I can help you find her again."

Old Ma tore it in half and threw it on the floor without looking at it. The Fortune Teller only smiled and doffed his new hat before ambling out the door. Later that night, when Old Ma reached into his jacket looking for his hotel key, he found another card, identical to the one he had ripped up, perfectly intact and tucked deep into an inner pocket. *JFA Fortune Telling*, it read in curly letters above a phone number and a Saigon address. Old Ma was too superstitious to throw this one away too.

He stuck it in a cabinet when he got back home, and then did not think of it again until one morning five years later, when his maid went to wake his fifteen-year-old daughter for school and discovered that she was gone.

The Mas were not originally from Ia Kare. In 1955, the main branch of the family had left Nghe An—the province forming the lower jaw of the North, forever on the verge of taking a bite out of Laos—to resettle in Dak Lak. They had built their house on top of the bones of the villa that had once belonged to the Frenchman Louis "l'Anguille" Lejeune, razing it and erecting a compound of gray cement with an appropriately Soviet preponderance of severe angles. In a few years, after the land reforms had had more time to kick in, the house would begin to sprout more stories and architectural ornamentation. But in 1986 the building was still relatively modest, and it took only a very brief search for the Mas to determine that the girl was not in the house.

The police combed through every pepper and coffee field, calling her name. They knocked on each door in the district and stopped all the buses at the Gia Lai border to see if she was being smuggled in one of their cargo holds. Posters of the girl were put up in Buon Ma Thuot. But after three days, when no ransom note had been sent, the detectives ruled out kidnapping. The only place they had not searched extensively was the old rubber plantation. This was because, in addition to being overrun by snakes, it was allegedly haunted by the ghosts of the two Frenchmen who had originally planted the trees, and the spirits of the half dozen bite victims from over the years—people unfamiliar with the area who had made the mistake of wandering in and stepping on something that was not a root. A few brave volunteers had ventured in at the edges, but they refused to go past the third row of trees.

Finally, the police chief told Old Ma that either the girl had gone into the plantation and was dead by now, or she had run away with a boyfriend and there wasn't anything they could do but wait for her to decide to come back.

Old Ma did not accept this. Of course his daughter didn't have a boyfriend, he snorted. She was his girl, and she was obedient. If she was in the plantation, he would hire someone to get her out. All of his hair had turned white over the last seventy-two hours; he would not concede defeat to the trees now. Of course, he had no intention of going in to get her himself. Old Ma dug out the card for JFA Fortune Telling, too desperate to let his pride stop him.

THE NEXT AFTERNOON, the Fortune Teller arrived in Ia Kare. He was wearing the cowboy hat he had won off the Russian, along with a too-tight denim jacket, too-baggy jeans, and rubber sandals. Unless his briefcase contained a pair of fang-proof boots, Old Ma did not think his outfit seemed like a wise choice in which to attempt to navigate twenty hectares of wild underbrush thick with concealed snakes.

The two men squinted at each other in the strong afternoon sunlight, with clear expressions of mutual dislike.

"Well?" Old Ma said, to break the uncomfortable silence. "Is there something else that you need? Equipment? Weapons?"

"What? Oh no," said the Fortune Teller, with mild bafflement. "I have everything in here." He patted the briefcase.

"Good." Another long and awkward pause ensued. Finally, Old Ma scowled. "Aren't you going to go find her, then?"

The Fortune Teller pointed to the sky. "I can't do anything until the sun sets," he said apologetically. But when he saw Old Ma's face begin to turn purple with anger, he quickly added: "But I'll go over to the cemetery to start setting up. If your daughter *is* in there, I will have her back at dawn." He loped away down the road, leaving Old Ma to roil in his own despair and ire and impatience.

At the cemetery he made himself comfortable on the ground in the shadow of Su-Su the elephant's tombstone, forty yards from the unruly edge of the rubber trees. No one else was around. There was enough time for a quick nap if he wanted. The Fortune Teller put his briefcase under his head as a pillow and tipped his hat forward to cover his face. He shifted a little in the grass and removed a pebble that was digging into his lower back. Then he abruptly sat up again and looked at his immediate surroundings cautiously.

"I know you're there," he said under his breath. "Yes, *you*. I can see you. You're watching me from that big gray stone." Now the Fortune Teller laughed. "No, don't go—come out here and meet me. I'd like to talk to you. I'll be right here; I'm not going anywhere until sunset. Please come." He leaned back against the elephant's grave, took out his lighter and three loose cigarettes from his jacket pocket, and waited.

Two hours passed. The sun began its descent and turned hazy at its edges. At last, the woman who had once been known as Odile came into view, walking slowly across the cemetery toward him.

The Fortune Teller stood up to greet her when he heard her footsteps on the grass. When he saw that she was leaning heavily on a cane, he hurried toward her so she would not have to keep walking.

"I'm sorry," he said. "I didn't realize that your body was unwell. I wouldn't have asked you to come if I had known it was so difficult."

The woman just glared at him with her magnificent tawny eyes. She leaned against a large gravestone to catch her breath.

"How long have you had the sight?" asked the Fortune Teller.

"I saw for the first time when I was twelve," she replied, still wheezing. "So, nearly forty years."

The Fortune Teller smiled at her. "We must be about the same age, then."

"Oh, don't start flirting. Cool that French blood of yours down."

The Fortune Teller's expression turned serious. "It's using you up too quickly," he said, with a nod that at once indicated the woman's cane, the trembling trunks of her legs, her straining lungs. "You shouldn't do it so often."

The woman met his gaze calmly. "Do you have the sight too?"

"No, what I have is, hmm . . . a slightly different condition," he said, pausing before the words, as if he was picking them out of his teeth with a bamboo splinter. "But I've met others with yours before. Not common though."

"How soon will it kill me if I don't listen to you and keep on doing it?"

"Oh, not for years and years. It will be slow, but it will be miserable."

She shrugged. "I am no stranger to slow misery. Now, what did you call me here for?"

The Fortune Teller looked at her sadly before turning away to face the rubber trees. "Have you been able to see the girl? Do you know where she is in there?"

"I turned the eyes on her this afternoon, before I saw you. She's in the old smokehouse. It's toward the center, in the gap between the north and west quadrants of the plantation. She can't move because she wrecked her ankle tripping in the dark. She's been kept safe, but she's weakening."

The Fortune Teller turned back to face her. "And why didn't you tell anyone else where she was?" he asked softly.

The sun was now balanced on the edge of the horizon. The woman gave the Fortune Teller a sharp look. "I'll give you three answers," she said. "And you can pick which one you like. Either I was too afraid of letting the others know what I was, or I didn't care enough about the life of that girl to bother, or I pitied her, because I saw the reason why she went into the trees that night and thought she was better off dead than in that house with that man. Choose the one that will make you hate me less."

"I don't hate you," said the Fortune Teller.

"Aren't you going to ask me why she ran away?"

The Fortune Teller couldn't meet her cold, gold gaze. "No," he finally said. "Because whatever it is, I can't leave her in there. I have to bring her back. You see? I can't risk wanting to change my mind. Does that make you hate me?"

The woman gave an ambiguous upward twist of her wrists. "I can't hate anymore. I can't really care very much at all." She took her cane in her hand and prepared to limp homeward.

"Wait," said the Fortune Teller, "Before you go, I want you to promise me something. Will you promise me something?"

"That depends what it is."

"Don't watch me tonight when I go in."

"Why not?"

"Because I'm vain," said the Fortune Teller. "I don't want you to see the creature that my affliction turns me into."

The woman turned away from him. "How is that fair," she said, half to herself, "when you've already seen what I've been turned into by my own?" She began walking away slowly through the graves.

THE FORTUNE TELLER NOW stood alone in the freshly fallen twilight by the edge of the trees. He knelt and removed his hat. Then he unclasped his briefcase, removed a small piece of folded paper from an inner compartment, and then locked it again. Fingers trembling slightly, he held up his lighter. A thin orange smear of flame caught the corner of the paper alight, and a furl of red-tinged smoke soon followed. The Fortune Teller closed his eyes, leaned over it, and inhaled.

It began the way it always did. The Fortune Teller opened his mouth and began to stretch. The bottom of his jaw dropped down, down, down, past his shoulders, down almost to his navel. And on cue, the smoke began leaching out of the orifice in red tendrils. But here the Fortune Teller reached down and hooked the fingers of his left hand securely over the set of teeth on his bottom jaw, where it was dangling by his stomach. Then, with his right hand, he reached up around his head from behind, brought it down over his face from above, and took hold of the teeth of his upper jaw. Gripping tightly, eyes still shut, the Fortune Teller now began yanking on his mouth in opposite directions, peeling the top half of his face backward, up and over his own head like a sweater, while simultaneously tugging the bottom mandible even lower, over his knees and his feet. He flipped the skin sack of his body completely inside out, swallowing himself in reverse. His interior lining had now become exterior. However, it was not composed of organ meat and pink wetness and capillary webbing but smoke. When it was over, the thing at the edge of the woods was still shaped like a man, but its flesh was made of dense, coppery cloud.

The red smoke drifted upward until it was hovering about two meters off the ground. Then it entered the forest and began moving through the trees. It changed its shape whenever it felt like it, adding more limbs to its humanoid form until it resembled an octopus more than a man, then re-absorbing its tentacles and becoming something amoeba-like instead. It noticed that it was being watched—on the forest floor, dozens of scaly heads looked up in fear as it passed, rearing back with flared hoods and hissing at the apparition. The smoke was amused by them. It adopted their shape out of curiosity, elongating itself into a snake the size of a giant anaconda and slithering on through the air. The moon was out now, bright on its opaque red smoke-flesh. It had been ages since it had been set loose. It felt like singing but it had no mouth of its own.

It had reached the center of the trees. The house was there, built of old, blackened brick, its roof partially caved in. The smoke coiled itself back into a more condensed shape as it entered—blobby and vaguely civet-like, but without a tail. It couldn't settle on how many feet it should have, so it alternated between four and six little smoke paws.

As it entered the house, the smoke thought it felt something like an old memory of dread flutter inside itself, even though this was impossible. The smoke could not have its own memories, because it was already a memory of a sort. It suspected that if it had come from anywhere, it had been a place much like this one.

Everywhere it looked, thin pelts of rubber in various stages of processing were draped over bamboo racks, ranging from the creamy white of the untreated sheets to a deep orange brown. Where was the girl? The smoke crawled over the edge of a tiled basin and peered inside. It still contained the forgotten curdy residue of coagulated latex from 1954. The building was frozen in time; everything was in the same place it had been left thirty years ago, when the workers had abandoned their posts.

Something rustled behind a door at the far end of the building. The smoke padded silently across the air toward the sound. Snake or girl? it asked itself. It grew an arm with a pincer-like attachment so that it would be able to pull open the door by its handle.

Both. Inside, curled up on top of a pile of the three-decade-old ashes in the latex-smoking chamber, was the missing girl, encircled by a two-headed cobra. The smoke jellyfished itself backward in surprise upon seeing the snake. But the snake seemed to have been expecting the smoke. It slithered tenderly over the body of the girl and then out the door.

The girl was unconscious. The smoke flattened itself into a thin, flat manta ray, intending to use itself as a trowel to scoop up her body. It managed to slip one of its wings beneath her but then only succeeded in shifting her forward a few inches before she flopped off again—she was heavier than anticipated. Frustrated, the smoke stretched itself snake-shaped again. It coiled one end of itself around the girl's ankles, ignoring the fact that one of them was swollen and discolored, and then heaved her ungracefully out of the chamber. The soft skin of her fragile human body squeaked as it was dragged over the dirty floor tiles, and the smoke felt sorry for her. It unwrapped itself from her legs. There was one option left.

The smoke drew itself out longer and skinnier, from the width of a snake to the width of an eel to the width of a rat tail to the width of a tapeworm—a shimmering red thread, thin enough that the girl wouldn't feel it. Then it floated over to the corner of her mouth, parted her lips, and began to slowly feed itself into her, inch by inch by inch. When all of the smoke was ingested, the girl's legs twitched. Her eyes remained closed, but her lifeless arms and legs were drawn upward until they were perpendicular to the ground. Then the rest of her body followed, and she slowly began to rise, her back leaving the floor tiles last. She hung in the air like a sloth dangling from an invisible branch.

Once all of her was aloft, the smoke realized from inside that the girl was facing the wrong way and recalibrated, aerially somersaulting her into an upright position. And then, with the jerky, boneless movements of a tangled marionette, she began to walk.

The smoke was clumsy at first. It was not used to the contours of this body, and it kept accidentally steering her into branches and tree trunks. It could feel the lacerations forming on her skin where thorns caught her; and though it did not understand pain, being unable to experience it, the smoke regretted causing it for the girl, even if she was unconscious. It wished that the girl could see herself walking through the forest in midair—as awkward as the movements were, she was a marvelous sight. Beneath the floating girl, down on the ground, the snakes raised their limbless bodies up as far as they could when she passed over, waving gently at her like the stalks of a strange plant.

DISMOUNTING WAS EVEN LESS GRACEFUL. When the girl's body passed through the final row of rubber trees and into the cemetery, the smoke dropped her to the ground with a careless thud and heard something in her delicate human connective tissue make a tiny popping sound. Ashamed, it began to rapidly wind itself out of her. Dawn was already approaching, and the smoke was in a hurry now. It patched itself back into a lumpy approximation of a man. It would do. Then, in a reversal of the self-swallowing at the start of the night, the smoke reached an arm into the place where a throat should be, latched on to something at the inner base of itself, and pulled the skin of the Fortune Teller out by his tongue, flipping him right way round again.

The suit of his body did not lie correctly on his flesh yet—he was still too loose for it, his mouth hanging open far too wide. But by the time the sun rose, it had tightened to fit him once more. The Fortune Teller donned his hat. Then he hoisted the girl in his arms and carried her across the cemetery and back to her home.

THERE WAS SOMETHING STILL nagging at the Fortune Teller, many months later, long after he had returned to Saigon. Something was amiss inside him. No, something was not amiss, something was *missing*. At night he prodded his stomach absently, trying to think of a way in which he could calculate how much smoke was in there. He had never considered before that the thing obeyed any laws of physics, or that it existed in a fixed amount. That there were liters of it, or cubic meters. He had assumed that it was regenerative, and therefore immeasurable. But for some reason, he could not get it out of his head that he had inadvertently left some of his smoke behind in the Highlands. And he was not eager to go back and look for it. The Fortune Teller could admit that he was not a very good fortune teller most of the time. But he had seen himself carrying the girl across the cemetery many years before he even learned of Old Ma's existence. This was why he had known that he must do it. He had already seen the day, far in the future, that Old Ma would be accidentally crushed when a chunk of the overelaborate second-floor balcony he would insist upon commissioning—ignoring the advice of his contractors—detached and landed on his head. He had seen that this would not be his last time in the Highlands, and he had seen that the forest was not finished with him yet.

BUT HE HAD NOT seen the child. At that very moment, in the hospital in Ea Sup, Old Ma's daughter was in labor. Old Ma was not there. He would never acknowledge the birth. He would not learn the gender, and he would not ask to know the name of the childless couple who had agreed to adopt it.

He was at home, instead, imagining the construction of a palatial new wing. He paused in front of a mirror in the hallway and studied his face, remembering what the Fortune Teller had claimed to have read in it. Then he smiled and continued walking, certain that the man had been wrong, and that he was the sole author of whatever future was written there.

EVEN THOUGH IT WAS STILL ONLY 9:45 WHEN TAN ARRIVED, the club was busy and the Worm was already occupying a stool at the downstairs bar. He was drinking his usual, a tumbler of rice wine on the rocks with a lime wedge, which he liked to term "neotraditionalist." Everyone else at the bar was drinking expensive cocktails that included at least three ingredients and was named after a place Tan had never been—singapore slings, long island iced teas, manhattans—but the Worm sipped his nasty *rượu* plain like an old village uncle.

There was nothing special about this club. It was a cement box without character or windows. It had flashing lights and a smoke machine and pulsing, wordless techno and a vaguely aggressive, monosyllabic English name like Lunge, or Thrust, or Jolt—Tan could never remember. This gave it a strange quality, more like a loose outline of a place than the real thing. He suspected that its utter unremarkableness was actually a deliberate choice on the part of the doctor. It did not attract attention, and so its main source of revenue—the various narcotic dealings of the Worm and his ilk—could continue unfettered.

The Worm had adopted his moniker because, growing up, he had worshipped Dennis Rodman. Those unfamiliar with basketball assumed that he had been dubbed the Worm because he happened to resemble one: tall and spindly and prematurely bald, with terrible eyesight too, just to make the comparison more inevitable. He hailed from some northern village within spitting distance of China and was adept at squiggling undetected across Vietnam's mountainous border with Laos and even going as far afield as northern Thailand and eastern Myanmar when required.

The Worm raised his glass in greeting. "Tan! My favorite captain! Why so grim?" he shouted over the music, forgoing the subtlety that Tan had understood to be traditional in drug dealing. "You look like shit! Have a drink with me, and then you'll get your boosters!"

Tan pushed past the beautiful young people with empty glasses who were clogging the vicinity of the bartender, half dancing, half pushing each other out of the way to get refills first. He plopped onto the stool next to the Worm with the fatigue of a shipwrecked sailor and leaned back against the bar. "Thanks," he said, even though he had no desire to drink anything.

A little hand flick from the Worm, and a bartender appeared within seconds holding a second glass of rice wine, to the silent seething of the queuing beautiful young people still waiting for drinks. Tan swirled the liquor, trying to get the ice to melt faster, the slice of lime batted around by the whirlpool like a tiny green boat. He did not like drinking rice wine, because it reminded him of his father. Tan's earliest childhood memory was of Duc Phan summoning him into the room where he and his friends sat, shirtless, in a circle on the floor. They were fanning themselves with folded paper—old maps and torn-up magazine pages—so this was before they had electricity in the house, and Tan must have been around five. The men had been too stingy to buy more than a bag of boiled peanuts and some green mangoes as drinking snacks, yet they all made a big show of fighting over who would pay for the next round of wine, grandly flourishing wallets and slapping crumpled bills out of each other's hands.

"Put your fucking money away, all of you! This is *my* house!" Tan's father had yelled, rising unsteadily and stepping across the middle of the circle and over the sad little bag of peanuts to stuff his own money into his son's hand. "Get us two liters!" he half belched, and gave Tan a hard pinch on the arm that could have been affectionate. Tan had walked the whole way to the shop holding the money as far away from his body and as high as he could, his arms stretched out in front of him and above his head like he was holding a cross at the front of a Catholic procession. If there was a reason for this, other than the usual strangeness of children, he had forgotten it. When he passed the front garden where his mother sat wiping away tears, she had looked up and seen his funny walk and smiled, and to this day, this was still the most gratifying moment of his entire life. The memory ended there. Tan swirled and swirled his glass.

The Worm was always nattily dressed. Tonight his suit was dark green, perhaps in the captain's honor, but the fabric was expensive, and the hue was not drab and ugly, like Tan's olive outfits, but lustrous, the color of an oil slick. He paired it with a silk shirt pimpled in magenta paisley and a pair of very pointy shoes. Tan looked at the Worm—who was surveying his little kingdom of the drunk, the high, and the sweaty, and nodding along to the music—and tried to imagine him as the old man he would've ended up as, had the doctor and the lure of a lucrative career in the Golden Triangle not interrupted the trajectory of his life. Tan pictured him squatting in front of a low one-room house. Toothless, wearing rubber sandals and knockoff Adidas shorts, a half-plucked, sinewy chicken in one hand and one of those enormous tobacco pipes made from half a bamboo branch in the other. And then Tan realized that this could have just as easily been his own narrowly avoided future. He closed his eyes and tried to push further into the vision, to enter that low little house and conjure up the Binh of an alternate world, alive, the old woman she should have become—his recalcitrant wife, saggy and gray and mean as ever, in fish-sauce-stained pajamas and a puffy jacket. He could only hold the image for about a second and then it was lost. Tan opened his eyes and took a big gulp of his drink to sear away with cheaply distilled alcohol what he had been in dangerous proximity of feeling. The lime wedge tumbled from the glass into his mouth when he tilted it back, and instead of spitting it out he just gnashed it up with his teeth, bitter rind and all, and swallowed it.

As he looked out into the crowd, he suddenly frowned. There was someone else in the club who was not dancing. She stood rigidly while people thrashed around her. It was not Binh. It was the girl with the strange face that he had seen earlier that evening at the snail restaurant, and she was looking straight at him. In her arms she cradled a small dog. The dapples of light from the machines on the ceiling flickered off and on to the pounding bass line; in the throng the girl's face was illuminated and then swallowed by shadow, illuminated and then swallowed, over and over again, and each time the light was on her face he could see that her eyes had not moved from him.

Tan dropped his glass. It shattered on the ground, but the sound was drowned out because the song that had been thump-thumping in the background up to that point switched without warning to something that must have been popular, because when it started the entirety of the beautiful young things in the club suddenly shrieked and began to flail with even greater conviction, and Tan lost sight of the girl and her dog in the churning mess of limbs. After the excitement had abated somewhat there was no sign of them anymore.

I am seeing things, Tan thought. *I am so tired that I am beginning to hallucinate. Dogs aren't allowed in nightclubs.* And he almost believed himself. He turned to ask for his drugs, but the Worm was already pulling a small plastic bag containing four rust-colored pills the size of lentils from the inner pocket of his jacket with a knowing smile.

"I want to pay you for these," Tan said as he closed his fist around the bag.

The Worm chuckled. "Oh, you will. You know that." He waved a bartender over to sweep up the broken glass on the floor.

"No, no, I want to pay with *money,*" pleaded Tan, "not with favors anymore."

The Worm's mouth twisted, as if hearing the terms of their transaction said aloud made what they did even dirtier. "You picked the wrong profession then, Captain. Or at least the wrong country to do it in."

At that moment, in his lower intestines, Tan began to feel an unwelcome, familiar bubbling. Unwelcome, familiar, and *urgent* bubbling, signaling a violent disagreement between the shellfish and his digestive tract. He opened his baggie and promptly swallowed two of the little red tabs, as if hoping that they were antacids in addition to being Burmese horse drugs.

"Easy there, cowboy," said the Worm, "This isn't your first time, right?"

"Is something supposed to be happening? I don't feel anything!" Tan said as his belly tightened and gurgled. He tried and failed to prevent a sulfurous fart from escaping, and the Worm pursed his lips and tried not to wrinkle his nose.

"How about I go and get you a glass of water to wash that down with?" he said to Tan, rising and walking over to queue at the bar, even though he could have summoned the bartender with a nod.

Tan did not feel embarrassed, which should have warned him that the pills were kicking in too quickly. His eyes alighted upon a staircase in a distant corner of the club, peeking through the thick clouds of cigarette smoke, the steps glowing faintly blue under the blacklights. It intrigued him, and without really being aware of what he was doing, Tan bounced down from his bar stool, legs briefly crumpling underneath him before he regained them.

The Worm called out to him. "Captain, where are you going? And why are you walking like that?"

"Up" was all Tan said, without looking back. The mystical blue staircase was calling to him. He knew that up those steps was where he would find what he needed. A toilet, primarily, but there was something else awaiting him there, he felt strangely sure. He had to go. Behind him the Worm sighed and waved his hand for another rice wine.

Tan was never good at weaving through crowds, even when he was sober, but that night, despite his accordion legs, he somehow moved through the dancing creatures untouched. They were all moving too quickly, or perhaps he was moving too quickly, and he couldn't tell the men apart from women, or the foreigners from the Vietnamese. Sometimes in the blur of faces there would be one that suddenly and sharply came into focus and he would be sure that it belonged to the girl with the dog, but then he would duck to avoid an elbow and it was lost again. His intestines gurgled to the beat of the music. It was when he attempted to actually mount the stairs themselves that the first real problem presented itself: Tan's body suddenly couldn't remember the appropriate way to walk up them, and he was struck by an acute case of the spins. Tan managed to continue on his quest by executing a sort of slow, upward crab scuttle while clinging to the handrail. He received many disapproving glances from the shot girls in little green dresses with trays of liquor who passed him on their way up or down.

The second level consisted of a lounge full of well-dressed people making unenthusiastic small talk while perched on uncomfortable-looking couches. Tan knew instinctively that this was not the place that the spirits were guiding him to, so he scanned the room, located the next set of stairs, and continued on. The third level was a large room of dancing people with a plexiglass ceiling through which, he would discover two minutes later, the fourth level could watch them. The fifth and final floor was all long intersecting hallways, dim pink lighting, and closed doors to private suites, attended to by security guards. One of them cracked his knuckles and strode over to Tan. "Who are you?" he grunted.

"Hello! I am the Cat!" Tan said cheerfully. He thought that he was being clever, using an alias—they wouldn't like a policeman poking around up here. "I'm friends with the Worm."

"Who?" frowned the meaty man.

The walls were vibrating and he could feel his blood moving too fast. There was a maelstrom in his veins. Tan was babbling. "He doesn't use his real name. Maybe he told you a fake one, like I just did. I also used to work for the doctor. Do you know him? I caught snakes for him! One of them had two heads! They fed the Australian man to the crocodiles, but they let me live!" His credentials did not seem to be impressing the security guard, who was scowling. But then by fortuitous accident Tan discharged another, even fouler cloud of gas, and all of the guards took a step away from him in unison. "Could you tell me where the toilets are?" he asked.

The bodyguard pointed him down one of the long hallways, holding his breath, and Tan was off again.

The restroom was only moderately clean, even by nightclub standards, but it was miraculously, gloriously empty. Tan could have wept with joy. He rushed into the single stall and exploded. As he emptied himself in noisy rivulets, he thought back to his days at the police training academy when he had shared a single latrine with twenty-five other boys. Compared to that, this bathroom was fit for the king of Bhutan.

Spent after his long and harrowing shit, Tan rested for a spell on the toilet seat. Then, while he was finally tugging up his trousers, he happened to glance at the ceiling and noticed that one of the large tiles above him was slightly askew, and that the just-glimpsable darkness beyond it was the night sky. *Aha!* He thought. *The next level!* He did not dwell upon why he had been incapable of walking up a staircase normally earlier yet now he was able to scale the toilet-stall walls without any difficulty at all, push aside the loose tile, then hoist himself up and out onto the roof. He had abandoned logic several hours earlier. Every inch of him crackled. He had never felt more awake in his life.

On the rooftop Tan rose to his feet, brushed the cement dust from his knees, and inhaled the muggy March air.

There was only a sorry sliver of moon in the sky, so Tan walked over to the edge of the building and looked down instead of up. This was the front of the building, the side facing the street and the line of bars across it. It was all a mess of headlights and bodies, and even from up here Tan could smell the smoke from the cigarettes of the idling taxi drivers waiting to catch people as they exited the clubs. There was a reveler throwing up into the gutter, and past him, several more pissing in it. A shadow that Tan could identify as a policeman by the shape of his hat was leaning against a wall in the alley between two of the bars. A woman in a wheelchair sold lottery tickets on a corner. Tan would have bet that her legs were actually fine and she just borrowed the chair in order to get more business. Acrobatic rats ran across the telephone wires.

Tan turned and stalked across the long, dark expanse of concrete to the other side of the roof. It was silent here; the bright and screaming world of the front did not exist anymore. The Saigon River spread out before him, inky and still and choked with clumps of water weeds and rusting barges. The sidewalk along the embankment was quiet; the only lights came from unoccupied noodle stalls, their dinner customers gone and their late-night customers not yet arrived. Saigon was probably the ugliest city in the world, thought Tan, but it was not so bad from above, where he was untouchable. If only he could avoid returning to ground level for the rest of his life. He peered over the edge, swaying slightly, and then he heard Binh's voice, very clearly, in his left ear. "Found you," she whispered.

TAN LEANED AGAINST A cement wall, panting. He did not know where he was, his head hurt, breathing hurt, his feet hurt too. He looked down at them; he was not wearing any shoes, and his socks were all bloody. Why did he always have to lose his shoes when he did drugs? His fingers curled into fists against the cement. Then he smelled incense—he was standing in the courtyard, leaning against the wall of his own apartment building. He had no idea how he had gotten home or where his bike was. His breath was calmer now but he felt painfully alert, like all of his nerve endings were slightly singed. He remembered the Worm, the strobe lights, the stairs, the toilet, the roof, Binh's voice. Then nothing. Had he fallen off of the nightclub? Was he dead? Tan felt too sore to be dead. His neck was throbbing, and when he touched it, his skin was wet. He held his fingers up to his face to see if there was blood on them, but his eyes wouldn't focus. He licked them instead— yes, blood. Step by aching step, he began making his way back inside and up to his room.

There were no lights on behind the doors of any of the apartments on the ground floor; Tan guessed that it was several hours before dawn, because he couldn't hear the monks chanting next door. He felt his way through the dark with one hand against the wall. As he passed the second-floor landing he saw a frail light at the end of the hallway—the painter was still awake.

"Vung!" Tan tried to call out, his voice a feeble bark. He limped down the hallway toward the light, his skin stinging wherever it touched a hard surface. Without knocking, he threw open the door.

The young painter was sitting cross-legged on the floor in drawstring pants and a faded Hai Phong FC jersey. When Tan came bursting into his room he was gazing at the portrait of Binh, which was now hung up on the wall. He did not seem to be too taken aback by the sudden appearance of the captain.

"Hello, anh Tan," he said, a little groggily. "You don't look so well. Your neck's bleeding. And your feet too."

"Yes, yes, I know! Listen, Vung," he said, "I want to buy that painting." The Binh in half-dry oils smirked down at him from the wall.

Vung chewed his lower lip for a long moment. "I've never actually sold anything before," he admitted, eventually. "I don't know how much a painting should cost."

"It doesn't matter—let me see what I've got on me . . ." Tan searched his wallet and all his pockets and managed to come up with almost 600,000 đồng in bills of varying degrees of crumpledness. He walked gingerly across the tile on his smarting feet and pressed the cash into Vung's hands. "Is this enough for her?" The painter's eyes bulged as he counted it, which Tan took as a yes. Tenderly, triumphantly, he unhooked her from the wall. "Let's go home," he whispered to the canvas, and left Vung smoothing out his money against a pant leg.

Tan walked down the dark hallway with the painting held high in front of him. He could not see, but he did not stumble or bump into the walls. It was not until he was back on the staircase that he first heard the footsteps behind him. Slow steps in the entranceway of the first floor, and strange-sounding ones—a shuffling first, and then something clicking on the tile, like the tapping of small, pointy shoes or very long toenails. He imagined someone walking on all fours, bare hands extending first, sliding against the floor, and then feet creeping up to meet them—repeating again and again like an inchworm on a branch. Tan would not turn around, but he quickened his pace. The echo of his own feet on the metal steps was too noisy; he couldn't hear if the other footsteps were quickening too. As his socks brushed the tile of the third-floor landing, he felt a new surge of energy and barreled forward down the hallway to his room, brandishing the painting before him.

His door was not locked, but he did not notice. Tan slammed it shut behind him and then knelt and pressed his ear against it, straining to hear the footsteps. And there it was—the quiet reverberation of something soft brushing against metal, trailed by the brisk little patter. It was going up the stairs now. Tan locked the door and leaned the painting against the kitchen wall while he went to turn on the lights. When he came back to pick it up again, the canvas was empty.

Binh was crouched underneath his kitchen table. She was paler than she should be, and a little cloudy around her edges, and—from what Tan could see—she was mostly wet hair. It spilled over her body, yards of it, falling on the floor in heavy tangles. He did not know what she wore beneath her hair, if anything. Where the hair ended, Tan could see that a puddle of water had formed beneath her. What took Tan aback most was the powerful odor of her—he thought her smell would be of paint, but instead it was of dampness and mildew and rotting wood. She smelled so cold.

Binh mimed combing through her hair with her fingers, and inclined her pointy little chin in the direction of Tan's bathroom. Obediently, Tan went and fetched a brush that had been Tram-Anh's. His hand shook as he held it out to Binh. She snatched it from him without letting their fingers touch and began to pick out her own damp knots.

As he watched her, Tan's face suddenly lit up. "Your arm!" he said. "You can use it again! Is it . . . is it still . . . ?"

In response, Binh partially drew back a sheaf of hair and extended her bare arm with a flourish, displaying both sides of it so that Tan could see the skin was now intact before returning to her brushing.

Tan sank down to the ground, fighting the dueling impulses to embrace her and to weep. He reminded himself that he was not looking at her flesh. She was not really here. This was a shadow of her that smelled like a flooded basement. He had forgotten to keep listening for the footsteps, but that did not mean that they had ceased.

The hair was now manageable, if not smooth. She smiled at Tan, nodded, and then turned to face away from him. But she was not shunning him; it was a familiar invitation.

"Just like old times, then," said Tan softly. He released his knees and scooted over to her on the floor. The puddle of water had been spreading slowly but steadily, and Tan sucked in his breath in surprise when the seat of his trousers made contact with it and soaked through. But his fingers did not tremble when he reached out to gather the first strands of the hair.

His skin grew slippery as he began weaving the slick, wet locks into thick plaits. He wanted to see what Binh looked like beneath her hair, but as much as he grabbed, there was always more concealing her. He tried sectioning off three braids first, each one as thick as his forearm. While he worked on one, he slung the other two over his shoulders to keep them neat. As the braids lengthened he had to squelch backward to accommodate them, and when he finally came to the end of the hair he realized he had nothing to tie them with, so he just knotted them around each other. The braids, disdainful of the laws of physics, held in place.

Tan tossed all three of the finished braids over his left shoulder, letting them dangle in a long U—down the length of his back and up again, over his right shoulder with the ends resting in his lap. He was about to reach for more hair when the front-door lock unlatched on its own. His door cracked open, and a head poked inside.

"Hello," it said in Binh's voice. "Hello, hello, hello." The body belonged, however, to the girl from the nightclub and snail shop. A few feet below it, the little dog's snout also thrust through the doorway. Tan turned to the Binh whose hair he was holding, and she merely looked at him over one shoulder and silently shrugged from her puddle beneath the table.

The girl at the door chuckled, opened it an inch wider, and stepped into the room. "Aren't you pleased to see me?" she said. "I didn't scare you too much back at the club, did I? I was just doing my best cat impression for you—they like to play with their food before they eat it. I was giving you a head start." Her canine companion had slipped inside the apartment too, and was barely fast enough to avoid getting its tail caught in the door when the girl shut it behind her and locked it. It trotted over to Tan's shoe rack in the corner and then curled up with its head on its paws. The girl brusquely scanned the apartment with undisguised disdain. Until this moment, Tan had been proud of his thirdfloor allotment of three hundred poorly lit square feet. "Thank you for bringing us to your home," said the girl. "I was curious to finally see where you lived. The city you love so much. It doesn't seem much better than a shack in a pepper field to me." She leaned back against the door and stretched her neck, rolling her head from side to side so that the cartilage crackled. Her movements were Binh's, Tan recognized with a sweet ache; they were just being performed by this new and slightly clumsier skeleton.

"It's confusing, I know," said the girl, as if reading his thoughts. "I'm just borrowing her; I needed a body. And she happened to have a very useful one. But it really is *me*, Kitty. You know that, don't you?"

Tan met her gaze defiantly. "This is a dream! I am still full of drugs!"

The girl licked her lips and grinned. "I *know* your dreams. I know them better than you do."

Tan narrowed his eyes. "How?" he asked, despite common sense telling him that it was a bad idea to get contentious with a ghost.

"Because I'm the one who has been sending them to you. There, look at your dreams!" she made a sweeping gesture with her left hand. "Look at her!"

Tan followed her hand with his eyes to the kitchen table and then bellowed in fright like a stuck bull. The silent Binh beneath it had grown a second, full-sized head next to the first, replete with its own cascade of half-braided hair. Both necks were now elongated like a pelican's. Her four eyes blinked at him and her two identical mouths smiled. Tan covered his eyes with his hands and whimpered.

"No, no, no," laughed the girl. "That's not how this works—you have to look! There's more! Do you remember this one?"

Tan peered through the cracks in his fingers. Now the double-headed Binh was gone, and in its place were two fleshless skulls, still attached to the sheaves of hair whose ends were draped over Tan's body. They were perched atop a heap of bones. Her beautiful, lonely bones. Her rib cage lay on its side like a rotting fish trap, and long, broken pieces of what were once Binh's sweet, swift limbs were messily strewn divination sticks around it. Tan wiped away stray tears. When he brought his hands back down to the floor, he found that it had grown even wetter than before. Water—cold, dark water—was seeping up from the tiles.

"It's too late for tears now; the next dream is starting!" reproached the girl. Tan's hands were submerged. The water was already five centimeters high and rising rapidly. Ten centimeters. Twenty by the time he managed to shake himself loose from the coils of Skeleton Binh's hair and then wobble to his feet. Tan splashed over to his table and clambered on top of it. "This is a dream, this is a dream, I am still full of drugs," he chanted to himself. "This is a dream." The water smelled septic and was the color of Coke and had now risen over a meter. Tan felt the legs of the table beneath him lifting off the floor, and then he was afloat, along with everything else in the apartment that was unmoored: his chairs, Binh's bones and the long braids they were still attached to, the broken chopsticks he had thrown on the floor earlier that evening, pots and pans and knives and a few bobbing sweet potatoes, his shoes and shoe rack—which the little dog was now using as its personal raft, perched at its prow and eyeing the floating bones with keen, piratelike interest—rolls of toilet paper, washed in from the bathroom on some malignant undercurrent. Teetering on the uneven surfboard of his tabletop, Tan grabbed hold of a curtain for balance.

What the girl was doing couldn't really be termed floating—she was crouched on top of the liquid-obsidian surface like a thread-legged water strider, her feet never breaking its skin. Tan had expected her to be delighting in the mayhem her dream was causing, but her expression was strangely somber. She met his eyes—*there,* that flinty look; it was her inside that body after all—and then, without smiling, lifted one hand and made a small flicking gesture. The apartment reservoir swelled suddenly and violently, knocking Tan off his table and into the black water.

It was cataclysmically cold. He spluttered and flailed, catching only half a gasp of air before going under. He tried swimming in the direction he thought was up, then second-guessed himself and started paddling the other way. His lungs couldn't stretch his last breath much further now, and he still couldn't locate either his floor or the water's surface. In fact, he was starting to doubt that either of them existed anymore.

Just as he could feel unconsciousness reaching out of the darkness to enfold him in its even darker arms, Tan's hand made contact with the end of one of Binh's long braids. His salvation; he clasped the hair, wrapped it around his wrist and waist, and used it to tug himself forward through the water, two mighty pulls with the last of his strength. On the second pull he felt his face finally leave the water. As he drank delicious air, Tan brought the hair to his face in gratitude, but what touched his skin felt different. Bristly. He opened his eyes. The apartment was no longer underwater. He was sitting on his kitchen floor where he had started, and what he was holding to his cheek—looped, too, around his waist and his shoulders—was no longer hair but a long, woven rope.

With impossible speed that did not belong to Binh anymore—or to any human—the girl sprang across the room and in one movement had Tan pinned beneath her, the rope tugged taught around his neck and the ends in her hands.

"This is the last dream," she said. "And this one is mine. I've dreamed it for two long years. Your throat and my hands around it. Now it's finally coming true."

A smile he recognized, on those lips he didn't. Tan wanted to stroke her cheek, but his arms were restrained by the rope. The best he could manage was to raise his hand half an inch and touch her calf lightly with the back of his fingers. It was not skin he knew.

"I don't mind," he said. "Because I brought you out of Ia Kare. You finally came to Saigon for me. This is how it should have been all along. Us. Together. Here. I was the one who set you free."

"No, you were the one who defiled me. You drowned me, burned me, and then buried me. Who else can say that they had three deaths? I was sacrificed for your pride. I am the one who is setting myself free, and I am doing it now."

The girl lowered her head and touched her lips to his wet forehead. Then she wrapped the rope ends around her hands a final time, and she wrenched hard.

"WHAT'S IN THAT BIG BAG?" THE OLD WOMAN POINTED to the green military rucksack on the floor by Tan's feet.

One of the bus's rear wheels skidded on some rocks and Tan gave a queasy smile. "Just my supplies—I'm in the Highlands on *business,*" he said, pleased by how cool and powerful he thought this made him sound, until it was undermined five seconds later by his needing to bend over and throw up into a small plastic bag for the second time. Tan was familiar with the twisty mountain route of the local bus from Saigon to Kon Tum, notorious for the amount of carsickness it provoked in its passengers, and yet he had still thought he could get away with eating an enormous predawn breakfast before leaving the city. He was paying for it now. The old woman held her breath and scooted a little farther from him on the seat. Out of the corner of her eye she thought she saw something twitch inside the rucksack, but she reassured herself that it was just the jostling of the bus.

It was not. Tan's rucksack was full of live field mice. They had been lightly sedated with ketamine (courtesy of the Worm) back in Saigon but were now beginning to stir. Luckily for both the mice and Tan's stomach, only about forty-five minutes now remained in his bus journey.

There was nothing to distinguish Ia Kare from any other arid, semi-inhabited patch of hill country; Tan knew he was approaching home only because he could feel how long they'd been driving since getting on the highway. He was always a little disappointed that nothing stirred within him as the landscape of his youth rolled into view.

The town's bus stop was at its sole intersection with a traffic light. The road on the left went straight to the Cambodian border, and the one on the right led to National Highway 14. Beyond it somewhere, the road that he and Binh and Long hadn't been able to find that day they'd tried to go to the beach when he was seventeen. The bus heaved to a sudden, hard stop, hurling Tan against the window and snapping him out of his old memories. The old woman braced herself against the seat in front of them with her horny-toed little feet. Eager to be rid of her seatmate, she bounced up as soon as she had regained her balance and bounded down the aisle to the door. Tan marveled at her agility as he trailed after her, lugging his squirming rucksack. The second his feet touched the ground outside, the bus's door groaned shut behind him. Then it continued lurching its way north, its wheels spitting dust and small stones.

The brick house where Tan had grown up was a fifteen-minute walk down the western road. But he was not here to visit his mother and grandmother. This was why he was glad to be arriving during the hottest part of the afternoon—most people were napping, and none of the nosy market ladies would see him. The only person out on the street was the old woman's son, who was waiting on a motorbike to pick her up. Tan studied the man's face but wasn't sure if he had seen him before. He bore all the hallmarks of a coffee or pepper farmer from the forsaken hilly outskirts of town—leathery skin, red dirt on the knees of his trousers, a faded twill work shirt. The man had grown out the nails on both of his thumbs to tapered, inch-long trowels and was using one to wiggle loose a bead of earwax. He did not pose much of a threat of gossiping and blowing Tan's cover. Still, Tan dawdled, adjusting his mouse sack, waiting for the pajama-clad old woman to clamber onto her son's bike. After they had driven away, he headed to the cemetery to meet Binh.

She was waiting for him by the statue, her motorbike parked be-tween two graves. He wished that he had worn his uniform to impress her, even though it would have been unwise to call attention to himself with it. And she probably wouldn't have been impressed anyway. Binh wore perfectly round, thick-framed sunglasses like a Cambodian pop singer from the sixties with her cashew-picking uniform of blue cover-alls and white rubber boots. Her hair was a mess, just as it should be.

"Meow," she said, and gave him a mock salute.

"Hello, Bé Lì."

The first stretch of silence. It was their first time meeting since the night at Fat Uncle's in 2005.

"How are your aunt and uncle?" Tan asked, just to break it.

"Oh, they're both alive," Binh said blandly. "I'm still helping them with the orchard, but a few months ago I moved into a cabin by one of the Mas' old pepper plots. Haven't told them where I am though—they think it's unseemly for an unmarried woman to be living on her own. They say they're praying for me!"

Concern crinkled Tan's forehead for a moment before he managed to control it. "Do the Mas know you're living there?" he asked, his voice creeping higher than he wanted it to.

Binh gave him one of her flat, cold-eyed lizard stares. "Of course not. That bastard owns more land than he knows what to do with. The field hasn't been farmed in years and the shack is abandoned. There won't be anyone to bother us. Get on," she said, restarting the motor-bike. "I'm glad you're here."

Tan hated how quickly he forgave her—for everything, for not even bothering to call once in the last four years—just by hearing those words.

IT DIDN'T FEEL RIGHT to be sitting on the back while a girl drove, even if the girl was Binh. Tan kept his arms crossed in front of his chest in what he hoped was a manly way for the duration of the ride, which became increasingly difficult as the topography of the dirt road grew more distorted with furrows and odd mounds—the result of years of flooding and subsequent rebaking of the mud by the sun.

There was no fence marking the perimeter of the Mas' fields, but it wasn't hard to tell which ones belonged to them in the long stretch of pepper plantations; their vines all grew higher and lusher, tended by an irrigation system and an army of workers that only their family could afford. The instant that Tan and Binh crossed over into their property, the leaves around them changed from a dull, seaweedy shade of green to a vibrant emerald, and Tan blinked frantically, thinking at first that there was something wrong with his vision. He was eager to catch a glimpse of the fabled Ma residence—a beige monstrosity of a modern villa with columns and faux Spanish tiles and a roof turret and French doors, with balconies that encircled each of its four stories and an enormous marble statue of Guanyin looming above the balustrade on the third floor. When he and Binh and Long were children, they had sometimes bicycled out as far into the fields as they dared and then climbed pepper posts to stare at the house in the distance. As the motorbike now rounded the crest of a small hill, the roof turret came into sight, rising above the blotchy fields, and Tan's breath caught in his throat. This was the closest he had ever been to it.

Binh did not turn her head to look at the house, but as more of it came into view she slowed down, leaned over, and spat in its direction without taking her eyes from the road. Tan could not stop himself from craning his neck to take in the full motley splendor of its architecture. He didn't know why he was still so in awe of the place—he lived in the city and could drive out to District 7 and gawk at rows of mansions twice the size of the Ma house any time he liked, and he knew that the truly wealthy Saigonese would be appalled by the gauche mishmash of French Colonial and Mediterranean flourishes—but even now, Tan found it utterly captivating. The afternoon sun was reflecting fiercely off of its pale walls, so Tan was squinting, but just before the motorbike began its descent of the hill and the Ma house dipped out of sight once more, he was certain he saw a slender figure standing out on the third-floor balcony, next to the Guanyin. He knew that no one would be able to tell who he was from so far away, but still he tilted his helmet forward to hide his face from them.

"I hate that hideous fucking house!" Binh yelled to him over the rattle of the engine once the villa was behind them. "All those pillars make it look like the biggest, ugliest birdcage in the world!"

They drove deeper into the fields. Workers were now starting to return from their midday breaks—Tan occasionally heard the *put-put* of their motorbikes coming down the other little dirt roads veining the plantations—but he and Binh did not cross paths with any of them. By the time they finally reached the shack, all of the mice in Tan's rucksack were awake and squeaking.

Binh hadn't lied: they were in a remote corner of the Ma estate, next to a patch of land that looked like it had been neglected for ten years. The house was a crooked little box constructed from bamboo, clay, thatched palm fronds, and some of the cobbled together remains of an older stone house that had stood here long before. Even though it hadn't rained recently, everything inside it felt damp. Binh had slung a wide hammock across the length of one wall. A rusty wire behind it was strung haphazardly with her clothing: an extra pair of work coveralls, an assortment of jeans and T-shirts that Tan suspected had been shoplifted from the market in Ea Sup, and an expensive dress Tan had mailed her a few months back—a gift for agreeing to help him, he'd written in the accompanying note. Truthfully, it was a gift for just speaking to him again. Tan had been so surprised when she'd actually responded to his message that he'd run out to a boutique and immediately bought the dress, carried away by the idea that Binh had become an entirely new person, someone forgiving and therefore, in his imagination, feminine, who would enjoy wearing something tight and lacy and lilac. Now, looking at the frilly purple thing as it dangled, with all of its tags still on, against a clay wall crawling with ants, Tan felt stupid for ever having sent it.

On the dirt floor there was a single-burner propane stove with a rice-encrusted pot and spoon on top of it. Another pot and a battered enamel strainer hung from hooks on the wall. The dirt floor was lit-

tered with used gas canisters, ramen noodle wrappers and empty pack-
ets of Mê Trang instant coffee, hot sauce in plastic sachets, cigarette
butts, several empty bottles that smelled of rice wine. There was exactly one neat corner in the whole house: a plank shelf above the hammock upon which a stack of books was carefully arranged in descending
order of height. Next to the books was a large flashlight, and next to
that, a wooden comb, which Binh grabbed and tossed to Tan.

She kicked off her boots and then sank into the hammock with her
back to him, shaking her hair free from the overtaxed rubber bands that
had been restraining it. "Not a bad place, huh?" she said. "Someday,
when that bastard Old Ma is down in hell, I hope he'll have to watch
me pissing on his precious pepper fields for all eternity. Be gentle when
you're untangling—I haven't brushed in at least a week."

Tan set down his noisy rucksack and squatted beside the hammock.
He did not tell Binh that he thought the lecherous Old Ma would probably enjoy watching her pee from the afterlife. He began to unpick the
snarls in her hair, and for a while they sat quietly. Then his curiosity got
the better of him.

"Where did you get all the books from?" he asked. "Did you go into
Pleiku?"

"Oh, Long mails them to me from Saigon sometimes," Binh said
absently.

"You've been talking to Long?" Tan said, a little louder than he
needed to.

"No." She shrugged. "Not yet. I just read whatever he sends me.
The books are his version of your dress. But maybe I should finally
write back to him. You're here, after all; maybe four years has been
long enough. Ow! Gentle, Kitty! You're pulling!"

"Oops. Sorry," said Tan. He detangled in sullen silence for another
minute, and then he couldn't contain his next question any longer:
"Did you actually like the dress?" He hoped desperately that she would
lie.

But Binh laugh-snorted so hard that she rocked forward in the hammock, and the comb—its teeth sunk deep into a knot—was yanked clean out of Tan's hand. "What am I going to do with that?" she hooted, flopping onto her back. "Dress up for manure days at the orchard?" Then she saw that she had hurt him and relented. "I'll wear it around the house. You didn't need to try to bribe me. You knew I would agree to this once you told me what it was." She grinned slyly. "You know I've always wanted to try and catch a snake."

"ONE THING STILL DOESN'T make any sense to me," Binh said to Tan. She had just returned from the forest and was untying the pillowcase that was dangling from the handlebars of her motorbike. "Why would anyone want to drink venom?"

"No, no, no," said Tan. "They're not drinking the venom." When he'd asked Binh for her help with the snakes, he'd been purposefully vague about what it was that the doctor actually wanted with them. They were now four days into the cobra hunt, and she was getting curious. "It's going to get dried and powdered and mixed with some other shit. Only a little of the venom is actually going into the pills, but it'll get you really high."

"How is that even possible?"

"Why don't you ask Long to send you a book about it?"

"Oh, fuck you," she said, but without any real spite to it. The pillowcase was starting to thrash. "Only a *Tây* would come up with an idea as stupid as this."

"He's not a Tây, he's overseas Việt," said Tan.

"Well, it's still a stupid idea. Someone's going to accidentally die from it."

"Who cares? They're going to make a fortune selling it to clubs in Bangkok, and then we'll be rich too. Since when are you the one with a conscience, anyway?" said Tan, which Binh did not argue with. "Just think about what you'll do with the money. A hundred million đồng." He had put it in Vietnamese currency because it sounded better than saying that it was only five thousand American dollars. "You won't have to live in a pepper shack anymore. You can buy a new motorbike. Imagine all the places you could go."

"The beach," said Binh without hesitating. "I already know what I'm going to do with the money. I'm going to the beach because I promised myself I would when I was fifteen and the three of us tried to go and never made it."

"Or," Tan tried to interject casually, "you could always come to Saigon. With me." Binh was staring off into the pepper field and did not reply, which was not the reaction Tan had hoped for. He knew that she was thinking about her family's cashew orchard. "Don't worry," he said, "our cut of the snake money will be enough to take care of your aunt and uncle too. They'll be able to hire someone to take your place." He did not actually know if this was true. He and the doctor had not agreed explicitly on what kind of payment he would receive. This was one of many wrinkles in Tan's plan.

"I'm not worrying about them," Binh sighed. She turned her attention back to unknotting the top of the pillowcase. "Besides, I don't have a conscience, right?" She opened it and extracted the snake—her third—by its tail.

"How do you catch them so quickly?" Tan asked, partly to change the subject and partly because he was curious. He didn't dare to go into the forest with Binh, even to watch. His only role in the proceedings thus far had been as the snakes' mouse catcher. The ones he'd brought with him from Saigon had all been eaten already, and for the past two mornings he had spent the mosquito-ridden predawn hours creeping around some unsuspecting farmer's rice paddy with an old hoe and his rucksack, whacking at the earth until he struck a nest and sent the mice scattering. Then he would leap on them in the darkness and hope that some ended up in the bag.

One of Binh's trademark bad-idea smiles shimmied across her lips. "Why don't I just show you?" she said, and without any further warning she released the cobra onto the ground.

This snake was slightly smaller than the others she had caught. It was inky black from its head to its belly, and from belly to tail it was marked with smudgy petals of white. It unfurled and recoiled itself over a three-foot span of grass, its head looking first at Binh, then at Tan, the edges of its hood visible but not fully spread yet.

Tan's blood had gone icy. His eyes hurt; he realized he had not been blinking. He was too afraid to, in case the thing struck in the split-second he closed them.

Binh screeched with laughter. "Your face!" she said, gasping for breath. "Oh, I wish you could see your face right now!"

"Put it back," Tan whispered, without taking his eyes off the snake. He wasn't even sure if she could hear him. "Put it back now."

Binh brushed the tears from the corners of her eyes and then wiped her fingers on her coveralls. Mirth was replaced with brisk composure. "The trick," she said, approaching the cobra, "is to become both the bait and the predator at the same time. And also, dry hands." It swiveled its head in her direction and then rearranged the sinewy rope of its body to face her. Binh dropped into a half crouch and began to creep side-ways. The snake followed her movements, and soon they were circling each other in a kind of counterclockwise, lethally focused dance that excluded Tan and the thatched shack and all of Ia Kare. This suited Tan fine—he slowly backed out of striking distance, heart still pounding.

Little by little, Binh had begun steadily elongating her gait, and her movements now grew slower and more erratic. She began letting her rubber-booted left foot extend farther and farther with each step, wiggling it in the air and letting it drag behind her on the ground, so that the snake's attention gradually switched from her face to the dancing boot. They were now within a yard of each other, Tan realized—Binh had also been slowly closing the gap between them with every rotation.

What happened next took place so quickly that he did not fully process it until the cobra was already in her hand: without warning, Binh, midstep, aimed a kick in the direction of the snake with her raised left leg. The snake snapped defensively at the boot. But Binh was simultaneously shifting her weight, drawing back the kicking leg—which the fangs had missed by only a centimeter—and then reaching in with her right hand, grabbing the snake while it was still preoccupied with her foot. She caught it behind its head, wrapping four fingers tightly around the top of its throat, her thumb pressed down on its skull to keep its mouth shut. Tan's fear of the snake biting him was now replaced by the fear that Binh would choke it to death.

She was panting. The veins in her forearm and neck were bulging and her pupils were huge and dark. When the snake had worn itself out trying to wrest free from her grip and was only twitching its tail feebly, something finally seemed to clear from Binh's eyes. She walked around the side of the house to the cluster of gasoline barrels, with airholes poked into the tops, that housed the other two snakes, found an empty one to stuff the limp cobra into, and then clamped on the lid. Then she dug out a pack of cigarettes from her coveralls. Tan watched her fingers to see if they shook when she lit one. They did not. She sprawled out in the exact spot where she'd had her showdown with the snake, the grass now trampled flat.

"See? Easy," she said between puffs. "They're not as aggressive during the day—they don't spit as much. I usually don't even have to go through the whole dance." With audible clicks and creaks she stretched out her joints, arching her back and rolling the stiffness from her shoulders and wrists and ankles. Then she closed her eyes with a satisfied little sigh and smiled.

In that moment, Tan lost control of himself. These past few days he had been waiting for his window, and he was sure that this was it. He rushed forward and dropped to his knees on the ground next to her. Seizing her face with both his hands, he pressed his own against it. The kiss was all teeth and lips mashed in the wrong direction, and his wildly overzealous tongue. Binh gave a smoke-laced shriek that was made mostly inaudible by Tan's smothering mouth. Her right arm was pinned beneath his body at an uncomfortable angle, but her left arm was free, and holding the lit cigarette. She brought the smoldering end of it down on the back of Tan's neck and he leapt back, cursing.

He looked at her, wounded. "I just wanted to show you . . . show you that I—"

"Show me what?" she spat. "You don't touch me like that anymore! You can only touch my hair!" Tan was taken aback when he looked in her eyes, and for a quick second he could see, beneath the obvious anger, a spark of real fear. But she blinked it away quickly. "I would die before I let you kiss me again," she snarled slowly. "Do you hear me? I would rather die." She took a drag of her cigarette to collect herself, and her voice, when she spoke again, was flat and betrayed nothing. "Now, how many more snakes did you say they want?"

How quickly she was able shift back to business Binh. This hurt Tan almost as much as her physical rejection of him. But he quietly replied, "We need eight to get enough venom. Though the doctor said ten would be better."

"Well then," said Binh, stubbing out her cigarette on the sole of her boot and flicking it into the bushes, "you've got a lot of mice to catch. I'm going back into the forest." She rose from the ground, swung the pillowcase over her shoulder, and left him there, smarting.

AT NIGHT THE SNAKES were always awake. Tan could hear them bumping around inside the rusting steel gas drums from the corner of the dirt floor where he slept. If one started hissing it would set the rest of them off, and the sound was amplified by their barrels. Tan would be roused several times during the night by what sounded like a symphony of broken televisions. Binh, snoring peacefully above him in her hammock, was somehow never disturbed by the noises. When he did sleep, Tan would dream about the containers tipping over and the snakes crawling out onto the ground, in through the gaps in the bamboo walls, and over to where he lay. He woke up in sweats, pushing imaginary coils off his body. At four he would leave on his daily rodent hunt, and at five he returned and roused Binh so she could feed them to the hungry snakes while he prepared instant noodles or porridge for their breakfast, humming loudly to himself while he cooked to drown out the sounds of the cobras enjoying their own meal. After they ate to-

gether, Binh would drive off to work in her uncle's cashew orchard. In
the afternoons, while everyone else was napping, Binh would sneak off
into the woods and look for the snakes. Tan would have dinner waiting
for her when she got home. Then at night she would quietly get rice-
wine drunk by herself, then select a book from her shelf and read it by
lantern light in the hammock. Before she went to sleep she would let
Tan comb and replait her hair. Neither of them mentioned the kiss—if
it could even be called that—again.

After Binh set off in the morning, Tan would compose his daily text
update for the Worm, who was waiting with the Australian herpetologist in a hotel fifty miles south in Buon Ma Thuot. When Tan had collected enough snakes, the plan was for them to drive up to Ia Kare in a
rented truck, collect Tan and the barrels, and then all head back to Saigon together. This, however, was where several more wrinkles entered
Tan's plan.

The Worm, the Australian herpetologist, and Dr. Sang did not
know about Binh. They believed that he was the one catching all of the
snakes, out in the woods by himself.

He also hadn't mentioned to Binh that she was a secret. Tan was
hoping to postpone having the conversation with her for as long as he
could. She was not going be pleased to hear that the doctor and company would probably insist on having her killed if they ever found out
about her. She was going to be furious. This was why Tan had decided
to wait until they had the eight snakes they needed before telling her. If
only Binh were a more rational girl, he thought, it wouldn't have to be
a problem. All she had to do was lie low for a little bit while he took
care of everything. Wait a few months to make sure that no one suspected anything. Then he would quietly send her some of the money.
But Binh was not a rational girl. She was unpredictable and she was
impatient and she had an atrocious temper. She was not a person who
would permit herself to be hidden.

By their tenth morning in the shack, Binh had already captured
seven cobras. For a week now the Worm had been asking Tan to send
him some pictures of the snakes, and Tan thought he couldn't put it off

any longer without risking suspicion. He wished that he could just wait for Binh to come home and ask her to take the photo for him, but he didn't want her getting curious about who he was communicating with. So, after doing a few pushups to invigorate himself, Tan made his way over to the gasoline barrels. Tan chose the fifth barrel from the left because he thought the number five was lucky, and because the barrel also did not smell like shit, like some of the other ones. He reasoned that this meant the snake inside had a slow digestive system and was therefore more sluggish and less likely to attack him. Holding his breath, he raised the lid half an inch. Nothing moved in the barrel. Nothing hissed sinisterly. He slid it open a little farther. Still nothing.

"No sudden movements, no sudden movements," Tan whispered to himself. He carefully dragged the lid open enough for the sunlight to get in, angled his cell phone with shaky hands, and snapped the photo. After he had closed the barrel securely once more, Tan emitted a little howl of victory and of pent-up terror, and then he sprinted over to the smelly old well by the edge of the dead pepper plants, a safe thirty yards from the barrels, and collapsed in the grass.

The photograph was grainy, and half of the cobra's coiled body was hidden in the shadows, but it was good enough for Tan. He sent it to the Worm, and then added:

Number 7

The Worm fired back almost immediately. *Wow! Looks like a big one! How are you catching them so quickly? What's your technique (Douglas wants to know. He says hi too!) haha!*

Tan hated texting with the Worm—his messages were inane and overly enthusiastic, and every single one of them ended with "haha!" He sighed and typed: *I use the Boot Trick. Will show you in person.* He didn't know why he had thrown in the extra lie, especially one so stupid. But at this point, he had already told so many that it didn't seem to matter anymore. The stress of all of his dishonesty, compounded by his diet of instant noodles, was wreaking havoc on his colon. He had been constipated for days now. His phone vibrated again. The Worm had sent him another gratingly chatty message:

Cool! Hope you'll finish soon so we can go home! Douglas and I have to share a hotel bed. He snores really loudly! I hate it! haha!

Exasperated, Tan snapped his phone shut and tossed it away from him. It bounced once before landing a little too close to the lip of the well, and for a second Tan willed it to bounce again and fall in.

He asked himself if what he really wanted was to abandon the plan and run away somewhere with Binh. In his heart, he knew that he didn't; he wanted the money. He wanted the doctor to be impressed by him and to include him in his future schemes. He wanted a reputation. He wanted his superiors at the police precinct to try and bribe *him*. And yes, he wanted Binh, had always wanted Binh, but he was not enough of a fool to believe that she wanted him back. Not yet. Right now she could still only see him as Ia Kare Tan, because she was still Ia Kare Binh. But once they had the money, once she got away from this tainted land that tried to ensnare everyone who was born here or unfortunate enough to set foot on it—Tan aimed an angry kick at a nearby thorny bush—that would change.

And yet at the same time, what he wanted more than anything else was for their strange shared life in the pepper shack to continue indefinitely: the quiet meals and evening hair combing; drinking instant coffee together out of empty condensed milk cans because Binh didn't own cups; their Sisyphean routine of boiling pots full of water on the gas burner to warm their baths, which would just get cold again while the next pot was boiling. It was not the kind of cohabitation with Binh that Tan had daydreamed feverishly about when they were teenagers, but it was oddly blissful. What made it so sweet was its unsustainability. They were teetering on the edge: the Worm was knocking on the door, Tan was going to explode if he didn't start eating vegetables again soon, and any day now, Binh would catch her final snake and he would have to tell her the truth. But he wished it could stay like this forever—always seven cobras in the barrels and a little more time before he had to ruin everything.

SNAKE NUMBER EIGHT WAS the most beautiful, with evenly spaced moonstone-colored bands, but it was also the most aggressive. It caught Binh on her inner arm with a spray of venom, and an angry red rash bubbled up the length of skin where it landed. The snake had attempted to gnaw through the pillowcase on the drive home and gotten its fangs hooked in the fabric; Binh narrowly avoided being bitten when she tried to free it. After she finally managed to dump it into its barrel, Binh looked spent for the first time in the twelve days that she'd been hunting. She was ready to quit and celebrate reaching the snake threshold, but Tan begged her to get just one more. She should end the hunt on a better note, he cajoled.

Binh agreed, somewhat reluctantly, and Tan rejoiced inwardly, thinking that he had managed to buy himself at least two more days in platonic shack limbo. But that very same afternoon, Binh went back into the forest.

When she returned after only a couple hours she was speeding. She was so excited that she hadn't even taken the time to fully knot the pillowcase—a scaly tail was poking out of the top while she drove. Tan's heart sank.

"Look, look, look!" she started calling to him before the bike had even come to a full stop. When she set the pillowcase down on the ground, Tan panicked and started backpedaling, remembering the time she had released snake number three. But Binh held up her hand. "Wait—it's okay. This one is different." She tugged the pillowcase away by its back corners and a cobra with two heads tumbled out.

Tan's fear turned to relief, then to amusement, as it attempted to rear itself up and promptly keeled over on its side in the grass. He snickered, which made Binh furious. "Don't laugh at her!" she snapped.

"*Her?* Oh, come on, you have no idea how to tell the boy and girl snakes apart." The cobra was now making a wonky, ovoid path in the grass, heads bobbing at two wildly different tempos. One of the heads was smaller than the other and kept turning to look at the other one, as if ineffectively trying to coordinate its movements. "Actually, it really looks like a boy to me. Both heads do. It reminds me of how my dad would walk when he went on a bender."

"Don't compare her to your terrible drunk dad," Binh said darkly. "Don't you see? This is the snake from the story—the snake that Old Ma's daughter saw, remember? The 'many-headed serpent' that found her in the forest."

That made the smile vanish from Tan's face. "Those stories aren't real," he said.

"Of course they're real. And now the snake has chosen me—it *let* me catch it. It wanted me to. This has to be the same snake. The Ma girl went missing, what? Twenty-five years ago? No, twenty-three—it happened the year before I was born. So the snake is at least as old as I am."

"Bé Lì, you know that's silly."

"You're right. Why would it age like a normal snake? It's probably been around for centuries."

"No, Binh . . ." Tan sighed. The two-headed snake had now accidentally flipped onto its back and was struggling to right itself. "Look at that thing—even I could catch this one. You know what you're saying is impossible."

She plucked it up from the grass easily and lowered it back into the pillowcase. "How can you say that? We both saw the same monster in the graveyard when we were children. Since that day I've stopped saying that things are or aren't possible."

"There was no many-headed serpent! This is just a deformed cobra! The Ma girl snuck off to meet some no-good boyfriend, got lost because she was a sheltered little rich girl, and later, when her parents found out she was pregnant, they made up a story about her going crazy to cover it up! That's the truth—that's what the ladies at the market think, and they know what really goes on in this place."

"The market ladies are full of shit. I once heard them tell someone that during the war, your grandma was an ivory trafficker. They spread the rumor that my parents aren't really dead, and my aunt and uncle bought me on the black market." Binh laughed and cradled the pillow-case. "We don't care what they think," she said, more softly. It took a long beat for Tan to realize that "we" meant Binh and the snake, and not Binh and Tan.

BINH DIDN'T WANT TO keep it in a gasoline drum like the others, so that night she went out and found an old woven fishing trap to repurpose into a cage for it instead. Tan protested, saying that it wasn't safe enough—the snake could spit venom through the slits in the bamboo and the lid didn't even latch properly.

"If you actually cared about my safety, you wouldn't have asked me to go catch cobras for you in the first place," Binh laughed. "Besides, I told you—this one won't hurt me." And as Tan watched, sick with fear, she hoisted the snake loosely by its belly, letting both of its deadly heads dangle free, and coaxed it into the basket. "You see?"

Tan didn't sleep at all that night, because Binh brought the fishing basket into the shack with her and placed it on the ground beside her hammock where he usually lay. He positioned himself as far as possible from them, against the wall by the entrance. Binh drank more than usual, raising her can of rice wine to first toast Two-Heads, then cobras one through seven (but not number eight), and then Tan, before passing out.

For two hours, Tan sat rigidly against the wall. Outside, he could hear the occasional hollow thud from the snakes, awake in their barrels, but there was no movement from the creature inside the basket. When Binh's breathing grew deeper and then coarsened into snores, Tan clicked on her lantern but held it against his chest to dampen the glow. He slowly rose to his feet and crossed over to her hammock, making sure to keep the light on Two-Heads so that he could see if it was looking spitty. It had looped itself into a surprisingly neat oval, with its heads resting on the end of its tail, and it stayed absolutely still even as Tan approached.

He extended his free hand and placed it on Binh's cheek, listening for a change in her snoring. When he was sure that she wouldn't wake up, he moved his hand down to her clavicle and let his thumb rest in the hollow at the base of her throat. Holding his breath, he lifted his hand and was preparing to place it on the soft jut of her hip next, when he saw a flicker of movement in the corner of his eye. Two-Heads was up. Its heads were now partially raised, though listing slightly to one side and bobbling in place. And it was watching Tan. He could not see its pupils, and he wasn't even sure if snakes' eyes actually had pupils, but he knew with a nauseous certainty that it was looking at him. Tan pulled his hand back from Binh and retreated to his old spot against the wall. He was not ashamed, he told himself. Why should he feel ashamed? It was unbearable to be in the same room as Two-Heads, and after only a few minutes Tan stood up again and went outside. He spread himself out in a spot in the grass and lay awake for the rest of the night.

It was hot even before the sun came up. Tan knew that he should get up to go mouse hunting, but he continued lying in corpse pose on the ground. If he moved then the day would begin, and today was the day he had to tell the Worm that the cobras had all been caught. Sunrise came, the color of a cantaloupe and nearly as sticky; it was going to be a humid and windless day. When Binh came stumbling out of the shack with a slight hangover around midmorning he still hadn't changed positions, but the backs of his knees were starting to sweat.

"What are you doing, weirdo?" she called to him amiably.

Tan considered this for a moment. "I'm trying to see what it's like to be a snake," he said.

"Well, stop it and come make breakfast."

Tan rolled his head to one side. He couldn't see her face from where he lay. But he could see her bare feet: small, spade shaped, archless and horrifically callused, big toes scrunching absently into the soft dirt (repulsive feet—how was it possible that he loved them so much?). He could see the fraying edges of her Hello Kitty–patterned pajamas, which she wore as a personal insult to him. And he could see the snake in the fish basket that was already dangling by her side.

She would not let it out of her sight or set the basket down anywhere beyond her reach. The instant noodles that Tan cooked were his best yet. Binh had come home with half a dozen duck eggs the other day, and Tan cracked two into the pot and swirled with his chopsticks until they became a creamy, hurricane-shaped curdle on top of the broth. The last meal that they would eat together here. No, not the last—there would still be lunch. Tan felt his phone buzzing in his pants pocket, but he did not open it to see what the Worm had written. He wanted to enjoy his breakfast first. But after only a few slurps, he looked up and saw that Binh was dangling two noodles down into the basket, trying to lower them into the snake's gullets. The sight was beyond sickening—the snake had its jaws wide open and was attempting to position itself beneath the noodle ends. Looking at the soft pink insides of its mouths made Tan want to throw up. He had an unobstructed view of its fishbone-thin fangs and the hollow, fleshy glottides above its forked tongues. Chicken-scented oil dripped off the noodles and onto the scales on its heads.

"Oh my god," said Tan. He dropped his chopsticks and pushed himself away from the pot. "Oh my fucking god! You can't do that!"

"What?" said Binh. "You didn't get any mice for them today. What else are they going to eat?" She had finally succeeded in getting the noodles into the snake's mouths; it swallowed them with a faint but disturbing gargling sound. Tan threw his chopsticks into the soup pot with disgust and stormed outside.

All he needed was some air, he thought. All he needed was a short walk. Tan turned his feet toward the pepper field. His phone was buzzing again. Tan wanted to scream but instead he grabbed two fistfuls of his own hair and yanked until his scalp was tingly and he felt composed again. He focused on breathing and walking. He would not think about the snake and its open mouths. He would not think about open mouths at all. He would not think about being nine years old in the cemetery. He would not. With a start, he realized that he had reached the well. It had never resembled a gaping, dark throat more. Tan closed his eyes so he wouldn't have to look at it and kept walking until he tripped over one of the remaining lumpy stones of the old, ruined wall that marked the former property and he knew that the well was now behind him. Then he found a pepper post to lean against and fished his phone out to face what the Worm had written. He opened the first unread message:

Tan my man! Did you get snake number eight yet? Really can't wait to get out of Buon Ma Thuot—all they drink here is Huda Beer. It tastes a bit like piss haha!

Tan rolled his eyes. He opened the next message. The Worm again:

Was just kidding earlier! I didn't mean to insult your local beer! Also, the doctor just called to check on your progress. Not rushing, just notifying haha!

Tan calmly shut his phone and placed it back in his pocket. Even though he hadn't slept all night, up until that point he hadn't felt the least bit tired. But exhaustion suddenly found him, there in the pepper field. Tan could not stand the thought of Two-Heads watching him sleep, so he dragged himself a bit deeper into the brush and then curled himself up on the ground. Part of him hoped that Binh would worry when she didn't know where he was. He wanted to wake up to the sound of her calling out his name frantically as she searched for him. Tan closed his eyes.

He did not stir until the sultriest hour of the midafternoon, and the only sound he heard when his eyes opened was the dull rasp of cicadas. Tan sat up and was surprised by how clear his head felt. Something was tickling his arm and he looked down: one of Binh's long hairs had gotten itself rolled up in his shirt cuff. Tan held it up in the air, waiting for a breeze to catch it, but there wasn't any wind to take it away. He wound the hair around a rusty nail sticking out of a post instead, tying the strand into a neat little bow. Then he stood up because he knew it was time to tell her about his assorted lies.

Binh was sitting out by the well, the basket at her side, and the top of her head came into view the moment that he rose to his feet. But she was facing the house, with her back to the pepper field, and could not see him walking toward her. Tan walked softly, taking care not to kick any pebbles or step on dry twigs. He didn't want her to hear him approaching.

The basket next to her was empty, he now saw; the snake was draped across Binh's lap. The end of its tail twitched in the grass and its two heads were resting on the underside of her forearm. In full sunlight the drab mud-splatter color of its scales took on a darker and more lustrous hue, like the cobra had been carved out of a thick slab of grass jelly. Binh had her face lowered nearly to its level, her head tilted to the side just enough that Tan could see her lips moving, but he was still too far away to tell whether she was speaking in Vietnamese or a made-up snake language. As he watched, Binh nodded her head, paused, nodded again. She was not merely speaking to the snake; she was listening to it too. It was a conversation.

Later, when Tan replayed the events of that afternoon, he was unable to recall what he had been intending to do when he walked out of the field. He just knew that he couldn't bear to watch any longer. Was he jealous of the snake for lying across her lap when he could not? Did he hate her for holding it so gently, after she had told him she would rather die than have him touch her? Had he planned to punish her for considering him less desirable than an actual animal?

Of course not. What kind of fool would be jealous of a snake? He hadn't wanted to startle it, he told himself. That was the sole reason he was walking so cautiously toward her.

Binh finally heard his footsteps when he was a few yards behind her and turned slowly. She squinted in the sunlight. When she saw that it was Tan, she smiled. He remembered her smiling. It was proof that she knew he would never have hurt her. His hands might have been raised, yes, but in the end, he wasn't the one who hurt her, was he? It was the snake. When Tan emerged from the field, it looked at him, raising both of its heads. It assessed Tan carefully. It had not been spooked; Tan knew this beyond a doubt. Two-Heads stared at him for a long moment, then it lowered itself slowly back down onto Binh's skin with undeniable tenderness. It rested there for a beat, and then it calmly sank both sets of its fangs into the crook of Binh's arm.

Binh did not scream. Her eyes, still fixed on Tan, widened. Her lips parted, and she gasped softly, a sound that Tan had never heard her emit before but had often longed to make her produce. For a split second he was so aroused that he managed to forget the snake that was still biting her. Then Binh dropped the hand that she had been using to shield her eyes, took hold of Two-Heads' neck, and pulled. She screamed then—the hooked fangs tore her skin as she tugged them free. Tan rushed forward now, his first impulse to crush the snake's skulls with his boots, but Two-Heads had retreated into its fishing trap.

"Leave her," Binh said, pressing her hand against the wound. The four little rivulets of blood streaming from the puncture marks were thread-thin. Tan dropped down onto his knees and tried to clutch Binh against his chest. She pushed him away roughly. "It's burning, Tan!" Cradling her arm, she got to her feet, slightly unsteadily, and began walking toward her motorbike.

Tan darted around her uselessly, plucking at her sleeves, Binh slapping him off every time he made an attempt to grab her. When they reached the motorbike she had to lean against the handlebars to catch her breath. Beads of sweat were forming on her forehead.

"The keys are on the shelf inside," she told Tan.

He raced into the shack and found her keyring next to the little stack of books from Long. When he returned her face had grown pallid.

"You'll have to hold on to me so you won't fall off," Tan said to her, straddling the bike and kick-starting the engine. Wordlessly, she climbed on and curled the fingers of her good hand through one of his belt loops. He was too thrilled by this to notice that her movements were already becoming slower and more labored.

There was no hospital in Ia Kare, only two small pharmacies and a clinic with a midwife and a doctor who was more of a dentist than a doctor. Ea Sup's hospital was closest, but Tan knew they wouldn't have antivenom on hand. He sped down the orange-dirt road through acres of pepper plantation, heading for the highway. Whenever they hit a pothole he reached behind him to keep Binh from flying off the seat. She still batted his hand away occasionally but didn't have the energy to do it every time; the road was all lumps and craters. By the time they reached the main road, she was leaning against Tan's back.

A few minutes later he felt a sharp little poke in his side. "Where are you going? This isn't the way to Buon Ma Thuot."

Tan kept his hands steady on the gas. "I'm taking you to Pleiku. It's closer."

"Only by ten minutes!" Binh spluttered. "And they're both a two-hour drive to begin with! It doesn't make any sense. Buon Ma Thuot has the bigger hospital—turn around."

"I can't. I already started going this way so we can't turn around. We can't afford to lose any more time." Tan sped up. They couldn't go to Buon Ma Thuot—the Worm and the Australian would immediately catch wind of someone showing up at the hospital with a cobra bite. And then it would be over for the both of them.

"It's like I'm on fire. All of me is filling up with fire." Binh's voice was getting shriller. "Where are your friends? The Tây people who started all of this? Don't they have a car? Can't you call and ask them to come help us?"

"I can't do that!" Tan yelled into the wind. He immediately wished that he had lied. He could have just said that they were still in Saigon, or they didn't have a truck yet.

"What do you mean?" Binh said into his back. The sweat from her forehead was soaking into his shirt.

"I can't do it! If I tell them, they'll kill you!"

Binh laughed. "But I'm already dying! Kitty . . ." Tan knew from her voice that she was fighting tears. "It hurts so much to breathe. It's like my lungs are filling up with smoke."

Tan had never heard or seen Binh cry before. He pulled over on the side of the highway and turned around to look at her. Binh's skin was the mottled gray color of gravel and her whole body was damp. Her breathing was shallow and noisy. When Tan looked down at her arm, he struggled not to dry-heave; it was bloated and purplish, the skin of her forearm had stretched so much that the puncture marks had become long slits. They were now leaking custardy puss instead of blood.

"It's fine," he muttered. "It's going to be fine. I know what to do." He reached down and started to unbuckle his belt.

"No! Get away from me!" Binh screamed, scrambling off the bike. Her legs couldn't support her and she collapsed on the side of the road, putting out her swollen arm to break her fall and howling with pain when it struck the dirt. "Don't touch me!" she shrieked, trying to roll away on the ground.

Tan leapt off the bike. "No, no, no!" he said. "I wasn't going to— I wasn't going to do something bad!" He had his belt in his hand and waved it at her. "For your arm! Come here . . ." He knelt down next to her and used the leather strap to form a clumsy tourniquet around her biceps. Binh no longer had the strength to pull her arm away. She was lying on her back, her hair in the dust and her eyes closed. The intervals between her breaths had gradually been growing longer, and when she inhaled it sounded like she was choking. Tan yanked the belt as tight as he could, grimacing to stop himself from crying.

"We're not going to make it to Pleiku, Kitten," Binh murmured without opening her eyes.

"I'll take you to the Ea Sup hospital instead," Tan said frantically, tying off the end of the belt. "It's only an hour away. Maybe the doctor can just drain your arm and keep you asleep until they get the right medicine from the city."

Binh laugh-wheezed. "They're going to chop off my arm," she said. "And then I'll look even sillier in that dress of yours." The movement of her chest rising and falling was now so slight that it was almost imperceptible.

Tan gathered her up in his arms and carried her back to the motorbike. Binh didn't even wince when he accidentally grazed her arm while he was positioning her on the seat in front of him. Tan drove with her flopped forward on the bike, her head on the handlebars. He held her by the waist with one hand and steered with the other. There weren't many other motorbikes on the road, and on the few occasions that one did pass, the driver slowed down to shoot a curious look at Tan and the barely conscious Binh but did not offer any assistance before speeding off.

Something smelled awful. Tan turned his head from side to side, looking to see if they were driving past a landfill or a pig farm. Then he felt something wet on his leg—Binh's bite had ruptured, and a hot, pinkish liquid was running out of it and dripping onto Tan. It was now clear that this was also the source of the smell. The skin below his poorly applied tourniquet was the color of an eggplant and the entire limb was distended almost beyond recognition.

"Fuck! Fuck!" Tan pulled over on the side of the road again. *"Binh!"* He shook her shoulder, but she was unresponsive. Tan clawed at the belt, trying to get it off, but the flesh had swollen too far on either side of it. With a jolt, he realized that it had been too long since he'd heard the ragged sound of her inhalations. He flopped her head back against his chest and held the back of his hand up to her open mouth to check for her breath. It took several minutes for Tan to be certain that he could still feel the slight tickle of air against his skin. But it was too faint to hope that it would continue for very much longer.

Tan leaned forward and buried his face in Binh's hair. He sobbed twice, loudly, and then stopped. This was the only time that he would cry. He raised his head, wiped his face, and gently draped Binh back down over the handlebars. Then he turned the motorbike around and started driving back toward Ia Kare.

The sun was beginning to set when Tan arrived at the shack once more. Instead of parking the motorbike in its usual place, he drove across the grass, over to the well. He saw Two-Heads still coiled up inside its basket and wondered why it hadn't bothered to escape. He briefly considered running it over. But he decided that it deserved the fate that awaited it with Dr. Sang more.

To his surprise, when he put his hand underneath Binh's neck to keep her head from flopping as he lifted her from the bike, he could still feel a very weak pulse. Tan laid her down on the grass and wondered how best to proceed—he had been counting on her death happening

while they were driving back so that he wouldn't have to know the moment it transpired. He didn't want to wait here, watching her chest
until it stopped moving, thinking about how long she might have left,
or the possibility that she could have lived if he had kept driving. Tan
stretched himself out on the grass alongside Binh and then reached
over a hand and gently turned her by the chin so that they were facing
each other, their noses almost touching. Her cement-colored skin was
spiderwebbed violet with broken capillaries. From her chin, he walked
his fingers up the side of her face and pried her eyelids open, using his
thumb and index as pincers. Beneath them, the eyeball was sightless
and glassy, the pupil inanimate. Tan pulled his hand back quickly, letting the eyelids fall shut again. Then he inched himself forward on the
ground and kissed her. It was not a quick kiss—Tan allowed himself to
excavate her mouth thoroughly, rationalizing that because Binh was
technically still alive, he was not being perverse—but really, he only
lingered because she was unable to resist and because he hoped that
Two-Heads was watching from its basket. The smell from her festering
arm was overwhelming. When Tan could not justify kissing Binh any
longer, he pulled his face back from hers and closed her slack jaw for
her. He stroked her hair one last time. Then he got up onto his knees
and rolled her body across the grass and over the lip of the well. It was
deep; he barely heard the splash she made.

Tan did not go back into the shack. He immediately marched off in
the other direction, through the slumped rows of pepper plants. For an
hour he cut through fields and walked down back roads. He could have
shaved twenty minutes off his walk by cutting through the graveyard,
but he went around it instead.

His mother was sitting in the doorway of the little brick house,
snipping the bad fruits from a pile of lychee branches by lamplight.
When she saw Tan she jerked back in surprise and dropped her shears.

"What are you doing home?" she said, looking over her son with
quiet alarm. He stank, his clothes were crusted with blood and puss,
and without a belt his pants were slipping down.

"Mother," said Tan warmly. He stooped to kiss her on the cheek and plucked a lychee for himself from the pile while he was bent over. He popped it into his mouth and used his molars and tongue to work the flesh free of its pit and rind. "I was in Pleiku on business," he said, spitting the discards out into his hand. "A big police conference. A symposium. I snuck down here for the afternoon to visit. Shall we have tea?"

Tan could see that his mother did not believe his story, but she gamely set aside her branches, wiped her hands, and went to boil water. It was not the first time he had come home covered in blood.

Tan immediately drained eight glasses of tea. He could not stop drinking. His mother had to go and refill the kettle. But other than this he was certain that he was acting perfectly normally.

"And will you see Binh while you're here?" asked his mother.

Tan smiled. "I'll drop in on her before I catch the bus tonight," he said. "I know she'd want to see me—every time we talk she tells me how much she wants to come visit me in Saigon. I think she might even want to move there."

When he said this, his grandmother began pounding on the wall with her stick from inside her room, aggressively and without rhythm. She did not usually make this sound. Even when Tan's mother went in to soothe her, the whacking continued. They were whacks of contempt. Whacks to shame him. His grandmother had always preferred Long anyway.

"I am going to go relieve myself!" Tan yelled in the direction of her door. He stood and went out to the backyard. While he was there he took a moment to poke around the odds and ends heaped up behind the toilet, mostly his late father's old tools. He selected a rusty trowel and tucked it into the waistband of his pants. Then he exhumed a long, sturdy length of rope from the bottom of the pile.

"You don't mind if I take these with me, do you?" he said, dragging it back into the sitting room with him. "I need them for my symposium. And I have to hurry off now—got to catch the bus to Pleiku." His mother knew perfectly well that there were no more buses to Pleiku at this hour, but Tan was barely registering the words that were falling out of his mouth. He meandered off into the clotting Highland twi-light, the enormous coil of rope around one shoulder making his gait lopsided.

The snakes were hissing in their gas barrels when he got back to the shack. "Hush now," Tan said, thumping a barrel with the knotted end of his rope. "Tomorrow the Worm will come and take us all south, so you have to be on your best behavior." One by one, he picked up the barrels and carried them across the grass, carefully arranging them in a semicircle that faced the well, assembling his scaly audience.

Two-Heads had not moved from its cage but had flipped itself over onto its back—it looked like it was stargazing. Tan lifted the fishing trap and hung it by its handle from the lip of one of the barrels. Then he retrieved his rope. He tied one end securely to a weed-strangled pepper post, dropped the other end into the well, and waited as gravity took the entire twisted length of it.

Tan finally walked over to the edge himself, sat on the ground, and removed his shoes. He took hold of the rope and he let his body drop. The fibers burned his palms and inner thighs as he slid down the line, and his elbows stung when they scraped the rocky sides of the well. When he struck the water he gasped at the pain. He groped around for her in the darkness. Binh was floating facedown, suspended just below the surface. Tan's fingers found her hair first, which he used to draw her to him through the water. Then he looped the rope around her waist. "I'll pull you up after me once I make it to the top," he whispered, brushing her stiff, waxy fingers with his lips. "Don't you worry—I was never going to leave you down here. I wouldn't do that to you."

Tan took hold of the rope once more and then began to climb. His hands were skinned and starting to blister but they did not hurt. Tan had always been a natural climber. He was seventeen again, putting the other cadets to shame on the police academy's agility training course. He was ten again, seven again, six. Shimmying up a lychee tree, a roof, the black, bowed statue in the cemetery. Binh beside him, always. When he looked down he half expected to see her climbing up behind him on her own.

Tan reeled her in easily, spooling the rope around the pepper post as he drew it up from the well. She weighed nothing at all. He didn't even realize that she had been pulled out all the way until he heard the squelch of her corpse dragging over the grass. Tenderly, reverently, Tan unbound her. He wrung out her wet hair onto the grass. And then he carried her in his arms back to the house.

The dirt floor was much harder than Tan had thought it would be. Even if he worked at it all night, he wouldn't be able to dig a grave that was deep enough. He threw the trowel away in defeat after managing to make a hole that was two feet by two feet, and then he unceremoniously scrunched as much of Binh's waterlogged body inside it as he could. It was like trying to stuff a live octopus into a pot. Her head and poisoned arm and one leg were all sticking out at hideous angles, and it looked even worse when Tan tried to cover her up with the loose dirt. He ran his fingers through his hair in anguish, then looked over and saw the gas burner.

TAN PLACED THE BURNER right on top of her heart, setting the flame as high as it would go. He had wheeled Binh's motorbike inside and shaken the gasoline from its tank out onto her, and then left it propped up in the corner of the shack—he wanted it to be part of her pyre too. Binh's half-buried body was surrounded by palm thatch that had been ripped from the roof, her woven hammock, the ripped and crumpled pages of all of the books—which Tan had taken great pleasure in tearing apart, a week's worth of old instant noodle wrappers, several loose boards that Tan had formed into a pyramidal configuration, and half a bottle of rice wine sprinkled on top of everything. When the fire started to take hold, the last thing Tan did was take the purple dress off its hanger and feed it, hem first, to the flames.

He retreated outside to observe the burning from the safe distance of his cobra semicircle by the well. It was so beautiful against the night, he thought. Binh would have liked it. The longer he watched, the more he regretted drowning her in the well; he should have just set her on fire to begin with. The flames were now up to the roof, and from the smell of burning rubber Tan knew that the motorbike was alight. He closed his eyes and listened to the hungry sound of it. The roar of the fire was indistinguishable from the roar of the sea. He opened his eyes again. He wondered if all of Binh's body had been consumed yet, and if so, whether her burning flesh was the reason the smoke above the house had turned an unusual shade of red.

The dog could not cross the river by itself. It sat politely at the edge of the crowd of motorbikes, all of them waiting for the Thu Dau Mot ferry. The city and the scent of its six million humans were on the other side of the weedy water, a barge ride away.

It did not have a plan. It was too tired to try and stow away inside a passenger's basket. The weariness that it felt in its legs transcended its muscle and bone. Another dog had ripped its ear two days ago in a fight over a pork bone. Its coat was matted around its torso like a leather jerkin. Were it not for the lottery ticket seller, the dog would probably have just trotted brazenly up the gangplank along with the motorbikes and laid its exhausted body down, hoping that the boatman would let it stay.

The woman with the carefully painted face was watching it from her chair at the very back of the queue. When the little dog felt her eyes on it, it turned, and then looked puzzled; the woman appeared to be in her early forties, but she smelled old, old, old. Older than trees. More like a rock, more like the river itself.

She crooked a finger at the dog. She was beckoning. The dog was too tired to remember not to trust. It briefly forgot that it was a dog. It left the safety of the half shadow by the benches where it had been waiting and pad-

ded over toward the woman, thinking that she might feed it, or let it ride to Saigon in her lap with her lottery tickets.

But when the dog was only halfway to her, the lottery woman suddenly stopped beckoning and raised her hand authoritatively, with the palm facing out instead. *Stay.*

Confused, the dog obeyed, stopping in the exposed center of the concrete wharf and plopping down on its haunches again. The lottery woman nodded. *Good dog.* She kept her hand raised. *Stay. Stay.*

The ferry was churning over the muddy water to the terminal now. On the shore, the passengers shouldered their bags and kick-started their motorbikes. The dog looked nervously at the lottery woman's face, waiting for a sign to move again. It did not pay attention to the bike engine quietly shutting off behind it.

The lottery woman smiled, and the dog met the darkness of a sack being forced over its head.

SAIGON,

THE DAY BEFORE THE DISAPPEARANCE

FIVE WEEKS AFTER RETURNING FROM IA KARE, WINNIE LEANED out over the bedroom balcony, looked down across the alley, and saw the dog.

It was past noon and the alley was deserted, overbright and shadowless. She had just woken up from a nap. Long was at work. The dog was in a rectangular cage, its snout muzzled. It had been deposited on the curb in front of the restaurant, destined to be eaten in one of the seven ways advertised on the sign. It was a small, skeletal thing, with jutting hip bones Winnie could make out all the way from the balcony, but it was so filthy that she couldn't tell what color it was supposed to be. And as she watched, the animal lifted its head and locked eyes with Winnie, and Winnie had to hold on to the railing to steady herself because there was such raw anger in those eyes that her whole body shuddered in response. In that moment Winnie felt something strangely akin to envy. There was something wild and unquenchable—even in a cage, in the last hours before it became someone's dinner—that the dog possessed, which Winnie had never figured out how to cultivate correctly inside herself. She did not pity the dog; she pitied herself, and this was why she knew she had to free it.

The restaurant was still shuttered—presumably, the man who had delivered the dog had gone around to the back to find the owners and get paid—and Winnie knew that she needed to act quickly. There wasn't time for her to put on proper pants or shoes, so she tore down the staircase on bare feet, wearing nothing but the oversized University of Economics T-shirt she had slept in.

"House, let me out!" Winnie whispered frantically to the air. Today was different; today it let her open the rusty metal gate, and today the gate did not screech. In ten seconds she had sprinted across the street, the gravel hot and painful beneath her feet. In another ten, she had snatched up the dog cage and made it safely back inside. She set the cage down carefully by the broken toilet and then darted back over to close the gate.

What Winnie thought had been a dog muzzle was actually a length of rusty wire that had been used to bind its snout. Another wire secured the door of the cage, and it was so tightly and erratically wound that Winnie could not loosen it with her fingers. She had to dig out Long's toolkit from upstairs and rummage around inside it for a pair of needle-nose pliers. Once she'd managed to get the cage open, the dog—quivering a little but remarkably composed—stepped out and calmly inclined its head toward her so that Winnie could free its jaw next. Its eyes did not bore into her with anger, as they had before, but Winnie imagined that she could see that fury pooling, ready and silent just behind its yellow-brown pupils.

"I'll be gentle, I promise," she whispered to the dog, taking its face in her hands. With horror, Winnie realized that the brown crusting around its mouth was not dirt but dried blood from where the wires had cut into its flesh. This set her hands shaking so badly that she had to put the pliers down for fear of hurting the dog further and start working with her fingers instead. Twice the sharp end of the wire pricked them and her own blood moistened the dog's snout—*Tetanus!* cried a frantic, very American-sounding voice in the back of her head, which she ignored. *Septicemia! Rabies!*—and several times the dog gave a soft, pained whimper through its clenched teeth while Winnie was untwisting, but the wire did eventually loosen and come off. Winnie rerolled the awful thing and shoved it away in the tool-box.

The dog tested its freedom, opening and shutting its mouth, wincing slightly, and gingerly poking out a pink tongue to lick at some of the scabbing on its snout. It did not bark, which relieved Winnie. The walls of the yellow house were thin, and she was terrified that the angry owners of "Dog Meat: Seven Ways" would come banging on the door at any second.

Holding her breath, she slowly extended a hand to its snout. The dog sniffed her fingers and gave them a brief and indifferent lick. It did not seem terribly affectionate, but Winnie told herself not to expect fondness from something that had so narrowly avoided a nasty fate at human hands.

"Sweetie, I think you need a bath and something to eat," she whispered to the dog, *her* dog now, she thought. She imagined being able to recount one day to the Cooks her story of rescuing it right from the doorstep of a restaurant. She knew they would be jealous because they had only found poor old Goji wandering around in the street. Then she remembered that she could never see the Cooks again, or Goji.

"No," said the dog. "No baths. And no more 'Sweetie' either. What I need is something to eat."

The dog sounded like it was a two-pack-a-day smoker. Its voice was undeniably female, but bizarrely low and hoarse, and this was almost as startling to Winnie as the fact that it had spoken in the first place.

"Wh-what would you like to eat?" Winnie stammered, awkwardly switching over to Vietnamese because it was the language that the dog had spoken to her in.

The dog cocked her snout and grinned. "Well, well, well," she rasped. "You're not afraid of me?"

"No, but I'm a little worried that I've lost my mind."

"If you have, it doesn't bother me." The dog raised her nose and gave two sharp sniffs. "There is sausage somewhere in the house; I'll have some of that," she croaked. Winnie went into the kitchen to slice up some of the spongy loaf of pork *chả lụa* that Long's mother had sent back with them after Tết, which they still hadn't managed to finish. "Don't even bother with a plate!" she heard the dog call from the living room as Winnie rummaged through the cupboards. "Just hurry up! I'm starving!"

Winnie arranged the discs of sausage neatly on the tiles, but the dog dispatched them all in a matter of seconds by tossing back her neck so that the pieces of pork went tumbling down her gullet without her even needing to chew.

Once it was all gone, the dog gave a satisfied sigh but then sniffed again with a surly wariness. "Where is the man that you live with?" she asked Winnie.

"Long's at work," said Winnie. She didn't think that she could call Long her boyfriend or her lover. "He'll be home sometime between five and seven. Later if he goes out drinking with his friends after they play cards, but he's always back before eight to bring me dinner. The situation is . . . a little unusual. But he likes to take care of me."

"What's so unusual about that?" the dog interrupted languidly. "It sounds like Long found himself a good little pet. You'll just have to find me a place to hide when he gets home. I'm going to be your secret, aren't I?"

Her secret. Winnie smiled. "What about the toilet alcove over there, underneath the stairs? Would you be comfortable there? There's no door, but it's dark. We can't use it because it's broken."

"Is it a wet place? It sounds wet. I don't like wet. I don't like the wet and I don't like fire and I hate cars."

"No, no," Winnie reassured her. "A little bit musty, but not wet. There's the attic too, but it's hot. The window doesn't open. But Long never goes up there."

The dog stretched out her front legs first, then her hind legs. The bony fins of her scapulae stabbed upward against her skin as they moved. "I'll take the attic," she said. "I'll be very quiet, and I promise not to shit on your floor." With that, the dog trotted off and began to mount the stairs, her toenails making little clicks on the tile.

"Wait!" said Winnie, running after her. "Do you have a name?"

The dog gave her a pointy-toothed smile. "You can call me Bé Lì."

"Belly?"

"Close enough."

Winnie couldn't help it—she mussed the fur on top of the dog's head and kissed the tip of her nose, which the dog tolerated patiently. "One day, someone is going to bite your face off when you try that," she chastised gently and then squirmed away, but not before Winnie managed to give her a tiny tickle underneath her chin too.

"Belly is a cute name. Mine's Winnie."

"Well, Winnie, I guess that since the man who feeds you isn't going to be back for ages, I should go explore." Belly turned and raced up the staircase, long body undulating, stoat-like, over each step. Winnie followed her, laughing.

Belly had gone into the spare bedroom, where she was rooting around in Long's unpacked boxes. She circled one several times, pressing her nose to the cardboard and sniffing loudly, then moved to another and did the same before returning to the first box. "Open this one for me," she commanded. Winnie picked at the edge of the tape with a fingernail until it came loose, then pulled it off with a noisy ripping sound that echoed off the walls. There were only two things inside. First, a rusting purple tin. The image on its lid indicated that it had once, many, many years before, held tamarind candies. And below the tin, nestled inside a clear plastic sack: two large, leathery squid—salted and dried and pressed flat, preserved whole, tentacles and all, the kind that were grilled and then slivered and sold with chili sauce by late-night street vendors.

"I bet that I can tell you what's in it," Belly said with a sly smile, tapping on the tamarind tin with a paw.

"Your nose is that good?"

"My nose is incredible. Let's make a bet." Her eyes flashed. "If I can tell you what's inside, I win the squid."

Winnie had a feeling that she was being tricked, and she worried that Long would somehow immediately know that his dried squid were missing when he got home—though she couldn't fathom how old they were, or why Long had kept them. But she said, "Okay, deal."

Belly took a theatrical sniff. "Candy wrappers."

"*I* could have guessed that there were candy wrappers in a candy tin . . ."

"I'm not finished yet! Colored pencils and a comic book. Rubber bands and a hair clip shaped like a strawberry. An unopened condom. Old money—paper bills, only two-thousands and five-thousands. Photographs. And a deck of playing cards that is missing . . . eight. No, nine cards."

"There's no way you can smell all that." The tin was light in Winnie's hands. She gave it a gentle shake and heard rattling from inside. Carefully she pried the lid off and was greeted by the rubber bands and the hair clip. It was indeed shaped like a strawberry. A couple of fine, longish strands of dark hair were still trapped in its metal teeth. She looked at Belly with disbelief and the edges of the dog's snout curled up very smugly.

"I don't know why you're so surprised," she said. "I told you I had an amazing nose. Why wouldn't you believe a talking dog?"

The bills—twos and fives, as predicted—were all crumpled; Winnie flattened them against her thigh, then rolled them up together and secured the fat little tube with one of the rubber bands. Then she placed it in the lid of the tin for safekeeping, along with the deck of cards, the pencils, the ancient-looking condom, and the strawberry, which she picked up carefully so as not to touch the hair.

"I don't see any photographs," she said.

"Look inside the comic book."

They were tucked between the pages at the middle, in a folded sheet of the thin, speckled-egg-colored paper that was used for wrapping bánh mì or found in rest-stop bathrooms in place of toilet tissue because it was less expensive. Winnie unfolded them carefully. They were the kind of cheap, blue-backgrounded 2x2 portraits taken for passports or visas or ID cards at quick-print photo shops.

She set them down on the floor tiles and started sorting them like mah-jongg tiles. There were a dozen photos but only three faces. Four photos of a teenaged Long, those convex fish eyes that she would recognize anywhere above a stubbleless jawline and a shirt with a white collar that gaped open around his thin neck. Three of another boy, with close-cropped hair—a teenager too, but with a shadow on his upper lip and a suggestion of brawniness in what was visible of his shoulders, a whisper of shrewdness in his narrow eyes. Winnie knew he had to be the estranged older brother—he and Long had identically sculpted noses and ears—but his face made her pause for a moment. She had a foggy, baseless half feeling that she had seen him somewhere before, but she told herself that it was just because, other than his eyes, he had the kind of everyman features that made him seem familiar when he was not. She had to guiltily acknowledge that he was slightly more handsome than Long. Winnie turned to the next photos: three of the same messy-haired girl. Her face did not resemble the brothers'. It was ferally charismatic, heart-shaped and tilted slightly to the left, which, coupled with the little smirk on her lips, gave the impression that she was mocking the camera. The book friend, the best friend, the friend who was now gone. As Winnie stared at her, she had the sensation that at any second, the girl in the photo was going to start moving.

Winnie arranged all of them into a long chain on the floor: Long-brother-girl-Long-brother-girl-Long-brother-girl-Long, lined up perfectly so that the seams wouldn't show.

Beside her, the dog suddenly cleared her throat. "I'm going up to your attic to nap now; I was almost eaten today, after all, and the experience was tiring." Winnie looked down at her. It was true—Belly's smug grin had faded and her canine face looked distinctly drawn. "I'll come and see you later tonight," she said, a bit more brightly, and gave Winnie a lick of reassurance on the wrist. "After your feeder goes to bed. Leave the squid on top of the box—I'm saving them for another day." With that, she pranced away daintily, leaving Winnie to clean up.

———

IT WAS LATER THAN USUAL—nearly ten—when Long came back, smelling like the watery lager and fried tofu of Bia Hơi Baby. Winnie knew it had taken him so long because he had pushed his motorbike home from the bar instead of driving drunk.

Winnie had been lying in bed for the past two hours, looking at the red light through the window and listening for any sign of the dog in the attic above, when she heard the gate scream as Long heaved it open. There hadn't been a sound from Belly since she'd gone upstairs; the afternoon and evening had seemed unbearably slow. Winnie had soaked in the bath for an hour, drowning more times than she ever had before and then swallowing a little too much water and choking it up onto the floor beside the tub. Now she followed the sound of Long's careful footsteps. Down the dark front hallway they came, pausing momentarily in the kitchen while Long drank a glass of water, and then up the stairs, to the bedroom door, where they stopped. He was checking under the door to see if a light was still on, thought Winnie. Bending down, seeing that it was dark, straightening back up, debating whether to wake her up and tell her that he had brought dinner. She imagined his hand resting briefly on the doorknob before he finally decided against going in. His feet managed to sound dejected as they brought him back to the kitchen.

Winnie felt bad for not calling out to him, but she knew that if she had let Long know she was awake, it would have been hours before he went to sleep. Winnie would have had to eat what he'd brought home, and he would have taken another three beers out of the fridge. Once they'd finally made it back to the bed there would be an additional twenty minutes of unproductive sex before she became the Mouth for him. Only then would Long fall asleep. Winnie didn't want to have to wait until then for Belly to emerge from the attic.

She listened to him crack open a beer and drink it while listening to something on his laptop with the volume turned down—Porn? Kung fu film? A new song he was learning for karaoke? Ten minutes later she heard him come upstairs and brush his teeth. Then he silently pushed open the bedroom door, eased himself gently down onto the mattress, and curled up beside Winnie. Long could always fall asleep immediately.

She decided to count a hundred of his snores before attempting to escape, but she was only at thirty when Belly's head popped up at the side of the bed, tail wagging so fast it was a blur and a grin on her face that looked faintly demonic in the fuzzy red light of the room.

Belly put her front legs on Winnie's pillow and pushed herself up, craning her neck to look over her body at Long. "Well, well, well," she said with a low, rattling chuckle. "He's a deep sleeper, isn't he? He'll be out until morning. Come on, come on, come on. We've got work to do." She prodded Winnie with a paw and then took off down the hall-way. Long didn't stir at all when Winnie left the bed and tiptoed after Belly in the same T-shirt she had been wearing all day.

When she passed by the refrigerator, Belly stopped and sniffed. "Ooh, he's brought back tofu," she said, a pink edge of tongue slipping out of her mouth.

Winnie opened the fridge and found Long's leftovers, wrapped up in crumpled napkins. She placed the whole bundle on the kitchen floor for Belly to eat. When the fried tofu was all gone, Belly licked at the grease spots on the napkins until they began to disintegrate.

"I wish there was more," she grumbled. "I'm still hungry; let's go out and get snacks. Can you drive Long's motorbike?" Before Winnie could answer, she was pitter-pattering away. When Winnie caught up with her, she had already hopped up on top of the motorbike's seat in the entryway.

"I'm not a very good driver," Winnie said. "The Suzuki is too heavy for me to steer." This was not quite true, but she didn't want to have to admit to Belly that she was worried the house would not let her outside again.

Belly snorted. "Well, that won't do at all," she said. "I'll just have to drive."

"How could you possibly drive?" Winnie cried. "You don't have fingers!"

Belly's canine teeth gleamed when she smiled. "A joke! But you're right—I can't drive, so I'll have to use your body to do it. Would that be all right?"

"What does that mean?" Winnie swallowed nervously.

Belly's grin widened a centimeter more. "It's not very complicated: we switch!"

"Switch what?"

"Bodies!"

Winnie did not know how to digest this information, so she just sat down on the floor. "I don't understand."

Belly mulled it over for a moment. "It's a little difficult to describe," she finally said. "Think of it this way: your body is a motorbike. You are driving it. Me, in my little dog body—it's more like somebody riding a bicycle. But the two of us can sort of . . . *trade vehicles* if we want to."

Winnie did not like dealing in metaphors. "So, you're asking me to let you take over my body?"

"Mm-hmm."

"And if you're me, I'll be a dog?" Would the house release her if she was inside a different animal?

"Aren't you at least a little curious?" There was that wicked glint in Belly's eyes.

"Is it dangerous?"

"Completely harmless."

"What happens if I die?" asked Winnie. "Or what happens if *you* die while you're in my body? How does it—" She broke off, momentarily overwhelmed, and buried her face in her hands for a quick second to collect herself. "Will it hurt?" she asked in a small, muffled voice.

Belly jumped down quickly from the motorbike and tenderly licked her kneecap. "Of course not. Believe me. Now, don't struggle."

The instant that the paw touched her skin, Winnie took a sharp breath in and felt herself go slack. It was like sinking into deep water, like when she played dead in the bathtub. Her mind fell out of herself. It was a release that felt like mental unlatching, like a tricky necklace clasp behind her neck finally coming free. She was suspended for one fumbling moment in soundless darkness before she came screeching back into the world, which was now hazier and much more gray. She tried to blink away the blurriness before she realized that it was just how she saw with the dog eyes. This faded, Vaseline-smeared version of her surroundings was even odder than the four legs. She peered up at the foggy version of what had been her face and watched it twist with wry amusement.

"That wasn't too hard, was it?" It was Belly's low voice that came out through Winnie's lips, with no trace of her American accent.

But when Winnie opened her jaws to respond, she found that her human voice was gone. She contracted her throat and tried again; a low wheezing sound came out this time. She looked up at Belly, bewildered. How did she do it when she was in the dog? How was she managing it now, with Winnie's vocal cords?

Belly clucked her tongue. "It takes practice. It'll come eventually. The first time I tried it after I was— Oh, now you're not even listening anymore? Well, fine then," she said, with more amusement than annoyance. "See if I care when you try swapping bodies again and end up stuck in the wrong one. Your boyfriend. A neighbor. A mosquito."

She was correct: Winnie had stopped listening, already preoccupied with testing out her new form. She tried to stand, but she could not synchronize all of her legs and they buckled. She contented herself with lying on the floor and just extending and contracting the muscles of her long tummy, like a concertina. To her delight, she realized that her tail had been wagging this whole time; it felt so natural that she hadn't even noticed.

Belly sighed and reached down to scratch Winnie behind an ear. "I suppose I should get some clothes on then, pup."

Winnie gave a happy bark. It erupted out of her without warning, like a surprise sneeze. She had no idea whether or not it actually meant anything. A little smirk uncoiled itself over Belly's face in response. Winnie tried to stand once more, and again her legs failed her, so Belly scooped her up by the stomach and carried her up the stairs.

Long was still fast asleep and his steady metronome of snores did not so much as waver when Belly cavalierly flicked on the lights, plopped Winnie onto the mattress, and pulled open the closet.

Winnie watched, fascinated, as Belly began to dress her old body—frowning at all of Winnie's sack dresses and finally reaching for one of Long's white shirts instead, leaving enough of it unbuttoned that, from some angles, the twin crescent shadows of her breasts were visible. She tugged on a pair of his trousers as well and then cuffed them twice to make them fit. Winnie had never found anything admirable in her ungenerous features before—stringy arms and calves, wide thighs leading to wide hips but a stingily apportioned ass, square shoulders and an even squarer jaw that was not softened by the smattering of American freckles above it. But now that she was no longer inhabiting it, she found the body much improved, even appealing. Belly imparted it with a ferocity and looseness that Winnie did not possess, traits that Winnie now smelled rather than saw. Smells were blooming at the outlines of everything, like blood in water—billowing, distorting the air where they met it. Belly was edged in aroma clouds of the chemical florals from Winnie's deodorant and shampoo, and the lingering, coppery musk of a period four days ago. Long was smothered by the bedsheets' laundry detergent, with warm and loamy top notes of sweat and beer breath. Winnie's nose caught veins of scent drifting in from other areas of the house—the stale air in the attic above, a murky wet smell from the broken toilet downstairs, and through the window, the soft street reek of asphalt, gasoline, piss, and roasting meat—some of it dog, from the restaurant across the alley, which caused her to shudder.

She found the odor of the dog body much more pleasant now that she was capable of picking up on its complexities. Her scent was not a cuddly one. She smelled like earwax and dirt, and her own hunger, hot and sour and prickling in her gums. She smelled kinetic; she smelled the way that itching felt. She had finally managed to pull herself up onto her feet.

After ten minutes of practicing up and down the length of the mattress, Winnie managed to get her four-legged gait more or less under control. Now that she was mobile, she was eager to leave the house and smell other things in the city. But Belly was savoring the experience of being in her new body a bit more leisurely. Winnie owned very little in the way of creams and lotions and makeup, but Belly slapped a glob of everything she could find in the bathroom onto her face. She took such delight in peeing—cackling with glee on the toilet and bending forward to peer between her thighs—that afterward she immediately ran to the kitchen and drank two glasses of water so that she would be able to pee again. She clumsily arranged her hair into a stubby braid and examined herself from all angles in the mirror.

"To be honest," she mused, half to Winnie and half to her own reflection, "I don't have a clue how it all works. The longer I think about it, the more I realize it's not actually like driving at all. You're not my vehicle, and you're not my puppet. It isn't . . . it's not a *clean* act. And each time it's different. Imagine water instead, water being poured out of and then back into many different vessels—sometimes it gets spilled or accidentally mixed with other things. I don't know what percentage of your you-ness belongs to your body, and what gets left behind when the rest of you is plucked out of it. Shit, I can barely tell what I am, or how much of me is dog and how much is what I was before."

Winnie managed to interrupt with a little nicker of impatience that was the nearest thing she'd managed to speech yet.

Belly turned away from the mirror and gave her a grin that was somehow identical to the smile she made when she was a dog. "Close!" she said. "You'll be talking soon. Now, show me where Long keeps his keys and let's go—I'm even hungrier in your body."

WHILE BELLY DROVE, WINNIE kept herself balanced on her lap, her head turned so that her snout rested atop Belly's left arm and the wind could flutter her ears and bring her odd cocktails of scent from the sidewalks and other motorbikes they passed. It was ecstasy. And when it became too much, when she could no longer bear the heady mix of odors—the rats and cigarette smoke and a hundred different kinds of soup and exhaust—Winnie buried her nose deep into Belly's elbow and snuffled up her skin scent, the slight salinity and yeastiness, and that rich half-American blood beneath. In a way, she had already forgotten that the body had been hers. Had been her.

Belly pulled over at a late-night barbecue cart by the side of the road in what might have been Phu Nhuan, Winnie guessed, from the smell of airplanes to the west. When she tried to squint at blurry street signs, she discovered that letters didn't make sense to her anymore. Belly ordered grilled tofu and quail egg skewers for her and miniature sausages on sticks for Winnie, and they perched on the seat of the motorbike to eat. The lady gave Winnie an extra sausage and scolded Belly about needing to give her dog a good scrubbing, and Winnie made barks that were almost laughs while Belly rolled her eyes and tore at her eggs with her teeth, her manners still more canine than human. When they were finished, Belly gathered all of the used skewers into a thick bundle in one hand.

"Auntie," she said to the woman, and the glint that Winnie was learning to be wary of was back in her eyes. "I'm sorry, but I don't have any money, so I can't pay you for these."

The barbecue woman was livid. She demanded that Belly leave her dog and the bike with her as collateral while she went to find an ATM.

"Nope," said Belly with a smile. "You'll just have to call the police."

"I'm not getting *them* involved," spat the woman, "I'm calling my husband, and he's going to come and drag you around by your fucking half-breed hair until you pay. And if you try and run away I'm going to dump this on you!" She reached for a bucket of still-smoking ashes beside the cart. Winnie trembled in Belly's lap.

But Belly's smile did not waver. "I'm not going to run. But I really would prefer it if you'd just call the police, like I told you to," she said calmly.

The woman had her phone in her hand.

"All right, hold on," said Belly. "If you're really not going to call the police, then I think you should see this, before you do something you'll regret . . ." She held up her fistful of bamboo skewers—nine or ten of them, the thick kind—made sure the woman was watching, and then contracted her hand and crushed them with ease. And she did not merely crack them in half—she opened her hand to reveal that the sticks had completely disintegrated under the force of her grip. She had crumbled them into splintery flecks, which she now casually brushed off onto the ground. "You wouldn't want me to have to do that to your husband's neck, would you?"

The woman's mouth had fallen open in shock; she did not respond.

"Oh, please," scoffed Belly, "That wasn't even close to my best trick." She started the motorbike and roared off down the street, only slowing down after about ten minutes when they had reached a wider street.

It was then that Winnie finally managed to speak her first human word. *"Whyyyy?"* She squeezed it out painfully, the word like a hot coal being slowly forced from her stomach up through her throat, barely more than a whisper by the time it finally made it to her mouth.

Belly looked down at Winnie between her knees and gave a throaty laugh. "It's all just part of my plan."

Plan? Winnie thought, but she could only manage to squeak out another, even quieter "Whyyy?"

Belly pulled the bike over to the side of the road. They must have been getting close to the river—Winnie could smell a whiff of something foul and clammy: cold, deep water, silt, the clinging, green overtone of algae. Belly stroked her head and gave one of her most frightening smiles yet. "I'm trying to track down an old friend."

"Whyyy?"

"He betrayed me. So I'm going to kill him."

So many words were burning at the base of Winnie's throat, but she couldn't twist them out no matter how hard she tried. "Whooo?" was the sound that she finally wheezed out, half by accident.

Belly fixed her dark pupils on her. "His name is Tan. He's a policeman here in Saigon. It's been two years since I last saw him, and for the past six months I've been following his scent, making my way to the city. I know he's here somewhere, but I can't always find his smell—

not in this sweaty rat nest. My plan tonight was to snag myself another policeman and use him to get to Tan somehow. But none of my plans are working. Getting nabbed by the poacher was certainly not part of any plan, but he brought me to you and to Lo—" She cut herself off and coughed quickly. "And to your body, so maybe it was part of another plan that I didn't know yet . . ."

Winnie was trying to focus but kept getting distracted by that same odd tendril of scent. She wasn't sure now that it actually was the river— there was something slightly different about it. Darker. A metallic edge to the smell that made her mouth water in an unpleasant way.

Belly was still talking, her voice growing faster, its growl thickening. "My first plan was to find him using dreams. I would send them to him, spooling them out into the darkness like fishing lines, trying to catch him on their tiny, sharp hooks so I could follow. But the dreams were always tangling. They would get snared on someone else who smelled like him. Or they would catch him, but I would lose hold of the thread before I could see him. Oh, I would get close, so close! I would feel myself closing in on him, until I got to the hallways—always the hallways, too many hallways—and then I would get lost again . . . Winnie? Hey! Are you listening?"

The smell had been growing stronger as Belly's talking had become faster and more incoherent, and Winnie was dizzy. There was now even less color in the world than there should have been. Then everything started to spin and all the lights went out.

And in the darkness, there was a wet hand.

WHEN SHE REGAINED CONSCIOUSNESS, Winnie was back in her body, in the yellow house, sitting on the floor of the kitchen. Through the windows she could see that it was still dark. There was sweat on her lower back and along the edges of her hairline. She looked at the clock. 4:39 A.M. With a sickening feeling, she realized that her stomach was swollen with food she had no memory of consuming. It was like a lethal hangover coupled with the delirium of a flu.

Belly appeared at her side, her furry head cocked at an inquisitive angle. Winnie tried to speak, but the effort it took to open her mouth used up the last of her reserves of energy. No sound came out, but she did lurch forward and retch down onto her lap. She could clearly identify the quail egg in it.

Belly frowned down at the foul puddle. "Should I fetch you a towel? Should I just lick it off of you? I really wouldn't mind—I'm feeling very doglike again."

"No, no, I can do it," said Winnie, wiping the corners of her mouth. Throwing up had made her feel better, but her throat was sore, and her lips felt clumsy and slug-like when she moved them to speak. She rose shakily to her feet and made her way upstairs, holding her shirt by the hem and keeping it fanned out so she wouldn't drop her vomit. In the bathroom she stripped and then crouched in the tub to rinse herself off.

Belly remained in the doorway. Her usual sly expression was gone, replaced by something uncharacteristically gentle. "You used to throw up all the time," she eventually said.

Winnie couldn't hear her over the running water. She turned off the tap. "What?"

"I saw it inside your head. You would try to make yourself throw up on purpose when you were fourteen and fifteen."

"Did you read my thoughts while you were in my body?" Winnie asked, wondering why she didn't feel more embarrassed. "Are they just written on the walls in there?"

"Well, you slipped," said Belly, matter-of-factly. "You fell out of the body, so I had to catch you and carry you in me while I brought us both back to the house. And while I was holding you, I could feel the shape of your memories a little bit. I didn't mean to rummage; a few of them just came loose. Maybe I accidentally dislodged them. It doesn't matter."

"Then you also saw that I wasn't very good at it. All the other girls in high school would talk about how they made themselves throw up, and I thought I would feel better if I did it too. Or at least feel more like them. But I couldn't do it. It was too hard and it wasn't working and I finally made myself stop." Winnie made a sharp little syllable of a sigh that she tried to pass off as a laugh. "I felt so pathetic for not even being able to do eating disorders the right way." She had never told anyone before. It wasn't really even a confession, she supposed, if Belly knew already.

Something occurred to Winnie. She perched on the rim of the bathtub, and before she was sure whether or not she wanted to know the answer, she found the question prying her mouth open for her. "A few months ago," she began, "I went out to a club, and I think someone . . . some people . . . I think something happened to me. When I woke up, that whole night was gone. I mean, sometimes when I drink I don't remember things, but this time was different." She swallowed. "Did you see that too? Do you know what happened that night, even if I don't?" She couldn't bring herself to say more.

Belly had eyebrows that Winnie hadn't noticed before. Or at least lighter patches of fur above each eye that resembled eyebrows. She furrowed them now, and then without warning she leapt onto Winnie's lap. She reared up and placed her forepaws on Winnie's shoulders and then leaned in to press her cool, wet nose against Winnie's forehead. When Belly spoke, her voice was a snarl. "The men who thought they could hurt you that night did not get to, Winnie. I saw you dancing, and I saw what you drank. I saw when you started to stumble, and when you didn't know where you were. I saw the marks they made on your arm when they tried to take you with them, but I saw you struggle, and I saw you get away. I swear you did. Even if I hadn't seen it in your head, I would be able to smell those men on you, even all these months later. You got away, Winnie. But if you hadn't, I would find them for you and we would tear them apart together."

Belly's toenails were digging into the skin on her shoulders, but she didn't flinch. She breathed in the warm, hairy stink of Belly's muzzle, and eventually her heartbeat began to steady. "Belly," she whispered, "If I took a bath, would you stay with me? I know you don't like water."

After a beat, Belly nodded.

Still wearing her underwear, one arm wrapped protectively around

Belly, Winnie lowered herself backward into the tub. When she turned on the tap, she felt Belly begin to quiver uncontrollably. "It's okay," murmured Winnie, stroking her fur. "I have you."

When the warm water had risen past Winnie's waist, she turned off the faucet and slowly lay back, with Belly curled on her chest. The dog's pointed little head—protectively tucked beneath Winnie's chin—was still dry, but Winnie felt her allowing her muscles to un-clench and her half-submerged tail to go limp, its long fur undulating softly in the water, like seaweed.

"The wrongness in me," said Winnie, "I'm not sure whether it's all from that night at the club, or if it started when I first came here, or if it started before then. Did I break, or was I broken from the beginning?"

"Listen to me, Winnie. No part of you is wrong."

"Every part of me is wrong," Winnie whispered, pressing Belly tighter against her skin. Dust and dried mud had loosened from her fur in the water and was turning it black. The bathtub was full of all the old Winnies she had never told anyone about, and now wouldn't have to, because Belly had seen them: Winnie, two months ago, with purple bruises on her arm. Winnie, five weeks ago, kneeling in the dirt behind the pigpen in Ia Kare. Winnie alone in a sex motel, alone in two hun-dred different Saigon coffee shops, alone by a traffic circle, alone in this house. Winnie in her college dorm room, a topographic map of wrin-kles on her sheets left by the first boy she had slept with. His asking her, from the door, not to talk to him if they saw each other in public. Win-nie in the girls' locker room, trying to knot her high school gym shirt where the curve of her waist should be, the way the others did. Winnie untying it ten minutes later, out of shame. Winnie in front of her bath-room mirror, watching herself stick her toothbrush down her throat. Winnie waiting for and never receiving birthday party invitations from Emily Hoang, from Christina Le and Victoria Vu, from two different Ashley Nguyens. Winnie at her brother Thien's graduation party, sit-ting by herself in the shadows at the top of the staircase of their split-level ranch. She had never learned his name, the friend of Thien's who had found her there. His quiet voice behind her—"You bad girl"—

when he saw the can in her hand. It was her first ever beer, stolen from the cooler behind a table of catering-company fried rice and papaya salad. "But you probably don't do anything else bad, right?" A quick smile, a quick hand running over the back of her first ever bra and around the side of her breast, like the careless swipe of a dishrag over a countertop. Winnie telling herself that it had to have been an accident, because he was white. They were all in the bath with her, always. But for the first time, Winnie didn't feel like drowning.

"It's this body," she said to Belly. "I know that if I could just get rid of it, I would be okay." Belly did not respond.

The windowpane started to turn from black to early-dawn cobalt. Winnie finally sat up and pulled the plug, and watched the filthy water drain away. She toweled Belly off first, then herself.

"Belly?" she asked as she turned off the bathroom light.

"Yes, Winnie?"

"What will happen after you do find your friend? After you . . . you know . . ."

Belly smiled. "After I kill him?" And then, softly, to herself, before turning and heading upstairs, leaving Winnie alone to walk herself to Long's bed: "Who knows?"

WINNIE WOKE UP TO the sound of Long dropping something downstairs in the kitchen. After she was certain that he had left for the academy, she kicked off the bedsheets, starfished her limbs out over the expanse of mattress, and gazed up at the old, yellowing ceiling, wondering how long she should wait before checking if Belly was awake. There was a new tea-colored water stain spreading in one corner, behind a cobweb. She felt clear-eyed and miraculously refreshed despite only getting two hours of almost-sleep.

"Beeeeeeelly?" she finally ventured, her throat still feeling furry. She waited, unsure if she had been too quiet for the dog to hear. Her ears felt funny. The itch was back again, but this time it felt different. Out of habit, Winnie stuck a finger into her right ear and scratched lightly, not expecting to find anything, but this morning she touched something. Winnie's eyes grew round. She gulped. And then, holding her breath, she reached in deeper with her thumb and index, pinched, and began pulling.

Slowly, her hand shaking, she drew out one end of a long, long human hair. The sensation of it being unspooled from deep inside her ear simultaneously felt like the sharp pinch of a needle sinking into a vein and the release of a full bladder that had been held for too long. Winnie's hand moved farther and farther away from her face as she tugged the strand out, her horror mounting with every inch that emerged from her, until at last, with a little popping sound, the other end appeared. It was over a foot long. She held it up in front of her face. The hair was not covered with blood or wax. It was clean, and it was fine and silky and such a deep black color that Winnie knew it didn't belong to her and could not begin to fathom the physics of what had transpired in her ear canal. She screamed.

There was a soft volley of toenail clicks, and then Belly slipped into the bedroom and leapt noiselessly up onto the mattress next to Winnie. "What's the matter? Up already?" she yawned. And then, "That's gross; put it away," when she noticed the hair. Winnie brushed it out of sight on Long's side of the bed and tried not to think about it. Tufts of Belly's fur stuck up at aggressive angles on her neck and back, and Winnie stuck out a hand to smooth them, but Belly flinched reflexively— lips drawn back to reveal teeth—before recovering her composure and giving Winnie's palm an apologetic lick. "Sorry, I'm jumpy this morning. My edges feel frayed. I don't feel like myself."

Winnie slowly reached out her index finger to graze one of Belly's toes, and this time the dog didn't shrink back. "I don't either," Winnie said softly. "And I think that's why I woke up so happy."

Belly narrowed her eyes, knowing what Winnie was going to ask next. "It's too soon to switch again; rest a little longer. Besides, your feeder is gone and we don't have a motorbike."

"We don't have to wait until tonight. We can take a xe ôm. We're losing time—we've got to get your friend!" Winnie managed to say this last part cheerfully, despite the little spasm of sadness that ran through her at the thought of Belly leaving her once the friend had been found.

Belly's eyes, inscrutable and crusting at their inner corners, bored into her. "Just remember," she said, "as we keep doing this, that this is changing you. In ways you can't anticipate. In ways *I* can't even anticipate. Are you sure you're ready for that?"

Winnie matched her gaze. "All I've ever wanted to do was change. That's why I came here. That's why finding you was the best thing that ever happened to me."

"Then that's what we'll do," said Belly. "I promise you, Winnie. I'm only doing what you want me to do." And this time when she approached Winnie with her outstretched paw, she moved slowly instead of taking her by surprise, as if giving her the time to prepare herself. This time Winnie was ready. But before the change, she did wonder, very briefly, if this had been Belly's plan all along, and she had just been made to think it was her own.

THE SAME XE ÔM DRIVER was always parked on the corner where the alley met the street, hunched atop his battered Honda and scouring the traffic. Belly headed straight for him, holding dog Winnie in her arms.

The burned-tar stench of the xe ôm man's White Horse cigarettes was so strong to Winnie that it destroyed most of the other smells within a twelve-foot radius of him. In the months that she had lived down this alley they had never interacted before, though, on one of the few occasions that she had left the house on her own in the beginning, she had felt his gaze slither over her in a cursory manner. She sensed his eyes—smelled them—lingering on Belly now, as they drew nearer.

"Older brother!" she cooed at him. "We need a lift."

When he heard her, a current of lust rippled the White Horse–scented cloud around him, and he grinned and ran the meaty, nicotine-stained fingers of one hand through his hair. "Long's girl, right?" he rumbled. "Where to?"

She gave him an address—Binh Tan District or Binh Thanh; Winnie was not really paying attention, because she was distracted by how badly she wanted to pee on the xe ôm man's bike.

"I'll take you for twenty. That's a discount," he said, handing her a spare helmet and kick-starting the old Honda so forcefully that the whole thing shook. "You and the mutt can hop on. Don't let it bite me."

Whenever they paused at stoplights Winnie would notice him resting his hand on Belly's kneecap. Her face betrayed nothing, but each time he did it her grip tightened on Winnie.

Even though it was just past noon, there was already a grisly traffic snarl at one of the larger roundabouts. They were moving too slowly for the bike to handle, so it kept dying, and each time the xe ôm driver had to kick it back to life he nearly knocked them all off.

"What's your business in that part of Binh Tan?" he shouted back at Belly. "Rough neighborhood for a little American thing like you, isn't it?" The yellow-taloned hand was on Belly's knee again, going so far as to give it a squeeze this time. A quiet, reflexive snarl tensed Winnie's body and set it tremoring. Belly scratched her under the ear in response.

"I'm going to the police about a missing friend," said Belly. "Binh Tan's the biggest station in the city, right? I figured I might as well start there."

The xe ôm man shrugged and clobbered the bike into gear again. The traffic was starting to move. "I guess it's the biggest because they've got the most bad guys."

Belly gave a quiet chuckle. *"Bad guys?"*

"Bad guys! All the gang members, pimps, bag snatchers, junkies. I can't believe that fancy Mr. Long is letting you go out there all alone." Traffic came to a screeching halt again and he turned and flashed a chipped-toothed smile at her. "I can stay with you if you'd like. For free. To protect you."

Belly threw her head back and gave her full, throaty laugh, punctuated with snorts. "Protect me from 'bad guys'?" she scoffed softly.

"I'm going *to* the bad guys; the police are the biggest gang in the whole country."

If the xe ôm man found this seditious he did not say so. He turned back around and remained silent for the rest of the journey and kept his knee molesting to a minimum. But when he dropped them off at the front steps of the police station—a squat cement building with peeling yellow paint—he insisted on unbuckling Belly's helmet for her, and his nails grazed her cheek in a horrible, deliberate way. "Are you *sure* you don't need looking after?" he purred. Belly did not flinch—Winnie did—though something hardened behind her eyes.

However, when she spoke, her voice was suspiciously bright. "All right, I'll take you up on it," she chirped. "Being here makes me nervous. Why don't you wait for me in that café across the street, and when I'm done you can drive me back home. I won't be long. And I'll pay you double for it. Maybe even more than that, since you're keeping me safe, hmm?"

The xe ôm man nodded eagerly. His White Horse stench seemed to thicken with how pleased he was by this.

"No!" Winnie hissed to Belly, once they were out of earshot and climbing the steps of the police building. (She could now pant out the word "no" in addition to "whyyy?" though it still felt like knives in her throat every time she spoke.)

"Don't worry," Belly whispered down to her, in a voice laced with stifled laughter. "That old letch can't hurt me. And we might need his motorbike." As she pushed open the door to the building, a gangly young policeman rose from his desk in the hallway and approached them, rubber soles squealing against the tiles. Belly's voice dropped even lower. "Now, I don't want you to be frightened by what happens next. I'm going to try something that I haven't done before. And I'm not really sure if it will work."

"What do you need, miss?" The policeman asked briskly. Then he saw Winnie in her arms and his gaze and tone turned frostier. "You can't bring animals in here."

Belly gave him a magnificently devilish smile. "Well, hopefully this won't take long." She shifted Winnie over onto one hip, took a step forward, and then abruptly shot out her hand and grabbed the young policeman's face.

Winnie squealed out a high-pitched "No!" There was something sickening about the action, even apart from the shock of the sudden violence. It was like a parasite latching on to its victim with its teeth; her palm covered the man's eyes and nose, and her fingers were splayed, each nail digging in where it landed—into jaw or scalp or cheek. But when Belly touched him the policeman did not resist. He did not move at all. For what felt like an eternity but was probably ten seconds, she held him. And then with a frown she withdrew her hand.

"He doesn't know him. We'll have to try someone else." The policeman remained motionless even after his face was released. His arms stayed at his sides, his eyes were glazed over, the pupils huge and dilated, and he did not appear to register the two of them anymore. For the first time in months, Winnie thought of her brief dalliance with the karaoke policeman. If she hadn't lost his hat, she could probably use the scent to find him now, with her dog nose. Maybe he could have led them to Belly's friend.

"I'm sure it'll wear off soon," Belly continued, "though I can't say I'll care if it doesn't." She started sauntering down the hallway, one hand trailing over every surface it came in contact with—the cinderblock wall, a small statue of Ho Chi Minh, the desk of the young policeman who was still frozen in place by the door. Winnie could not be certain of this, because her dog vision was so poor, but Belly's fingers now looked slightly longer than usual. Or perhaps it was just the new poise with which she imbued Winnie's body that made them appear more elegant.

Belly selected a room at random and walked in. There were two officers seated behind a desk. They started to rise when the door opened, but Belly plopped Winnie down on top of their paperwork, stretched out her hands, and seized the faces of both men in that same leech-like way as before. After a beat, she dropped first one and then the other, disappointed. They remained dead-eyed and motionless.

"Piss on the desk," she sighed to Winnie. "Chew on their papers. Destroy something to cheer me up. I'm tired of digging around in their sick little minds and not finding anything useful."

Happy to oblige, Winnie kicked all of their pens onto the floor, and Belly gave a flicker of a smile, which then brightened into something wider and much less trustworthy. "You know, I've just thought of another way we could try this," she said to Winnie, stroking her chin with one hand. There was no question now that the fingers had grown to an unnatural size; they were at least an inch longer than they should have been, and tapered at the tips. She traced one over the cool, damp ridges of Winnie's nose. "You still trust me, don't you, my furball?"

Winnie swallowed nervously but nodded.

"That's right; that's my brave girl. After all, what do you and I have to be frightened of anymore? Men have a habit of just taking what they want, don't they? *Particularly* when the thing they want is a woman's body. In the spirit of fairness, I think we should be able to take whatever we want too, and right now what we want is a man's body. So, what I need is for you to jump into it for me." And before Winnie could protest, Belly had grabbed her by the scruff of the neck with one hand and was reaching for the larger of the two policemen with the other.

The change was much less clumsy this time. Winnie was knocked loose from the dog easily and spent only a moment in that jarring, dark, bodiless limbo before finding herself inside flesh again. But she felt nauseous when she opened her eyes and found herself so much higher up from the ground than she was used to, and hairless and slick—the man was sweaty. Being him did not feel nearly as natural as being the dog. The uniform was too tight at the neck. He had eaten some sort of spicy soup for lunch, and so her stomach felt swollen, her tongue numb.

Belly's peals of laughter echoed off the walls. "Ooh, this just got more fun! Hey—how big is it?" she said, making a sudden grab at the policeman's crotch with her creepy spider fingers.

Winnie dodged the hand, protecting her new genitals. She hadn't actually gotten around to noticing them yet—she had been preoccupied by the strangeness of having an Adam's apple.

"Oh, come on. Don't be a prude, Winnie," Belly teased, pressing her body—*my body*, Winnie remembered, both repulsed and experiencing an involuntary twinge of arousal—against her with an exaggerated hip grind.

"Cut it out!" Winnie said, and it was her true voice that emerged, high and clear and American-accented, and without the pain that had accompanied it when she was the dog.

Belly pulled away, laughing. "Fine, let's find a computer. This is my new plan: we'll look up Tan, put you back inside this dog, and then get out of here." Winnie glanced down at the table and was surprised to see the dog there, awake but a little dazed, on the table. A very normal, slightly dirty mutt. She wasn't sure what she had expected to happen; perhaps, self-centeredly, she thought it might just disappear—or stay slumped over, inanimate, without her inside it. She reached out one of her thick-fingered man-hands—they felt massive, like oven mitts, after the experience of having little paws—and rubbed the dog behind one of its ears. It tilted its head back into her hand in contentment. When Winnie looked into its eyes, she saw no glimmer of recognition.

Belly snatched up the dog. "Well? Let's go, Sergeant Tuyen!"

Winnie looked down at the name tag pinned to her chest. She was in the body of Nguyen Gia Tuyen, whose scalp itched, whose bladder was nearly full, who had a blister on his left pinkie toe, and most importantly, who she could feel beginning to stir in the distant corner of his own mind that he had been squeezed into. Winnie was aware, instinctively, that it was only a matter of time before he began to push his way back in.

There wasn't a computer in the small office where they had found Tuyen and his colleague, so Belly and Winnie and the dog went back out into the hallway in search of one.

"Make it look like you're escorting me somewhere," she said, "but don't talk. You can't, not with that voice. If anyone comes up to you and asks you something, just fake a coughing fit."

Luckily, it was just after lunchtime and the building was largely empty; the few police and staffers that they did encounter in the yellow corridors were in a state of dreamy digestive contentment and paid them no heed. There was an unattended computer on a desk in the hallway of the second floor, and Belly coolly slid into the chair behind it.

"What if there are security cameras watching us?" whispered Winnie. She was beginning to feel the pinch of an encroaching headache.

"There's no one behind them," Belly snarled, without looking away from the computer. The machine was taking ages to wake up. She grabbed the monitor and shook it, which did nothing to help. It was obvious that she had very little experience with computers. "Everyone is eating or napping or on their phones or drunk or having a quick motel fuck during their lunch break. There isn't even a password to get onto this. Don't you see?" She waved a hand around, gesturing to the walls and empty hallway around them. "It's all just decoration—the big building, the statues, the uniforms—a fancy paper house for paper dolls in green paper uniforms. That's all it is." The computer screen finally lit up, and her fingers began moving rapidly across the keyboard, like praying mantis legs. Her face hovered centimeters from the monitor, bathed in white glare.

"Ahhh," she hissed suddenly. "I found him!" She raised her index finger, which was beginning to resemble a string bean, and traced a line of text on the screen with it. "But which one is he? There are five. I've got their addresses and motorbike plate numbers right here; now if I could just find a photogra—"

The sound of approaching footsteps made them both jump. Belly snatched her hand back from the computer, and Winnie knocked an elbow against the wall and dropped the dog.

"Anh Tuyen?" A policewoman poked her head through the door. "What are you doing up here? Why is everyone acting so weird?"

Luckily, she didn't have to answer; the dog chose this moment to attempt an escape. It sprinted through the legs of the policewoman and down the hallway, and Belly and Winnie tore after it.

They caught up with the dog at the bottom of the stairs; Belly scooped it up from the ground like a loose football without having to slow her gait. She made for the exit. "We've got what we need," she called to Winnie. "Let's get out of here. Hurry!"

Winnie's aching skull was slowing her down—that kernel of Sergeant Tuyen again, trying to climb back into the driver's seat of his mind. She stopped for a second and shook her head roughly from side to side, thinking it might release some of the pressure. The policeman they had first encountered on the way in was still standing more or less in the same spot, but he was now unfrozen—as they passed him, he was rubbing his temples. He frowned as they ran out the door, eyes blinking, clearly trying to remember where he had seen them before but unable to.

Belly didn't pause when she reached the road—she plunged straight into the busy street, clutching the dog against her chest, and cut a steady, seamless line through the traffic. Winnie waded in clumsily after her, arms waving and raised in the air so that the drivers would avoid her. She could barely see where she was going. Sunbursts of light kept blooming in her line of vision, and the asphalt felt untrustworthy beneath her feet. Halfway across the road, she stumbled, lost her footing, and landed on her knees amid a chorus of horns and tires screeching as they swerved out of the way. Gravel tore through both her pant legs and stung her palms. But with the traffic coming to a halt around her, Winnie was able to pick herself up and limp the rest of the way across the road.

Belly was waiting impatiently for her at the coffee shop. She had already found the xe ôm man, who gave Winnie a distinctly unfriendly look as she approached.

"Who's this? Different Vietnamese lover?" he muttered. "Is he here to arrest me?"

"He's helping me find my missing friend," said Belly. "He'll have to come on the bike with us."

The xe ôm man tossed a few bills at a waitress to pay for his coffee. "Doesn't he have his own bike? He's too big for mine! And he's bleeding. Look!"

Winnie took a napkin from the table and dabbed at her skinned knees with it. Belly took hold of the xe ôm man's arm. "Don't worry," she said sweetly,. "I'll just have to squeeze in closer to you so we can all fit."

The xe ôm man cracked a coarse smile. He didn't even notice the disturbing length of her fingers. "It'll still cost you extra," he said.

They all piled onto the Honda, the xe ôm man scooting up as far to the front of his seat as possible, hunched over the handlebars. Belly was in the middle, her arms wrapped around the xe ôm man's waist, and Winnie nearly falling off the tail, shoes dangling just centimeters from the ground, because she didn't have any foot pegs to rest them on. The dog was squashed between her chest and Belly's back. They were not heading in the direction of home. Winnie didn't know where their destination was and couldn't remember whether or not Belly had already said it—her head felt like it was splitting open, and she could barely keep herself from toppling off the bike. There was an encroaching darkness at the edges of her eyes, and black spots swam in front of her. She needed to tell Belly that she wouldn't be able to hold on for much longer, but she couldn't say anything in front of the xe ôm man.

They crossed a river, skirted a roundabout, crossed what might have been the first river again or a different one entirely; rivers, storefronts, motorbikes, people, noodle carts, roadside poincianas were all blending into each other. Winnie pinched her own thigh as hard as she could to keep herself from losing consciousness, but she couldn't feel any pain.

"There." She heard the jagged tenor of Belly's voice above the traffic. "Take us there, and then stop."

They dismounted—Belly swinging herself down from the bike with gamine grace and Winnie dropping from it like a sack of rice, setting the dog down on the ground and then staggering away, half blind, to find something to prop Sergeant Tuyen's body up with. She made her way to a railing that was surprisingly wet and slimy when she touched it; when she forced her bleary eyes to open further, she discovered that they were parked at a riverbank. Even though Winnie was no longer the dog and all her senses were fading, she could still make out the smell—water and stone, silt and sewer, rust and rot, mildew and bone. It was Saigon's marshy underbelly: her skyline hovered, huge and hazy in the smog, just to the west, but seemed worlds away. They were on a grassy outcrop that could have been a romantic spot, were it not for the garbage everywhere—old cans and half-empty Styrofoam containers and a pile of old ashes. Beneath a bridge farther down the river, Winnie could see a little encampment made out of boxes, and blankets and laundry hung to dry on ropes suspended from the pylons, but apart from that, and the rats scurrying around by a trash can, they were the only ones there.

"Are we alone?" she heard Belly ask.

"We would have been if you hadn't brought along a cop," snorted the xe ôm man. "What's the matter with him, anyway? Is he drunk or something?"

Winnie couldn't make out what Belly's reply was. Sounds were growing muffled, like she was sinking underwater. She found an old beer can on the ground and stepped on it. She saw the metal crunch. But she did not hear anything. Panicked, Winnie got down on her knees in the soggy grass and searched for another can. This one she held right up to her ear and crushed in her fist. Again, there was no sound.

As the blackness began devouring the last of her vision, Winnie turned on all fours to look at Belly, willing her to come and help.

The afternoon sunlight revealed the American in her hair, burnishing it orange. Had it gotten longer? Yes, like her fingers, Belly's hair had grown inexplicably longer. It was past her shoulders now, almost to her mid back. She was silhouetted against the city—the spear of the Lotus Tower, the squatter rectangles of new buildings under construction, crisscrossed by cranes, a distant airplane that from Winnie's perspective looked like a little insect flying out of Belly's ear. Her mouth had turned cavernous, the bottom jaw opening all the way past her sternum, a massive, dark oval. She was in the process of swallowing the head of the xe ôm man, who was unconscious and wreathed in smoke.

With a final crack of pain in her head, Winnie was expelled from the body of Nguyen Gia Tuyen, out to where there were no more thoughts, or pain, or feeling, or fear, or much of anything at all.

IT IS THE SAME WORLD, but she is no longer in it. She knows this because for the first time since arriving in Vietnam, Winnie is not hot or sweating. Even when she was in the dog she would sweat out of her nose and paw pads. She has no skin or pores now. She has no eyes, and yet she is still able to see the riverbank perfectly clearly—the water; broken glass in the weeds by the shore; long rat tails threading through trash; the policeman, now back inside his own mind but still far from his old self, lying on the ground, cradling his head in his hands and coughing periodically; the void-mouthed thing that Winnie's body has become, which has now devoured half of the xe ôm man. Only his camo-cutoff-clad legs are still visible. Winnie exists in a semidissolved state. She is static, a disturbance in the air. She is finally what she imagined becoming, on the nights she sat on the windowsill in the Cooks' apartment.

Unbound, she looks back at the riverbank and at the orange-and-white dog. She can nearly remember the sensation of being inside that skin, and aches for it, but she knows that she is too weak now to reenter the world through that portal.

As Winnie watches, Belly finishes ingesting the xe ôm man. Her mouth gradually shrinks back down to human size. Her stomach has grown slightly rounder, but not nearly enough to indicate that she has just consumed a large human male. She picks up the dog and grins down at the policeman, still on the ground. Sergeant Tuyen has not seen what has befallen the xe ôm man behind him and is not able to recall anything from this afternoon; he is suffering from the worst headache and nausea of his life, and after today will never be able to fully shake the feeling that he has misplaced something important. Belly leaves him and walks directly up to the litter-strewn spot by the ash heap where what is left of Winnie lingers.

"Start with something small," she says, "and work your way up from there."

Then she gives a little wink, mounts the motorbike, and she drives away.

She will start small. On the riverbank, one of the trash can rats is approaching. She waits until it has meandered innocently onto her patch of grass. She can feel the hum of its quick heartbeat. The rat suddenly straightens up onto its hind legs and scans its surroundings, as if it is able to sense Winnie's presence. But it is too late—she is already reaching for it.

THE SKIN BETWEEN THEIR worlds was punctured, and the sudden noise and heat and stink of Saigon were a sweet assault. She was back. The world seemed enormous now, but wasn't this the sensation that she had been trying to find all along? It felt like there was an entire orchestra vibrating on her whiskers. Each of their filaments was an eye, an ear, and a tongue all at once. The textures that Winnie drank in just from sweeping them over her little speck of sunlit grass were already richer than anything she ever experienced in her human body. Her eyesight was poor, but what did it matter when she could hear an individual blade of grass waving in the wind?

Winnie had never felt so beautiful before, or so powerful. If she could have wept, she would have; she was that exquisite. She was sleek and nimble and had just discovered that she could rotate her nose around like a satellite dish. She wriggled her little pink hands and clicked the tiny nails against each other, delighted by her stubby fingers. Her tail! It had been trembling behind her this whole time without her noticing until now. She wrapped the silky, naked noodle of it around her body and then unfurled it again with a deliciously serpentine flourish. Her teeth had started to ache sweetly; she needed to gnaw something.

She twitched. She was ready now. She began to run. The city was waiting for her, and it was made up almost entirely of small, dark spaces where she would fit perfectly.

LONG WOKE IN THE MIDDLE OF THE NIGHT TO WINNIE STAND-ing over him. When he opened his mouth she clamped a hand over it. Shook her head. Long tried to speak her name into her palm anyway, and she pressed her hand down even harder on his lips, with a force that surprised him. She was wearing a motorbike face mask that he had never seen before. A Hello Kitty–patterned one. Winnie lifted her hand from his mouth but raised her index finger over her face mask. *Shhh.* Then she beckoned for him to follow her. Down the staircase, through the kitchen, over to his motorbike.

"Where are we going?" Long whispered in the darkness of his foyer. He didn't know why he hadn't attempted to embrace her, or demonstrate in some other way his relief at her return. It occurred to him that he might be dreaming, and he looked around his house for some sign of trees.

Winnie had pulled open the gate. "The beach." Her voice was muf-fled by the face mask. She handed Long a bag that he hadn't noticed her holding, and when he took it in his arms it wriggled, and he nearly dropped it in surprise. Long looked down and saw that there was a small, filthy dog inside the bag with its head poking out of the zipper flap at the top.

"Winnie, wha—"

She held her finger up to her face mask again. *Shhh.*

WINNIE HAD BECOME A better driver, and Long didn't know how or when it had happened. She sailed smoothly down the highway to Vung Tau in the dark. Maybe this was what she had been doing for the past three days. He was still groggy, and he tightened his arms around her waist. For some reason, he did not want to ask her where she had been, or even where the dog had come from. None of it felt like it mattered. The dog was sitting obediently on his lap between them. They were one of only a handful of motorbikes traveling at this hour, but occasionally a truck or a bus would howl past and Long's baggy raincoat sleeves would flap noisily in its slipstream. Before they left, he had accidentally grabbed Winnie's jacket from the seat compartment instead of his own, but didn't notice until after he had already tugged it on. His hands were cold now, so he took them off of Winnie's waist and stuffed them into his pockets, where one of them brushed against something papery. Long passed the time by studying the shadows flashing by on the side of the road and trying to identify them: the dark, hulking outlines of tire factories and textile warehouses and packaging plants, the small apartments where the people who worked in them lived, the last of the spider-legged mangrove swamps this far north of the Mekong. And then finally, he smelled salt.

They reached Vung Tau just after dawn. It had already begun waking up, its eyes blinking in the morning light; motorbikes were being loaded with hot bread, the morning swimmers were already performing their calisthenics on the sands of Bãi Sau. But Winnie was not stopping yet; she drove them down the entire length of the spindle of a city, to the very tip of the peninsula, to the lonely beach that lay at its end. When there was no more road to follow, she parked the motorbike and they dismounted. In the daylight, Long could see now that Winnie was wearing new clothes in addition to the face mask. She was all in white.

She stared out at the sea in the milky new morning, and she did not blink or move or even breathe for what felt like two minutes. Long twisted his head all around, looking at a group of haggling fishermen, looking at the sky, looking at the rock formations by the water, their edges dizzyingly sharp. He turned to look at the sun-whitened façades of the hotels behind them, at the symmetry of their balconies, at the enormity of the shade cast by their awnings. Behind the hotels, the hills. Somewhere at their top, a lighthouse that the French had built a hundred years ago. Long put his hands into his pockets absently and reencountered the piece of paper inside one of them. He took it out and gave it a brief and indifferent examination—it was a blank slip of paper, the size of a bill or a receipt or a lottery ticket, but there was nothing written on it—before folding it back up and putting it away.

Winnie was moving again. She stepped onto the sand and began walking away from the cluster of fishmongers, taking the dog out of the bag and letting it trot alongside her. Her hair was blowing in the briny air, and Long could see, ruefully, that it had grown long again without his noticing. He hadn't been paying enough attention to her lately. All along, he thought to himself, he had been waiting for her to become someone else for him—to turn into Binh, probably—instead of loving the real Winnie in front of him. He was going to change, he decided. Why not move here? The sea would heal them. He could find a job at a different school, and Winnie would be happy by the beach. This was what they should have done all along.

It was low tide now, and the sand was glittering with all the unsellable things that the fishermen had drawn in with their nets and then discarded—jellyfish and already-dead slipmouths and old shoes and sea cucumbers and one pike eel that was still alive, but barely. As they passed, Winnie nudged the eel back within reach of the tide with a sneakered toe.

She led them to a sheltered spot by the rocks and then set down her bag. The dog was now entertaining itself by chasing a small crab it had found. Winnie looked out at the water again, and then at Long. There were tears in her eyes. Then she finally removed her face mask for the first time, and she smiled at him.

"Do you think you would recognize me anywhere?" she said.

Long frowned. "Winnie, what's wrong with your voice?"

Winnie held his gaze. "I mean, if you saw me, would you know it was *me*?"

Her timbre had completely changed. Her accent had completely changed. How could the face mask have done this? "Winnie," stammered Long, "what happened to you?"

She shook her head and she reached into the bag. From it she removed the two large dried squid that Long had purchased for her six years ago in Ia Kare, withered and brown and slightly larger than the length of her hands. Long could not put a name to what had transpired, but he felt the edges of the truth brushing up against each other. "No," he said softly, though he wasn't sure yet what he thought he was refuting. She whistled to the dog, who promptly dropped its crab and frisked over to her across the sand. She flicked one of the dried squid to it like a Frisbee, and the dog caught it in its mouth and quickly retreated to the rocks to gnaw on it before she could change her mind.

She paused at the water's edge before entering and took a deep, shaky breath. Then she took her arms and wrapped them around herself, embracing her own body tightly for a full minute. And then finally, she stepped in, Long two paces behind her. They waded through the shallow, foamy spittle to finally reach the point where the water came up to their knees. She crouched down. Long watched as she held her squid beneath the surface of the waves.

"It's dead, silly," he said with a smile. "What are you trying to do to it?"

She was rehydrating the squid. He still didn't understand why. Then Long frowned. The squid's body had grown bigger. Paler, too. *That's not right,* he thought. Its skin had expanded to the size of a very large plastic grocery bag.

The tide was starting to come in now. A wave knocked her off her feet, and Long sloshed over, hindered by his sodden pantlegs, to help her back up.

But she was not trying to get up again, he realized, too late. She was lying back in the water, her hair floating all around her, and she had inserted her legs into the sack of the squid's body, which had now become the size of her own.

She pulled its head over hers as a second wave came crashing in.

The skin of the creature glimmered momentarily beneath the surface of the water, and she was gone.

BECAUSE MAX'S VAN IS OLD AND SLOW, WE DO NOT ARRIVE until it is almost sunset. The light turns the spume into gold. Both the shore and the sea are full of people—families and lovers and friends and the stray suntanning foreigner. The Fortune Teller squints down at them all from beneath the brim of her hat. It is too crowded for her to try and sense the girl. We will have to return tomorrow. If her spirit is here, we will find her. But if she is not dead, or if she has become something in between, it will not be so simple.

The Fortune Teller did not want to tell me about the missing girl at first, when her parents called us from America. Years ago, they had come to Saigon to speak to the police and look for her themselves, back when she first went missing. But after a long search that uncovered nothing, they decided to turn to the Saigon Spirit Eradication Co. All they could track down was the motorbike belonging to a boyfriend she had been living with, before she'd disappeared. It was discovered here, in Vung Tau, with an illegal new license plate and no sign of its old owner. It had changed hands many times. Something was not adding up, the family told us. The Fortune Teller's suspicion was that the arithmetic in question had been tampered with by the spirit world.

She'd asked me if I wanted to stay in the city, saying that it might be too difficult for me, as a former missing girl myself. Of course I'm coming with you, I said. My Fortune Teller, my love, my lucky ticket. I just cannot bear to tell you that I am not a former missing girl; I still am one. I have given you all that remains of me, and you have granted me joy I did not believe was possible, but I disappeared long before I ever set foot in that forest when I was fifteen. Here, the secrets engraved on my body: my father's bed was the traditional, carved kind, uncushioned and made from an endangered species of rosewood. It weighed five hundred pounds, and he attributed his posture and the suppleness of his joints to it. I know that the child I grew inside of myself as a child was sired by at least one monster, but I do not know how many. One of them left something burning and corrosive behind inside of me, that I could never get rid of even after the baby had torn its way out. On the day that our father was crushed by his balcony I was standing above it, and just before I whispered the word "die" and the stone began to crumble when it heard the word, I tasted ash in my mouth. Every night I still dream that I am surrounded by trees and flying. My love, you know so many ghosts, but you cannot know mine.

Yen, she calls to me from the van. Let's go somewhere.

We drive up the mountain, to the whitewashed lighthouse above the city. We park the van and walk around it with our arms linked, pretending that we are at this seaside resort for our honeymoon instead of the dark work that has really brought us here. We lean over the railing and look across the water. I like to imagine that my child ended up far from that dry, lonesome place. I like to think that she escaped.

I hear a bark.

The dog lies in the shade of a plumeria, at the end of a long rope whose other end is tied to an ice cream seller's cart. Its muzzle is white, its belly round and clean and contented. It is an old dog now, but its tail smacks the ground excitedly like a puppy's when it sees me, the years falling away from it. The dog barks again, and the Fortune Teller turns and sees it too.

Her hand tightens on mine, and we begin walking toward it together.

ACKNOWLEDGMENTS

——

MY FIRST AND ENDLESS THANKS TO MOLLY FRIEDRICH, WARRIOR agent, for your wisdom, grace, and belief in me. I could have never built this house without you. Thank you to the crack team at the Friedrich Agency: the peerless Heather Carr, Lucy Carson, and Hannah Brattesani.

Thank you to my editor, Caitlin McKenna. I am so grateful for your brilliant eye and very large heart, and for the alignment of stars that brought this book to you. Many thanks to everyone at Random House and beyond who helped *Build Your House Around My Body* out into the world, including Emma Caruso, Jennifer Rodriguez, Barbara Bachman, David Lindroth, Elena Giavaldi, and Mimi Lipson.

Thank you, Cindy Spiegel, for supporting this story when it was just a seedling.

Many thanks to David T.K. Wong and to the University of East Anglia and the MacDowell Colony, for generously allowing me to haunt your premises.

Build Your House and I owe so much to the love and support of many friends and writers. I am especially grateful for this book's early readers: Adelina, Bill, Emily, Khine, Laura, Valerie, and Vincent.

Thank you to my family, *luôn luôn, mãi mãi*.

PHOTO: © ADRIANA DE CERVANTES

VIOLET KUPERSMITH is the author of the short story collection *The Frangipani Hotel*. She previously taught English with the Fulbright program in the Mekong Delta and was a creative writing fellow at the University of East Anglia. She has lived in Da Lat and Saigon in Vietnam, and currently resides in the United States.

violetkupersmith.com

Twitter: @vmkupersmith